Lawrence tucked Glory's hand into the crook of his elbow, smiling at her as if they shared a delicious secret. It was the most intimate look she'd ever known from a man and it sent a rush of heat through her body.

He guided her on to the dance floor. For a few minutes the intricate steps demanded all her attention. Had she been more experienced, she would have recognised the controlled sensuality of his every move.

He propelled her into a spin that sent her to the furthest reach of his arms, then pulled her tight against his chest. Feeling a hungry surge of desire, he made himself back away. Glory might look as if she'd been born to make love but the way she hesitated before she spoke – as if she were unaccustomed to the company of men – told him she was no casual flirt.

Also by Alexandra Thorne

Creative Urges
Past Forgetting
Sophisticated Savages
The Ultimate Sin

About the author

Alexandra Thorne has spent her life in the arts. She majored in music at the University of Pennsylvania, went on to a career as an acclaimed sculptor, and wrote her first book in 1987. She is the author of four previous novels published by Hodder and Stoughton: *Creative Urges*, *Past Forgetting*, *Sophisticated Savages* ('good rauchy stuff' – *Publishing News*) and *The Ultimate Sin*. She lives on a lake outside Houston, Texas with her husband and two Weimaraner dogs.

To Speak of Triumph

Alexandra Thorne

CORONET BOOKS
Hodder and Stoughton

First published in Great Britain in 1995
by Hodder & Stoughton
A division of Hodder Headline PLC

A Coronet paperback

10 9 8 7 6 5 4 3 2 1

ISBN 0 340 62470 1

Printed and bound in Great Britain by
Cox & Wyman Ltd, Reading, Berkshire

Hodder and Stoughton
A division of Hodder Headline PLC
338 Euston Road
London NW1 3BH

To the keepers of the flame, Peggy Webb, Helen Cavanaugh, Marie Tracy, Laura Taylor, Olivia Rupprecht and Suzanne Forster, may your lights burn ever brighter.

This book grew out of my personal experiences as a sculptor. Special thanks are due to Lawrence Lee and Mary Wyant who share a studio and a marital bed and make both work. I am also indebted to Shirley Estes who always makes research a delight, and to my husband Bill for driving me down California Highway 1 to Big Sur and Monterey. Last but not least, I owe my editor Philippa Pride my gratitude for her patience and her belief in me.

Why speak of triumph?
To endure is everything.

Folk saying

PART ONE

Noble Girard

Nature never deceives us;
it is we who deceive ourselves.
Rousseau – *Emile*, 1762

CHAPTER ONE

San Francisco 1906

Rebecca O'Meara was standing at the kitchen window gazing down Taylor Street towards the waterfront, when a cramp radiated from a point low on her back and knifed through her abdomen. Dropping her arms to cradle her belly, she took a slow, steadying breath. At last, she thought. The baby, her first, was two weeks late.

'Please God, help me to be brave,' she murmured, swallowing the fear that clotted in her throat.

She rubbed her back until the ache ebbed and then, turning away from the thin April sunshine, looked around, forcing herself to concentrate on all the things she needed to do while she still could. The apartment – a parlour, bedroom, kitchen and bath – was too small to be both living quarters and artists' studio. No matter how she tried to keep it neat and tidy, her efforts never equalled her intentions.

This morning proved no exception. Sean had worked on a painting after dinner last night. The canvas still sat on his easel in the middle of the floor. She'd kept Sean company for a while, sketching him as he painted, almost capturing his intensity as her love for him flowed through the charcoal stick on to the thick manila paper.

Exhaustion had driven her to bed at ten. Now her own discarded sketch-pad sat on her rocker. A paint-encrusted wooden palette, tubes of oils, a jar of brushes, and a redolent tin of turpentine lay where Sean had left them when he finally retired for the night.

The dust from San Francisco's construction boom coated the furniture. Tidying up would be a morning's work. First things first, she thought, heading for the bedroom to make the bed.

Sean stood in front of the clouded mirror that hung over the chiffonier, struggling to attach a wing-tipped celluloid collar to the neck

3

of his shirt. A beam of sunlight glinted on his mahogany curls. *Shanty Irish hair*, he called it disparagingly whenever she admired the colour.

Sean O'Meara was a short, heavily muscled man with a thick neck and a broken nose that made him look more like a pugilist than an artist; at least that's what she had concluded the first time they took a class together at the Chicago Art Institute.

She smiled to herself, remembering how quickly he'd proven her first impression wrong. While more aesthetic-looking men talked endlessly about the creative process, Sean's drawings and paintings offered mute proof of his genius. She'd fallen in love with his talent before she'd fallen in love with the man.

'I hate these Godforsaken things,' he muttered, finally attaching the collar to his shirt.

'Don't take the Lord's name in vain,' she chided.

He turned to face her. 'You're looking a big peaked this morning, colleen.'

Walking around the bed, he took her in his arms. She relished his muscled strength, the soapy scent of his skin, and tried to snuggle closer. However, her swollen abdomen prevented a true embrace.

'I'm just a little tired,' she replied, deciding not to tell him her labour had begun. If he knew he might not go to Munson's and they needed every dime he earned at the photography studio.

The concern in his eyes told her how reluctant he was to leave. 'Swear you won't over-do today.'

'I don't swear. That's your department.' A gentle smile masked her apprehension.

His parting kiss was so passionate that she forgot everything but the sweet pressure of his lips against hers. For that brief moment she was swept back to the time when, heedless of the consequences, they had fallen in love. They had paid dearly for it. But looking back, Rebecca knew she'd joyfully pay the price all over again.

Sean hurried downstairs, passing several school children on his way to the ground floor. 'Good morning, Mr O'Meara,' they politely piped.

'And a good morning to you,' he replied, patting the smallest on the head. He and Rebecca had been right to come here. San Francisco was a young city, full of young families. It would be a fine place to raise their own bairns.

Out on the pavement, he turned to look up at the second floor window where Rebecca – a glorious Juliet to his unlikely Romeo – waited to wave goodbye. Lord she was beautiful with her ebony hair, smoky eyes and dimpled chin, far too beautiful for the likes of him. He didn't deserve her by half. Yet here she was about to have his baby, never complaining even though he'd taken her far from home.

Although Munson's was some twenty blocks away on Market Street, he walked there every day to save the cable-car fare. Rebecca didn't know of this or any of the other sacrifices he made to give her a few luxuries.

Damn. He didn't care how he lived. He'd lived far worse in the past. It was seeing his beloved Rebecca do without that hurt.

She wouldn't have had to if that stiff-necked father of hers had been more understanding. But Saul Hersch would never forgive his only child for marrying a Mick.

Rebecca completed her chores between labour pains. Keeping busy was preferable to sitting around with nothing to do except contemplate her fear of childbirth. If only she hadn't been kept so ignorant about the workings of her own body.

She'd known next to nothing about the sex act when she married – and even less about how babies were born. If she had a daughter . . . Another contraction cut off the thought.

At noon she finally asked one of the neighbourhood women to fetch Mrs Ames, the local midwife. Then, unable to stay on her feet any longer, she'd collapsed into her rocker.

Now, assaulted by another wave of pain, she hoped she hadn't waited too long. A sharp longing for home and family swept over her. She missed her parents terribly. Considering her father's fury when he learned she intended to marry outside the Jewish faith, she doubted if they would ever reconcile. He had even said the Kaddish, the prayers for the dead, as though she had left this life instead of just leaving Chicago with Sean.

She grimaced, thinking she had never been more full of life than she was at this very moment. The baby kicked and stretched inside her, demanding entrance to the world. Let me be a good mother, she prayed. Let this child have a good, full life, one filled with love. How she wanted that. If only she could give him or her the material comforts she had enjoyed as well.

5

Rebecca had never been one to dwell on the things she didn't have. Thrusting her current poverty to the back of her mind, she made herself catalogue her blessings. Although the roof over her head lacked the opulence of the Lakeshore Drive mansion that had been her childhood home, she loved the apartment – the first home she and Sean had shared.

They had food in the cupboard, a little money in the bank, and the hope of an even brighter future. One of these years the rest of the world would recognise Sean's artistic genius and they'd never have to count pennies again.

In the meantime, he was doing so well. Just last week Mr Munson had said no one could tint photographs the way Sean could. Two weeks ago Sean had sold a seascape to the owner of a nearby restaurant for ten dollars and the man had hung it in his establishment for all the world to admire.

Most importantly, she would soon give birth to their first child. For the rest of their lives, 17 April would be a day to remember.

As if to remind her of what lay ahead, another pain, sharper than any of the others, forced a groan from her throat. A warm liquid gushed from between her thighs. Good Lord, she'd wet herself, she thought, staring aghast at the spreading stain on the faded Persian rug. What was wrong with her? Trembling, she clung to the rocker's arms.

At that moment she heard a firm knock on the door accompanied by a warm female voice. 'Mrs O'Meara, it's me, Martha Ames.'

'Come in, it's open,' Rebecca called out.

The door swung wide and the midwife came bustling in. The artist in Rebecca automatically catalogued the pleasant contrast between Mrs Ames' salt and pepper hair and her rosy complexion. A worn purse and a small satchel hung from her meaty arms. She had a take charge expression in her brown eyes.

Looking Rebecca up and down she said, 'I see I didn't get here a minute too soon. When did your birth sack break?'

So that's what happened, Rebecca thought with relief. 'Just now. I was on my way to the kitchen to get some rags.'

Making a sound like a clucking hen, Martha Ames skewered Rebecca with her gaze. 'You won't do any such. It's time to get into your night clothes. I'll clean up.'

Grateful to have all decision and responsibility taken from her inexperienced hands, Rebecca assayed a weary smile and did as she was told. While undressing she heard Mrs Ames moving around the small apartment. The midwife was humming a popular aria from Leoncavallo's opera, *Pagliacci*.

As Rebecca hung her skirt and blouse in the wardrobe, she recalled that Enrico Caruso was appearing in San Francisco's Grand Opera House that very night. Rebecca Hersch would have had front-row tickets.

Mrs Sean O'Meara had more important things to do.

Noble Girard rose from the rumpled satin sheets, walked to the bureau and took the bottle of Dom Perignon from the silver ice bucket where he had left it to chill an hour earlier. Making love satisfied one appetite while arousing others. He was damnably thirsty.

'Are you going to the opera tonight?' Greta Saxlund asked from the huge sleigh bed that dominated the room.

He turned to gaze at his mistress. Her blonde hair fanned across the pillows like wheat shimmering in sunshine. The sheets he'd carelessly tossed aside moments before exposed her upper body. Her flawless complexion glowed from their recent love-play.

She crossed her arms behind her head, thrusting her pink-tipped breasts upwards. Delectable, he thought, Greta was utterly delectable. Better still, she regarded the act of love with the same single-minded devotion that his wife gave to an act of contrition.

Anna spent a lot of time on her knees in prayer. He'd never seen Greta on hers unless she was giving him a blow job. None of the women he'd bedded had a more gifted tongue. Remembering the things she had done with it today sent an icy shiver up his spine and a rush of warmth to his groin.

'Well?' Greta prompted.

'You know I have a box,' he replied, filling two Waterford flutes.

'I wish I could go with you. I'd love to hear Caruso. He's the talk of the town,' Greta replied wistfully.

Ordinarily Noble fulfilled all her requests and delighted in the ways she found to thank him. He'd purchased and furnished the North Beach town-house in keeping with her opulent taste. Her wardrobe boasted extravagant clothes and furs. The jewel box in her wall-safe

7

overflowed with costly trinkets. The best crystal, the finest china, and the heaviest silver filled the pantry cupboards.

Lavishing money on a mistress was perfectly acceptable for a man in his position. Being seen with her at the opera was not.

'Anna is going with me.'

Greta's brows lifted over her blue eyes. 'I thought your wife didn't like going out socially.'

'You forget yourself, my dear Greta. What my wife does or doesn't do is none of your business.'

'It's just that I can't understand why any woman in her right mind would treat you the way she does. I would never lock you out of my bedroom – but I might lock you in.'

'Enough,' he commanded in the tone that never failed to send his employees scurrying for cover.

He'd made the mistake of confiding in Greta once, telling her how much his failed marriage troubled him – and he'd regretted it ever since. He didn't need or want her sympathy. The only thing he required from her was sex on demand. A man expected nothing less from his mistress.

Greta bit her lip when she saw deep lines bisect Noble's brow. Shit. He was angry. You'd think by now she would have learned to watch what she said. Men didn't like women who overstepped the bounds. They didn't appreciate being confronted with uncomfortable truths either – and Noble was more prickly about it than most. He had a short fuse and a hot temper.

'I'll have that champagne now,' she said throatily, giving him a seductively wet-lipped smile that was guaranteed to distract him.

His night-dark eyes were stormy with anger barely held in check. Tall and well built, he had a dangerous aura that enhanced his appeal. Handsome. God. He was handsome. And rich too.

In the years since his father's death, he'd cleverly invested and reinvested his inheritance. Today the Girard Company owned a fleet of steam ships serving the Hawaiian sugar trade, a dozen ferries that carried passengers to the burgeoning cities of Oakland, Berkeley and Richmond, and a series of warehouses on the Embarcadero. At thirty-four he was one of the wealthiest men in a city where outrageous fortunes were commonplace.

'Isn't the champagne to your taste?' he asked.

'I was saving it for you,' she replied, languidly lowering her lids.

She tipped her glass so that a few drops splashed on her nipples. 'Help yourself.'

To her relief, Noble didn't have to be asked twice. He bent his head to one of her breasts, sending ripples of pleasure along her nerve paths as his tongue circled the rigid tip.

Noble was an extraordinarily inventive lover. He knew when to dawdle, when to diddle, when to attack and when to retreat. This afternoon he seemed to be in the mood to take his time. Greta quivered as her body became a chalice for his questing tongue. He trailed champagne down its length, lapping the golden liquid from her nipples, the deep valley between her breasts, her navel.

'Oh Lord, that feels good,' she groaned when he reached the tender flesh between her legs.

She would have been content to lie there forever while he lapped the nectar from her body's most intimate places. But she knew that being a mistress had more to do with giving pleasure than getting it.

With a final shiver, she sat upright and said, 'Turn about is fair play, sir.'

Now it was her turn to dapple his body with the effervescent liquid, her turn to nibble and tease, giving him an agony of pleasure with her mouth. His skin tasted of bay rum, soap and perspiration, all mingled with the wine. She feasted on him with gluttonous pleasure, drunk with the power she had over him. Although she was dependent on him in every way, this afternoon he belonged to her, body and soul.

When at last he thrust inside her, she cried out in triumph, glorying in the knowledge that despite his money and power, he was but a man in thrall to her sex.

And then she thought no more.

Sean hurried home at the end of the day. He had great news for Rebecca – a promotion to assistant manager of Munson's and a four-dollar-a-week pay rise to go with it.

Although Rebecca didn't like going out in public now she was so heavy with child, he hoped to talk her into dinner at their favourite Italian restaurant. His mouth watered in anticipation of an antipasto followed by a hearty spaghetti Bolognese. They could splurge and have some Valpolicella to go with it.

When he reached the third-floor landing he heard a primal moan that raised the hair on the back of his neck. The eerie sound came from behind his own door. If anything had happened to Rebecca during his absence, he'd never forgive himself he thought, working his key in a fever of impatience.

The last rays of the setting sun tinted the parlour with a bloody hue as he walked into the room. 'Rebecca, where are you?' he called out.

'We're in here,' Mrs Ames answered, appearing in the bedroom door.

It took a moment before the reason for the midwife's presence registered. 'Is my wife all right?'

'She's as well as any woman can be in the last stages of labour.'

Another moan punctuated the midwife's comment.

Sean felt sick. He fought for breath and a slick of perspiration sheened his forehead.

'You're looking a bit green around the gills, young man. Go down to the corner pub and have a beer. Birthing is women's work,' Mrs Ames declared, attempting to shoo him out of the apartment.

'Sean, Seaaan,' Rebecca cried out.

Sean brushed past Mrs Ames. 'My wife needs me. We made the baby together and we'll damn well bring it into the world together.'

Hurrying into the bedroom, he saw Rebecca sprawled on the bed. Her face was pale. Dark shadows coloured the delicate skin under her eyes. Seeing him, she managed a smile and held out her arms. 'I'm so glad you're home.'

He sat on the edge of the bed and pulled her close. 'How long has this been going on?'

'All day.'

'You should have sent for me.'

He could feel her trembling and then another pain gripped her body and she writhed in his embrace.

'I told you, this is woman's work,' the midwife said from the doorway.

Sean ignored Mrs Ames. He held onto his wife, willing his own strength into her. The paroxysm seemed to last forever. When it finally subsided, Rebecca fell back against the pillows.

Mrs Ames gave Sean a peremptory tap on the shoulder. 'If you'll excuse us I'd like to examine my patient.'

Only after Rebecca nodded her acquiescence did Sean reluctantly get to his feet.

'You might make yourself useful,' Mrs Ames said, 'and put a little more water in the kettle on the stove. It's probably half-boiled away by now.'

She ushered him out and shut the bedroom door firmly behind him. He barely made it across the parlour when he heard Rebecca's tormented cry again. Weak-kneed, he collapsed onto the sofa.

Mother of God. If he'd known the price Rebecca would pay in pain, he wouldn't have been so thrilled when she told him she was carrying his child. Whoever said women were the weaker sex had never seen a baby come into the world. It would kill him, he thought grimly.

Five eternal minutes later Mrs Ames opened the bedroom door, a disapproving frown on her face. 'It's almost time, Mr O'Meara. Your wife says she wants you with her when the baby comes. If you think you're man enough, come on in. But if you think you'll faint, I'd appreciate it if you did it someplace else.'

'I'll be all right,' Sean replied, wishing he felt as self-assured as he sounded.

'All right then. Before you come in, take off your jacket and tie, roll up your sleeves and scrub your hands. I may need your help. This isn't going to be a tea party.'

Sean meekly did as he was told. When he returned to the bedroom, Rebecca's wide-spread legs were modestly draped with a sheet.

'Now the real work begins.' The midwife sounded far too cheerful to suit Sean. 'Rebecca, the next time you feel a pain, I want you to push as hard as you can and keep on pushing until I tell you to stop.'

Rebecca nodded her understanding.

'What can I do?' Sean asked in a tremulous voice he barely recognised as his own.

The midwife gave him a look that clearly said, *stay out of my way*. 'Hold your wife's hand and give her some encouragement. And you could wipe her brow from time to time.'

As the next pain transformed Rebecca's face into a tortured mask, Mrs Ames deftly twitched the sheet aside. 'Push,' she exhorted.

Sean had known more than his share of hardship. He prided himself on having a stalwart nature. But the next half hour made him doubt his own courage. The forces that racked his wife's body punished

11

him too. His own muscles tightened involuntarily with every contraction.

As the struggle went on and on, his respect for Martha Ames grew. She was at one and the same time the friend Rebecca needed, the mother she missed, and a competent midwife.

'It won't be much longer,' she said when Rebecca begged for release from her pain. 'I can see the head. A few more pushes and you'll be holding a beautiful baby in your arms.'

Sean mopped his wife's damp brow and helped her sit up so she could push even harder.

'It's coming, it's coming,' Mrs Ames encouraged. 'I've got the head now. Push, Rebecca, push.'

For the next minute the only sound in the room was Rebecca's long, guttural 'aaaahh'.

'It's a girl, a great big girl,' Mrs Ames crowed, emerging from between Rebecca's legs with a birth-slick infant in her arms. Turning the baby over with practised care, she gave it a stinging slap on the buttocks. The tiny child wailed in protest.

It was, Sean thought, the most beautiful sound he'd ever heard.

Enrico Caruso's magnificent tenor voice filled the San Francisco opera house with a sound so sweet and pure that women in the audience were moved to tears. But Noble Girard cared nothing for music and only kept his own box at the opera because it was the ideal place to see and be seen.

From the vantage of his gilded chair, he ignored the action on stage to survey the glittering audience. San Francisco's *haute monde* in black-tie and ball gown, filled the auditorium. Across the hall the district attorney was a guest in Mayor Schmitz' box. Down below a noted New York financier sat front row, centre, with one of Leland Stanford's minions.

More deals had been made in San Francisco on social occasions, more power peddled at dinners, balls and concerts than around boardroom tables. An astute man with an active social life didn't need a fortune teller to anticipate future business activity. All he needed was a good tailor, a well-born wife, and entree to the right places.

Noble possessed them all. His clothes were made in London by a renowned Savile Row tailor. His aristocratic wife carried the blood of Spanish grandees in her veins. His fortune and her breeding guaranteed their place in society.

Anna Mendez Girard was high born, high strung, perhaps a bit inbred. Tragedy had scarred her mind but not her face. Tonight, in her black velvet Worth gown with diamonds at her throat and ears, she looked especially lovely.

Before their baby daughter's death, he and Anna had shared an all-consuming sexual passion. She had been almost feverish in her desire to know all of life – all of him. But then little Isabel passed away in her crib while he and Anna were making love *soixante-neuf* style in their boudoir.

Afterwards everything changed. Anna blamed him for the tragedy. She withdrew from him, from her friends, from everything but the Church. And there wasn't a damn thing that Noble or all the specialists he consulted could do. *Melancholia*, that was their diagnosis, a persistent depressive condition for which there was no cure.

Damn her, he thought, glancing sidelong at Anna's aristocratic profile. He had suffered too. He had needed the solace of her love – and been forced to settle for Greta's bought-and-paid-for passion.

Damn all women, he concluded with growing anger. High born or low – one way or another – they found a way to make a man pay for his pleasure.

CHAPTER TWO

At midnight Martha Ames stowed the tools of her trade in her bags and put on her coat. Giving Sean a motherly smile she said, 'Frankly, young man, you look a little the worse for wear. Get some rest. I'll be back to check on your ladies in the morning.'

'Don't worry about me. I'll do just fine,' Sean replied, giving her a peck on the cheek. 'Thanks for everything. We couldn't have managed without you.'

After she left he tidied up the kitchen and parlour, then turned out the lights. She was right, he thought, wearily rolling his shoulders to ease the knotted muscles in his back. He really should get some rest. But an overwhelming joy still pulsed through his veins. He felt too drunk on life to sleep.

By God, he was a father now. The word sounded all the sweeter in his mind when he remembered his own orphan upbringing. He'd been so alone before he met Rebecca.

'Father. Dad. Papa.' He tried the words out, then grinning from ear to ear, tiptoed into the bedroom carrying his sketch-pad.

He stripped to his underwear, hung his clothes up and put on a threadbare robe and slippers. A small lamp glowed on the chiffonier. Its soft light fell on Rebecca's face. She slept soundly, her cheeks flushed a rosy pink, her hair tumbled around her face. Despite her recent ordeal she had never looked more beautiful.

The baby lay swaddled in a small cradle on the floor beside Rebecca. Emotions seemed to chase each other across the infant's tiny face as she dreamed a newborn's unknown dreams. Sleep well little one, Sean thought, pulling a chair close.

As long as he was too keyed-up to sleep, he might as well begin her first portrait. He had barely enough light to work, but was soon engrossed in his task and oblivious to the passage of time. The infant woke at two in the morning, startling him with its lusty wail.

14

Rebecca stirred, rousing with surprising speed considering what she'd been through. 'Is the baby all right?'

'Just hungry, I think,' he replied.

Sitting up, Rebecca began to get out of bed.

'Stay put, colleen,' Sean admonished. 'I'll get the babe for you.'

He lifted the infant out of her cradle, being careful to support her head the way Mrs Ames had shown him, and handed her to Rebecca. His manhood stirred as she exposed a swollen breast. A moment later the baby was nursing greedily.

'What a picture you two make. Now I know why so many artists have painted the madonna and child.'

Rebecca laughed softly. 'As you well know, Sean O'Meara, I'm no madonna.'

'You're everything in the world to me.'

'Why aren't you in bed?'

'It isn't every day a man becomes a father. I just wanted to watch the two of you for a while. Since we're both awake, why don't we give her a name? I've been thinking two Rebeccas in the family wouldn't be half bad.'

'That wouldn't be fair. This little girl needs her own name to help her be her own person. I have a feeling she's going to be very special.'

'Well . . . I do have another name in mind. I'd like to call her Joy,' he hesitated, hoping Rebecca wouldn't think him foolish, 'because that's what she's given me.'

'Joy,' Rebecca said, trying out the sound, 'Joy O'Meara.' Just then, the baby smacked her lips as if putting her seal of approval on the choice.

Sean laughed. 'I think she likes it.'

Before the baby's birth his love for Rebecca had been so all consuming that he wondered if there'd be enough left over for a child. Now he knew he had love to spare. God, he was a lucky man.

In the days to come Noble Girard would recall that there were no signs or portents on the night of 17 April, no comets streaking across the darkling sky, no birds of ill omen roosting in the windswept trees. It had been, in fact, a night like any other.

Following the opera he and Anna had gone to Delmonico's for a late supper. The usual after-theatre crowd occupied the plush booths and damask-covered tables. He'd ordered the Chateaubriand for which the chef was justifiably famous and a bottle of fine Burgundy.

As was her custom on their rare nights out, Anna had been infuriatingly taciturn throughout the meal, barely responding to his conversational gambits. She picked at her food and refused the wine. But he ate hungrily and finished the bottle. Their chauffeur delivered them back to their Nob Hill mansion at midnight.

Clarence Ashton, their English butler, stood at rigid attention when they walked in. Despite the late hour, he was impeccably dressed in a swallow-tail coat and dark trousers. His mousy brown hair looked freshly combed, his cheeks just shaved. No matter the time of day or the circumstances, Noble had never seen him less than perfectly groomed.

Clarence was the ideal servant, punctilious to a fault. Although it must have been obvious that the Girard home wasn't a happy one, Clarence never reacted – not by so much as a lift of his brow – to what went on within its walls.

'Did you enjoy the opera, madame?' he asked, relieving Anna of her ermine wrap.

She looked at him, then through him, and hurried towards the stairs without replying.

Clarence didn't bat an eye. 'And you, sir?'

'I'm sorry to say I'm tone deaf.'

'Is there anything more you'd like, sir?'

'We'll be retiring for the night. You can go now. I'll turn out the lights.'

'Sleep well, sir – madame,' Clarence said, turning on his heels with military precision and moving towards the wing that contained the servants' quarters.

Noble followed Anna up the stairs. He took them two at a time and caught her by the arm as she reached the second-floor landing. Tormenting her with his unwanted touch was a game he indulged in when he'd had too much to drink. Considering the champagne he'd consumed at Greta's, the whisky between acts at the opera, and the Burgundy at Delmonico's, that was certainly the case tonight.

'Thank you for a delightful evening, light of my life. I don't know when I've had a more amusing dinner companion.'

Anna gazed down at his hand and then up at him as if he were a

16

nightmare from which she hoped to wake. 'You've had too much to drink.'

'You're right. I have had too much to drink. Spending an evening with you is thirsty work.'

She jerked her arm free and headed down the hall to her bedroom without a backward glance.

He thought about following her, but what was the point? Fighting with Anna was as unsatisfying as trying to bed her. He'd as soon sleep with a corpse. What he needed was another drink. He made his way back down the stairs and through the mansion's echoing halls until he reached the library.

It contained hundreds of leather-bound volumes, many of them first editions. Dickens, James, Thoreau, Melville and Thackeray – Flaubert, Hugo, and Dumas in the original French, he'd read them all. A Rembrandt self-portrait, part of his treasured collection of Old Masters, hung over the fireplace. The room's rosewood panelling and comfortable leather furniture gave it a homey atmosphere despite its generous proportions.

Taking a decanter from a seventeenth-century English side table, he poured a large measure of the finest Napoleon into a delicate snifter, breathed in the bouquet, and drank the liquor down without pausing for breath. Refilling the glass, he sought refuge in a well-upholstered chair and sat staring into space.

Sean O'Meara was dozing in the chair by the cradle, his sketch-pad fallen to the floor, when the sound woke him – a sound like no other he'd ever heard. Before his mind had time to identify it, the chair began to move.

Coming fully awake, he tried to stand. The floor undulated under his feet as if it were riding on the back of a giant serpent. In the brief seconds before the lamp went out, Sean saw Rebecca sit up, an expression of terror contorting her lovely face.

'Sean,' she cried into the sudden darkness. 'Sean, what is it?'

'Earthquake!' he shouted back, knowing instinctively what was happening.

Furniture danced across the floor and the curtains thrashed as if they'd been caught in a gale. He had just started towards Rebecca when the chiffonier jolted into his back, knocking him flat. He lay momentarily stunned, hearing her call his name.

The sound galvanised him. He had to get Rebecca and the baby out of the building before it came crashing down around them. Muscling the chiffonier aside, he struggled to his feet. The pale light of the moon cast eerie shadows as he lurched across the heaving floor.

'Thank God you're here,' Rebecca moaned, seeking the comfort of his arms.

He longed to hold her but there wasn't time. The terrible noise escalated. Dishes crashed from cupboards. Pictures fell from walls and lamps hit the floor.

'Can you walk?' Sean shouted.

'I'll try.' Rebecca's eyes were huge with fear.

He picked up the cradle and helped Rebecca out of bed. She staggered. Her nightgown billowed around her legs as she fell to her knees.

'I can't make it by myself. Take Joy downstairs and come back for me. Don't worry,' she said, trying to reassure him despite the quaver in her voice. 'I'll be fine.'

Sean barely managed to stay upright, hanging onto his daughter's tiny bed with dogged determination as he made his way across the parlour. Coming into the hall, he heard people screaming in other apartments, children crying for their parents, husbands for their wives, their agonised sounds adding to the hellish cacophony.

Please God, don't let anything happen to my wife and baby, he silently prayed. A light fixture came crashing down, grazing his elbow, and the stairwell canted dangerously, but Sean kept his balance long enough to reach the first floor. The apartment door loomed ahead, crazily askew. He put the cradle down and pulled the handle. The door was stuck, the frame badly sprung.

Tears of frustration welled in his eyes as he tried to power the door free with his shoulders. The ground movement seemed to accelerate, the frame twisted to the left and the door suddenly burst open. A guttural growl of triumph burst from his lips as he scooped up the cradle.

The sight that met his eyes reminded him of Dürer's etchings of Hades. Taylor Street was unrecognisable. The pavement undulated as if it had been laid on the breast of the ocean. Sturdy trees whipped to and fro like frail flowers in a gale. Many of the buildings had great gaping wounds where brick and stone had fallen away.

He gazed around, frantically looking for a safe haven to leave the tiny bed. But there was no refuge in a world gone mad. Fighting down his terror and despair, he carried the cradle to the kerb and put it down ever so gently. Bending low, he kissed the child.

'God bless you and keep you safe from harm, Joy O'Meara,' he murmured, taking comfort in saying her name out loud. Then he raised his face and his voice to heaven. 'Lord, take care of my little Joy,' he bellowed.

He didn't have time to do more to assure his daughter's survival, not if he wanted to save Rebecca too.

Noble woke when a shower of books landed in his lap. Earthquake – a bad one – he thought, instantly leaping to his feet to avoid the volumes plummeting down around him.

He'd been in the city during the April, 1898 quake, and the stronger one in January of 1900 when the Saint Nicholas Hotel had been badly damaged. But those quakes felt minor compared to this one. Lurching into the hall, Noble almost collided with Clarence. With his clothes and hair in disarray, the butler had lost his air of unflappable calm.

'Is it an earthquake?' Clarence asked, forgetting in his agitation to add, 'Sir'.

'Damn right. A bad one. I've got to see to my wife. Can you get the rest of the servants out of the house?'

'I'll manage,' Clarence replied through clenched teeth.

Noble looked into Clarence's eyes. The determination he saw there reassured him.

'They ought to be safe in the garden,' Noble said, giving Clarence an encouraging clap on the shoulder. Then, hurrying down the hall, he put Clarence and the servants out of his mind.

He estimated fifteen seconds had passed since the falling books woke him. Unlike previous quakes, this one gave no indication of diminishing. It seemed to be getting worse.

At one moment the floor rose up to meet his feet and the next, it fell away like the deck of a ship in a storm. Using his hands to keep himself from crashing into the walls, he burst into the hall. Overhead, the enormous Baccarat chandelier swung to and fro like a glittering pendulum.

Staying close to the walls, he staggered around the octagonal room to the nearest flight of stairs. He hung onto the banister, pulling himself upward with sheer brute strength. His heart pounded. His pulse raced. Not from fear, though. The danger exhilarated him. He felt incredibly alive.

As he reached the shelter of the second-floor landing the glass roof over the hall gave way in a deadly cascade. Noble didn't take time to contemplate the destruction or his own escape from certain death. A few more steps brought him to Anna's door.

As he had feared, she had made no move to save herself. She cowered in her canopied bed, her eyes glazed, a rosary in her hand, mumbling a Hail Mary.

'Damn it, Anna,' he shouted, reaching her side, 'you can pray later. We've got to get the hell out of here.'

'The blasphemers, the unbelievers, the fornicators, shall all perish,' she declared, sounding like a crazed Old Testament prophet.

His booming baritone rose above the tumult. 'This sinner has no intention of perishing and I'm not going to let you die either.'

Sean listened to his child's frantic wails as he hurried back to the apartment building. The pitiful sound tore through him, bringing tears to his eyes. But then he realised why he could hear it. The earth-quake seemed to be ending.

The apartment building had barely survived. The foyer looked crazily askew like a reflection in a fun house mirror. The tongue-and-groove panelling had come loose, exposing the building's wooden frame. The stairs had pulled away from the wall in places and a few treads were missing.

When he stepped on the bottom riser it shivered under his feet. The whole thing felt insubstantial, as if one more shake would bring it crashing down. He clenched his jaw and began climbing upwards, moving with exquisite care.

The cries of survivors echoed in the stairwell like the sound of lost souls, but he saw no movement in the hallways and no one appeared. Were they too badly injured to try and escape?

Using all his young strength, he pulled himself past missing risers, battling his way to his own gaping door. 'Rebecca,' he called out, 'where are you?'

Dust thickened the air, making it impossible to see across the parlour. 'Rebecca,' he called again, his voice taut with dread.

She appeared out of the murk, a pale wraith in the gloom. 'I'm here, Sean. Is Joy all right?'

'She's fine,' he replied, pulling Rebecca into his arms.

They clung together wordlessly. He loved her beyond imagining, beyond reason – and he'd come so close to losing her.

'Is it over?' she asked, her face buried in his neck, her breath warm and alive against his skin.

'I think so,' he replied. 'We've got to get out of the building and we can't use the stairs. The fire escape is our only chance.'

Rebecca's reply was lost as the earthquake suddenly struck again with renewed fury.

A despairing cry burst from Sean's lips. He put his arm around her waist and helped her to the door. The floor jolted up and down under their feet, threatening to topple them at any moment.

They crab-walked down the hall, fighting for balance. The building was being torn apart but Sean refused to give up. As long as they kept moving towards the fire-escape, they had a chance.

The floor continued to buck and heave and the ceiling dipped overhead. Ahead he saw a ghostly grey light coming from the fire-escape window.

Sean's blood roared in his ears. His legs and arms ached from the constant strain. Behind them, he heard something heavy crash to the floor. The earth's motion increased, the pandemonium grew louder. Now he could see the fire-escape silhouetted in the window.

He didn't have the breath to urge Rebecca on, to tell her salvation was at hand. Ten feet to go. Then eight. The window had shattered and glass shards covered the floor. He heard a howl coming from the building's wooden timbers. When he looked up, he saw the ceiling give way.

The floor shuddered and dropped from under their feet. They fell, locked together. Their agony was instant and merciless as all four storeys came crashing down with them.

Finally, they were beyond pain.

Noble Girard took a pragmatic view of life – and death. When his time came, he hoped he'd accept it like a man. But he'd be damned if he'd run open-armed to meet it. Let Anna prate about God's will. The only will Noble cared about was his own. He'd made up his mind to save his wife, whether she wanted him to or not.

'It's the apocalypse,' Anna moaned.

Noble didn't reply. He could deal with the earthquake, or with his wife. Not with both. She continued to buck like a green colt as he pulled her towards the servants' staircase. They were halfway down it when the temblor returned full force, tumbling them to the bottom in a tangle of arms and legs.

The fall stunned Anna. Noble clambered to his feet and gathered her up. The nearest outside door was more than fifty feet away through the kitchen. Widening his stance for balance, he began the tortuous journey.

The cupboards had opened to spew china, glasses and canned foods on the tile floor. Shattered jars of jams, jellies and preserved fruit contributed sticky splashes of colour to the litter. Copper pots and pans clanged overhead, adding their own harsh carillon to the din.

Noble juggernauted his way through the debris, his leg muscles burning from the incessant struggle to keep his balance. The kitchen door beckoned. He paused on the sill, looking out. The house sat on five well-groomed acres at Nob Hill's highest point. The estate had been famous for its view, its extensive manicured lawns and stately terraces.

Now the lawn moved like a green sea, the flagstoned terraces had buckled, and a malevolent, particle-laden cloud obscured the city. Every few seconds a horrendous noise, like the cannonading of heavy guns, sounded in the distance. Noble kept his head down, doing his best to dodge roof tiles as he carried Anna from the house.

He didn't see Clarence until the butler was just a few feet away. 'Is Mrs Girard all right?' Clarence asked.

'She will be,' Noble replied. 'Did you get everyone out of the house?'

'They're in the garden, sir.'

The quake was subsiding again. It had been by far the longest Noble had ever experienced and certainly the most severe. For the first time since the tumbling books had woken him, he thought about the rest of the city – about the people he knew. Had Greta survived – or was she even now buried under a building?

While Anna and Clarence went on ahead he turned to look back. His once proud estate had a derelict air. Large chunks of pink stucco had fallen away, leaving scabrous wounds. Jagged glass shards in the shattered windows looked like dragons' teeth.

He'd have to go through the house room by room to make sure

it was structurally sound. Then and only then would he instruct the staff to begin the monumental clean-up. Once the work was underway he'd go on down to the Embarcadero and see what, if anything, was left of the Girard Company's warehouses, wharves and ferries.

It was going to be a hell of a day, week, month and year.

The cradle rocked madly, threatening to expel its tiny occupant. Suddenly the air seemed to expand, pushing outward as another apartment building came crashing down with a crazed shriek of shattered timbers and torn walls. The din drowned the infant's unhappy cries.

Eight hours earlier Joy O'Meara had been forcibly expelled from the moist warmth of her mother's womb. She missed the comforting beat of her mother's heart. She missed the constant, life-giving nourishment she received through the umbilical cord.

She hadn't been fed for three hours. She was hungry and soon she would be dehydrated as well. She wailed in protest, instinctively using the only means she had to control her world. But there wasn't a soul on Taylor Street to hear the orphaned child. San Francisco, the gayest, most carefree city on the continent, had been reduced to a charnel house.

A thick miasma of plaster dust enveloped the baby's crib. She gasped, coughed, choked. Kicking the blankets that held her fast, she was a miserable bundle of unsatisfied needs. She found her own fist and sucked greedily. Although it gave her no nourishment, it soothed her. Exhausted, she drifted off to sleep.

Half an hour later dazed survivors were moving down Taylor Street, some headed for the Embarcadero's ferries and others for the open spaces of Golden Gate Park. They were too preoccupied with their own families, with saving the pitiful remnants of their belongings, to give any thought to the crib they passed on their journey.

Had Joy O'Meara cried out, someone might have looked in and found her. But she slept on.

A large dog wandered past. The dog was hungry, thirsty and bewildered, hunting for food, shelter and companionship. Hearing a mewling sound coming from the cradle, it came over, wagging its tail. At last it had found something warm, alive – perhaps edible.

Nuzzling the covers aside, it sniffed carefully. A rich aroma of infantile faeces and urine filled its nose, sparking messages along its memory banks. Envisioning another baby it had grown to love, the dog sat down and licked at the infant's face.

Her eyes opened wide but she was too young to control their focus. She gazed upward, seeing a blurred shape. Feeling the soothing wet tongue on her cheeks, she cooed with delight. The dog stayed with her, curling up by the crib to take a brief nap. Twenty minutes later, still hungry, still thirsty, it got up and ambled away.

A strong after-shock rumbled up Taylor Street at eight-fourteen in the morning, rousing the baby. Her empty stomach ached and her throat felt dry. Her tiny buttocks burned from the urine and faeces that had accumulated in her nappy. She began crying again.

But her voice was weaker and she didn't have the energy to cry very long.

It had taken dozens of skilled craftsmen fifteen months to finish the interior of the Girard mansion. Nature only needed three minutes to destroy their handiwork. Tumbled antiques, jammed doors, cracked frescos, splintered floors and panelling attested to its power. The octagonal entry hall was ankle deep in its own glass roof and one of the staircases had collapsed. Bad as it looked, though, the basic structure had survived intact.

Noble had been toiling side-by-side with the servants for three hours, shovelling broken glass and carting it out of the house, boarding up windows, setting the furniture back in place.

At eight-thirty, he was in the library putting his priceless first editions back on their shelves when Clarence walked into the room. 'A Mr Auden from the mayor's office is here to see you, sir.'

A few minutes later, Clarence ushered the mayor's emissary into the library. Although Noble had met Auden several times at City Hall, he barely recognised the man. Auden's complexion looked pasty, stubble darkened his cheeks, and his mismatched jacket and trousers were grey with dust.

Noble realised he probably didn't look any better. 'Can I offer you a brandy?' he asked.

'I'd appreciate it.'

Auden's manicured fingers shook as he took the glass. He gulped the liquor down without pausing for breath. When he finished, a little colour had returned to his face.

'Now, what can I do for you?' Noble asked.

'The mayor is forming a citizens' committee to deal with the emergency. He'd like you to be a member.'

'I'm at the mayor's disposal.'

'The committee will meet in the Fairmount Hotel later this morning.'

Noble's eyes widened. The Fairmount Hotel was still a few months from completion. 'Why the hotel instead of City Hall?'

Auden bit his lip. 'Oh God, that's right. You wouldn't have any way of knowing. City Hall is gone, destroyed.'

Noble's chest tightened. The six million dollar building had been an important landmark, a signal to the world that San Francisco had left its rough and tumble past behind.

'What about the rest of the city?'

Auden shook his head in despair. 'We just don't know. The telegraph and telephone lines are down. The mayor was hoping I'd catch you before you went down to the Embarcadero to inspect your own properties. He'd like you to check out North Beach and Chinatown while you're in the area.'

Memories of the next few hours would forever be etched in Noble's mind. Driving past the Spreckels' mansion, he saw the financier's family camped out on the lawn. The women were seated in armchairs, dining from a silver service laid out on the grass. Seeing Noble, they waved, as if *al fresco* pavement meals were an everyday occurrence in their household.

He laughed out loud at the sight. It would be the last time he laughed at anything that day. Nothing, certainly not Auden's brief comments, prepared Noble for the things he observed driving down California Street. What had been one of the city's loveliest thoroughfares was in ruins.

Horses lay dead in their traces, human corpses littered the pavement where ornamental brick and stone facings had crushed them. Live wires dangled from electricity poles, broken water mains spouted like gushers and fire had begun to hopscotch from ruin to ruin.

A few other vehicles, horse-drawn carriages as well as automobiles, moved down the street. A six-cylinder HP Standard rolled by, carrying a cargo of corpses piled up like carcasses in a butcher's wagon. The destruction worsened as Noble headed into Chinatown.

The three-by-six block area had been the most crowded in the city, home to over thirty thousand people. Nothing remained of the joss houses, opium dens, gambling resorts and houses of prostitution for which the area had been infamous.

Resuming his journey through the stricken city, he turned the Rolls north on Taylor. The street, built on land reclaimed from the bay, had suffered some of the most severe damage he'd seen so far.

When debris blocked the road he let his car mount the pavement. A cradle lay directly in his path. He'd already driven over more formidable barriers that morning and knew this one would prove no obstacle to the heavy vehicle.

At the last minute he slammed on the brakes. He had seen enough destruction. He couldn't bring himself to add to it. Leaping from the car, he walked up to the cradle and gazed inside, expecting to see a doll.

Sweat bathed his forehead and bile welled in his throat. Another foot, just twelve fatal inches and he would have run over a baby. Who in God's name would leave a helpless infant out on the kerb?

He looked up and down the street as if the parents were honour-bound to show themselves, then headed for the nearest ruin. Before the temblor it must have stood three or four stories tall. The floors had pancaked and the resulting rubble was no more than fifteen feet high.

'Is anyone alive in there?'

The only response was the susurrant sound of the fire-driven wind.

Drawing closer, he peered inside. Furniture, plumbing fixtures, timbers, and what looked to be human bodies, were inextricably twined in the debris. His heart jolted as he caught a flicker of movement out of the corner of his eye. But it was only a torn lace curtain fluttering in a shattered window frame. Nothing else stirred.

With a groan, he returned to the cradle. This was a hell of a time to be saddled with a baby. He didn't have any choice though – he'd have to take it home before he reported to Mayor Schmidt.

Twenty minutes later he brought the Rolls to a stop at the rear of the Nob Hill mansion and got out of the car, carrying the cradle under one arm. The staff were eating lunch when he walked into the kitchen.

Clarence was the first to be aware of his arrival. 'How were things in the city, sir?' he asked.

Noble set his burden down on the counter. 'There are fires everywhere and the earthquake destroyed the water system. Thank God we've got our own cistern. I want you to organise a bucket brigade and start wetting down the—'

A lusty wail interrupted him.

'What have you got there, sir?' the housekeeper, Ellen Delaney asked, getting to her feet.

In his hurry to return, Noble hadn't taken time to look at the infant again. Now he lifted it from its resting place. The pungent odour rising from its soggy bottom made his nostrils twitch.

'Good heavens, sir, you'd better let me have the little one,' Ellen said.

Noble gladly handed the smelly, squirming bundle to her.

Cooing and clucking like a mother hen, Ellen pressed the baby against her bosom. 'I need towels, a basin of warm water, and some corn starch.'

The parlour maid hurried to obey as Ellen lay the child down on the table and stripped off its wet garments. 'It's a girl, sir, a bonny girl.'

Noble's heart constricted. A girl – just like Isabel. While Ellen bathed and changed the infant, he stood at a distance, wondering what the hell to do with it.

Ellen surprised him by returning the child to his arms. 'The Chinese believe you're responsible for someone if you save their life,' she said.

From what he'd seen of Chinatown, there wouldn't be any Oriental gentlemen around to enforce that particular belief.

Just then, the baby wriggled, kicking and stretching after her long confinement. He looked down to find her staring back at him with a pair of smoky grey eyes fringed by thick lashes. A halo of red-gold curls circled her head. Her features were surprisingly well-defined, and she had a deep dimple in her chin.

He couldn't help smiling as she waved her arms in his face. In that unguarded instant, she sparked a tiny fire inside his frozen heart. He gazed at the foundling, experiencing a tenderness he had never expected to feel again – a melting warmth that invaded his chest and sent tendrils right down to his toes.

He had longed for another child after Isabel's death. When Anna banished him from her bed he even considered asking Greta to bear

27

one for him. But he had wanted a child he could claim as his own in front of the whole world so he abandoned the ill-conceived idea.

Now fate had placed a beautiful little girl in his arms. He made up his mind then and there to do everything in his power to keep her.

CHAPTER THREE

Three weeks after the quake, Noble Girard sat behind his desk enjoying a brief respite from work. For once there were no junior executives awaiting his decisions, no secretaries presenting him with documents to read or letters to sign, no emissaries from the mayor demanding that he come to yet another meeting of the emergency committee.

He rocked back in his chair, stretched out his long legs, pyramided his fingers on his chest and closed his eyes. Although his weary body begged for rest, he couldn't quiet his thoughts.

He had come through the disaster far better than most of his peers, he mused. His mansion had survived the fire that swept San Francisco. His Embarcadero offices only need patching plaster and a coat of paint to be good as new. His ships at sea hadn't been harmed.

The ferry business was booming due to the evacuees who aimlessly crossed and recrossed the bay. His wife and his mistress hadn't been injured, and his work on the emergency committee had even made him into something of a local hero.

And then, there was the child.

'Glory – Glory Girard,' he murmured, feeling a peculiar frisson of pleasure at the sound of her new name.

'Who the hell is Glory Girard?' came a gruff male voice from across the office.

Startled, Noble rocked forward, jumped to his feet and spun ninety degrees to face the office door, wondering who had the temerity to intrude on his privacy. A huge man – at least six feet two and almost half as wide – bulked in the doorway like a granite monolith.

It was Willard Bevan, the Pinkerton detective Noble had hired to look into the child's background. The investigator was a study in grey, from his brush-cut hair to the stubble on his cheeks to his soiled tweed suit. He looked as out of place in Noble's luxurious office

29

as a chimneysweep at a banquet. Presumptuous bastard, barging in like that, Noble thought.

'I'm sorry, sir,' Noble's harried secretary quavered from over Bevan's shoulder. 'I told Mr Bevan you were busy but he insisted on seeing you.'

'It's all right.' Noble dismissed her with a wave, then motioned the detective into the room.

'I have very little time for you today. State your business, Mr Bevan.'

Bevan's smile revealed a dismal lack of dental hygiene. 'All in due time, Mr Girard.'

Noble returned to his desk and sat down behind it. Bevan's rank body odour – a combination of sweat, male musk, and cigar smoke – added to his displeasure.

'I wouldn't get too comfortable if I was you,' Bevan warned, pulling a stained manila file from under his grimy jacket. 'I figure you'll want to hear my report in private.'

Noble's glance went to the closed door, then back to Bevan. 'This is private enough.'

'Not for me it isn't. And it won't be for you once you hear what I've learned.'

So the man did know something. Noble had been so sure no one would be able to trace Glory's family. Hiring the world's most prestigious detective agency had been a gesture designed to soothe his conscience, rather than an action he expected to produce results.

'My car is out front. We can go for a drive.'

Noble made no attempt at sociability as he led the way through the building and out onto the pavement. He didn't bother to reply when Bevan oohed and aahed over the Rolls.

'Is this private enough for you?' he asked a few minutes later as he parked on a deserted side street.

Bevan's bloodshot eyes darted back and forth as though to satisfy himself that no one could eavesdrop. Only then did he speak. 'You sure as hell gave me a bitch of an assignment. Do you have any idea how many people are looking for lost relatives?'

Noble eyed the detective up and down, noting the bad haircut, the cheap suit, the dirty linen. 'Are you making excuses for your failure?'

Noble's gimlet gaze had reduced men to quivering children awaiting punishment. It didn't have that effect on Bevan, though. 'No, sir. I wouldn't be wasting your time or mine if that was the case.'

The man looked serenely confident – too confident to suit Noble. What the hell had his investigation uncovered? Silence stretched taut between them while the Pinkerton man lit a cigar and took a deep puff. The aroma of cheap tobacco did nothing to sweeten Noble's mood.

'I know everything there is to know about the baby you found on Taylor Street,' Bevan began. 'It's one hell of a story if I do say so myself.'

Noble detested braggadocio. 'If you're trying to get more money from me, you can forget it.'

'You ain't the only man with money, Mr Girard.'

'But I'm the one paying for this job.'

'Maybe. Maybe not,' Bevan replied cryptically.

'What the hell is that supposed to mean?'

'It means I found the child's family.'

'I don't believe you. I saw that building. No one got out of it alive.'

Bevan's smile was totally devoid of humour. 'The baby did. And she sure as hell didn't get out by herself.'

'Give me that file. I'll sort it out myself.'

'Not so fast, Mr Girard,' Bevan warned, holding the file tight in a ham-sized fist. 'I didn't put everything I know in here – not yet anyway. If you want the whole story, you'll have to hear it from yours truly.'

'Get on with it, then.'

Bevan gave him a mocking salute. 'After you hired me I went straight over to Taylor Street to look through the ruins. A Martha Ames was there and we got to talking. I told her I was looking for relatives who lived in the building. She said she was a midwife and that she delivered a baby girl to a couple in that very building the night of the quake. Said they was real fine folks by the name of Sean and Rebecca O'Meara. Artists, both of them. She talked about them like they was family, even shed a couple of tears.'

'That's a very sad story,' Noble interrupted, 'but I don't see that it's relevant.'

'Oh, it's relevant, all right. According to Mrs Ames, she'd never seen a prettier newborn. I guess she's partial to red hair and a dimpled chin.' Bevan gave Noble a long speculative look. 'Are you partial to those traits too, Mr Girard?'

Noble's gut tightened. The son-of-a-bitch had done it; he'd found Glory's parents. Were they dead – or alive? 'Get on with it, Bevan. What else do you claim to know?'

'It seems that Sean and Rebecca died when the building came down. Mrs Ames identified their bodies. But there was no sign of their child. Now why would that be?'

Noble didn't realise he'd been holding his breath until he let it go. The news couldn't have been better. 'I have no idea. As far as I'm concerned you haven't established a convincing tie between the child I found and the O'Mearas. However I'll be sure to tell your superiors you gave the case your best effort.'

Bevan raised his hands in protest. 'Not so fast, Mr Girard. Here's where the story gets really interesting. While I was on Taylor Street talking to Mrs Ames, my boss assigned me to another case.'

'Your caseload doesn't interest me.'

'It should. Have you ever heard of the Hersch Department Store in Chicago? I hear it's the kind of place rich folks like you shop in.'

'I have,' Noble replied through clenched teeth. He longed to snatch the file from that huge fist and throw Bevan out of the car – to drive away from his insolent smile and repugnant odour. But Bevan wouldn't have mentioned the Hersches unless he had a reason – a damn good one. Noble had the sick feeling he wouldn't enjoy hearing it.

'Saul and Miriam Hersch employed the Pinkerton Agency to look for their missing daughter. I hear Jews don't come any richer,' Bevan continued. 'It seems she ran off to San Francisco when they refused to let her marry. Now they'd give anything to get her back. They promised a handsome bonus on top of our regular fee if we found her. You see, the last they heard she was pregnant. She was an only child. Her baby will inherit a fortune.'

'Are you suggesting their daughter and Rebecca O'Meara are one and the same?'

'I'm not suggesting. *I know*. The Hersches' missing daughter was named Rebecca. She ran off with Sean O'Meara, a Mick artist she met at the Chicago Art Institute. She wrote to her mother from time to time so her mother wouldn't worry.' Bevan shrugged. 'Who can figure it out? What would make a rich Kike heiress run off with a poor Mick?'

'I believe it's called love,' Noble answered, wishing he had the power to make Willard Bevan disappear from the face of the earth – and even more, wishing he had never hired him.

Bevan let go a mirthless chuckle. 'Hell, Mr Girard, I feel like King Solomon, trying to decide who should have the baby. The way I see it, here's the problem in a nutshell. The Hersches would sure want their granddaughter if they knew she had survived. With their money, they're in a position to take care of her real good. On the other hand, they're sure old to be raising a baby girl. I can't forget that you found her – that you've been looking after her all these weeks. I imagine you've become quite attached.'

Noble felt as empty of hope as a beggar's purse. Bevan was toying with him – and he was powerless to stop it. 'I don't need to read the fine print. What's the bottom line?'

'It's simple, Mr Girard. Do you want to keep the baby – or shall I wire the Hersches that I found her? I sure could use the bonus money the Hersches promised.'

Noble knew an extortion attempt when he heard one. He was tempted to tell Bevan to go straight to hell. But then he remembered the way Glory had looked at him when he stopped by the nursery to check on her before going to work that morning.

Her solemn gaze had brimmed with trust. Her tiny hand had curled around one of his fingers as if she never wanted to let him go. Her scent – a *mélange* of baby powder, milk and innocence – had been far more alluring than the most seductive French *parfum*. He hadn't wanted to leave her then – and God knew, he didn't want to lose her now.

When Isabel died a part of him – the loving, gentle part – had died with her. He'd always been a hard taskmaster in business. After his daughter's funeral that hardness had permeated all his actions. But three weeks of coming home to a cooing, contented infant had thawed his frozen soul. He didn't want to lose that warmth.

What would it cost him to keep it? What was Bevan's price?

Suddenly, he realised the money didn't matter. He had more than he could spend in one lifetime. He'd lost his child and the love of his wife when Isabel's tiny coffin had been lowered into the ground. Settling for Greta's counterfeit affection had never filled that void.

With Glory he had a chance to start fresh – to raise the child of his heart if not of his loins – to be loved for himself rather than his fortune. He wanted all that and so much more.

He wanted to be there when Glory took her first steps, he wanted his ears to be the ones that heard her first words, he wanted to shape and mould her into everything he admired most in her sex. He pictured her growing to dutiful loving womanhood under his tutelage. She would be the most devoted daughter in all the city, and he would be the envy of other fathers.

He would do anything to make those images a reality. Lie to the world about who she really was. Bribe Bevan. Such incidentals didn't give Noble pause. Nor did cheating Glory of her true identity, her birthright, her inheritance. He could do much more for her than a pair of elderly grandparents. Besides, they didn't deserve the child after the way they had abandoned their daughter.

'How much did you say the Hersches were willing to pay?'

'I didn't,' Bevan answered.

'It doesn't matter. I'll double the amount and then some. How does fifty thousand dollars sound?'

Bevan's manner was instantly transformed. If he'd been wearing a hat, he would undoubtedly have taken it off and held it against his heart. Lacking an appropriate prop, he nodded his head repetitively. 'More than fair, sir. More than fair.'

'There are a few strings attached to my offer. I want every piece of paper on the case, every single record. And don't even try to hold out on me.' Noble extended his hand for the file. This time Bevan passed it over.

'It's all there, sir.'

'I want your office to wire the Hersches today, telling them their daughter died before giving birth and their son-in-law perished with her. And I want a copy of the telegram.'

'It's as good as done, sir.'

'I'll have the money in my office at the end of the business day. I want you to leave town after you have it, and I never want to see you or hear from you again. Is that clear?'

'I'll be gone before you know it,' Bevan replied with a snaggle-toothed grin.

Noble felt in control for the first time since the detective had appeared in his office. 'Mr Bevan, have you ever wanted anything so much that you would run any risk to have it?'

Again, the detective's head bobbed on the thick stem of his neck. 'This may surprise you, Mr Girard, coming from a man like me – but I've always wanted to travel.'

Noble's smile deepened. 'Bevan, your dreams are about to come true.'

And so are mine, he silently added.

From the day the news burst on the world, Miriam Hersch had read every word the *Chicago Tribune* published about the San Francisco earthquake. After she finished the local paper, she sent the chauffeur to get out of town editions.

But all the newsprint in the world couldn't satisfy her need to know what was happening in the beleaguered city on the bay. She wouldn't be content until word came from the Pinkerton Detective Agency.

Miriam had been pacing the parlour. She walked to the windows, closed the velvet curtains against the chill wind blowing in off the lake and resumed her pacing. The days of waiting and worrying had been so taxing that she felt far older than her thirty-six years.

Would she ever be able to forgive Saul for ordering Rebecca from her home? Was this God's punishment for marrying him for his money rather than love? Surely the Lord wouldn't be that cruel. She hadn't done it for herself. She'd done it for her family.

She had just turned fifteen when she got a job in the stockroom at Hersch's dry goods store. The pay had been a Godsend to her family. For the first time since they had arrived from Russia there was a hot meal on the table at the end of the day, and a few lumps of coal to heat the dismal room the six of them shared.

Then Saul had seen her and all their lives had changed. A confirmed bachelor twenty years her senior, Saul had been instantly smitten with her ripening body, her grey eyes and her jet curls.

A couple of weeks after she went to work at Hersch's Mercantile, Saul had asked to meet her parents. He had seen how they were living and instantly waved the magic wand of his wealth over her family, moving them into a comfortable six-room apartment a few blocks from his own magnificent mansion. Then the wooing began in earnest.

He had loved her madly and wanted her to love him in return. God knew, she had tried. But love couldn't be pried from the human heart like a pearl from an oyster's shell. She hadn't loved him until their daughter had been born, twelve months later.

Tears oozed from her eyes as she recalled holding Rebecca in her arms, nursing her, watching her grow and thrive. Nothing could have kept her from reliving those moments with her daughter and grandchild – certainly not Saul's objections. A few more weeks, just a few more weeks and she would have been in San Francisco.

Knuckling her tears away, she turned abruptly and bumped into Saul. In her preoccupation she hadn't heard him come home. He had aged since the quake, but tonight he looked worse than ever.

'What is it?' she asked. 'What's wrong with you?'

'I heard from the Pinkerton Agency.'

'Thank God. I don't know how much longer I could have stood the waiting. When will we see Rebecca? When will our darling girl come home?'

To Miriam's horror tears began to slide down Saul's cheeks. 'It's all my fault,' he moaned.

'What's your fault? Is Rebecca hurt?'

Saul moaned again.

Miriam knew she ought to be concerned about him. The more she tried, though, the angrier she became. But for Saul, Rebecca wouldn't have been in San Francisco in the first place. 'I'll take the next train to San Francisco and nurse her myself.'

'That won't be necessary,' Saul finally managed to say.

'Damn you, Saul, tell me what you know.'

His mouth opened again and this time four fateful words emerged. 'Our daughter is dead.'

'What about Sean?'

'The son-of-a-bitch died too.'

'And the baby?'

Saul trembled like a sapling in a gale. 'The baby was never born.'

'I don't believe it. I'd have known if we'd lost the three of them. I'd have felt something.'

Saul reached inside his coat pocket, took out an envelope and offered it to her. 'It's all here in a telegram from the Pinkertons' San Francisco office. Their apartment building was destroyed. A neighbour identified their bodies.'

Miriam stared at the envelope long and hard before she had the courage to take it from Saul's hand. When she did dread crawled across her skin, turning her flesh to ice. She opened the envelope, removed the single sheet of paper and read it carefully. She could almost feel her heart breaking.

Daughters weren't supposed to die before their mothers. Grandchildren weren't supposed to perish in the womb.

Her vision narrowed. She felt feverish and cold at the same time. If Saul hadn't taken her arm, she might have fallen.

'You need a drink,' he said, guiding her to a chair as though she'd lost her sight. 'We both do.'

He shambled to the sideboard and filled two glasses with whisky.

'The Pinkertons are wrong,' she said so quietly that she might have been speaking to herself, 'I know they're wrong.'

Saul returned to her side and held out a brimming glass. When she refused it he drank his own whisky down and then hers too. 'I know it's hard, Miriam, but we've got to face the truth.'

'You face it. Go to the synagogue and say the Kaddish again the way you did after Rebecca left. Tear out your hair, rend your clothes. Do what ever you have to do. But don't expect me to do it with you. I'll never give up hope. Never.'

Noble led Father Tremaine to the front door and opened it wide, hoping to speed the youthful prelate on his way. He had no further use for him now that the christening was over.

'It's a fine day,' Father Tremaine observed.

Noble gazed at the impossibly blue sky. It was the exact colour of the sky in Raphael's painting of the *Alba Madonna*. Noble smiled, recalling how he had outbid the Hermitage for the canvas. 'Indeed it is.'

'I wasn't talking about the weather,' Father Tremaine said, his ascetic features lit by a smile. 'I was thinking about your wife. She seems better.'

Although Noble didn't believe in discussing family matters with strangers, Anna's personal confessor was privy to the fact of her melancholia. 'Having a child in the house has done more for her than all the doctors she's seen.'

Tremaine nodded. 'I have often advised Mrs Girard to consider adoption.'

The priest's words banished Noble's euphoria. 'You won't forget your promise to keep silent on the matter?'

'You can count on it. Your daughter will never hear the truth of her birth from me.' Tremaine put his slender hand on Noble's shoulder. 'It's perfectly understandable for a couple to keep adoption a secret – and far better for the child. I'm sure you can count on your friends to guard your confidence. I do, however, worry about your servants.'

Meddlesome bastard, Noble thought, but managed a thin smile. 'It's kind of you to concern yourself. My butler and housekeeper are absolutely trustworthy. The others have been transferred to out of town positions in my company. They have been well compensated for any inconvenience.'

'You're wise to do so, sir. And kind too. I don't know many men in your position who would open their home and heart to a child they knew nothing about. God will bless you for it. You can be sure of that.'

Noble almost gagged at the priest's unctuous tone. He had always wondered how men of the cloth felt free to speak for the Lord. Although Noble was accustomed to wielding power, to shaping lives and events, it would give him pause.

Thank heaven the chauffeur chose that moment to drive up in the Rolls. 'My man will take you back to the parish house.'

'I hope we will see you in church soon with your wife and child,' Tremaine said before Noble could shut the front door between them.

Noble couldn't resist answering, 'You surely know what the New Testament says about rendering unto God that which is God's and unto Caesar, that which is Caesar's. God is my wife's department. I take care of Caesar.'

He closed the door on the startled priest, spun on his heels and headed back to the parlour where the christening had taken place. Anna and Mrs Wilder, Glory's nurse, were still there. Glory slept soundly in the nurse's arms.

'It was a lovely service,' Anna declared. 'Quiet and dignified just as I wanted. In these uncertain times, it's good to know the child will go straight to God if her life comes to a sudden end.' It was so like her to imagine the worst possible eventuality. Anna lived in a world where disaster and tragedy were just a heartbeat away.

'I'm sure our little girl will have a long and happy life,' he said.

'One devoted to her Lord and saviour,' Anna amended. 'If you will excuse me Noble, I'll go up to my room. I'm quite tired.'

Noble had made up his mind to be on his best behaviour around Anna for the child's sake. 'Of course, my dear. I'll look in on you later.'

Although they hadn't discussed it, Anna's behaviour told him she shared his resolution. She actually gave him a peck on the cheek before leaving the room. Her lips were dry, her touch as light as a hummingbird's. So much for passion, Noble thought as he took a handkerchief from his pocket and wiped at the spot.

'Shall I take Miss Glory up to bed?' the nurse asked.

'I'd like to hold her for a while,' Noble replied.

'There's nothing more soothing to an infant than her father's arms,' Miss Wilder cooed.

'I'll bring her up to you when she wakes,' Noble replied, taking Glory's sweet weight in his arms.

He walked to a chair that afforded him a view of the gardens and settled into it. Glory slept on peacefully, her rosebud mouth forming words she had yet to learn.

Noble's gaze stayed riveted on her as he thought how well things had turned out. Willard Bevan was on a steamer bound for the Orient. Father Tremaine would never break his vow of silence. Only Clarence and Ellen remained from the original staff. Even Anna's reclusiveness had worked in his favour. A few months from now few would recall that Anna hadn't carried the child. Glory was his – truly his in the eyes of God and the law.

Late afternoon winged into evening with only the deepening shadows to mark the boundary as Noble sat with the child in his arms, dreaming of the future with his perfect daughter by his side. Glory would be his life's crowning achievement.

PART TWO

Glory Girard

The obstinacy of human beings is exceeded
only by the obstinacy of inanimate objects.
Alexander Chase – *Perspectives*, 1966

CHAPTER FOUR

San Francisco – 1924

Honour, honesty, fidelity, and trust. The words had been engraved on Glory's heart and mind as far back as she could remember. Her father wanted – no, he insisted that she exemplify those virtues. Yet here she was, turning her back on all four.

Guilt soured her stomach as she opened her bedroom door and tiptoed into the hall. She knew giddy girls who snuck out of their homes to dally with a forbidden beau. However no would-be Romeo awaited Glory in the garden. Her goal was far more high-minded. She was teaching herself to draw.

If only she could make her father understand how much being an artist meant to her. But how could she when she didn't understand it herself? Sometimes she felt like an alien in her own skin – an alien who had no true tie to the life or the people around her.

She wanted to be an artist despite her father's opposition. The need to recreate her vision of the world was as much a part of who she was as her red hair and dimpled chin. She had been drawing from the day she was old enough to hold a crayon, not colouring inside the lines of a drawing someone else had done like most children. She had insisted on creating the lines herself and then filling them in with colour.

At first art had been no more than an occupation, a way to wile away time. By her tenth birthday it had become a preoccupation. Now she saw it as her vocation – the thing she had been born to do.

Widening her eyes in the predawn gloom, she gazed down the corridor to her father's room, relieved that no light seeped from under his door. He rarely got up before six-thirty when Clarence delivered a tray laden with coffee and freshly squeezed orange juice.

When she was little she thought Noble was a farmer because so much of the food they ate had been raised on Girard land. Newly picked citrus arrived weekly from the Girard groves in the Sacramento Valley. Vegetables came from their farms in the San Fernando Valley and beef from their ranch outside Blythe.

She'd been stunned when she finally understood the full scope of Noble's business interests – and that she would one day inherit them all. Noble embodied the word *tycoon* and yet he'd always had time for her. He was the sweetest, most generous, most understanding man in the world – with one exception.

She had flung the lance of her ambition against the shield of his intransigence time and again and never made a dent. His extensive art collection attested to his love of art. Why didn't he want her to be an artist?

She tiptoed down the hall, careful to avoid all the places where the stout oak floors squeaked underfoot. Those creaks and groans were the only reminder of the great quake. As she slipped past her mother's room she tried to imagine what it must have been like for Anna on that fateful day.

Anna had been alone and in labour, her bedroom lit only by the fires that consumed the city, her cries for help unheard above the holocaust's fearful din. A shudder ran the full length of Glory's five foot eight inch frame as she tried to imagine herself in Anna's place. How terrified her mother must have been, giving birth by herself. Did she cry out for Noble?

Glory couldn't imagine Anna needing any saviour other than the Lord. In her mother's lexicon duty to *Him* superseded everything else. Anna prayed from morning to night, from vespers to compline like a nun. God knew, she lived like one.

Glory couldn't recall ever seeing a single sign of affection between her parents. Yet they must have felt something for each other – passion if not love – or she wouldn't have been born. She felt her face heat up. She shouldn't be thinking about her parents that way. It wasn't *comme il faut*.

According to Madame Gilot most of the things she thought about weren't *comme il faut*. And yet she couldn't seem to control her thoughts. In her bed at night she felt stirrings she didn't understand, needs she couldn't label, desires that made her skin seem too tight.

What did it feel like to be kissed by a man, to be held?
To make love?
And how, exactly, did a man and woman go about it?
Why hadn't anyone told her?
Her knowledge of male genitalia came from the Greek and Roman sculptures she'd seen in museums, most of them adorned with fig leaves. Her knowledge of the sex act had been gleaned from giggling conversations with her best friend, Cal. And for all Cal's pseudo-sophistication, she didn't know much more than Glory.

Glory felt her blush deepen. She longed to break free of her circumscribed existence, to leave the last trappings of childhood behind, to explore the boundaries of her woman's heart and soul. Most of all, she ached to define her talent – or lack thereof. But everyone from her father to the help still treated her like a child.

She tip-toed down the servants' stairs, through the back hall and into the kitchen. The room was empty but for the lingering aroma of last night's supper.

A voice stopped her in her tracks. 'Good heavens, Miss Glory,' the housekeeper said, emerging from behind the pantry door, 'what are you doing up at this hour?'

Ellen Ashton quivered with sympathy at the sight of Glory's shoulders hunched protectively over a sketch-pad. For the life of her, Ellen couldn't see what harm there was in the girl drawing a few pictures, especially when Mr Girard took such pride in the gloomy paintings of saints and the like he had hanging throughout the house.

Old Masters, he called them. Old disasters was more like it. It fair gave Ellen the shivers, seeing Anna Girard look at a painting of the crucifixion with the same hungry longing other people displayed when they gazed at a juicy steak.

Still, Ellen thought, heaving a sigh, she had best remember Mr Girard paid her salary. She had to do his bidding and so did Glory – or there would be hell to pay.

'You promised your father you wouldn't draw pictures any more.'

Glory's generous mouth firmed and she hugged her sketch-pad even closer. 'I promised my father I wouldn't go to town to sketch. But I didn't say anything about not sketching in the grounds.'

Lord, she was strong-willed, a regular chip off the old block, Ellen thought, then let go a nervous titter. So many years had gone by that she thought of Miss Glory as the Girards' natural born child.

45

'I don't mean to get you in trouble,' Glory was saying. 'I'll take the blame for my actions if my father finds out about them. But I'd really be grateful if you didn't tell him you saw me this morning.'

'Don't you worry, dear girl. I think the Lord will forgive me if I don't volunteer the information. My immortal soul won't burn for one sin of omission.'

Glory couldn't help smiling. Ellen was one of those rare individuals who radiated good cheer no matter the circumstances. She had an abundance of affection that she lavished on everyone, from her husband, to Glory, to the lowliest maid.

If only Anna could have been more like Ellen, Glory mused with an inward sigh. Glory's love for her mother had beaten against the stone wall of Anna's indifference for as long as Glory could remember. The last time her mother had kissed or held her had faded from her memory, it had been so long ago.

'You've got an hour before your father comes down for breakfast,' Ellen reminded her. 'Best make the most of it.'

Glory didn't give Ellen a chance to change her mind. She opened the door and stepped outside. The sky, a subtle union of gold and crimson, reminded her of pink champagne. Would she ever be able to duplicate that colour on canvas?

From his bedroom window Noble had a perfect view of Glory as she headed down the drive. She was a splendid young woman, as perfectly formed as a Praxiteles' Aphrodite. He couldn't help but envy the man who would one day run his fingers through that wild Titian mane.

He had been delighted when she refused to cut it in the short shingle that was all the rage. He'd applauded her independence then almost as much as he objected to it now. His once dutiful daughter had become a rebel through and through.

Although he filled her closet with designer clothes by Lanvin, Drecoll, Chanel, and Patou, Glory preferred less ostentatious clothing like the simple cotton blouse and pleated skirt she wore this morning. It swirled around her as she walked, exposing tantalising glimpses of her legs.

His stomach knotted as he thought how Glory's tapered ankles and well-formed calves might entice some rogue male. She was so innocent – so vulnerable. She knew nothing of men's needs and desires. Had he made a mistake raising her that way?

His fists clenched as he imagined some lust-driven youth promising her anything to get her into bed. Damn and double damn. There were times when being the father of a beautiful girl was pure hell.

Although he couldn't see her face he knew all too well the look of almost orgasmic pleasure that would appear on it as she began sketching. He'd first seen that look when, at the age of seven, he found her tucked in a chair in the music room, trying to copy Raphael's *Alba Madonna*.

Over time art had become more and more important to her, until now he felt as if he ran a poor second in her affections. Nothing in his past life, not even Isabel's death, unnerved him the way Glory's single-minded determination to become an artist did. In it he scented loss and disaster, the way a fox scents his own death when the wind carries the aroma of hounds to his den.

A knock on the bedroom door interrupted his morbid introspection. 'Come in,' he called out.

Tightening the belt of his velvet robe, he managed a cheerful smile as Clarence walked in. The butler's marriage to Ellen had brought a contentment that permanently softened his features.

'Good morning, sir. I trust you slept well,' Clarence said, depositing a tray laden with a Limoges coffee service, a crystal decanter of fresh orange juice and a copy of the *Wall Street Journal*, on a table near the window.

While Clarence decanted the juice and coffee, Noble picked up the paper and glanced at it. He was so preoccupied with Glory that headlines about the ongoing Tea Pot Dome oil leasing scandal failed to capture his interest.

After Clarence left Noble dropped all pretence of reading and returned to the window. He stared out at the figure in the gazebo wondering where he had gone wrong with her.

He'd done everything in his power, everything he could think of to mould her character according to his own precepts. He'd hired her nannies, chosen her schools, guided her choice of friends, even filled her wardrobes with clothes suited to a proper *jeune fille*. But over the last few years he had felt his control slipping away, almost as if Glory's talented parents had risen from the dead to claim their daughter.

47

Did Glory suspect the truth? Could that be the cause of the widening rift between them?

Six people had been privy to all the facts. Bevan had died aboard the *Titanic* and the others, Anna, Clarence, Ellen and Father Tremaine had been sworn to secrecy. Despite all the precautions he had taken the truth seemed to be crowding closer, and all because Glory wanted to follow in her parents' footsteps.

He couldn't let that happen – ever.

CHAPTER FIVE

Wisps of fog curled around San Francisco's hills like kittens circling a woman's skirts. The freshening breeze carried with it the briny scent of the Pacific. The view and the aroma were at once familiar and exotic, a reminder to Glory of the places she had been and places she longed to go.

Squinting to narrow her field of vision, she gazed at the nearest group of buildings, plying the charcoal with almost feverish haste. She much preferred going to the waterfront to draw stevedores at work, or housewives coming to buy seafood with string bags dangling from their wrists.

She seemed to have an innate understanding of anatomy in motion while rigid rectangular cityscapes continued to evade her. How do you draw a wall without outlining every brick? How do you reproduce the sheen of a window pane where the sun glances from it?

Glory gazed down at her sketch, her lips curling in disgust. It was all detail and no feeling.

There had to be a way to capture what the eye saw without pencilling in every single thing. But the technique remained as elusive as her mother's affection. Commitment and desire were no guarantee of success – or she'd be another Rembrandt.

Half an hour later she returned to her room and hid her morning's work at the back of her wardrobe. A cursory glance in the dressing table mirror showed her how ill-kempt she looked. She didn't have time to repair the damage properly, though. Instead she hurriedly smoothed her skirt, tucked in her blouse and finger-combed her wind-tossed hair.

Her racing feet kept time with her heart as she made her way to the dining room to join her father. Its classic proportions and frescoed ceiling had always delighted her. Not this morning. Concern slowed her step as she approached the enormous mahogany table. Did her father know why she was late?

'Good morning,' she said, sliding into her chair.

'Good morning,' he replied, his face hidden by the newspaper.

One of the maids appeared as if summoned by a genie. 'What would you like for breakfast this morning, Miss Girard?' the maid asked cheerfully.

For a moment Glory wished she could change places with the girl. How wonderful it must be to earn your own living, to come and go as you pleased, to be mistress of your fate.

Although the fresh air had given her an appetite, the thought of her father's displeasure made her queasy. 'Just toast and coffee, thank you.'

She waited for the maid to leave, then turned to Noble. 'Did you sleep well?'

He lowered the paper and folded it carefully, smoothing the creases as if he had nothing more urgent on his mind than preserving the pages. 'Very well – and you, sweetheart?'

'I overslept.'

She almost choked on the lie. However he'd be furious if she told him she had risen early to steal an hour with a sketch-pad. She couldn't understand why he objected to her drawing when so many of her peers went to speakeasies where they danced half the night, drank bathtub gin until they couldn't see straight and smoked like chimneys on a winter day. Unlike those things, art wasn't illegal, immoral, or even unhealthy.

She saw charcoal smudges on her fingers, lowered her hands beneath the table and wiped the telltale stains with her napkin. 'Where's Mother?'

'She's a little under the weather. Ellen took a tray up to her room,' Noble replied.

Although he still seethed over Glory's disobedience, the rigours of business had long since taught him to conceal his emotions. He prided himself on being in control at all times.

'Is she well enough to go to morning Mass?'

Noble almost felt sorry for Glory. How tired she must be of going to Mass every day. A daily dose of religion would drive him mad. But he and Anna had come to a *quid pro quo* years ago. In exchange for giving him a free hand with Glory's upbringing, he permitted Anna to oversee the girl's religious training. It had been rigorous.

'Your mother hasn't missed a morning Mass since . . .' he almost said since Isabel's death and quickly substituted, 'since the 1906 earthquake. Now that you've graduated from Madame Gilot's you know she expects you to go with her.'

Seeing Glory's crestfallen expression, he postponed the lecture he'd been planning. 'Why don't you have lunch with me afterwards? The chauffeur can drop you at my office before he takes your mother home. There's a terrific new French restaurant near Union Square you might enjoy.'

A quiet corner table would be the perfect setting to tell her he'd seen her that morning, to explain he only wanted what was best for her – and it in no way included a career as an artist.

Glory rewarded him with a radiant smile. 'I'd love to have lunch with you, Daddy.'

'It's a date, sweetheart.'

He took a last swallow of coffee before getting to his feet, then stopped by her chair and kissed her cheek on his way out. She smelled of fresh air and femininity. She smelled like a woman.

His little girl had grown up. He knew that losing her was inevitable, but he'd be damned if he'd forfeit her to the precarious, licentious lifestyle of a female artist.

Anna was in the hall, pacing impatiently when she heard Glory approach. 'It's about time,' she said, checking the diamond watch pinned to her dress. 'Another minute and I would have sent one of the maids to see what was keeping you.'

She looked Glory up and down, taking in the wild mop of hair, the dowdy blouse and skirt, the muddy shoes. 'Surely you don't plan to go to Mass like that?'

'What's wrong with it? I look perfectly respectable.'

'Don't talk back. No Girard goes to church looking the way you do. I want you to change into your new navy dress with the matching cloche – and make it fast.'

The girl was hopeless, Anna thought as she watched Glory take the steps two at a time. She was too tall, too bosomy, too outspoken, too full of herself – too everything except devout. Despite Anna's best efforts, Glory was sadly remiss in that department.

'Father told me you weren't feeling well,' Glory said when she rejoined Anna a few minutes later.

'I was up half the night with a sick headache and being kept waiting hasn't helped. But I'm sure I'll feel ever so much better after Mass. By the way, Monsignor Carruthers wants us to join him and Father Tremaine in the rectory for tea afterwards.'

'Must I?' Glory burst out. 'I'm supposed to meet Daddy for lunch.'

'You'll have more than enough time to do both. I don't think you've been paying enough attention to your religious duties, young lady. Besides, I told Monsignor you would be happy to help Father Tremaine with the widows' and orphans' clothing drive. You need something to keep you busy. Idle hands do the devil's work.'

'My hands wouldn't be idle if I could go on with my education.'

'Watch your mouth, Miss. You learned everything a proper female needs to know at finishing school. Madame Gilot has trained three generations of San Franciscans – myself included. Madame does a superb job of preparing women to be the sort of wife any man could be proud to call his own.'

Dealing with Glory had worsened Anna's headache. Why couldn't Glory ever do as she was told without a war of words? Between her rebellious attitude, her unseemly height, and that blatant mop of red hair, she seemed more like a shop-girl than a Girard, let alone a Mendez. Glory's behaviour and appearance made a mockery of both family names.

Anna had but to close her eyes to envision how well-mannered her own Isabel would have been, how obedient, how *soignée*. Sometimes her dead daughter seemed more real to her than the living one. Not that Glory was her real daughter.

If only Noble had been able to find out something about Glory's background before the adoption, they might have been spared a lot of grief. Now it was painfully obvious she'd come from the gutter where Noble had found her. She should never have let Noble talk her into keeping the girl.

As Anna settled in the back of the Rolls, her thoughts returned to the day of the great quake. The nightmarish trembler had given her a dreadful headache – and having Noble abandon her to set off on a mission for the mayor while aftershocks continued to rattle the house hadn't helped. At the time she'd been convinced he'd run off to see to his mistress's safety. What a fool he'd been, thinking she didn't know about Greta Saxlund – or that she'd have cared if she did.

She'd taken a little laudanum to soothe her shattered nerves, then spent half an hour at the *prie dieu* in her bedroom waiting for the drug to work. She was lying down, half asleep, when she heard a knock on the door.

'Anna, may I come in?' Noble called out.

Not having the energy to deal with him – or anything else considering what she'd already endured – she didn't answer. The sound of the door opening made her groan with displeasure. The least Noble could do was respect her privacy.

The bed sagged as he sat down beside her. 'Wake up, Anna. I've got something wonderful, something truly glorious to show you.'

'Can't it wait? I'm exhausted.'

'It can't. You see my dear wife, I have a little miracle here – a genuine gift from God.'

Damn him. He'd known just how to pique her interest. She'd opened her eyes to see him holding a bundle in his arms. 'What is it?'

'A baby. I found her on Taylor Street an hour ago. That part of the city is doomed. What the quake didn't destroy, the fires will. I think God meant me to find her and bring her home.'

Before she could object he thrust the child in her arms.

'I know no child can ever replace Isabel,' he rattled on, 'but this little girl has just lost her family. We can do so much for her, and maybe – just maybe – she can do something for us. Do you remember how happy we were when this house had a child in it?'

'How cruel you are,' she replied, refusing to look down at the baby. How dare he imagine a child he'd snatched off the streets could hold the shadows at bay, the way her darling Isabel had?

'I know your illness isn't your fault,' he said. 'You've done everything the doctors suggested, taken every conceivable medicine, but none of it made you better. I've watched you suffer, watched you retreat from the world. Perhaps you're holding the perfect antidote in your arms.'

Anna finally looked down at the child, feeling its warmth through the thin blanket. It couldn't be more than a day or two old. She studied it carefully, taking in the red hair, the tiny dimple in its chin. Could this foundling lift the despair that had shrouded her mind since God called Isabel to heaven?

'We're here, Mother.'

The sound of Glory's voice returned Anna to the present. Blinking, she gazed out the car window at Saint Mary's stately façade. Now she knew the answer to the question she'd asked herself that day. Raising another child hadn't helped. Only God could ease her torment.

Melancholia had such a lilting sound the first time she'd heard the word on a doctor's lips all those years ago. *She'd get over it in time*, they told her. But they had been wrong – so very wrong.

Since Isabel's death she had lived in a tenebrous gloom that no one else saw – poised on the precipice of a bottomless pit of depression, with only prayer to keep her from falling into it.

But for her faith in God, she would have given up long ago.

Noble couldn't help noting the appreciation in men's eyes as Glory followed the *maître d'* to the quiet corner table he'd requested. The sober navy dress she wore failed to conceal her lush figure, while the russet curls escaping the edge of her cloche added a piquant note to her stunning appearance. His little girl had grown up to be everything he'd dreamed of all those years ago – everything and more.

It was the *more* that troubled him.

The day Bevan told him about Glory's Jewish/Irish lineage, about her parents' artistic genius, Noble had been enthralled. Beauty, talent, passion, intelligence, a fiery spirit – they were all part of her heritage. He'd imagined himself as her Pygmalion, sculpting the raw clay of her genealogy into magnificent womanhood, never dreaming that her patrimony would one day threaten to undo all he'd achieved.

After the amenities of seating and ordering had been attended to – as was his habit, he chose for them both – he gave her the benefit of his total attention. 'How was your morning?'

'All right,' she replied, although the expression in her eyes said it had been far from pleasant. 'After Mass we had tea with Monsignor Carruthers and Father Tremaine. Mother told them I'd help with the widows' and orphans' clothing drive.'

The mention of Tremaine got Noble's attention. 'You don't sound very happy about it.'

'It's not the work I mind. It's just that there are other things I'd rather be doing.'

Widows and orphans be damned. 'I'll speak to your mother on your behalf.'

Noble didn't want Glory to work side by side with Tremaine any more than she wanted to work with the priest. Tremaine meant well. However he might say something in an unguarded moment that would cause Glory to ask questions Noble wouldn't want to answer.

The arrival of their mussels ravigote put an end to Noble's introspection. He kept the conversation on neutral ground until the dessert dishes had been cleared away. Only then did he broach what had been on his mind since he'd seen Glory heading down the drive with her sketch-pad.

'I asked you to join me today because I saw you this morning. I'm deeply hurt. It's not like you to disobey me.'

'Perhaps if I understood why you—'

Noble didn't permit her to finish. 'There are some things you're not mature enough to understand.'

'You make it sound as if I'm still in nappies. I'll be eighteen in a few months. Have you forgotten you married Mother when she was my age?'

'I live with the consequences every day,' he replied grimly.

Glory could have handled his anger. The sadness in his eyes swept away her defences. 'I'm sorry. I had no right to say something like that.'

'You have every right. You live with the consequences too. If I hadn't been in such a hurry to marry your mother I might have realised she wasn't well enough to take on the responsibility of being a wife.'

Glory ached to comfort him the way he had comforted her through all her childhood illnesses and hurts. But she had too much at stake.

'Just because you and Mother made a mistake doesn't mean I will. Remember the day you found me in the music room copying the Raphael. When you praised what I'd done I felt ten feet tall.'

'There's a vast difference between a child spending a pleasant hour or two crayoning and a woman devoting the rest of her life to art.'

At least he had admitted she was a woman. It was a step in the right direction. 'It's not as if I'm some silly creature who wants to run off to Hollywood to become a movie star. I know the odds against my becoming a successful artist. All I'm asking for is the chance to try.'

'You're asking for heartbreak,' Noble thundered, then lowered his voice when other diners looked their way. 'I won't let you do that to yourself – or to me. You're a lovely young woman but a very naive one. You think you know your own mind and I can't help admiring your determination. You're very like me at the same age. I had dreams too and I fought just as hard for them.'

'What were they?'

'I wanted to be an explorer, to live a life of adventure.'

'Oh Daddy, you should have,' she burst out, sorrowing for his stifled ambition as much as her own.

'You're wrong, sweetheart. My father insisted on my joining the Girard Company and I've never regretted it. He was right about my future just as I am about yours. Someday – although I can't help hoping it won't be too soon – you're going to fall in love, get married, and have a family. Being a wife and mother is the most important thing a woman can do.'

'I don't agree. The world is changing . . .'

'Some things will never change,' he interrupted. 'I want your promise that you'll forget all this nonsense about being an artist.'

Her love for her father and her passion for art fought a short battle inside her. Neither won. 'I'll think about everything you've said. But I want you to think about something too. Will you at least consider the possibility that I'm old enough to know what I want?'

'You certainly know how to drive a hard bargain.'

'Of course I do. After all, I am your daughter.'

Calpurnia Pompeia Flaminia Blackstone sat at her dressing table, plucking her eyebrows into the pencil thin arch that current fashion demanded. Her father – a professor of Roman history – only refrained from adding a fourth Latin tongue-twister to her name because there wasn't enough room on the birth certificate.

Most motherless girls would have withered under the professor's absent-minded parenting. Calpurnia Pompeia Flaminia had thrived. At five she had told him she wanted to be called *Cal* and enforced her decision by refusing to answer to anything else. From then on she had taken her life into her own hands.

She was strong-willed, as affectionate as a puppy, loyal unto death to her friends, and desperately anxious to become a sophisticated woman of the world. Somehow it never occurred to her that those traits might not go together.

'Ouch,' she squealed as a particularly recalcitrant hair finally suc-
cumbed to her insistent tugging.

Wearing peach satin tap pants and a matching bra, her ebony hair
cut in a straight slash just below her ears, her lips painted a deep
carmine, her complexion as pale as milk, she looked every inch the
flapper she hoped to become – as soon as she convinced her father
she was old enough.

She leaned so close to the mirror that her breath steamed the
glass, lifted first one eyebrow and then the other and managed a
seductive pout at the same time. It was her version of a vampish
come-hither look and she practised it regularly. The first time she
set foot in a speakeasy she intended to be ready.

'Theda Bara, eat your heart out,' she declared, then took a bottle
of blood red polish from the dresser. She applied two coats to her
nails and was waiting for them to dry when she heard a knock on
the door.

'Cal, are you decent?' came Glory's voice.

'Not really – but come in anyway,' Cal answered. She practised a
hip-swiveling lubricious glide as she crossed the floor and opened
the door. Glory stood there looking like she was in a blue funk and
had dressed accordingly.

'Who died?'

'No one. I went to Mass with Mother.'

'It's a wonder you don't have calluses on your knees considering
all the time you spend on them.'

Glory unpinned her hat, kicked off her shoes, then sat on the edge
of Cal's bed, preparing to unburden herself. Cal had a devious mind
that had got the two of them out of scrapes in the past. 'I need some
advice.'

Cal batted her lashes. 'Please tell me you've taken a lover and
want to know how to make him your sexual slave.'

Glory couldn't help laughing. 'If I had, what would your advice be?'

'Advice? I'd be dying to know what it felt like to lose your virginity.'

'No such luck. I want to talk about my father.'

'Again?'

'Again.' Glory sighed. 'He saw me sneaking out of the house to
go sketching this morning.'

'Why should that bother him? I just don't get it.'

'Neither do I. He gave me his standard lecture and then added a new twist. He wants me to get married.'

'He what?'

'He said being a wife and mother is the most important thing a woman can do.'

Cal collapsed on the bed with a dramatic glazing over of her china blue eyes. 'Eeeyuck! He's even worse than my father. Dad may spend all his time thinking about ancient Rome but even he knows this is the twentieth century.'

Glory couldn't help squirming. Hearing her father criticised always made her uncomfortable. 'He's just looking out for me.'

'Looking out for you, my ass. Your father is a famous collector. He thinks of you as another one of his possessions like his art and his first editions. The question is, what are you going to do about it?'

'I'm going to think things over the way I promised.'

'Damn it, Glory, it isn't fair. You've known you wanted to be an artist all your life. But your father acts like you want to become a second Josephine Baker and dance in the nude wearing a couple of banana skins. There has to be a way to get through to him.' Cal narrowed her eyes. 'Have you tried crying? That always works with my Dad. And I don't mean a few ladylike like tears. I mean bawling your head off.'

'He'd just send me to my room until I got over it. Besides, he's only trying to save me from heartbreak. And who knows – he may be right. I don't even know if I have any talent.'

'Of course you have talent. You've always been special.'

'You mean different, don't you?' Glory didn't wait for an answer. 'If you only knew how much I wished I could be like you.'

'Like me? I don't have any talent, except maybe for flirting and making boys want to get in my knickers. And my father doesn't have any money. I wouldn't have been able to go to Madame Gilot's if he hadn't been on the staff.' Cal propped her head in her hands. 'You know your Dad better than I do. What's the best way to make him take you seriously?'

'I suppose facts and figures might do it. He's a business man first, last and always.'

Cal abandoned her pose, jumped off the bed and fetched a silver flask and two shot glasses from a dressing table drawer.

'Now don't make a face, Miss Priss,' she said, filling both glasses and handing one to Glory, 'It's only sherry and according to *mon père*, sherry is medicinal. It will help me to think.'

Glory couldn't help laughing. Although Cal had failed French twice – loudly proclaiming that a well-bred woman only needed to know enough French not to be intimidated by a sommelier – she loved to sprinkle a word or two in her conversation.

'*À votre santé*,' Cal said. She took a sip, then ran her pretty pink tongue around the inside of the glass. 'That's more like it. Now let's get back to the problem of convincing your father that wanting to be an artist isn't the same thing as wanting to be a prostitute.'

'I'm afraid it's a lost cause.'

'My father says your parents are so old-fashioned that they probably equate studying art with running off to Paris, starving in an attic, drinking absinthe, and screwing your brains out. Of course Dad didn't quite put it that way. He doesn't have my way with words. He suggested you talk to them about attending a school that has an outstanding reputation, both in the art world and in academic circles.'

'What school?'

'The Chicago Art Institute. According to Dad, it's the *crème de la crème*. Unless I'm mistaken, he has their catalogue in his office. You can take it home with you.' Cal jumped up suddenly and Charlestoned towards the door. 'You said facts and figures would impress your father. Wait until he gets a load of that catalogue. It should make him see being an artist in a whole new light.'

CHAPTER SIX

Greta Saxlund liked to boast that no man had ever thrown her out of bed. It had taken the 1906 earthquake to do that. Lately though, she couldn't help wondering how much longer Noble Girard would want her in his bed and be willing to pay for the privilege.

He'd been less attentive the last few years, his visits shorter, his ardour more difficult to awaken, although she had tried every trick in her repertoire. If he had been any other man she would have known he'd found another woman. But Noble was far too ruthless to continue paying her bills if he'd fallen in lust with someone else. Perhaps at fifty-two he was simply too old to get it up the way he used to.

Maybe the fault was hers. Taking off her maribou-trimmed robe she gazed up at the mirror over her bed, studying her body with the dispassionate interest of a surgeon evaluating a prospective patient.

Her tits had sagged a little, her stomach wasn't as flat as it used to be and just last week she had plucked the first grey hair from her pubic fleece. Still, she looked damn good for forty-four. Maybe she was too old to be a ragtime doll but she was much too young to be cast off like an old rag.

By the time Noble drove up to her townhouse at three that afternoon she had set the scene for seduction. The curtains had been drawn, the air liberally sprayed with Chanel No. 5.

Although an unseasonably cold wind rattled the windows, she had recreated summer inside. Pots filled with gardenias and camellias, and vases overflowing with sweet scented roses added cheerful splashes of colour to the parlour. In case Noble developed a post-coital appetite the delicacies in the ice-box included such warm weather fare as lobster salad, oysters Rockefeller, and chocolate mousse.

She had taken even more trouble with her own appearance. Noble favoured an almost virginal look – not an easy thing to achieve considering her age – but she had given it her best. Her skin glowed from a hot bath followed by an icy shower. Her make-up had been expertly applied so only the most practised eye would realise she wore any at all. She had released her hair from its pin curl prison, then barely run a comb through it so that it appeared sleep-tousled.

From her vast stock of expensive lingerie she had chosen a white eyelet bra with matching tap pants. Under them she wore a white lace garter belt and ivory stockings that came halfway up her thighs.

She was trying to choose between a satin robe and an antique lace négligé when the doorbell rang and she hurried to answer it as she was. The appreciation in Noble's eyes told her she had chosen wisely.

'You're looking exceptionally well,' he said, letting her help him out of his coat.

'It's because I'm happy.'

'What have you got to be happy about today?'

'You're here,' she replied, throwing herself into his arms and covering his face with kisses.

Her ardour was no sham. She had learned to love him despite his faults. At times he was dictatorial, demanding and thoughtless. But he could also be warm, tender, generous – and incredibly passionate.

It was his passion she hoped to arouse when she led him up the stairs and helped him undress. Despite the grey hair at his temples, chest and groin, he showed few signs of ageing. His nude torso would have done credit to a man ten years his junior.

She gave herself up to kissing him, delving deep inside his mouth, tasting the lunch he had eaten, the mouthwash he'd used afterwards, the cigarettes he'd smoked. She teased his nipples with one hand, fondling his penis with the other, waiting for the predictable response.

His nipples hardened. His penis didn't.

Before embarrassment had a chance to overtake them both he pushed her away. 'I'm not in the mood just yet.'

'I'm sorry. I didn't mean to rush you.'

The line should have been his, she mused ruefully. Twenty years ago or even ten, it would have been. He had been a hot, hungry, hasty lover who always came back for seconds and sometimes thirds.

He looked ill-at-ease. 'I've got a lot on my mind.'

Perhaps a glass of champagne and a little conversation would put him in a more romantic mood. She uncorked the Dom Perignon with

61

practised expertise, poured the chilled wine into a pair of flutes –
expertly twisting the bottle so not a drop spilled.

Noble usually took time to hold a vintage up to the light to survey
it for clarity, lowering his nose to experience its scent before taking
his first sip. This afternoon, though, he simply put the glass to his
lips, drank it down and then belched.

Greta didn't acknowledge the gaffe. She'd long since abandoned
any romantic notions about men. Even the richest of them belched,
farted, and scratched their balls.

'Maybe talking about what's troubling you will help,' she said.

Greta gave him a reassuring smile although she had yet to meet
a man who really wanted a woman for conversation – unless he was
worried sick about something. But of course they didn't truly want
conversation; not if by that you meant an exchange of opinions. What
a man wanted when he talked to a woman was reassurance – a
sounding board with tits.

'I'm worried about Glory,' Noble said.

'Fathers always worry about their daughters. It goes with the
territory.' And he worried more than most, she silently added as she
refilled his glass, then walked over to the bed, sat down and propped
herself up on the pillows.

'You can't be too concerned about an innocent child,' he retorted.

'What's Glory done now?' she asked, feeling a twinge of sympathy
for the girl. Being seventeen was confusing enough without having
Noble and Anna for parents.

'I caught her sneaking out of the house at the crack of dawn.'

Greta was about to tell Noble that her father used to catch her
sneaking out of the house too. But then, considering how she'd spent
her life, she decided it wouldn't be very reassuring. 'Did you find
out where she went?'

This time it took Noble two swallows to empty his glass. And he
didn't belch. 'She didn't go anywhere.'

'Then what are you worried about?'

'She was drawing.'

The way he said it, you'd have thought he'd caught the girl screwing the chauffeur on the front lawn. 'The last I heard, drawing wasn't
one of the seven deadly sins. Why are you so upset?'

'I'm upset because she deliberately disobeyed a direct order.'

'But that's what seventeen-year-olds are supposed to do.'

'Not my daughter,' he replied vehemently. 'I've given as much time and thought to her upbringing as I have to running any of my businesses. Perhaps more. And this is how she repays me. It makes me sick, thinking about all the hours she's spent mooning over that damn sketch-pad.'

Greta listened with increasing concern. Here was the passion, the fervour that had disappeared from their relationship. 'You're afraid, aren't you?' she blurted out before she had a chance to consider what she was saying.

'Don't be ridiculous. I've never been afraid of anything in my life.'

'Oh yes you are,' she insisted. 'You're afraid Glory is more like her real parents than she is like you.'

Noble moved so quickly, she didn't have time to ward off the blow. Tears spurted in her eyes as the diamond ring he wore cut into her cheek.

'Jesus Christ,' she gasped, 'what the hell was that for?'

'I told you never to talk about the adoption. Glory's my daughter – *my* daughter damn it – and don't you ever forget it.'

She'd been wrong about no man ever throwing her out of bed. Noble pushed her aside so brusquely that she landed on the floor.

'I'm sorry,' she cried out, holding her hand against her throbbing cheek.

'Who the fuck are you to analyse my motives or question my behaviour?' While he talked, he struggled into his clothes. 'Obviously you've forgotten who pays your bills.'

'I haven't forgotten. Please don't leave. I didn't mean to make you angry.'

'Angry doesn't do justice to what I'm feeling.' He buttoned his shirt so hurriedly that one of the buttons popped off and fell to the floor.

She snatched it up. 'At least let me sew this back on before you go.'

Noble didn't seem to hear her. Although she knew he prided himself on being impeccably dressed at all times, he ran from her bedroom in total *déshabillé*.

She flew down the stairs after him, wondering what in the world she could say to lessen his anger. Damn, she must have been out of her frigging mind – speaking out like that.

'Noble,' she wailed futilely as the front door opened and then slammed shut.

She threw herself down on the nearest chair, lowered her head into her hands and wept. Her father used to warn her that her big mouth was going to get her in trouble some day. The no account bastard always followed up the warning with a roundhouse punch so she wouldn't forget.

Well, she had to give him his due – her big mouth had really got her into trouble this time. God, she hoped Noble didn't wind up doing something really stupid. But she wouldn't put anything past him in his present mood.

Experience had taught her that men only knew two ways to get rid of their anger. Either they fucked you silly – or beat you senseless.

Noble had spent every Thursday afternoon with Greta for the last twenty years, sometimes staying late into the night. As he slammed from her house and hurried to his car he had no idea where to go or what to do.

He was much too upset to return to his office. He couldn't return home in his present emotional state either. Much as he could use a drink, his dishevelment ruled out stopping at his club. Thanks to Prohibition, the bars had closed five years ago.

He was one of the richest men in San Francisco yet he couldn't think of a place to go. Putting the car in gear, he pulled away from the kerb and drove aimlessly, barely taking in his surroundings.

A dark winter of the spirit ruled his heart and mind as he finally headed towards Golden Gate Park. It had served as a refugee centre after the quake. It would be his refuge now.

But for tourists, few people patronised the park on a workday afternoon. He took South Drive past Stow Lake and parked in the shade of a Monterey pine just off Overlook. Cutting the engine, he pounded the Rolls's panelled dashboard, releasing a fraction of his fury.

He wasn't the sort of cad who took pleasure in hitting a woman but Greta had driven him to it. Damn her for making him lose control. That was the trouble with women. Give them an inch and they'd take a mile. He should have got rid of her years ago, instead of trusting her with so many of his secrets.

However she was the least of his problems. He could dismiss her with a cheque and send her far away. But what was he going to do about Glory?

He used to take pleasure in her talent, even boasting to friends about it. Now, though, her fixation with art was driving him mad. He had nightmares about her becoming so famous that the Hersches would see her picture in the paper, put two and two together and realise she was their granddaughter.

After returning from Saint Mary's, Anna spent the day in prayer in the private chapel Noble had built for her in the first onslaught of grief over Isabel's death.

Running her rosary beads through her fingers while repeating the familiar words of the litany usually helped to hold the darkness at bay. Not today though. She didn't know how much longer she could keep up the charade of being a wife and mother when her heart longed for the peace she only found in Holy Mother Church.

Although every nerve in her body cried out for laudanum, she had to keep her wits about her. She had made up her mind to talk to Noble about Glory when he came home, to resolve for good and all the problem of the girl's existence.

Anna's knees ached as she rose from the tiled floor. She backed out of the chapel, keeping her eyes fixed on the magnificent altar which Noble had imported from Italy. The sorrow on Jesus's face was the last thing she saw before she shut the door.

She made her way through the darkened halls, passing a series of rooms that would have done credit to Versailles. While the house was under construction Noble's agent had attended estate auctions throughout Europe, buying a Louis XV *bureau de roi* here, an Elizabethan table there. She had long since stopped taking satisfaction in any of it, though. Worldly pleasures were Noble's province – not hers.

To her surprise, Noble was home earlier than usual. He stood in the hall taking off his coat, hat and gloves. Clarence was waiting with outstretched arms to receive them.

'Ah, Mrs Girard, I didn't realise you were still up,' Clarence said. 'Do you need anything, madame?'

'Only privacy. I'd appreciate it if you left us alone.'

Clarence cut a glance at Noble. 'And you, sir, do you require anything? Ellen has your supper in a warming oven.'

'I'm not hungry. You can go now.'

Noble didn't seem to be in a very good mood. His eyes were slightly bloodshot and his shirt wasn't properly buttoned. Today was the day he always visited his mistress. What in the world had he done with that Saxlund creature to produce such a sorry result? On second thought, she didn't want to know.

'What are you looking at?' Noble asked.

'At you. I want to discuss a matter of some importance.'

'If you want me to raise my annual donation to Saint Mary's, I'll take your request under advisement. But I'm not in the mood for a discussion right now.'

How predictable he was, she thought, watching him head for the library. It was his *sanctum sanctorum* – the place where he went to be alone – just as the chapel was hers. She trailed behind him, feeling like Daniel walking into the lion's den.

Noble paid her no heed as he headed straight for the sideboard where a silver tray held decanters filled with his favourite liquors – Scotch, brandy, and a blended whisky. Tonight he chose the Scotch, filled a glass to the brim and drank the contents down, then looked at her.

'I told you, I'm not in the mood for conversation tonight.'

'And I told you we need to talk.'

'We haven't *talked* in years so you'll forgive me if I fail to see the urgency. Can't it wait?'

'No, it can't. I've been having a problem with Glory. She doesn't listen to me at all any more. She's been very lax in her duty to the Church too. Just this morning she told Father Tremaine she thought organised religion caused more problems than it solved.'

Had Anna complained about Glory twenty-four hours earlier, Noble might have applauded his daughter's audacity. But he'd already had his fill of female insubordination. 'What else has she done?'

'She's been rude and argumentative. Her behaviour has got completely out of hand. You really must do something before she disgraces us.'

'What do you suggest?'

'I think it's time we arranged her marriage.'

Noble gazed at the woman law and God had bound to him, hating the prissy expression on her face, the prim way she pursed her lips.

'Arranged marriages went out with the horse and buggy. We married for love. Shouldn't Glory –'

'Perhaps arranged isn't the right word,' Anna interrupted. 'If we insist she take her proper place in society, I'm sure she will eventually settle down with a suitable young man.'

At lunch, he had told Glory he wanted her to marry someday. Could that someday be so close? A husband would keep her mind off art.

He refilled his glass and then, remembering his manners, said, 'Can I get you a drink?'

Anna crossed the room and settled in one of the wing chairs that flanked the fireplace. 'I'd like some sherry.'

Noble poured for her too. Carrying both their drinks, he took the chair opposite hers. 'How do we persuade Glory to take her proper place in society? She's already refused to have a formal debut.'

'You've always been too lenient with her. A girl who has stopped doing her parents' bidding needs a husband to keep her in line.'

Noble had known he and Anna would have this conversation one day. But when he got up that morning, he certainly hadn't expected to have it tonight. 'Do you have someone in mind?'

'The Aspromantes' son graduated from college last year and went into the family business. He's quite presentable.'

'The Aspromantes' son is an addle-pated twit with bad skin and worse breath! Glory wouldn't give him a second look.'

'Perhaps you're right. But there must be dozens of other acceptable bachelors in our circle.'

Much as he hated to admit it, Anna might be right. If he had to choose between two evils – a career as an artist that would take Glory God knew where with God knew who, and marriage to a well-bred young man – he would choose marriage.

CHAPTER SEVEN

'Give a Christmas ball?' Anna's pursed lips and her furrowed brow told Noble she thought it was just another of his unreasonable demands. 'I haven't entertained in years.'

He struggled to control his temper. 'You said it yourself. Glory has ignored her obligations as a Girard far too long. It's time she took her proper place in society. And I can't think of a better way to introduce her to a large group of eligible young men.'

'Christmas is just three months away. The best caterers, florists, and orchestras are already booked.'

'They can be unbooked. All it takes is money.'

'The people in our circle plan their holiday calendar a year in advance. All the suitable dates are taken. No one will come. We'll be a laughing stock.'

That was Anna for you, he thought with a glower. He should have known she would think of a dozen reasons not to cooperate. 'You brought up the subject of Glory's marriage. I'm merely suggesting a way to bring it about as speedily as possible. I'll be happy to assign two or three people on my staff to help you with the details. As for our circle having prior engagements, you seem to have forgotten who I am. No one will refuse an invitation from Noble Girard.'

Anna's once lovely mouth twisted in a bitter smile. 'No one but Glory. She's already refused your offer of a coming out party, and she's turned down heaven knows how many opportunities to go to cotillions and debutante balls. She has the foolish idea that the money would be better spent if people gave it to charity.'

He rose, stood in front of the hearth and gazed down at the ashes of the evening fire. 'This time she isn't going to have a choice.'

'I never thought I'd hear you talk that way about Glory.'

'Don't tell me you're feeling sorry for her.'

'I assure you, it's a new experience. But I've seen the same look in your eyes when you're planning a competitor's ruin.'

'That's ridiculous. I love Glory.'

'I suppose you do in your own way.'

'My own way. What's that supposed to mean? No father ever loved a daughter more. I've done everything in the world for her.'

'True. However whether Glory welcomes it or not, she's as good as walking down the aisle.' Anna shrugged as if the matter didn't concern her. 'All right. We'll do it your way. Have a couple of your most obedient, socially acceptable employees come to the house after Mass tomorrow and we'll get to work. But I want something in return.'

'As long as it's within reason, I won't object.'

'Our ideas of what's reasonable haven't been compatible for a long time. I want your promise that I'll be able to join the Sisters of Mercy after Glory is married.'

'You've gone on retreats before. I have no problem with your doing so again.'

'This time the retreat will be permanent. I won't be coming back to this house – or to you.'

'Are you sure that's what you want?'

'I've never been more certain of anything in my entire life. I'll play the proud mother and devoted wife long enough to see Glory married. Afterwards I plan to petition the Church for an annulment.'

Anna had managed to surprise him. 'Isn't that a bit extreme after all these years?'

'You and I haven't had a real marriage since Isabel died.'

Noble sat in silence, surrounded by the ruins of his private life, while Anna rose and walked out of the room. In one day he had lost the three women who had given his existence meaning for good or evil. He had given his body to Greta, his heart to Anna and his soul to Glory.

He never intended to see Greta again, not after the things she had said that afternoon.

If his plan for Glory succeeded, she would soon leave the house on her husband's arm.

And then, Anna would leave too.

So be it. The three of them – by their actions, words and deeds – had made their own beds. They could wallow in them for all he cared.

He stayed up long after Anna left, walking through the mansion's memory-crowded rooms, drinking from the decanter of Scotch he carried with him. He had said all he intended to say to Greta by way of goodbye when he slammed out of her townhouse, and Anna had escaped his purview the day Isabel died.

Anna would go to God – and Greta could go to hell.

Now he said a sad farewell to his daughter.

As a rosy-cheeked toddler she had loved playing hide-and-seek with him, running from one room to another, trailing a tell-tale stream of laughter while he counted to ten.

Far too quickly the laughing toddler had grown into a serious child who seldom smiled, who attacked every task as if her very existence depended on its successful completion. He blamed Anna for that.

He would never forget the pride on Glory's face the day she showed him the first of a series of perfect report cards – or her glow when he praised her. She had responded to his approval like a spaniel eager for its master's hand.

When had she stopped putting his feelings first?

He walked into the music room, tugging on the decanter with the urgency of a famished infant at its mother's breast. But the liquor didn't fill the emptiness inside him. Nothing could.

Glory had given piano recitals in this very room. How sweet the songs had sounded, even when she hit the wrong notes.

Gone.

All those precious moments gone, never to be lived again.

She'd been so excited that fateful day when he found her copying the Raphael, as if she had just discovered her personal kingdom. Had he known what a turning point it would be he would have snatched the crayons from her hand and broken them into bits, instead of hanging her drawing in a place of honour alongside the Raphael.

For all his watchfulness he'd been caught unaware when the serious child had blossomed into a determined young woman. And now all the Glorys he had known and loved – the laughing toddler, the serious child, the stubborn young woman – would soon be lost to him.

His restless wandering finally halted in the vast, glass-roofed hall. The moon cast chiaroscuro shadows on the marble floor. The restless soughing of the wind spoke to his loneliness.

No, he decided, draining the last of the Scotch. He couldn't, he *wouldn't* lose Glory to just any man. He had planned every detail of her existence; he would choose her husband with the same exquisite care.

There had to be dozens of likely candidates who would jump at a chance to wed the heiress to the Girard fortune – men whose blue-blooded parents had squandered the family's wealth – men whose ambition would permit them to fall in love on command. For love Glory they must. Noble would settle for nothing less.

It shouldn't be too difficult to groom such an individual to be an ideal mate for her. A magnificent wedding present, perhaps a neighbouring mansion along with an executive position in Girard enterprises, would guarantee the most adoring husband a woman could want.

Swaying on his feet, Noble chuckled to himself. Instead of losing a rebellious daughter he would gain a dutiful son. As a married woman, Glory would have to give up her notions about being an artist. In a year or two she'd present Noble with his first grandchild – perhaps a boy.

The thought inspired him to do a jig. He need never worry about the great deception he had carried out all those years ago. Glory would forget all about art once she had a baby in her arms.

Yes, he mused, he would retain control of his daughter through her husband and her children. It was a compromise he could live with. So why did he feel half sick? He had manipulated grown men. Why did he quail at the thought of manipulating his daughter, especially when it was for her own good.

The question echoed through the chambers of his mind with the plaintive power of a lost child seeking a parent. A ragged sob burst from his mouth as he fled to the library in search of the nirvana he would find in another bottle of Scotch.

Glory returned late from her visit with Cal and went straight to her room. Too excited to sleep, she dozed fitfully for a couple of hours, then tossed and turned for a couple more before turning on the Tiffany boudoir lamp on the night table by her bed.

She had hidden the catalogue from the Chicago Art Institute in her dresser. Retrieving it, she returned to bed and clutched it to her breasts like a talisman.

'Once your father has a chance to see the quality of the school, to read its history, its list of alumni, not to mention its outstanding curriculum, he's certain to let you attend,' the professor had said at dinner, nodding his shock of white hair for emphasis.

Could it really be that simple? Were Noble's objections based on ignorance? Did he really imagine her starving in a garret somewhere or taking up with all sorts of low-lifes if she became an artist? Did he want to shield her from the shock of seeing a nude male model in a life drawing class, as Cal's father had suggested?

What other reason could there possibly be?

Although she had already gone over the catalogue from the first page to the last she opened and read it all over again, smiling the entire time. Founded in 1879, the Institute included a highly respected art school and a world class museum. Photographs showed a building whose classic architecture demonstrated a reverence for the task of training artists.

The curriculum included classes in every medium as well as offerings in related fields. Many of the professors were respected painters, sculptors, and academics in their own right. The tuition was reasonable and scholarships were available to worthy but needy students.

A full page boasted of the enormous Hersch Endowment which funded various activities in the name of the Hersches' dead daughter. Best of all from a parental viewpoint, carefully supervised living arrangements could be provided for out-of-town students. And it was only a two-day train ride from San Francisco. She could easily get home for all the important holidays.

By the time Glory joined Noble for breakfast, she had carefully marshalled every argument in favour of her going to the Chicago Art Institute and tried to anticipate every objection. She would only ask for one year – just two semesters – to prove herself. If she didn't have any talent she'd know by then and come straight back to San Francisco. She'd even agree to a coming out party if that's what her parents thought best.

Noble was at the table in the dining room, spooning sugar into his coffee when she walked in clutching the catalogue. She considered falling on her knees and begging him to let her go. However he was more likely to respond to reason than emotion.

A frisson crawled down her backbone at what she was about to do. 'Hi, Dad,' she said, slipping into her usual chair.

'Good morning,' he replied, gazing at her through red-rimmed eyes.

Although he was wearing the new navy pinstripe suit that had just arrived from his Savile Row tailor, he looked as rumpled as though he'd slept in his clothes. His hand shook when he picked up his cup.

'Is something wrong? Are you angry because I stayed at Cal's so late?'

'Of course not. It gave your mother and me a chance to have a long talk.'

Glory couldn't have been more surprised if he'd told her Anna had run off with the Sheik of Arabee. Her parents talking? What in the world about?

'Your mother told me what you said to Father Tremaine yesterday.'

So they had been talking about her. 'I suppose I shouldn't have been so outspoken – but you must admit I was right. There have been more wars fought in the name of organised religion, more—'

'That's quite enough, young lady. I'm not interested in your opinion and neither, I might add, was Father Tremaine.'

Glory wanted to remind him that it was he who first voiced that particular opinion to her, however there were far more important issues at stake this morning.

Her parents must have had a terrible fight about her last night. She couldn't think of anything else that would have left her father so out of sorts.

Perhaps this wasn't the right time to broach the subject of the Chicago Art Institute after all, she decided, suddenly aware that she was holding the catalogue in plain sight.

Seeming to read her mind, his gaze fell to her hands. 'What have you got there?' he asked before she could lower the incriminating document to her lap.

'Just something Professor Blackstone gave me.'

He held out his hand. 'I'd like to see it.'

Obedience warred with her instinct for self-preservation – and obedience won. She offered the catalogue for his inspection.

He glanced at the cover long enough to read the title, then cast the booklet aside. 'You promised to forget all about this art nonsense.'

She had grown up avoiding confrontations, doing her best to please

73

both her parents despite the dichotomy of their tastes. An inner voice warned her not to turn away from this one.

'It isn't nonsense. And I haven't broken my word. I promised I would think about what you said and I have. But I can't turn off my feelings the way you turn off a tap. I want to be an artist. It's all I've ever wanted – and you have the power to help me. I don't understand why you won't.' She picked up the catalogue and offered it again. 'If you love me at all you'll take a minute and look this over. Please, Father.'

Noble had wakened with a killer of a hangover. His head ached. His eyes felt like they'd been poached over a slow fire. He suffered from dehydration and he had a deplorable taste in his mouth – as though he'd dined on dirty socks.

He remembered very little of what had happened after Anna had gone to bed and had absolutely no recollection of getting to bed himself. The sound of Glory's voice pounded into his brain like a hammer on an anvil.

Wanting nothing more than to silence her, he took the catalogue and riffled through the pages. The Hersch name appeared so suddenly that he let go his breath in an audible gasp. Glory's parents had attended the Chicago Art Institute. But he had no idea her grandparents had endowed the school so heavily.

Rising so quickly that his coffee cup fell over, he walked over to the fire blazing on the hearth and thrust the catalogue into the flames.

'Daddy, don't!' Glory cried out, hurrying to his side.

She bent to retrieve the catalogue and would have burned her fingers if he hadn't grasped her shoulders and lifted her to her feet. The anger in her eyes almost matched the fury he felt.

'You had no right to do that,' she declared.

'I'm your father. I had every right.'

'That catalogue wasn't mine. It belonged to Professor Blackstone.'

Still gripping Glory's shoulders, he gazed down to make sure the flames were doing their work. The catalogue was too thick to burst into flames. Instead the pages caught fire one by one, writhing like souls in torment as they smoked, then curled into brittle parchment, then turned to ash. For a moment, the name *Hersch* flared blood red before it too burned away.

Noble felt as if a great weight had lifted from his shoulders. He hadn't been absolutely sure he'd come to the right decision concerning Glory's future. Seeing the catalogue and the Hersch name had resolved all his doubts.

His grip on Glory's arms didn't falter as he guided her back to the table and shoved her into her chair.

'You had no right to talk about family affairs with Professor Blackstone. And he had no right to meddle in our business. I have half a mind to forbid you to see Cal.'

A couple of years ago, Glory would have withered at the reproach in his eyes. Although tears ran down her cheeks she locked her gaze with his. 'Why are you being so unfair? You've never treated me this way before.'

'Perhaps I should have. Your mother told me you've been out of control. I'm sorry to say I agree with her. In a way it's my fault. I've been lax about your discipline. I spoiled you when all I wanted was to show my love. But those days are over and done. There's one thing you had better understand. While you live under my roof you will do as I say. If you cannot live by my rules you can go – now – today. I'll not go through another scene like this one.'

Her father had never been so dictatorial before, so unjust. An angry rejoinder leapt into Glory's mind. She longed to shout her defiance. But the words died still-born. If she had loved him less she would have bolted then and there. However the bonds of affection and duty bound her in place as firmly as steel shackles.

'I didn't mean to make you angry,' she said in a small voice. 'I don't want to leave home – or you. I love you, Daddy.'

'That's more like it.' Noble returned to his seat, righted his cup and filled it with fresh coffee. 'About the talk your mother and I had last night, we've decided to give a ball at Christmas to introduce you to society.'

'But Daddy—' Glory burst, out, unable to contain her dismay any longer, 'I could go to art school for a year and it wouldn't cost near as much as a ball.'

'Don't you *but* me! And don't ever talk to me about art school again. I've had enough of your disobedience, young lady. What you need is a husband to take your mind off all that foolishness. We'll be inviting every eligible young man in San Francisco to the ball. You can damn well take your pick.'

*

75

An hour later Glory sat in the Blackstones' parlour with Cal, shivering as she recounted the quarrel. Her challis dress had done little to ward off the chill and her flimsy sandals hadn't been made for hiking up and down San Francisco's hills.

The cold had numbed her extremities and her feet hurt like the devil. But her physical discomfort didn't hold a candle to her emotional wounds. She felt as though her life were over.

'I've never seen my father look so angry or sound so irrational,' she said. 'I can't believe he burned your father's catalogue.'

'Dad won't miss it.'

'One minute he was throwing the catalogue into the fire and the next, he was talking about my getting married. You should have heard him. He's planning to put me on exhibit at a Christmas ball in the hope that some man will be foolish enough to propose.'

'It's not the end of the world. I'd kill to have the kind of party your parents will throw,' Cal said wistfully.

Glory had been so intent on her own unhappiness that she hadn't given a thought to anyone but herself. A wave of guilt washed over her as she took in the genteel poverty of her surroundings. What in the world was she doing whining like a spoiled brat when Cal had grown up without the advantages and luxuries she took for granted?

She had grown so accustomed to Cal's home that she didn't really see it any more. Now she realised the Persian rug had worn down to the backing in places and the stuffing showed through the sofa's upholstery. 'I must sound so self-indulgent.'

'You are – but I don't hold it against you. Look at it this way. A husband isn't likely to be as unreasonable as your father. If you play your cards right, you'll be able to wrap him around your little finger.' Cal's eyes glittered with mischief. 'I imagine there are all sorts of ways to persuade a man to do what you want after you get him in bed. Once you're the mistress of your own house what's to stop you from studying art – or bellydancing if it suits your fancy?'

Glory couldn't help grinning. 'You always make me feel better.'

Cal grinned back. 'I know.'

'So what do I do now?'

Cal put her index fingers at the corner of her eyes, pushing them into an upward slant. 'We Chinese have saying. The mighty oak breaks in the storm. The fragile bamboo bends. You, my plum blossom, are going to be the bamboo.'

'How do I do that?'

'You start acting as if the party is the hottest idea since Rudolph Valentino played the sheik. You accept all those invitations you've been turning down – provided I'm invited too. It's time we had some fun. No more being good little girls. Sin and sex, here we come.' She jumped from her chair and shimmied across the floor in a knee knocking Charleston. 'You can be the toast of the town and I'll be the toastette. We'll have men lined up waiting to drink champagne from our slippers. And then when you find one who suits your fancy, it will be twenty-three skiddoo as far as Noble and Anna Girard are concerned. You'll be free.'

'You make it sound wonderful.'

'It will be,' Cal said with all the confidence of a woman of the world.

Wonderful? Could Cal be right? She made the search for a husband sound like a cross between a treasure hunt, a dance marathon, and a glittering adventure into the unknown realm of womanhood.

Suddenly Glory couldn't wait.

CHAPTER EIGHT

'Christmas – bah, humbug,' Greta Saxlund muttered. She stood at the living room window, gazing out at San Francisco's ever present fog. She no longer believed in peace on earth, goodwill towards men.

The cold and damp seemed to have worked their way into her bones. God, she wouldn't miss the city – or the life she had lived here.

Noble's letter of dismissal hadn't come as a surprise. The ten thousand dollar bank draft it contained had. Coupled with her own savings and the money from the sale of the house, she had no financial worries.

After spending the last three months with no one to cater to but herself, she realised how demanding being a mistress had been. Manufacturing passion regardless of her own mood or time of month, pretending to orgasms she didn't experience, and all the while looking her very best, qualified her to be an actress. Perhaps she ought to be heading for Hollywood instead of Arizona.

The ringing of the doorbell jerked her from her reverie. Who the hell was that? she wondered, automatically smoothing her hair. Her few goodbyes had been said, her final bills paid. It must be the estate agent come for the keys, she decided, hurrying to the door.

Her paperboy stood on the steps, shivering in the wintry air, his acne flaring red against his pale skin.

'I just wanted to say goodbye – and thanks again for the tip you gave me yesterday. I'm going to miss you, Miz Saxlund.'

More likely he was going to miss her generosity. He unfolded the morning paper and held it out with an expectant smile as if he were offering up a dozen roses instead of yesterday's news.

She looked down to see a picture of Noble with Glory on his arm and gasped, feeling an unexpected sense of loss that took her breath away.

Noble was still the handsomest man she'd ever seen. He looked for all the world like a proud father – except for something pinched and narrow around the eyes.

Beneath the photograph, the caption read, *Noted philanthropist and business man, Noble Girard, is fêting his daughter, Glory Girard, at a Christmas Eve ball tonight in the Girard home.*

'She sure is pretty,' the paper boy said.

'Yes, she is,' Greta agreed, and heaven help her for it. Being pretty could be a woman's passport to heaven – or hell.

'I guess Mr Girard is just about the richest man in the city.'

'I suppose so,' Greta replied, still studying the photograph as if it were the Rosetta stone and trying to read the truth about Noble in it. Had he ever cared for her, or was he one of those men who only cared about himself?

'I wonder if rich folks are anything like the rest of us,' the paperboy said.

'I don't know anything about rich men like Noble Girard,' she said on a sigh. 'I don't understand them and I guess I never will.' She took one last look at the photograph, then folded the paper and handed it back. 'I won't be needing this. I'm leaving today.'

Her throat felt swollen the way it always did before she cried. But that certainly wasn't the case today, she told herself. She couldn't wait to be on her way.

Ellen Delaney checked the breakfast trays lined up in the butler's pantry, making small adjustments to each one. When she finished she sent Clarence off with the tray for Mr Girard and a maid off with the one for Mrs Girard. She would take Miss Glory's up herself.

Preparing the trays was a lot more trouble than serving the Girards in the dining room, but the caterer had declared the dining room out of bounds for the entire day. Talk about pompous, self-important men. The caterer had turned the staff upside down with his demands.

Ellen had been pleasantly surprised when the Girards announced they were planning a ball. At the time she'd thought it was a sign that the family was finally returning to normalcy. But there had been nothing normal about the frantic haste with which the event had been planned.

Ellen could hardly wait for the evening to be over so the household could return to its accustomed routine. She'd bet that the fancy caterer would be nowhere in sight when it came to the time to clean up.

She knocked on Glory's door, waited until she heard a response, then let herself in. A constant hum, like the sound of bees, wafted through the door with her.

'What's that noise?' Glory asked, yawning as she propped herself up on the pillows.

'It's Monsewer Alfonze and his crew. He brought so many people with him, they're tripping over each other.'

'You mean Monsieur Alphonse,' Glory said.

'Whatever,' Ellen grumbled.

Three months ago, the girl wouldn't have corrected her pronunciation. She had changed – and not necessarily for the better. Before all the hubbub about her taking her proper place in society, she wouldn't have dreamed of staying out 'til all hours of the night and then lollygagging in bed the next day.

She looked and acted just like the flappers in those John Held cartoons in McClure's. Why, she had even cut her hair in a flapper's shingle. But her appearance didn't upset Ellen half as much as her air of almost frantic gaiety.

'Where are Mother and Father?'

'In their rooms, same as you. Monsewer Alfonze said he won't be finished with the decorations and such before five. He wants all of you to stay out of his way until then.'

'That won't be a problem. Madame Renée will be here in half an hour for a final fitting. I have an appointment at the beauty salon at eleven and Cal and I are having a late lunch afterwards. I don't expect to be back until four.'

'Do you want your tray in bed or shall I set it here on the table?' Ellen asked.

Glory yawned prodigiously. 'In bed. I'm just too tired to move. I had no idea dancing was such hard work.'

Ellen was tempted to say if Glory hadn't been so busy proving what a good time she was having, she wouldn't have had to stay up all night dancing like one of those poor girls who entered Charleston marathons for the money. But that was something else that had changed. Ellen didn't dare speak her mind to this new Glory the way she would have to the old one.

'Enjoy yourself today,' she said, placing the tray on Glory's lap, 'and tonight too, in case I don't see you before the ball.'

'I'm sure I will. Before you go would you be a darling and bring me my cigarettes? They're in the beaded bag on top of the dresser.'

Ellen did as she was asked and then hastened from the room. For the life of her, she couldn't figure out what had got into Glory or her parents.

Noble gazed at the photograph in the morning paper, smiling with satisfaction. He'd never seen a debutante ball written up on the front page before.

Although Lenin's death had left the communist world in chaos and Calvin Coolidge was putting together a new government, the paper had treated the party like important news. It had to be Hearst's doing. He'd have to remember to thank him tonight. Although, come to think of it, over the years he'd spent enough money advertising in Hearst papers to merit a *thank you* from Hearst himself.

Just as he'd promised Anna all those weeks ago, the invitations had been snapped up, even by those couples who had cancelled their own affairs so as not to conflict with the Girards'. Everyone who was anyone from William Randolph Hearst to the Spreckels to the Lelands, had promptly sent an RSVP. There hadn't been any problem booking Ted Lewis and his band, even though they had already accepted an engagement at the Waldorf Astoria. As Noble had told Anna, all it had taken was money.

Ultimately everything came down to money. Love, loyalty, religion, politics, sex – especially sex. Over the years he'd bought and paid for a series of desirable women. And now he'd negotiated a deal with his daughter's future husband – a man she would meet tonight and not a moment too soon. He'd been worried that she might conceive an inappropriate attachment to some damn fool while he searched for the ideal candidate for her hand.

Just last week, when she returned from a tea-dance, he'd asked her if she had met someone special.

'Not yet,' she'd replied blithely. 'I afraid you've set a very high standard. I haven't met a man who compares to you.'

It had been months since she'd given him such a nice compliment. She looked happier than she had in a long time. He'd been right to insist Glory forget being an artist. Indeed, he thought as he finished dressing, it would be a memorable night for them all.

Putting the paper aside, he settled his shoulders in his jacket, buttoned his cuffs and left his room.

'Who ees it?' Madame Renée called out when he knocked on Glory's door. Unlike Monsieur Alphonse, her French accent was the real thing.

'It's Mademoiselle Glory's father. I'd like to speak to her.'

'But it ees not possible. We are having a fitting.'

Not another intransigent woman, Noble thought. His temper, so easily triggered these days, threatened to erupt. A headache pulsed into life behind his eyes.

He'd had far too many headaches the last few months, both figuratively and literally. Not having anyone to talk to hadn't helped. He hadn't expected to miss Greta so much. But he'd been right to send her away.

After Glory's future was assured and Anna had taken herself off to a nunnery, he was going to have to find a replacement for Greta, preferably someone young and malleable. In the meantime, he'd be damned if he'd stand outside his daughter's room like some unwanted swain.

He twisted the knob and flung the door open so forcefully that it thudded into the wall. Glory was standing on a stool, facing the windows. Her ball gown gaped open to the waist, revealing a back as smooth and white as cream.

Madame Renée whirled to face him, holding a pincushion in front of her body as if it were a talisman that was sure to ward off an evil spirit. 'Monsieur Girard, your daughter ees not dressed to receive guests.'

'I'm not a guest. I'm her father. Zip her up and let me take a look at her gown.'

God knew, he'd paid enough for it. Getting Lanvin's personal assistant to travel half the globe to ensure Glory had the proper clothes for her debutante season had cost a small fortune.

'Very well,' Madame Renée replied, displeasure riding her aquiline Gallic features.

For a second the closing of the zipper was the only sound in the room. Then Glory pivoted on the stool and faced him.

'Here's looking at you, big boy,' she said.

Her pseudo-sophistication hit a raw nerve – but it didn't upset him half as much as her appearance. The dress had transformed her into an elegant stranger. Transfixed, Noble stood rooted to the spot.

'Permit me to explain the design,' Madame Renée said into the awkward silence. 'Since Madame Girard chose white and silver for the ball's theme colours, Monsieur Lanvin picked a complementary white chiffon. It does convey a *merveilleux* sense of innocence, *n'est ce pas?* And yet it clings to the body like a second skin. It's all in the cutting. As you can see the gown is medieval in style. The chiffon is oversewn with crystal beads and belted low with a band of pearl and diamanté embroidery. It's lovely, ees it not?'

The sound of Glory's voice finally roused him. 'What do you think, Daddy?'

Noble's fury escalated as he took in every detail of her appearance. The dress didn't suit her at all. She looked far too old in it.

'What the hell have you done to my daughter?' he demanded, rounding on the couturier.

Madame Renée appeared to be dumbfounded. '*Je ne comprends pas.* I don't understand, Monsieur. This is one of Lanvin's most beautiful designs. He created it with the Duchess of Sforza in mind but then your cablegram came.' She gestured at Glory like a ringmaster. '*Et voilà!*'

The ache in Noble's head thundered like tympany. God, he needed a drink. 'How old is the duchess?'

'She is, as we say, a woman of a certain age. It would not be proper to ask.'

'Do you mean to tell me Lanvin designed this dress for a mature woman and fobbed it off on my daughter. If it weren't too late—' He left the threat unfinished. He wasn't the sort of man to indulge in idle threats and time had run out. 'I repeat, what have you done to my daughter? She looks as stiff and flat as a dressmaker's dummy.'

Comprehension finally dawned on the couturier's face. 'Ah, you are referring to the line of the bodice. In keeping with current style I have bound your daughter's breasts as tightly as possible. It may be a trifle uncomfortable but, I assure you, it ees necessary. It ees not fashionable to be so large as Mademoiselle Glory.'

'Keep this in mind, madame.' Noble's voice ricocheted through the room. '*Girards don't follow fashion. They make it.* I will not have my daughter trussed up like some pigeon on a spit. Fix the damn dress!'

He turned on his heels and strode out of the room without giving either woman a chance to reply, slamming the door behind him.

Glory stayed sitting on the stool after he had gone, quivering with shock. Her father had acted like a madman.

'I'm so sorry, madame. I don't know what to say except my father is under some strain, with the ball and everything.'

'*Zut alors*, you don't need to apologise. Your father ees not the only man to unravel the first time he ees forced to look on his daughter as a desirable woman. And *chérie*, in this gown, that's how you look. But he must love you very much, *vraiment*? Why else would he take such an interest? Now my dear, we have much work to do if thees dress ees to fit as he wishes.'

How easily Madame Renée explained Noble's behaviour, Glory thought, marvelling at the older woman's worldliness. The couturier had burst into her life like a cyclone six weeks ago, dispensing information and advice in a delightful *mélange* of English and French that somehow gave her every pronouncement the ring of truth.

'You must not let thees little *renversement* spoil your day,' Madame Renée said, beginning to mark up the alterations. 'A man such as your father, a man with great power and wealth, needs special handling.'

'I'm afraid I don't know very much about men.'

'They may be difficult to understand – but we certainly can't live without them. Permit me to give you some advice. When dealing with a man just bat your lashes, lower your eyes, wet your lips, and smile. And always tell him how smart he is – even if he's as dumb as an ox. Trust me, *chérie*. It works every time.'

'I don't know if I can do that. I'm not good at flirting.'

Madame Renée stepped back and tilted her head, eyeing her handiwork. 'Your father was right. Such a figure shouldn't be hidden. Tonight my dear, you won't need to worry about flirting. No man will be able to resist you.'

CHAPTER NINE

Lights blazed in every one of the Girard mansion's windows at nine o'clock on Christmas Eve, creating a constellation of their very own against the night sky. A line of chauffeur-driven Lincolns, Pierce Arrows, Duesenbergs and Cadillacs queued up in the drive, waiting to disgorge their passengers.

The muted growl of well-tended engines, the lilt of cultured voices, the airborne vibrato of stringed instruments and the clatter of servants hurrying to and fro, blended in a discordant overture to Glory's debutante ball. Society mavins had predicted it would be the event of the year – perhaps of the decade.

Outside the wrought-iron gates reporters clustered with curious citizens, hoping to catch a glimpse or exchange a word with the rich and powerful guests. All of them, from invitees to members of the fourth estate, to casual bystanders, whether they arrived in luxurious limousines or aboard Shank's mare, had the same question.

Why had the Girards chosen this holiday season to end their long exile from society?

The attendees soon abandoned such speculation and surrendered to the hedonistic pleasure of being entertained in magnificent surroundings. Monsieur Alphonse, despite his pretensions, had carried out Anna's white and silver colour scheme with a sure hand, transforming the elegant mansion into a scene of wintry splendour.

Glitter was the watchword of the night. Evergreen garlands twined with silver and ivory ribbons and twinkling with hundreds of lights adorned the hall's twin staircases. White poinsettias clustered under the risers. At the apex of the stairs, a blue spruce decorated with silver and white ornaments sent its branches soaring towards the glass ceiling.

Smaller trees graced the four corners of the ballroom, while potted gardenias and white orchids forced into early bloom turned the conservatory into an exotic jungle. Scented candles in giant candelabras added their own aroma to an atmosphere already heady with expensive perfumes and gourmet food.

In the dining room a shimmering ice sculpture reflected off silver trays laden with Beluga caviar, pâté de foie gras, oysters on the half shell, eggs à la russe, and salmon in aspic – among other delicacies. Despite Prohibition, Noble's bootlegger had supplied a variety of alcoholic beverages from the best champagne to the finest liquor to aperitifs for every taste.

Three bars, one in the library, one in the conservatory and one at the far end of the ballroom, guaranteed no guest would go thirsty. Uniformed waiters bearing canapés circulated through the crowd, ensuring no one would go hungry before the midnight buffet.

Pandemonium reigned in the kitchen where Monsieur Alphonse commanded a seemingly endless array of sous chefs, sauciers and their helpers. From the chaos emerged ambrosial foods that would have been the envy of any five star restaurant. This was the most important event the Brooklyn-born caterer had overseen, and he intended to make the most of the opportunity to gild his reputation.

Glory was unaware of the hubbub in the other parts of the house as she stood in the hall, her father to her left, her mother to her right, welcoming guests. They had been at it for an hour. Her fingers ached from all the hands she had shaken and her smile felt frozen. But she was determined to make her parents proud of her, to show that no matter how much she'd resisted having the ball, she appreciated the fact they were doing it for her.

Her mother's aplomb astonished Glory. Anna greeted their guests with such *sang froid* that a stranger might think she hosted lavish parties several times a year, when in reality she hadn't seen many of her former friends in a decade.

Noble was even more impressive. He never failed to associate the right name with the right face and managed to produce some tidbit of information about each one. His charm never flagged as he spoke of golf handicaps, mergers, anniversaries, and asked after children and grandchildren as if he really cared about each and every answer.

He was in his element and, certainly, he had never looked more handsome as San Francisco's *haute monde* paraded by in a bounteous display of starched shirt fronts and deep *décolletage*. Contrary to the natural order of the animal kingdom, the ladies looked like peacocks in their best jewels and couturier gowns, while the men reminded

Glory of an assemblage of crows. How she would have enjoyed sketching them!

'Sweetheart, you know the Aspromantes and their son Leslie,' Noble said, introducing yet another group.

'Of course. It's lovely to see you all again,' Glory replied.

'I h-h-hope you'll keep a place for me on your dance card,' Leslie stuttered, his sallow skin turning bright pink.

Not giving Glory a chance to reply, Noble reached for Leslie's upper arm and propelled him past her. 'Sorry son. You're too late. My daughter's dance card is already full.'

Before Glory had time to think about her father's blatant lie, another person took Leslie's place in the receiving line and then another. At last Cal and Professor Blackstone reached her side and the smile that had been pasted on her lips became genuine.

'I've been wondering when you'd get here,' Glory said, taking Cal's hand.

'Late? Are we late? I was reading Scaevola's *Annales Maximi* and I'm afraid I lost track of time.' Professor Blackstone's bushy white eyebrows moved up and down like an agitated yoyo. Although he wore the required black tie he looked as though he'd put it on in the dark.

'You're not late at all, is he, Father?' Glory gently passed the professor on to Noble so she could have a moment alone with Cal.

'Your dress is pure dynamite!' Cal exclaimed with her habitual enthusiasm. 'Talk about a red hot Mama, you'll knock them dead tonight.'

'And you look more like the toast of the town than the toastette.'

Cal widened her eyes until the whites showed all around, then gave her bare shoulders an insouciant shrug, doing her best Gloria Swanson imitation. 'Oh, it's just some old thing I had in my closet.' Leaning closer, she whispered, 'Are there any terrific looking men here?'

'Gobs.' Glory burst out laughing. 'You just missed Leslie Aspromante.'

'Be still my heart. I can hardly wait to see the handsome devil.' Cal was still giggling as she led her father away.

Glory sighed, wishing she could be there to see the swath Cal was bound to cut through the young men in the ballroom. But the receiving line showed no sign of slackening.

A few minutes later Noble surprised her by greeting a strange young man with a hearty bear hug. He took a step back and looked the young man over. Approval was evidenced by his broad smile. 'It's good to see you, Jeremy.'

'I wouldn't have missed tonight for the world, sir.'

'Permit me to introduce you to my daughter. Sweetheart, this is Jeremy Montclair. He interviewed with the firm last week. The only way I could persuade him to take a job as my personal assistant was to promise him a couple of dances with you tonight.'

Flattered, Glory turned to face the newcomer. He appeared to be in his early twenties, of average height, with a football player's heavily boned body and a baby's blond curls and innocent blue eyes. Cute, she thought – very cute. 'It's nice to meet you, Mr Montclair.'

'Please call me Jeremy. Your father and I have talked about you so much that I feel I know you.'

How peculiar, Glory mused. Noble usually made a point of keeping his business and his private life totally separate. 'Then you must call me Glory.'

'About those dances, your father was mistaken. He promised me three.'

Glory laughed at his temerity. She liked the bold young man. 'No wonder my father hired you. You're just like him.'

'I'll take that as a compliment. There isn't a man I admire more.'

'I say, Jeremy, how about an introduction,' a tall stranger at Jeremy's elbow interjected.

Glory glanced his way. His gaze locked with hers, sending an electric ripple along her spine. With it came the prescient feeling that here was the man she had hoped to meet when she and Cal first talked about the ball.

'This is Lawrence Wyant, my pushy former Stanford room mate,' Jeremy said, laughing.

The newcomer stood well over six feet tall. His chestnut hair was parted on the side and an errant strand fell forward over the greenest eyes she'd ever seen. He had the high-bridged nose, arrogant cheekbones, and sun-bronzed complexion of a Spanish grandee in one of Goya's paintings.

His broad shoulders and slender build reminded her of the athletic matinee idol, Douglas Fairbanks. But it was his mouth that captured her attention. His full lips contrasted with the ascetic elegance of his other features. She shocked herself by wondering what it would be like to kiss him.

'Former room mate?' she asked, feeling herself colour.

'We both completed our master's degrees last year,' Jeremy explained. 'Mine was in business. I went to work but this no good bum decided to chase coeds and live off his parents a little longer.'

It was Lawrence's turn to laugh. 'Fortunately my parents didn't quite see it the way you do, Jer. They agreed that having a doctorate in art history might be an asset to the family business.'

'And what business might that be?' she asked, her interest in the stranger intensified by the mention of art.

Noble intervened before Lawrence Wyant could answer. 'Gentlemen, you'll have plenty of time to talk to my daughter during the party. But there are other guests waiting to meet her now.'

Half an hour later Noble stood in the hall by the giant blue spruce, waiting for his wife and daughter. He had sent them to their rooms to freshen up under Madame Renée's critical eye when the receiving line came to an end.

Now, watching them descend, he experienced a proprietary sense of ownership. No matter their differences they were *his* women, and tonight they were magnificent.

In honour of the occasion, Anna had eschewed her habitual black for a gown of ivory Alençon lace. The famous Girard parure – a diamond and emerald tiara with a matching necklace and earrings – framed her delicate features. Such beauty would be wasted in a permanent religious retreat, he mused with unexpected sadness.

However even Anna's loveliness faded into insignificance when compared to Glory's. His daughter came down the stairs with the easy grace of a young lioness. Her startling colouring, her height, her magnificent figure, made an indelible impression on everyone.

Jeremy Montclair was a lucky devil, and not because of his new and privileged position at the Girard Company. Noble had handpicked young Montclair to be his future son-in-law.

Montclair wasn't yet privy to Noble's plan and in view of the stunned look on his face when he met Glory, he would never have to know. From Noble's perspective the romance was off and running.

'Ready, ladies?' he asked, linking his arms with theirs.

Glory and Anna nodded in unison. As the three of them walked into the ballroom a musical flourish announced their entrance and two hundred pairs of eyes turned their way. Noble felt his chest inflate with pride.

He had spared no expense to ensure the evening's success – and his beloved Glory was worth every penny. Tonight she had fulfilled his fondest hopes. He smiled, thinking he'd spend even more on her wedding to Montclair.

As he helped Anna and Glory onto the dais at the end of the room, waiters bearing trays of champagne circulated through the glittering throng. Clarence delivered Noble's champagne in person, then acting totally out of character, gave Glory a wink before returning to his other duties.

Noble had planned this moment as carefully as he planned a raid on a rival's company. He gazed down on the assemblage, commanding their silence by the sheer force of his personality, then walked to the microphone and cleared his throat.

'Ladies and gentlemen, friends old and new,' he begun, 'I'd like to take this opportunity to welcome you to our home. Although we haven't given a party for more years than I care to remember, you must admit this one was worth the wait. I want to thank my dear wife for working day and night to make sure all of you would enjoy yourselves.'

He nodded at Anna, waiting for the applause to die down. 'And now if I may beg your indulgence, I'd like to present my daughter with an early Christmas present.' Reaching into his jacket pocket, he produced a pair of diamond drop earrings whose ten carats elicited an appreciative gasp from the female onlookers.

Glory's eyes sparkled even brighter than the gems as she put them on. 'Daddy, I don't know what to say.'

'A simple thank you would do,' he said into the microphone to a burst of laughter.

Dozens of board meetings had taught him how to mesmerise a crowd – and when he'd worn out his welcome. It was a fine line, one he had no intention of crossing tonight. He lifted his glass. 'Last but far from least, I want all of you to join me in a toast to my daughter. May she remember this night as long as she lives.'

Putting his glass aside, Noble signalled Ted Lewis to begin playing the waltz he had personally chosen for the occasion. He took Glory's hand and led her to the centre of the room for the customary father-daughter dance.

'What do you think about having a debut ball now?' he asked.

Her grey eyes glittered with pleasure. 'Can't you tell? I'm having a wonderful time. I didn't realise you were the wonderful dancer you are, Daddy.'

'And I haven't danced for so long, I'd forgotten the pleasure of holding a beautiful young woman in my arms.'

'Oh Daddy, you're such a flatterer.'

But it wasn't flattery. From the top of her sleek mahogany hair to the tips of her satin slippers, Glory outshone every woman in the room. After she and Jeremy were married, she would take her proper place as a leader of San Francisco society.

When the music ended, he reluctantly relinquished Glory to the first of the partners whose names crowded her dance card and walked over to Anna. She was engrossed in conversation with Father Tremaine as usual.

'If you'll excuse us, Father, it's traditional for a debutante's parents to have the second dance.'

He offered Anna his arm and, ever so slowly, she took it. How long had it been since they'd stood so close let alone moved as one, he wondered as he twirled her around the floor. For a moment he remembered what it had been like between them before Isabel died. Where had all that love gone? It had been buried with the child, he answered himself.

'Are you feeling all right?' Anna broke his reverie.

'Why do you ask?'

'You look quite bilious tonight.'

'How kind of you to worry about my health,' he replied. Anna might resemble the woman he had loved so passionately but her querulous voice was a reminder of the unhappy woman she had become.

'You should have consulted me about Glory's gift,' she said. 'It was terribly gauche of you to give such large diamonds to an eighteen-year-old girl.'

'They suit her.'

'You've spoiled her before. This time though, you've gone too far.'

'For God's sake, Anna, it's not as if I couldn't afford them.'

'One or two carats would have been adequate. Gaudy baubles like those earrings belong on your mistress – not on our daughter.'

Noble felt the blood drain from his face. He hadn't realised Anna knew about Greta. What else was the damn bitch keeping to herself?

By the time Jeremy Montclair came to claim the first of the three dances he'd requested, Glory had circled the floor with a dozen young men. Tall, short, thin, husky, talkative, shy – she had Charlestoned, tangoed, foxtrotted, and waltzed with a shopping list of San Francisco's most eligible bachelors.

'I've looked forward to this moment ever since your father introduced us and thinking about doing bodily harm to every one of my rivals,' Jeremy said.

'Why Jeremy, are you giving me a rush?' she teased.

'I'm planning on it being more like a whirlwind,' he teased back.

'You didn't look as if you were pining away when you danced with Cal,' Glory commented, recalling what a splendid couple they had made – and the way they had stared at each other.

'I spent the entire time talking to her about you.'

Glory doubted it. While Jeremy held Cal in his arms, he'd had eyes for no one else.

'The day I walked into your father's office has turned out to be the luckiest day of my life – in more ways than one.'

'I know my father is pleased about it. He seems very taken with you.' She tried not to giggle as he struggled with the simple rhythms of a foxtrot. Unfortunately Jeremy's feet weren't as nimble as his tongue. She cried out when one of them came down on her instep.

'Oh God I'm sorry,' he said, losing the rhythm completely. 'Did I hurt you?'

'It's nothing, really.'

'Perhaps we ought to sit this one out.'

Thank heaven, she thought. 'I could use some fresh air.'

'Hunky-dory. I've been dying to get you alone.' He put a proprietary arm around her waist and led the way to one of the french doors on the east side of the ballroom.

When they stepped out onto the terrace Glory shivered involuntarily as the night air chilled her bare shoulders and arms.

'Here, let me put this on you,' Jeremy said, removing his jacket and draping it around her shoulders. For a moment, she glimpsed something so sad in his gaze that she couldn't help wondering what sorrows he hid behind his ready smile.

'I don't run with the social set the way I did before my father died,' he said, 'and I imagine your father will keep me quite busy. But I'd very much like to see you again.'

'I stop by my father's office once or twice a month.'

'I had something more personal in mind. The Museum of Fine Art will be opening an exhibition of Plein Air painters next weekend. I'd be delighted to escort you.'

Considering the way Jeremy and Cal had looked at each other, Glory would have refused any other invitation from the young man. However she couldn't pass up a jaunt to an art museum.

She was about to ask if Cal could go too when she heard a masculine chuckle. 'Since when are you interested in art, Jeremy?'

Glory tracked the voice to its source. Her heart bumped as she saw Lawrence Wyant coming towards them. The moon silhouetted his lean figure, highlighting his striking features and glittering in his green eyes.

'Don't let Jeremy snooker you,' Lawrence said. 'He wouldn't know a Plein Air painter from an Impressionist. Bonds and debentures are more his style. If you want to tour the exhibit with a knowledgeable guide, I'm your man.'

Lawrence took both her hands in his. The contact sent an electric jolt through her. 'And now, Miss Girard, I believe the next dance is mine.'

Glory forgot all about Jeremy Montclair.

'I do believe you're right, Mr Wyant,' she replied even though every dance on her card had a name next to it and not one of them was his.

'Mr Wyant is my father. My friends call me Lawrence.'

'All right, Lawrence it is.'

'If you'll excuse us, Jeremy?'

Lawrence took Jeremy's jacket from around her shoulders and gave it back to its owner. Then he tucked her hand into the crook of his elbow, smiling at her all the while as if they shared a delicious secret.

It was the most intimate look she'd ever received from a man and it sent a rush of heat through her body, completely banishing the chill she'd felt just a moment before.

The orchestra was playing a tango when he guided her onto the dance floor. For a few minutes the intricate steps demanded all her attention. However Lawrence was a superb dancer and she soon found herself relaxing in his arms.

She had tangoed with other partners, never once realising the dance had been perfectly designed for seduction. Her hips brushed against Lawrence's, her breasts touched his chest. They moved in silence while she struggled to think about something else.

'When we were introduced, you said something about studying art because of your family's business,' she said, hoping to get him to talk about himself as Madame Renée had advised. And not because she wanted him to think she was a fascinating conversationalist but rather, because she found him fascinating.

'My family is in the art business. That's why I'm taking my doctorate in art history. Perhaps you've heard of the Wyant Gallery. It's on Fifth Avenue.'

'No,' Glory answered, wishing she could say she had been there – or better still, that she had plans to go, 'but I've only been to New York once.'

'It's of no importance. I'd much rather talk about you.'

'I'm afraid you'd be bored,' she replied with utter sincerity, wondering why the handsomest man in the room had singled her out. 'I'm just your average deb.'

'You may be many things, Miss Girard, but I'm quite certain boring isn't one of them.'

His gaze locked with hers and she felt it clear down to her sandalled feet. She had read about what the French called *le coup de foudre*, love at first sight, but she had been too sceptical to believe it existed. Dancing with Lawrence banished those doubts.

The words they spoke had less significance than the subtext they conveyed with their eyes and hands. That sweet language was as old as time. Had she been more experienced, she would have recognised the controlled sensuality of his every move. And correctly identified the answering throb deep in her abdomen as awakening desire.

He swept her into a deep dip, then lifted her back up with effortless strength. 'There's nothing average about you, Glory Girard. Tell me why your face lights up at the mention of art.'

'I want to be an artist,' she answered simply.

Glory's answer took Lawrence by surprise. Could there be a serious intellect, let alone genuine talent behind those gorgeous grey eyes? Girls who looked like Glory Girard usually dreamed about becoming movie stars.

He propelled her into a spin that sent her to the furthest reach of his arms, then pulled her tight against his chest so that their bodies touched from chest to thigh. For a moment he permitted himself to concentrate on the contact, to revel in the erotic cushion of her breasts and the heat he sensed between her legs. Then, feeling a hungry surge of desire, he made himself back away.

Glory might look as if she'd been born to make love but the way she hesitated before she spoke, as if she were unaccustomed to the company of men, told him she was no casual flirt.

'Why an artist?'

'When other little girls were playing with dolls and pretending to be their mothers, I spent all my time drawing. I'd give my soul to go to art school.'

The sadness in her voice aroused his protective instincts. He pulled her close again, wishing he could shield her from . . . from what? He tore his gaze from her to take in the opulent setting. If ever a girl had everything – looks, wealth, devoted parents – she was it.

'I doubt your soul will be required under the circumstances.'

'What circumstances?'

'It's perfectly obvious your father could afford to buy an art school, let alone send you to one.'

'He doesn't think art is a proper career for a woman.'

'What does he think you should do?'

'Get married.'

Hoping to suppress the spiralling warmth in his groin, he shifted his body sideways so only their cheeks and shoulders touched. 'I imagine you've already had your share of proposals.'

'Not yet. How about you?'

'Not a one. But then, women don't usually do the proposing.'

'I would – I'd propose to you,' she blurted in a breathless rush.

He was tempted to discover where this enchanting flirtation would lead. Sorely tempted. He longed to take her out on the terrace and kiss her – and suspected she felt the same way. But he had been well schooled in honour and duty and they urged him in the opposite direction.

'I said no one ever proposed to me, Miss Girard. I didn't say I hadn't proposed. I'm engaged. My fiancée lives in New York.'

Just then the music came to a halt and he felt a peremptory tap on his shoulder.

'I hope I'm not interrupting anything. The next dance is mine,' Jeremy said.

'You're not interrupting anything. Mr Wyant and I are quite finished,' Glory replied.

The disgust in her voice cut into Lawrence like a sabre slash. His jaws clenched as he watched her submit to Jeremy's graceless dancing. A waiter bearing a tray of brimming champagne glasses walked by. He helped himself to two, drank them both straight down, then made his way back to the hall.

What the hell had got into him? Debutantes weren't his type. Besides, he'd just met Glory Girard. He wouldn't have met her at all if Jeremy hadn't said he needed moral support tonight. Even then, Lawrence had only agreed to attend the ball because he wanted to see Noble Girard's famous art collection.

Damn. He didn't have the time or the temperament for an ill-advised infatuation. He'd finish his degree, return to New York, take his place in the family business and marry Beth. She needed him in a way that a woman like Glory never would.

He left the party without a backward glance. He'd make his apologies to Jeremy in the morning, congratulate him on meeting a terrific girl, and then get on with his own life. It was the right thing – the sensible thing to do – the only thing to do.

And yet his heart ached at the thought of never seeing Glory Girard again.

CHAPTER TEN

Noble stood in the hall with Glory and Anna by his side, watching the last guests leave, feeling more content than he had in years. The ball had banished his concerns for Glory's future. It had gone off like clockwork in every respect from the first dance to the last.

Montclair had been as attentive to Glory as Noble could have wished. They made a handsome couple, he mused, although they would have looked even better together if Montclair were a couple of inches taller.

The compliments he'd received about Glory's appearance, her behaviour, her maturity, assured him he'd made all the right choices about her upbringing. Her chic, her social graces, her *joie de vivre* proved she was his daughter through and through, no matter who her birth parents had been.

A man might win the world and take it in stride. Hearing his progeny praised, knowing he'd set them on the road to a satisfying future was far more rewarding. Despite the lateness of the hour he felt far too stimulated to retire for the night.

Euphoria prompted him to offer Anna a rare compliment. 'It was a very successful party. You did a magnificent job.'

She cut a sharp glance at him. 'I hope the evening served its purpose. I don't have the energy to repeat it.'

'What purpose?' Glory questioned.

'Ask your father,' Anna said. She gathered her skirts and made her way up the stairs with a brisk step that denied her professed exhaustion.

Glory turned to Noble. 'What was Mother talking about?'

He pretended ignorance. 'God alone knows what your mother means half the time. Certainly I don't.'

Glory's eyes brimmed with concern. 'You mustn't let it spoil your evening.'

'Not a chance. I'd like another glass of champagne before I call it a night and a little conversation with my daughter.'

'I'd like that too,' Glory replied. Although it was two in the morning she looked as fresh and lovely as she had in the receiving line.

'Did you have a good time tonight? Was it everything you dreamed it would be?' He meant it as a rhetorical question, one that didn't require an answer.

'It was fine,' Glory said with less enthusiasm than he expected.

The library was the only room in the house that had been off limits to Monsieur Alphonse and his crew. Noble went to the sideboard to pour their drinks while Glory walked to the window and gazed out at the night.

'You were certainly the belle of the ball. Did any of the young men you met strike your fancy?' Another rhetorical question he thought with an indulgent smile. He felt certain he knew the answer.

'Jeremy Montclair seemed nice.'

'Nice? He strikes me as a great deal more or I wouldn't have given him such an important position in the company. He's bright, intelligent, and ambitious.' Noble ticked off Jeremy's virtues. 'He comes from a good family even though they fell on hard times after his father died. I realise I can't see him through a woman's eyes, however my secretary tells me he's quite attractive.'

'You're right, Dad. Jeremy is all those things. I like him, but that's as far as it goes.'

'You don't need to hold back. I'm your father, remember? I saw the way the two of you danced, the way you stared into his eyes and hold onto him.'

'What you saw had nothing to do with romance. Jeremy's a terrible dancer. I was just trying to help him. Believe me, that's all there was to it.'

The headache that had plagued Noble off and on for weeks returned full force. 'Apparently you're not capable of knowing a good thing when someone hands it to you on a silver platter.'

'Perhaps I'm just not cut out for love and marriage. I know you don't want to hear it, Dad – and heaven knows I don't want to say it – but the last few months haven't changed a thing. I can't imagine spending the rest of my life serving tea to boring women just because they're in the social register, or going to parties to further my husband's career. I want a career of my own. I want to be an artist.'

Noble couldn't believe his ears. After all he'd done for Glory – the compromise he'd reached with Anna, the dozens of young men he'd interviewed before finding the right candidate for her hand, the huge expense of the ball, this was how she thanked him. He shoved his fists into his pockets to prevent himself using them.

'How dare you defy me?'

'I'm not defying you. I'm trying to be honest the way you taught me.'

'I taught you to be obedient too.'

'I've tried. I've been to more parties than I can remember. I've flirted with every eligible young man in town. And I haven't so much as drawn a line in weeks. But I'm not ready to get married – at least not to someone like Jeremy. We don't have a thing in common.'

Noble's blood pounded in his ears. 'You have everything in common. Class. Status. To say nothing of the fact that I hand-picked him to be my successor. Don't you care that Jeremy is going to run the Girard Company someday?'

'Then why don't you marry him?'

Noble's control snapped. For the second time in his life, he struck a woman – only this time the woman was his daughter.

She made him do it, he told himself, just as Greta had. 'As long as you live under my roof I expect you to obey me. You will, I repeat, you will see Jeremy Montclair again and I don't mean casually. I want you to call him tomorrow and ask him for dinner.'

'If you insist on my dating him, I'll leave. I won't be your puppet. I won't let you make me as unhappy as you've made Mother. You can't ruin my life the way you've ruined hers.'

Noble threw his champagne glass across the room. It crashed into a shelf of first editions, sending tiny spears of glass into the leather bindings. The sight enraged him even more.

'How dare you blame me for your mother's behaviour. She's certifiably crazy.'

Glory sprang to his challenge like a pugilist to the sound of a bell. 'Is crazy your euphemism for miserable? I don't want to be like her. If that means I have to leave this house, so be it.'

'You aren't capable of living on your own.'

'If I'm helpless it's your fault. You raised me. You kept me from growing up. But I'm not afraid of living on my own. Anything would be better than staying here.'

'On your own? You're as crazy as your mother. You wouldn't last a week in the real world. I've had enough of your fucking nonsense for one night. Get your ass up to bed.'

'You can curse all you like but I don't have to listen,' Glory shouted back, spinning away from him. She couldn't stand breathing the same air.

Although she had overheard other men describe her father as a hard man – and occasionally a profane one – she had never seen that side of him before. To think he had actually hit her. If that was his idea of love, she wanted nothing to do with it – or him.

Has this hideous argument been waiting for years to ambush them both?

Had he hidden his hostility beneath the pretence of love?

Had she ever truly known her father?

She had to escape from the house before guilt eroded her courage, she decided as she burst into the hall.

Ellen stood there with her hands on her hips and a horrified expression on her face. She must have overheard every word.

'What is it, child? What's happened?'

Glory skidded to stop. 'Father and I had a fight.'

'Anyone with ears knows that. But why tonight of all nights? The two of you seemed so happy.'

'Oh Ellen, he hit me,' Glory burst out.

'You must have made him very angry.'

'He doesn't understand me. He won't even try.'

'All young people feel that way sooner or later. It's part of growing up. I used to feel the same way about my own Da. We argued all the time about my coming to America. But there is no winning or losing when it comes to families.'

'You're wrong where my father is concerned. He has to win every argument whether he's right or wrong.'

'I know it must seem like life is a battle and your father is the enemy. But my mother, bless her soul, had a saying I've never forgotten. Why speak of triumph, to endure is everything, she'd tell me when I threatened to run away. That's what you have to do now, dear girl. You must endure. If that means giving in to your father, I don't see you have any choice.'

'I appreciate what you're saying, Ellen, believe me I do. No one in this house has been kinder to me.' Glory blinked away the tears pooling in her eyes. If she broke down, she'd be lost. 'Times have changed since you were my age. I don't have to put up with being hit or cursed at. I'm entitled to my own life just the way you were when you left Ireland.'

'But I was a grown woman and my father was dead.'

'How old were you?' Glory demanded.

'Eighteen.'

'I'm eighteen too, old enough to know what's best for me.'

'I don't mean to make you feel bad. You've had enough of that, I suspect. But you know nothing of life beyond your own privileged world. The girls in my village married at thirteen. Most of them were mothers at fourteen. I went to work myself as soon as I was old enough to handle a broom and a dust pan. I was ready to go.'

'You left home and you did just fine and so will I,' Glory declared although her legs trembled beneath her couturier gown. It was one thing to say she was leaving in the heat of argument with her father and quite another to tell Ellen.

'What in the world are you saying, child?'

'My father hasn't given me a choice. He wants to marry me off even though he damn well knows the only thing I care about is being an artist.'

'He loves you, dear.'

'He thinks he owns me. It's not the same thing.'

'You don't know what you're saying. You're angry at him but you'll see things differently in the morning.'

'The morning won't change things. This didn't start tonight. It's been going on for years. The difference is I never saw it before.'

'Do you think I'm crazy the way my father does?' Glory asked Cal.

They had spent the last hour in the Blackstones' shabby parlour while she recounted the bitter quarrel that had driven her from home.

'No. But there are times when you seem determined to be your own worst enemy.' Cal's fingers picked at a loose thread on the Blackstones' worn sofa. 'I'm not sure you realise how much you're giving up. Does your decision have anything to do with Lawrence Wyant?'

'Of course not. Why would you even suggest such a thing? He doesn't mean anything to me.'

'Glory, this is Cal you're talking to.'

'All right. I was terribly hurt when he told me he was engaged. But I hardly knew him. This is about my father and my wanting to be an artist. I've spent the last few months trying to forget it. You know that better than anyone else. And I can never be one while I live under my father's roof. He wants me to marry Jeremy.'

Cal's cheeks flushed. 'You make it sound like a fate worse than death.'

'I don't mean to. He's a terrific guy.'

'Then you do like him?'

'Not the way you do. I hope the two of you will go on seeing each other.'

'So do I. But that's not the point of this discussion. What in the world will you do for money?' Cal asked.

It was a question Glory had been asking herself. She didn't know which frightened her more. The thought of being on her own, or of going back home.

'I have some savings.'

'How much?' the ever practical Cal demanded.

'A hundred dollars. No, make it ninety. I gave ten to the cab driver who brought me here.'

'Ten! He shouldn't have charged more than a dollar.'

'He didn't. But he was so sweet that I couldn't resist giving him a big tip.'

Cal shook her head. 'What in the world am I going to do with you? Ninety dollars won't last a month unless—'

'Unless what?'

'Unless you move in with us. I've always wanted a sister.'

'So have I,' Glory replied.

It would be so easy to accept the invitation. She wouldn't have to be on her own. The professor might even help her get a scholarship to a local art school.

But Glory couldn't do that to the Blackstones. They couldn't afford to have her live with them – and not just because of the extra expense. Her father wielded a lot of influence in San Francisco. She wouldn't want to see him use it against Cal and the professor. And she had no doubt he would if they gave her a refuge.

'Well, what do you say?' Cal's eyes sparkled with enthusiasm. 'We'd make a terrific team.'

'I appreciate the offer but I have other plans for my future – big plans.'

'Name one,' Cal challenged.

Glory improvised. 'For starters I'm going to sell the diamond earrings my father gave me last night so I won't have to worry about money.'

'What then? Will you go to the Chicago Art Institute the way you wanted?'

Glory shook her head. 'I'm not ready yet. Besides, I could learn so much more if I had private lessons.'

'Here?'

'I don't want to take a chance on my father tracking me down. I've been thinking about heading south,' Glory declared as if she'd been contemplating such a move for weeks, although the idea had just popped into her mind. Cal must never know how much she wanted to stay. 'I wouldn't mind seeing sunshine and palm trees for a change.'

'What will I do without you?'

'Marry a rich young man the way you've always wanted and have lots of kids.'

Tears glittered in Cal's eyes. 'It won't be the same after you've gone. I'll worry about you every minute.'

'I'll be fine,' Glory replied as though it were a certainty instead of the longest of long shots.

Cal's concern was so seductive that she knew she wouldn't have the courage to leave if she waited much longer. 'I had better call a cab.'

'So soon?' Cal wailed. 'I thought you'd at least spend the night.'

'My bags are packed. It would be a shame to go to the trouble of unpacking and then packing them again.'

'I can't believe this is happening,' Cal moaned. 'We were both so happy last night.'

'Last night, one of us was living in a fool's paradise. Please, Cal, don't make this any harder than it already is. I don't want to leave you,' Glory said, heading for the phone, 'but it's for the best.'

When the cab came half an hour later Glory insisted on taking it to the train station alone.

'Write to me every day,' Cal called out as the cab pulled away from the curb.

Glory knew her heart would break if she looked back at her friend. Instead she kept her eyes firmly fixed straight ahead on a future she couldn't see.

'Glory's gone,' Anna announced when she joined Noble in the dining room for breakfast.

'I know,' he replied, not bothering to look up from the newspaper. He refused to let Anna see how upset he was. The pain in his head was blinding in its intensity.

'Did you see her leave?' Anna asked.

'I was sleeping. Ellen told me she was gone.'

'Do you know why Glory left?'

He rustled the paper. 'Can't you see I'm reading?'

'I think you owe me an explanation. After all, she's my daughter too.'

He wanted to say she had never acted like a mother but what was the point? Suddenly a searing pain made him gasp. His right arm felt so weak that the newspaper dropped from his hand. But he'd die before he let Anna have the last word.

'Glory will be back.'

Anna gave him a cold smile. 'Oh no she won't. You see, my dear husband, you raised her to be just like you. She'll never admit she's wrong. We've seen the last of her.'

With the last ounce of his failing strength, he rose to leave the room and the mocking sound of his wife's voice. The last thing he remembered was hitting the dining room floor. He came to in bed, at least he thought it was his bed.

'He's coming around,' he heard someone say. A hand clasped his wrist and he realised someone was taking his pulse. Prying his eyes apart, he saw his doctor standing over him.

'What the hell happened?' he managed to say although the words came out slurred.

'You've had a mild stroke, nothing that bed rest won't repair,' the doctor replied.

Anna appeared at the outer edge of Noble's vision. 'You'll be fine in a few weeks.'

'Fine, hell. I can't see out of my right eye.'

'We have every reason to hope the condition won't be permanent,' the doctor responded. 'Now that I'm sure the crisis is past I'm going to leave you to your wife's care while I see about getting you some nurses.'

Noble considered asking him not to leave, then decided against it. He and Anna would have to talk sooner or later. It might as well be now. He waited while she walked the doctor to the bedroom door, wondering what they were whispering about.

Probably his condition. Well, he'd show them. He'd be on his feet in record time.

'Can I get you anything?' Anna asked when she returned.

'No.'

'Should I call the office and tell them you're sick?'

'The fewer people who know, the better.'

'Our friends would want to send flowers.'

'No.'

'Glory would come home if she heard.'

'No,' he said more forcefully. He didn't want Glory to return out of pity.

'How will I explain her absence, to say nothing of yours?'

'Tell people I took her to Europe on a surprise trip. When I'm on my feet and back at my desk I'll say she decided to stay abroad.'

Anna pulled up a chair and sat down. 'I'll stay with you until a nurse gets here.'

He closed his eyes.

'Don't pretend to be asleep, Noble. I want to put your mind at rest. I spoke with Father Tremaine while you were unconscious – and I've come to a decision. I wouldn't be in a state of grace if I abandoned you in your time of need. I've written to the Sisters of Mercy to tell them I've decided not to join them.'

Noble tried to turn away from her but his body wouldn't cooperate. He felt weak and totally disorientated. He'd never expected to lose Glory and keep Anna. He'd have been better off if the stroke had killed him.

PART THREE

Dimitri Konstantine

You cannot create genius. All you can do
is nurture it.
Ninette De Valois – *Time*, 26 Sept., 1960

CHAPTER ELEVEN

Monterey, California, 1926

The wind churning Monterey Bay's sapphire water did nothing to relieve the August heat. Cannery Row sizzled in the relentless sunshine as Glory made her way down the wide dusty road. Hungry, thirsty and tired, she longed to find a shady place to rest. But she knew once she did, she wouldn't have the courage to continue searching for a job.

She shivered despite the heat as she considered her circumstances. She'd spent the last couple of months looking for work, first in San Diego and then Los Angeles. But none of the employers who had interviewed her considered the ability to plan an elaborate menu, to arrange flowers, or to speak a smattering of French as desirable job qualifications.

Time and again she'd been told she couldn't get work until she had experience. But how could she get experience unless someone was willing to hire her? The conundrum tugged at her weary mind as much as the heat tugged at her weary body.

The shrill cries of herring gulls wheeling overhead intensified her foreboding as she reached the corrugated metal building that was her destination. A pungent aroma announced its purpose even before she read the *Konstantine Cannery* sign.

She'd taken the night train to Monterey because she'd overheard two women talking about how the canneries were hiring. Now, squinting in the fierce sunlight, she took a tissue from her bag and mopped her streaming brow. Squaring her shoulders, she opened the door marked *Office*.

It took a moment for her eyes to adjust to the gloom. She was in a small wood-panelled room crowded with two scarred desks, a couple of metal filing cabinets, and three mismatched chairs. A fishing net lay in one corner like a tangled spider web.

A fan on one of the cabinets stirred the malodorous air. The stench – a blend of sardines, machine oil, and toiling human beings – was stronger inside than it had been on the street.

A middle-aged woman seated behind one of the desks looked up and said, 'If you've come to meet your boyfriend, the boats aren't in yet.'

Although Glory's knees were shaking, she gave the woman what she hoped was a confident smile. 'That's not why I'm here. I heard you were looking for workers.'

The woman got up and came around the desk, her lively brown eyes studying Glory from head to toe. 'We don't need any office help, young lady.'

'I heard you needed help in the cannery. If you'd just let me talk to the owners . . .' Glory's voice trailed off. In the year and a half since she'd left San Francisco she had known fear, loneliness and despair. Now all three crowded her close.

'I'm one of the owners. My name's Elena Konstantine,' the woman said. Her eyes, as she looked Glory over for the second time, managed to be both appraising and sympathetic. 'I don't think you're right for the job but I'll get my husband. It's really his decision. He runs the cannery and I take care of the paperwork.'

Before Glory had time to say thank you, Elena Konstantine disappeared through the room's only other door. Although Glory was desperate to sit down, in her determination to make a good impression, she stayed on her feet at near military attention.

Elena Konstantine reappeared minutes later with her husband.

Glory expected to see a well-dressed businessman in a suit, someone like her father. To her surprise Mr Konstantine wore a faded shirt, denim trousers, rubber boots and an oilcloth apron. He looked like the other cannery workers she'd seen that day.

'I'm Spiro Konstantine,' he said, giving her the same appraising look his wife had minutes earlier. 'My Elena tells me you want a job. Have you ever worked in a cannery?'

Glory had been asked the same question in the four canneries she had already visited. 'No, but I'm a hard worker.'

He nodded, then said, 'Let me see your hands.'

Glory held them out.

He wiped his stained hands on his trousers, then took hold of hers and turned them palm up.

His palms boasted thick calluses.

Hers were as silky and useless as a chiffon gown in a blizzard.

'You say you're a hard worker but your hands tell me you haven't done a lick of work in your life. I'm sorry, miss. You wouldn't last an hour on the line.'

Glory's shoulders sagged. Her head drooped. She chewed on her lips to keep from crying. She knew she looked like a whipped cur but she didn't care. She'd run out of pride along with more mundane things like money.

'Thank you for your time,' she managed to say past the choking lump in her throat.

She had opened the door to the street when Elena Konstantine called her back. 'Just a minute, miss. We don't have a job for you but you might try Tina Czernik's boarding house. She's looking for someone to wait at tables and help in the kitchen.' She scribbled an address and directions on a piece of paper and handed it to Glory. 'Tell her I sent you.'

Please don't let this be another dead end, Glory thought an hour later as she gazed up at a whimsical Victorian house whose pink siding, rose-coloured trim and elaborate woodwork reminded her of a birthday cake. Surrounded by well-kept lawns and bordered with flowerbeds, the boarding house looked as homey as a warm fire on a cold night.

Home, she mused, grateful that the word no longer had the power to pierce her heart. It would be heaven to live in a home again instead of a third-rate hotel.

On her way to the boarding house she had stopped at the train station to retrieve the luggage she'd left in the care of the station master. Her underarms had dampened during the long walk. Madame Gilot had been wrong, she thought with sour frustration. Women didn't glow – they sweated just like men.

Madame Gilot had been wrong about other things as well. She had taught her students that worrying about money was a man's province, and that a lady never looked at a price tag. Glory had mistakenly followed that advice when she first left San Francisco. She had sold

111

her diamond earrings and used the proceeds to pay for lodging in good hotels and meals in nice restaurants.

Now all her worldly possessions were contained in two cheap cardboard suitcases whose weight tugged at her shoulders. Would arriving with luggage in hand make her appear over anxious? Or over confident?

By now she'd been turned down at so many potential work places – from coffee shops to five and dimes to the canneries – that she should have been accustomed to rejection. But her chest felt tight at the thought of being turned down again.

Smoothing her dress, she started up the drive. A wide porch beckoned her into its shade. Pots overflowing with geraniums added their own spicy scent to the aroma of fresh baked bread wafting through an open window.

She salivated involuntarily. Last night she'd been unwilling to pay the outrageous price of dinner in the train's dining car and had gone to sleep hungry. This morning she'd been afraid to go into one of the rough cafes near the canneries. If only she had learned to manage her money earlier, she wouldn't be in such desperate straits.

She felt faint. Her knees seemed as insubstantial as clouds as she climbed the six steps to the porch where a calico cat snoozed in one of six rocking chairs.

The front door boasted a well-polished brass knocker in the shape of a ship's anchor. Before Glory could lift it the door swung wide to reveal a woman cooling herself with a cheap palmetto fan. Although the woman was several inches shorter than Glory, she filled the opening.

Her girth seemed magnified by the pink cabbage roses printed on her dress. Her plump face made it hard to guess her age. She could have been anywhere past thirty but surely not yet fifty.

'My goodness,' the woman said, blinking in surprise, 'I didn't know anyone was here. I hope you didn't come for a room. I don't have any vacancies.'

She crossed the porch on a pair of surprisingly dainty feet, scooped the cat up in her meaty arms and sank onto a rocker, settling herself as ponderously as an ocean liner snuggling into a berth. Then she motioned at an adjacent rocker.

'As long as you're here, you might as well sit a spell. It isn't often I get a chance to chat with a lady of quality like yourself.'

For the third time in less than an hour, Glory found herself being eyed up and down.

'If you don't mind my commenting,' the woman said, 'that dress and those shoes certainly didn't come from the Sears catalogue. They look like New York to me – or even gay Paree.'

'They're from New York,' Glory mumbled.

'I knew it,' the woman replied contentedly. 'If you aren't looking for a room, what brings you to the Czernik boarding house on the hottest day of the year?'

'Elena Konstantine sent me. She said you needed someone to wait at tables and help in the kitchen.'

Tina Czernik fluttered her palmetto fan even harder. She couldn't have been more surprised. Why would a girl who could afford such finery want a job as a maid? 'Are you in some kind of trouble?'

'I don't know what you mean?'

'Man trouble? Cop trouble?'

The girl shook her head, sending her red hair – the real thing, not the kind you got from henna – flying. 'No. But I will be in terrible straits if I don't find employment soon. I'm almost out of funds.'

Tina had never heard such a refined accent or such an elegant use of words. But she believed in calling a spade a spade. 'You mean you're broke?'

This time the girl nodded yes. She certainly was a pretty thing, even if she did look more forlorn than a newly weaned pup.

'Do you have experience waiting at tables?'

'No.'

'Do you know your way around a kitchen?'

'No. The truth is I don't have any work experience of any kind.'

'I'm sorry, miss, but I really do need someone who can start right away.'

'Please,' the girl said with a catch in her voice, 'just give me a chance. I promise you won't regret it. I'm a quick learner.'

'I imagine you are. You do have a right smart look to you. But I just don't know. You see, I have a very good trade here. My boarders are like family and the last girl – well, I caught her in bed with her boyfriend. The way they were making the mattress springs squeal would have roused the dead. My boarders didn't appreciate it and neither did I. Do you have a steady?'

Most girls would have blushed or bridled at the question. This one went white as a sheet. 'I don't go out with men!'

Tiny's brows elevated at the vehement response. 'Don't tell me you're one of those lesbians.'

The girl looked shocked. 'I'm not interested in women that way. And I don't trust men. I don't see any reason to spend the rest of my life trying to catch one.'

'Good for you,' Tiny replied, softening a little. She liked a girl with spunk. 'Men are nothing but trouble. Take my dear departed husbands, all three of them. It was always Tiny fetch this and Tiny fetch that, as though I were a damn dog instead of a wife. My first husband ran off with another woman. The second one decided he liked boys better. My last husband took sick a month after we got married and expected me to nurse him to the end. He bought a big insurance policy to pay for a fancy funeral but I used it to buy this house. I imagine he's still turning over in his grave – in a plain pine box I might add.'

She burst out laughing at the mental image she had conjured up. 'Oh dear, there I go running off at the mouth again. I'm sorry. I'm forgetting my manners. My name's Tina Czernik but my friends call me Tiny.'

Seeing Glory's confusion, she grinned. 'Not for my size, honey. For my feet. The good Lord made my body ten sizes too big and my poor tootsies four sizes too small. You'd think he would have had better sense. But then, what can you expect from a man?' Without skipping a beat, she extended her hand. 'And your name is?'

Glory hesitated a moment. When she first left San Francisco she had used a false name. But something about Tiny inspired trust. Besides, after so many months she doubted if her parents were looking for her – if they ever had. 'I'm Glory Girard.'

Tiny's clear-eyed gaze gave no indication that the name meant anything to her. 'I don't know about the job, Glory, but you look as if you could use a cold drink.'

Glory followed Tiny inside past a comfortably furnished parlour and a large dining room dominated by a table that could easily seat sixteen. The upholstered pieces were pleasantly overstuffed and the wooden ones gleamed with coats of wax.

Within these walls, Glory mused, the art-deco age hadn't happened and Queen Victoria still reigned supreme. The colour scheme, from the pale pink walls to the deeper red of the curtains to the dark crimson of the mohair chairs and sofas, echoed the rosy exterior.

At the end of the hall, swinging doors opened into a spacious kitchen. A large enamelled stove dominated one wall. Across the floor a modern refrigerator sat side by side with an old-fashioned icebox. Counters, cupboards, a pie safe, and a porcelain sink occupied the rest of the wall space. An enamelled table surrounded with mismatched chairs and laden with newly baked bread and rolls took up the centre of the room.

Glory's stomach growled and her mouth watered. It took all her will not to snatch up a loaf and bite off a chunk.

'Take a load off,' Tina said, pointing at one of the chairs.

Glory obeyed instantly. Although she would have liked nothing better than to lower her head to the table top and drift off to sleep, she squared her shoulders and sat ramrod straight.

The heat, the sleepless night, the hours spent going from cannery to cannery, had taken their toll. She closed her eyes for just a moment. When she opened them again a frosted glass of lemonade sat in front of her and Tiny was looking at her with concern.

'Drink up, girl. You looked parched. Tired too.'

She took a sip, savouring the thirst-quenching combination of sweet and tart. 'Thank you very much. The lemonade is delicious.'

Tiny took a cigarette pack from her apron pocket, lit up and blew a perfect smoke ring. 'If I'm going to take you into my home – I'm not saying I will – you're going to have to tell me a little about yourself. For starters, where are you from?'

The icy beverage combined with the prospect of a job to revive Glory. 'I grew up in San Francisco but I spent the last few months in Los Angeles.'

'Trying to break into the movies were you?'

'No.'

'Is that where your folks live?'

'My parents died last year.' Glory hated lying. But Noble and Anna were as dead to her as if she'd seen their coffins lowered into the ground. She had no idea what had happened to them after she left – and no desire to know.

For months after leaving San Francisco, memories of the easy life she had known there had beckoned with all the seductive charm of a Lorelei luring sailors to their deaths. The only way Glory could ignore that siren song had been to slam the door shut on her past, the good along with the bad.

'That explains it then.' The sound of Tiny's voice interrupted Glory's train of thought.

'Explains what?'

'The good clothes. The cheap suitcases. The look on your face like your best friend just died. It's obvious you're used to the finer things. I guess your folks didn't leave you much.'

'No they didn't. Forty dollars is all I've got left. I really need a job, Mrs Czernik.'

Tiny blew a contemplative stream of smoke at the ceiling. She could be making a big mistake – hiring someone who didn't even have references – but what the hell. In this man's world, girls had to stick together.

'I'll tell you what. I'll give you a month's trial. The pay is five dollars a week plus room and board. Mrs Garcia does the heavy cleaning but I expect you to dust and run the Bissell in addition to changing linens, waiting at table, and helping out in the kitchen.'

Glory didn't know what a Bissell did but this certainly wasn't the time to ask.

'I serve three meals a day six days a week and breakfast on the Sabbath. I do all the cooking and I'm a damn fine cook if I do say so myself. You can eat all you want here. You get Sunday afternoons off. How does that sound? Fair enough?'

'More than fair, Mrs Czernik.'

'Tiny, call me Tiny.' She heaved to her feet with considerable effort. 'Let me give you the grand tour and then you can unpack.'

Five hours later Glory finally opened her suitcases in the tiny fourth floor bedroom that was now hers. She could hardly believe her good fortune. Despite the cumulative exhaustion of the journey from Los Angeles, the time she'd spent job hunting and the grand tour of the boarding house which turned out to include setting the table, serving dinner, clearing the table and doing the dishes while Tiny filled her in on the boarders – Glory felt like dancing for sheer joy.

She loved Tiny. She loved the house. She loved the feeling of security that came from having a job. She loved her room.

Delighted, she turned a full circle taking in the quilt covered brass bed, the eyelet curtains, the rocking chair and the mirrored chifforobe. The furnishings were old fashioned and inexpensive but, like everything else in the house, they gleamed with loving care.

She hung up her dresses, put her underwear in the drawers and set her few toiletries out on the dresser. After a quick wash in the tiny bathroom off the hall, she returned to her room, took out some notepaper and wrote to Cal as she had every night since she last saw her.

She had written in the heat of anger, recounting how she had sold the diamond earrings because she couldn't bear to look at them only to learn later how badly she'd been cheated.

She had written with her heart still jolting from being accosted by sailors when she was staying at the Roosevelt Hotel in San Diego.

She had written with disgust about the charlatans who took her money and claimed to be qualified art teachers.

She had written in the depths of despair over her inability to get a job.

But she had never written when she was happy.

Dear Cal, she began, *Guess what? Good news for a change. I have just joined the ranks of the gainfully employed.*

Her pen skimmed over the page as she described the house. *You should see the colour scheme. With the pinks and rose reds, it's like living inside a four layer birthday cake. In addition to the living, dining room and kitchen, my new boss, Tiny, has her own suite on the ground floor. Six bedrooms and two bathrooms take up the second floor. Four more bedrooms and a single bathroom occupy the third.*

An additional two bedrooms are tucked under the fourth floor's slanting roof. One is mine. Tiny told me she only rents the other one to overnight guests because it's too small for a longer stay.

I wish you could meet her. She's really quite pretty despite her size. She has slanted green eyes like her calico cat, naturally curly brown hair, and the sweetest smile. Best of all, her irreverent sense of humour reminds me of you.

Perhaps being a maid in a boarding house may not seem like much of an achievement in view of the lofty ambitions I used to have but it's certainly a step in the right direction.

She finished the letter with X's and O's, signed her name and folded it. And then she tore it to shreds just as she had all the other letters on all the other nights.

Pride had kept her from letting Cal know about the education she had received in the school of hard knocks and now the same pride kept her from letting Cal know she was a maid in a boarding house.

But one of these days, when she was a successful artist, Glory vowed she would walk back into Cal's life.

CHAPTER TWELVE

Glory scrubbed the last of the pots and pans, put them on the rack to dry, then wiped her hands on the apron snugged around her waist. They certainly weren't the useless hands of a lady any more, she thought with pride.

Her body had changed as well, firming and tightening even though she had never eaten more. She felt as though she had been in perpetual motion since going to work, racing from one task and one chore to another as she changed linen, dusted, swept, set the table, washed dishes, served at every meal, and yes, even cut and arranged the profusion of flowers growing in the garden.

There was, she had discovered, a certain satisfaction in physical labour – a sense of accomplishment she had never known before. She could scrub and wax almost as well as Mrs Garcia. And she could set a table and deliver a meal with speed and aplomb. All twelve boarders had complimented her on her gracious service.

'Why, it's just like being served at that fancy club over at Pebble Beach,' Mr Johnson, a retired railroad engineer, had declared just last night.

The kitchen represented her only failure. When she peeled potatoes she always managed to cut herself. When she grated cabbage she grated her knuckles too. And if she set something on the stove to simmer, it always boiled over.

'Do you know what day it is?' Tiny's voice interrupted Glory's self-appraisal.

'It's Sunday,' Glory replied, turning to face her employer.

'But not just any Sunday. You've been here a month and you know what that means.'

Glory lowered her gaze. The trial period had ended. The thought that she might be asked to leave sent her stomach plummeting to the vicinity of her knees. She didn't want to wander the streets

119

looking for a job again. She loved it here. If only she had done better as a cook's helper. But it was too late improve now.

'Are you trying to tell me something?' she asked in a small voice.

'I damn sure am!'

'If you aren't satisfied with my work, I'll try harder. Just give me another chance.'

Tiny burst out laughing. 'You'd need four arms and legs to do more than you already are.' She lifted one dainty foot and stared at in amazement. 'You do so much running around for me that I can't remember the last time my tootsies hurt.'

'It's the least I can do. If you hadn't given me a chance—' The tears pooling at the back of Glory's eyes suddenly spilled over.

'Hell. I didn't mean to make you bawl.' Tiny pulled a rumpled dollar bill from her pocket, held it out with one hand and used the other to lever herself to her feet. 'Here. Have a good time on me. I'll finish drying the dishes. Go on. Skidaddle. You deserve it.'

Knuckling her tears away, Glory took the money, said, 'Thank you', and fled the room before she made a complete fool of herself.

She raced the three flights to her room without losing her breath the way she would have a month ago, then changed into one of her remaining good dresses. Putting the big sketch-pad and the new pastels she had bought with her first pay into a canvas tote, she raced back downstairs and hurried from the house.

She had been a stubborn, naive idiot when she left San Francisco. Now at twenty, she saw herself as an adult woman with her own agenda. Aside from buying art supplies and a few inexpensive work dresses, she had been saving her earnings with miserly frugality.

Fifty-six dollars had already accrued in a bank account in her name. Every week four more dollars joined her hoard. If she kept on saving at the same rate she could afford the trip to Chicago in another year. Once she got there she would find another job and apply for one of those scholarships she had read about in the Chicago Art Institute's catalogue. And this time she wouldn't let anything, not even insecurity about her talent, stand in her way.

She had used previous Sundays to explore the town, seeking out intriguing vistas to draw. Although small in population, Monterey was a giant in natural beauty. Claimed by the Spanish in 1602 when Sebastian Vizcaino sailed around a rock-girt peninsula to discover a calm bay, the city still had a Spanish flavour.

She loved the shady plazas, the mission, the old Presidio and the sun-baked adobe homes with their stucco walls and red tiled roofs. She enjoyed the work-a-day world of the sardine canneries and had even hiked into the rugged hills surrounding the town. From there the vista of land and sea had been sublime.

Eventually she hoped to draw them all. But today she headed for the Konstantine Cannery, feeling far more confident than she had when she first saw it. The building had a simple geometry, a picturesque utilitarianism she hoped to reproduce in pastels. If the drawing came out well she intended to have it framed and give it to Elena Konstantine as a token of her appreciation.

Glory hated to think what might have happened if Mrs Konstantine hadn't sent her to Tiny. In the months she had lived alone she had seen the fate awaiting attractive girls like her who were down on their luck. Selling their bodies may have kept them alive, but she had looked into their dead eyes and sworn to die before she suffered a similar fate.

However she refused to permit such dark thoughts to ruin this beautiful day. She strolled down Cannery Row seeing beauty in the ramshackle chandleries and the huggermugger of the boatyards, deserted now in the Sabbath calm. Even the trolley squealing down the track in the middle of the street seemed to move at a more leisurely pace.

As she reached her destination the distant tolling of mission bells enhanced her hard-won serenity. She glanced around for a place to sit, saw a sturdy-looking crate and dragged it into the shade across from the Konstantines' building.

She decided to do a sketch first before using the pastels. Setting the pad on her lap, she took a stick of charcoal from her tote and began drawing.

Two hours and several discarded drawings later she realised that what had seemed a simple task held unexpected complexities. Erasures smudged the sketch where she had corrected her mistakes. The pastels had smeared far more than she had anticipated.

Intent on her work, she was oblivious to everything else until she heard a lightly accented masculine voice over her shoulder. 'Your composition is faulty, you put the focal point in the wrong place, and you need a fixative.'

Faulty composition? Focal point? Fixative? He sounded like an expert.

She turned to confront the would-be art critic, expecting to find a scholar cast in the same mould as Professor Blackstone. Instead she found herself not a foot away from a ruffian whose curly black hair spilled over his collar – a primal looking male whose impossibly broad shoulders threatened to rip out his shirt seams.

A shirt, she might add, that was unbuttoned halfway to his waist, exposing a hairy torso. No decent man would parade around in public like that – and yet she couldn't help noting that his chest had the exquisitely defined musculature she had seen on Greek statues. His thighs, revealed by an embarrassingly tight pair of trousers, promised to be equally well-muscled.

Her father and Lawrence Wyant had been the two men she used as a yardstick of masculine good looks. This intruder lacked her father's aura of authority and Lawrence's visible good breeding. He had something else though, something Glory couldn't define.

Sex appeal – that was it, she realised as his brown eyes crawled over her with lazy familiarity. Although he didn't say a word, she could read his opinion in his eyes. He was attracted to her.

What in the world could a man like him, a man whose clothing and demeanour alluded to a lower class origin, know about art? And yet he had sounded so knowledgeable.

She felt herself flush, then pale as she realised how aggressively masculine he looked. She had seen stevedores who were less intimidating. And she was alone with him.

Seeming to read her thoughts, he said, 'I'm not a masher if that's why you're frowning. In fact my family tells me I'm a real pussy cat. I just thought you could use a little help with your drawing.'

Help indeed! Of all the egotistical . . . ! Too angry to consider the impropriety, let alone the danger of talking to a complete stranger, she said, 'I suppose you think you could do better.'

'I know I can,' he declared as if he were Da Vinci in the flesh.

Before she could object he took the pad from her hand, flipped the page, and began sketching with a sweeping motion that contrasted radically with her own cramped efforts.

She would have liked to get up and look over his shoulder the way he had been looking over hers. But she'd be damned if she'd give him the satisfaction.

Instead she found herself studying his profile. He had the high forehead and prominent brow of a scholar, the broken nose of a boxer, and a courtesan's long lashes. His lips were so full as to appear almost fleshy. And yet the composite result was not unpleasant. Some women might find him quite attractive.

He was so intent on drawing that he seemed to have forgotten all about her. She envied his sureness, the facile coordination of hand and eye that told her he had done this many times before.

What seemed like an eternity later, although it couldn't have been more than a few minutes, he handed the pad back. Her mouth gaped open as she looked down. He had done what she only dreamed of, using simple bold lines to breathe life onto the page, creating a vision that was far more real than her own meticulous rendering.

He had moved the cannery to the side of the page while she had put it dead centre. A lone gull perched on its roof. An ancient Ford squatted in the left foreground, looking even wearier and more careworn than the building. She could almost feel the laziness of the day and the warmth of the sun.

'How in the world did you do that?' she asked, her curiosity overcoming her antipathy.

'Like I said, the big problem with your drawing was the focal point. You have to entice the viewer's eyes to move around the entire picture rather than nailing it dead centre the way you did. That's why I set the cannery off to the side and put a car in the foreground.'

He was right. Why hadn't she seen it? She'd been sketching all her life and she had paid a small fortune for private lessons and yet a passing stranger, a fisherman if she was any judge at all, had easily surpassed her hard-won skills.

She must have been out of her mind, thinking she had any talent. Embarrassed, humiliated and distraught, she threw her things back in the tote and fled up the street, not even bothering to look over her shoulder to see his reaction.

'See you around, Rouge,' Dimitri Konstantine called out, enjoying the view her precipitous retreat afforded him.

If she knew the effect it was having on him, he felt damn sure she'd slow to a crawl. The faster she moved the more her buttocks bounced. And what buttocks they were. Round yet firm like perfectly ripe peaches.

Were they peach-coloured too, like her complexion? Or would that be asking too much of the Gods? And was that Titian hair natural? He'd love the chance to find out.

He was tempted to catch up to enjoy a frontal view. Her breasts were probably bobbling too. And those long legs of hers had been made to wrap around a man's back – his back.

Who the hell was the glorious red-head?

He'd spent enough time in Monterey to have made a thorough survey of the female population. A girl like Rouge wouldn't have escaped his discerning eye. Her clothing and cultured voice marked her a lady. Perhaps she lived in Pebble Beach and had been slumming, seeing how the other half lived.

He'd never been interested in her type before, had never wanted to test his sexual prowess on the ice goddesses of the upper class. He much preferred women with a more earth-bound approach to life. But he couldn't help wondering what it would take to thaw such a creature.

She'd been so flustered when she saw his drawing. Envious too. She had been smart enough to know real talent when she saw it – and female enough to know a real man too. He smiled, remembering the way her eyes had lingered on his chest and crotch. She'd wanted him all right, even though she'd never admit it.

Undoubtedly she was one of those rich girls who amused herself doing prissy little sketches destined to hang in some maiden aunt's parlour. He doubted their paths would ever cross again. Girls like that didn't frequent the bars and cafes on Cannery Row. But he knew she'd haunt his dreams for quite a while.

Someday, he promised himself, rich society women like Rouge would stand in line to meet him. Someday the whole world would kneel at the altar of his genius.

Someday soon.

Tiny was sitting in one of the rockers on the front porch, her beloved calico in her copious lap, when Glory returned to the boarding house.

'You're back early,' Tiny said. 'Lord a mercy, you sure worked up a sweat. You look as though you ran all the way back here.'

'I did. I was accosted by the most dreadful man on Cannery Row while I was sketching there. I was afraid he was going to follow me so I ran all the way back.'

Her chest heaving from the recent exertion, Glory collapsed on the rocker next to the one Tiny occupied. She didn't know what had upset her more, the stranger's crude but compelling appearance, or his careless display of talent.

'It's a damn shame a woman isn't safe on the streets these days. You'd think things would have got better since Prohibition. But they've got worse,' Tiny declaimed with righteous indignation. 'Speaking of men, I should warn you I rented the room across from yours to the Konstantines' nephew. He lives up in Big Sur but he comes to town every month to lay in supplies.'

'Why doesn't he stay with the Konstantines?' Glory asked out of idle curiosity. 'They seem very hospitable.'

'They'd love to have him. With six kids in a four bedroom house though, they really don't have room.' Tiny smiled and her voice softened. 'Besides, he's not the type to impose.'

'You sound as if you like him.'

'Indeed I do, and so does half the female population in town. He's a real looker.'

'I thought you didn't care for the opposite sex.' Glory was surprised that Tiny seemed to have done a complete about face.

Tiny burst out laughing, her excess flesh shaking like jelly. 'There are men – and there are *men*!'

'What's the difference?'

'Come on, sugar. We're friends now. You don't have to go on pretending you don't like men. A looker like you must have had her pick. I may be old and fat, but I'm not dead. I haven't forgotten that there's a certain itch only a man can scratch. And believe you me, if I were younger I wouldn't mind having Dimitri Konstantine scratch it. And that, as we both know, is the difference.'

Glory's face heated up at the older woman's candour. She couldn't imagine herself wanting a man in the biblical sense when she hadn't even talked to one after her brief but disastrous flirtation with Lawrence Wyant. She could no more envisage herself welcoming a man's sexual attention than she could picture herself crawling back to her father.

'Seeing as how you're back early, how about taking in a matinee and then having dinner?' Tiny said. 'There's a new Clara Bow movie playing.'

*

When Glory woke up at five the next morning and headed downstairs, the door opposite hers was shut. She tiptoed past so as not to wake the Konstantines' nephew. Having a quiet cup of coffee with Tiny had become a morning ritual. The ever ebullient Tiny never seemed to run out of small talk and Glory had discovered she was a very good listener.

This morning Tiny kept up a steady stream of chatter, commenting on last night's films, the Chinese dinner they'd eaten – and how she could have fixed it better. All Glory had to do was nod at the appropriate places. It left her mind free to take its own journey and, this morning, it returned to the stranger on Cannery Row.

His talent attracted her almost as much as his appearance repelled her. The memory of both burned in her brain. Were there other undiscovered artistic geniuses wandering the streets? Was she kidding herself about becoming an artist? And what would she do with the rest of her life if her dream had no basis in reality?

'Time to get up and at 'em,' Tiny said, signalling the end of their coffee break and the beginning of the work day. 'Oh, and Glory, don't forget to set an extra place at the table.'

Glory rinsed their cups and saucers while Tiny assembled the ingredients for the buttermilk pancakes. Glory squeezed the three dozen oranges it would take to satisfy the boarders' thirst, and Tiny cut slices of bacon from a thick slab of side meat and put them in a skillet. Minutes later the kitchen was filled with the mouthwatering aromas that always accompanied Tiny's culinary efforts.

Glory had no time to savour the scent, though. She headed for the dining room and set the table, using the blue willow dishes that Tiny's first husband had brought back from Japan. By the time she finished, Helen Davidson, a spinster school teacher in her forties, had walked into the room. Glory was surprised to see she wore a dress she usually saved for church.

'I hear Dimitri Konstantine is with us again,' Helen said, patting her marcelled hair although every rigid wave was perfectly in place.

'So Tiny tells me, although I didn't see him last night.'

'He's such a lovely man. We're all so fond of him.'

Just then Mary Beth Kimbrough, a widowed book keeper in her late fifties, walked into the room. This morning the severe suit she habitually wore to the office was softened by the addition of a colourful paisley scarf. Her expression changed from anticipation to disappointment as she looked around.

'Oh dear,' she said, 'I was so hoping Dimitri would be down by now. I just love hearing about his adventures.'

What sort of adventures could a sardine fisherman have had? Glory wondered as she headed back into the kitchen. Did he enthrall the ladies with tales of the big fish that got away?

The paragon had yet to put in an appearance when she returned a few minutes later, carrying a tray laden with a pitcher of orange juice and a pot brimming with fresh coffee. However the rest of the boarders were in their seats, the men engrossed in the morning paper, the women chatting with unusual verve.

Glory moved one to the other, filling glasses and cups. Suddenly the chatter came to an abrupt halt. 'Good morning, Dimitri,' Mary Beth Kimbrough trilled.

Glory looked up to find herself face to face with the man from Cannery Row.

CHAPTER THIRTEEN

Dimitri couldn't have been more surprised if Aphrodite had served him breakfast. 'I told you I'd see you around,' he said.

The girl ignored him and went about her business. However her scent lingered. He inhaled it hungrily, detecting soap, oranges and female musk. She smelled as good as she looked.

Pretending a nonchalance he didn't feel, he took a seat at the table. Aunt Elena had mentioned something about Tiny's new girl at dinner last night. 'She's very *omorfoseeo*,' Elena had said.

'That's nice,' Dimitri replied, paying more attention to the baklava than his aunt's words.

Elena didn't have a mean bone in her body. A girl could have a face that would stop a clock and still be lovely in Elena's opinion if she was well-mannered. His own taste ran to tits and ass. He regarded himself as a connoisseur of both.

This Rouge didn't disappoint in either department. Who would have guessed that the Cannery Row ice goddess would turn out to be Tiny's new girl. Things were looking up – in more ways than one, he thought, feeling his erection pressing into his jeans.

He smiled at Rouge across the table. He might not know how to woo a lady – but he certainly knew how to seduce a maid.

Glory had never expected to see him again and certainly not here in the little piece of the world she had won for herself. She was so unnerved that cups clattered in saucers every time she picked one up to pour coffee. The laden plates felt so heavy that she could only manage to carry one at a time instead of the usual two or three.

Fortunately no one seemed to notice. Every eye was riveted on Dimitri Konstantine and every ear bent to hear what he said, as though he were a Greek oracle who could foretell the future instead of a simple fisherman.

Glory had never been more conscious of a man and she didn't like the feeling. His presence was as irritating as a chigger bite. Couldn't he afford a two-bit haircut? she fretted, noting the way his jet curls tumbled down his brow and over his collar. A gentleman would never permit his hair to riot that way. But then, Dimitri was clearly no gentleman.

Not that it bothered Helen Davidson or Mary Beth Kimbrough, Glory noted with disgust. They couldn't take their eyes off Konstantine or his hairy muscles. Despite being at least twenty years his senior, Mary Beth flirted with him so outrageously that Glory felt her face heat up on Mary Beth's behalf.

Although it was Glory's habit to stay in the dining room so she could quickly respond to the boarders' needs, this morning she hurried to the kitchen on the smallest pretext and lingered there as long as she dared.

'Is something wrong?' Tiny asked the third time she returned to refill the cream pitcher.

'Wrong? What makes you think something's wrong?' Glory asked, heading for the icebox.

'You look feverish.'

'I'm fine. It's just hot in the dining room.'

Tiny flipped the pancakes over so expertly that they landed on the griddle with geometric precision. 'Does Dimitri Konstantine have something to do with the sudden rise in the temperature?'

'Of course not!'

'These pancakes are just about ready. Hot or not, would you mind fetching the platter from the dining room?'

Glory promised herself she wouldn't look at Dimitri when she returned to the dining room. But her gaze winged his way as surely as a well-aimed arrow heading for a target. He was cutting his pancakes with a dainty precision that belied the strength implicit in his broad hands. His nails looked surprisingly clean in view of his trade.

'Anyone for seconds?' she asked as brightly as her dry throat permitted.

The male boarders all answered in the affirmative – the females in the negative, although she knew they would be the first to help themselves.

Dimitri Konstantine didn't answer at all. His attention was riveted on Mary Beth Kimbrough. She liked to expound on the intricacies of double entry bookkeeping – a topic that struck Glory as being about as fascinating as watching grass grow.

You couldn't tell it by Dimitri's behaviour though. He kept his dark eyes fixed on her as though the two of them were alone at the table. She responded by batting her lashes, gesturing expansively, and tossing her grey hair back like a girl instead of a fifty-some-year-old woman.

Dimitri Konstantine didn't seem to mind her obvious adoration.

He did have a certain crude appeal. Glory felt it herself. But she would never lower her standards so far as to let him know. *Never.*

She returned with the replenished pancake platter a few minutes later, put it down so hard that it almost broke, and beat a hasty retreat to the kitchen.

In Glory's absence, Tiny had filled plates for the two of them. 'Eat up,' she said between mouthfuls.

Glory took the chair opposite Tiny's, decorated her pancakes with fresh butter and maple syrup as though they were a work of art and forked a bite into her mouth. However she didn't taste the delicious mingling of flavours. Thanks to Dimitri Konstantine, her appetite had evaporated along with her good mood.

While Glory toyed with her food, Tiny swallowed her last bite, pushed her plate away, and lit a cigarette. 'What do you think of Dimitri?'

'Not much.'

'Not much?' Tiny chuckled. 'The way that man fills out a shirt – to say nothing of a pair of trousers – sure gets my vote.'

'I thought you didn't like men.'

Tiny blew a thin stream of smoke into the air. 'In general, no. In particular, yes. Dimitri's more man than anything I've ever run across. If I were twenty years younger and a hundred pounds lighter, I'd give him a run for the money.'

'But shouldn't you be in love before . . . ?' Glory's voice trailed off.

She had been about to say a woman ought to be in love before she had sex – only she wouldn't have said sex, she would have said *intimate relations*. She may have run away from home, she thought sourly, but a part of her continued to be Daddy's little girl.

'Honey, even you can't be that naive.' Tiny snorted. 'This is the twenties, honey bun. Women have the right to vote, to own property, and to damn well make love with any man that suits their fancy as long as they can handle the consequences. Besides, there are such things as french safes.'

Although Glory didn't have the vaguest idea what a french safe was, she pasted a knowing smile on her lips. 'How could I forget?'

'Dimitri's a looker, he's smart, he makes a decent living and he's built like a brick shit house. And if that ain't enough, he speaks French like a native.' Tiny sighed. 'I always did want to hear love-talk in French.'

'You really like him, don't you?'

Tiny rolled her eyes, then leaned closer. 'I'm not ashamed to admit I wouldn't mind getting in his pants.'

Glory felt herself crimson. The girl talk she had shared with Cal hadn't prepared her for this conversation. 'Remember my telling you about the man who corrected my drawing yesterday.'

'You were madder than a wet hen when you came home.'

'That man was Dimitri. How does a fisherman know so much about art?'

Tiny let go a roar of laughter that made her body quiver like a half-set Charlotte Russe. 'A fisherman! Is that what you think he is?'

Glory nodded.

'Honey, he's a sculptor, and a damn fine one.'

Although Dimitri never acknowledged Glory's comings and goings, he watched her covertly throughout breakfast. Where in the world had so lovely a creature been hiding before she appeared at Tiny's?

He had made it his business to know every unattached female in Monterey – and quite a few of the attached ones too. However none of them promised more pleasure than this Rouge. He wanted her in his bed with those long legs open to receive him. He smiled to himself, thinking he'd earn a slap from her if she knew.

He couldn't understand the American attitude towards sex. Growing up, it had been as much a part of his life as eating and sleeping. As a little boy he'd heard his parents' noisy couplings in the next room. He and his brothers had even spied on them once or twice.

He had swum nude in the Aegean with his sisters and been fascinated by the way their bodies differed from his. Then at thirteen, he'd finally had the chance to appreciate that difference for himself.

His parents had sent him to do chores for a distant neighbour while her husband was at sea. She'd been a lonely twenty-five-year-old who needed someone to talk to as much as to do the heavy work.

Over the next few weeks she revealed her life to him in bits and pieces. Her body too. She enticed him in a hundred ways, leaving her door open when she undressed, unbuttoning her blouse on the pretext of being hot, asking him to massage her shoulders.

Her marriage had been arranged by her parents. Her husband was a good provider. However she confessed had never loved him and feared he was too old, at fifty-five, to give her a child.

She talked to Dimitri as though he were an adult instead of a callow boy and he responded by giving her his complete and undivided mental and physical attention. In the course of their time together he learned what he said didn't matter to a woman as much as how well he listened. She had taught him to be a very good listener and an even better lover.

She had been his first. He'd lost count of all the others since. There were so many ways to woo a woman, he mused as Mary Beth Kimbrough droned on and on.

Being an artist gave him certain advantages. He had convinced many a modest woman to take off her clothes in the name of art. Sometimes he was so engrossed in sculpting her body that he forgot all about making love.

But only sometimes.

Could he talk Rouge into modelling for him? It was certainly worth a try.

'If you ever need a book keeper,' Mary Beth was saying, 'I'd be happy to come up to Big Sur.'

'You're very kind to offer,' Dimitri dutifully replied.

Encouraged, Mary Beth rattled on, leaving him to his thoughts. They were all of Rouge.

'I'd like some more coffee, please,' he said the next time she came into the room.

For a moment he thought she was going to tell him to help himself. However Tiny had trained her well. With an almost imperceptible nod, she picked the coffee pot up from the trivet on the buffet and carried it over to him.

A polite man would have handed his cup back so she wouldn't have to lean over him to fill it.

Dimitri left his where it was. He wanted to feel her nearness, to breathe in her scent.

She hesitated, then reached around him. Her body heat enveloped him. Her breasts brushed his back, sending a jolt of desire straight to his cock. It came to instant attention.

He couldn't remember the last time he had wanted a woman as much. Hell. He had never wanted one the way he did this Rouge – this house maid with the body of a goddess, the face of an angel, and the demeanour of a queen.

Which road to seduction would be the shortest, he wondered as she returned to the kitchen. He continued the pretence of listening to Mary Beth while he considered the possibilities.

Despite Rouge's proud carriage and lady-like speech she was only a sweeper of floors and a washer of dishes. She probably didn't have the time or the money to enjoy herself. It shouldn't take more than an inexpensive meal in a road house and a moonlight drive in his car to win her over.

He could hardly wait to test his theory.

'I wouldn't want you to be late for work on my account,' he said, interrupting Mary Beth in mid-sentence.

'I forgot all about the time,' she replied coyly. 'Talking with you makes me lose track of time.'

He rose, helped her from her chair and propelled her towards the door. After she'd gone he returned to his place to await Rouge. Happily she didn't keep him waiting long.

'Let me help you clean up,' he said, getting to his feet.

'There's no need.'

As she picked up the serving platters he caught a tantalising glimpse of bountiful cleavage. He was fascinated by breasts and buttocks – and all the parts in between. They were wonderful to sculpt – to look at too. He had never quite got over the wonder of being paid to do both.

'I hope you're not upset because I didn't introduce myself yesterday but you really didn't give me the chance,' he said.

She shook her head, loosening tendrils of hair that clung to her forehead and neck. 'I had no desire to meet you.'

The chill in her voice was even more cutting than her words. Who the hell did she think she was to look down on him?

She reminded him of the haughty upper class bitches he'd met in Paris. He had learned more than sculpting while he lived there. He had learned about status. His had been low.

He hadn't known how poor the Konstantines were until then. Everyone on Santorini lived in ancient whitewashed houses devoid of luxury – houses that had sheltered the same families for generations.

Paris had been a shock – and a challenge. He had coveted its riches and its beautiful women, and had nothing to win them with but his talent and his cock. The six years he had studied there had taught him to use both to advantage. But he had never bedded a wealthy woman.

In the years he had lived and worked in America, first in New York and then Big Sur, no woman had made him feel worthless the way those French women had – until Rouge. He would enjoy teaching her humility, he thought, imagining her underneath him begging for satisfaction.

'I'm going to visit the Konstantines later on,' he said, making sure to keep all hint of temper from his voice. 'I'd be honoured if you would go with me.'

'I have to serve supper here.'

'I wouldn't mind waiting. A woman who looks the way you do is worth waiting for.'

'You can save your compliments. I won't go out with you tonight or any other night.'

Another man might have been discouraged. He wasn't so easily put off. All was fair in love and war – and this had the makings of both. Beneath Rouge's *hauteur* he sensed latent passion. He intended to be the man to unleash and control her fire.

He stayed at the table after Rouge left, waiting for his erection to subside, then left the house on the business that brought him to town every month. When he returned after dark he went straight to the door to Tiny's suite.

She answered his knock wearing a flowing house coat that made her look like a ship under full sail. 'Come on in,' she said, grabbing his arm and pulling him into the parlour.

He produced the bottle of whisky he'd hidden behind his back, bent down and kissed her cheek. 'This is for you, my love.'

'You sweet thing, you didn't need to do that.'

'Oh but I did.' He wanted her to be in a receptive mood when he put his plan in action.

She went to a cupboard, took out two glasses and poured with a liberal hand.

134

'*Steen eeyeeah sahss,*' he said, saluting her in his native tongue.

'*Na zdrowie,*' she said in hers, taking an appreciative sip. 'Now, young man, although I would like to think you stopped by for the pleasure of my company, I'm too old and experienced to be that foolish.'

'You look irresistible tonight, *ma chère.*'

'Don't kid a kidder, Dimitri. What's on your mind?'

He took Tiny's free hand in his, led her over to the sofa and pulled her down beside him. The springs sagged beneath their combined weight. 'I came to beg your help.'

'Sure thing, honey. All you have to do is ask.'

'It's Rouge,' he began hesitantly.

'Her name is Glory Girard.'

'Rouge suits her better.' He paused. 'Did she tell you we met down by the waterfront yesterday?'

'She mentioned it.'

'I can imagine what she said. I don't think I made a very good impression on her. However she certainly made one on me. I know it sounds insane but I'm in love with her.'

Seeing a glow kindle in Tiny's eyes, he knew he'd been right. Beneath her tough-talking exterior beat the heart of a true romantic.

'I thought there might be some sparks between you two,' she said.

'It was more than sparks on my part. Unfortunately Rouge doesn't feel the same way. Is there another man in her life?'

'Not that I know. She's skittish when it comes to men. I have the feeling some man hurt her real bad in the past.'

'Has she ever talked about it?'

'I've tried to draw her out but she's real close-mouthed about her past. I'll tell you this. She comes from quality.' Tiny's eyes narrowed. 'I'm not sure I want you sniffing around her. I wouldn't want to see her hurt and I know your reputation where women are concerned.'

'I would never hurt her,' he declared. 'I told you, I'm in love.'

'In lust is more like it. Now what's this favour you want?'

'Tell her what I've told you.'

'Tell her yourself.'

'She won't listen to me. Hell, she won't even stay in a room with me. Please, Tiny, help me.'

'You swear you're on the up and up.'

'On my honour as a man.'

'In my experience, a man's honour is a lot less reliable than his dick. Once he gets inside a woman he forgets all the promises that got him there.'

Dimitri wanted to laugh but managed to look hurt instead. God, he loved women – all women. Young or old, fat or thin, he loved their bodies, the way their minds worked, the eternal mystery between their legs.

'My honour is longer than most men's,' he said with a straight face. 'If I only wanted a woman for my bed there are many in town who would be happy to oblige. I tell you, this Glory of yours has got to me.'

Tiny downed her drink and came up sputtering. 'Oh hell, I never have been able to say no to a sweet-talking man.'

An artist! Dimitri Konstantine was an artist, Glory thought the next morning as she dressed. No wonder he'd sounded so knowledgeable when he corrected her drawing. His quick pencil gave evidence of a skill that far surpassed hers. She wanted to know more about him and yet his blatant masculinity made her uneasy.

He was undoubtedly the sort of man her father feared she would meet if she studied art. The sculptor had every trait she'd been taught to detest in a man. He epitomised the word *uncouth*. Yet she couldn't stop thinking about him.

Fearful of another encounter, she tiptoed past his door on her way to the kitchen. When she walked in two steaming cups or coffee had been set out on the table and Tiny was having the first of the many cigarettes she would smoke that day.

'You're looking a little peaked,' Tiny said.

'I didn't sleep very well.'

Tiny gave her a knowing look. 'I guess it's a little unsettling, having a virile man like Dimitri on the other side of a thin wall.'

'I'm not used to having anyone in that room.'

'He's afraid he offended you when you ran into each other down by the Konstantine Cannery.'

'He made me feel like a fool. He should have told me he was an artist.'

'He's very sorry about that.'

'How do you know?'

136

'He paid me a visit last night. He's very taken with you. In fact he claims he's in love with you.'

Glory pushed away from the table so abruptly that coffee sloshed over the edge of her cup. 'That's the most ridiculous thing I've ever heard. He doesn't even know me.'

'Honey, men don't fall in love with their minds. The part of their anatomy involved is considerably south of their foreheads.'

'That's not love,' Glory objected.

'Maybe it's not the sort of love women dream about but it's as close as most men come to the emotion. They look. They like. They want.'

'If that's all there is to them, they're no better than animals.'

'I know the good book tells us we were created in God's image but the truth is we're *all* animals. Men want sex. Women want a father to care for their children. The rest of it is just window dressing.'

'You make it sound cut and dried – like a business deal.'

'In a way it is. I'm as fond of hearts and flowers as the next woman but I know the way men think. It didn't stop me from marrying three of them. There's nothing sweeter in this world than a man in the first heat of desire.'

'I'm not interested in men that way.'

'How about Dimitri? I told you he was an exception to the rule.'

'I'm not the least bit interested in him. But I am in knowing more about his work. Have you ever seen it?'

'He's shown me photographs. I'm no expert but they impressed the hell out of me.'

'What does he sculpt?'

'Nudes. Mind you, they're very tasteful.'

Nudes. She should have known. But she was interested despite herself. 'What medium does he work in?'

'Medium?'

'Bronze, clay, stone?'

'Like I said, I'm no expert. Why don't you ask him yourself?'

Why indeed? Glory mused. It would be silly to let anything get in the way of her being an artist. Dimitri might be able to help her.

She kept a watchful eye on him throughout breakfast. Yesterday she had reacted to Dimitri the way her father would have wanted, judging him on his appearance without knowing a thing about him.

137

By lunch she had convinced herself she'd been wrong to be so rude to him.

By supper, she was anxious to make amends.

She served him the juiciest cut from the roast beef and anticipated his every need during the meal, offering seconds the minute he cleaned his plate and keeping his coffee cup full. After the dishes she searched him out to apologise.

She found him standing at the far end of the porch, his back towards her as he gazed towards the mountains.

'I love the light at the end of the day,' he said at her approach. 'Do you, Rouge?'

'How did you know it was me?'

'You have a light step. It's as distinctive as your scent.'

A frisson rippled over her skin at the intimacy of the comment. He must have smelled her when she poured his coffee that morning. Dear God, she'd been dripping with nervous sweat.

'What's so special about the light?'

'It has an incandescent quality that permits me to see things with my heart as well as my eyes.' He turned to face her. 'Take you, for instance. The first time we met down on the waterfront, all I saw was a beautiful girl I wanted to kiss. Now I see a young woman so full of hopes and dreams that she fears they will spill from her lips.'

It was the most romantic thing any man had ever said to her. Mesmerised, Glory took a tentative step towards him and then another until only a few feet separated them. 'Tiny told me you're an artist. But you talk like a poet.'

'Which would you like me to be?'

'An artist. It's what I want to be too,' she blurted out.

'So that's why you were drawing yesterday.'

'Yes, but I'm not very good.'

'You need training.'

She bridled. It certainly wasn't the response she expected from a man who claimed to be in love with her. 'I have had training. I took private lessons with a portrait painter.'

'Ah, a portrait painter – a man who flatters people with paint and brush. Did he flatter you too, Rouge?'

Dimitri's question came as a surprise. 'He said I had talent.'

'Did he have many students?'

'About twenty.'

She flushed remembering the crowded studio, the eager pupils waiting for a word from the great man. Her flush grew hotter as she recalled how little time he had for any of them and how quick he was to take their money.

'A *successful* artist teaches by example,' Dimitri said softly, 'by letting a few students watch him at work, by explaining what he does and why he does it. When he thinks his pupils have absorbed his knowledge he lets them under-paint his canvases or rough in his sculptures, closely supervising their work. An *unsuccessful* artist fills his atelier with paying pupils whom he ignores until it's time to take their money. The man who taught you wasn't a teacher, he was a business man.'

'How do you know so much about it?' she challenged.

'Because I met both kinds when I studied in Paris.'

'You studied in Paris?'

'From 1916 to 1922.'

'You were there during the war then?'

A soft laugh rumbled in his chest. 'I was so ignorant, I barely knew about the war when I left home. Once in Paris I cared nothing for distant battles. I was too busy watching an artistic revolution unfold. Fauvism. Cubism. Expressionism.' He spat the words out as though they were epithets. 'They are vehicles for men who create art with their minds and not their souls. Picasso, Braque, Duchamp, I knew them all.'

Glory felt like a fool – a rude one at that. The man she had taken for a crude fisherman had actually associated with the greatest figures in the art world. She moved a step closer as if she could absorb his experiences through her pores. 'You sound as if you didn't especially care for them.'

'As men, I did. As artists –' He shrugged eloquently. 'Duchamp could never convince me a urinal any plumber could buy was a sculpture because Duchamp chose to call it one and enter it in an exhibition. He had more ego than talent. But enough about Paris. I would rather learn about you. Do you really want to be an artist? It's a hard life, especially for a woman.'

'I've never wanted to be anything else.'

'I felt the same way growing up. My father was a stone cutter, a maker of tombstones and monuments to the dead. I learned to work stone from him – then took what he taught me and began creating sculptures. The next thing I knew, I was in Paris.'

'I'm sure it wasn't that simple.'

'Nothing worth having ever is,' he answered, giving her a long speculative look.

He stood so close she took in his aroma with every breath – just as he must be taking in hers. Did intimacy begin with the nose? she fretted, then giggled at the thought.

'Do I amuse you?'

'No, I mean – well, I'd love to see your work someday.'

'Come back to Big Sur with me. You could model for me and I could be your art teacher.'

His boldness took her breath away. 'I couldn't do that. It wouldn't be right.'

He chuckled. 'You mean it wouldn't be proper.'

'It wouldn't.'

He reached out and touched her cheek for an instant, then lowered his hand. 'You're a very sweet girl but girls don't make good artists. Stick to your little drawings, *ma chère.*'

He brushed past her before she could say a word in her own defence, walked down the porch steps and off into the night. Little girl indeed, she thought angrily. How dare he judge her? He didn't know the first thing about her.

You didn't know anything about him either and you didn't hesitate to judge him, her conscience reminded her.

She hurried inside, slammed the door and went to her room. But she found no peace in solitude. Every nerve taut, she listened for Dimitri's return. Was it the artist who fascinated her with his stories of Paris – or the good looking man?

CHAPTER FOURTEEN

An October storm woke Glory before dawn. The wind whistled around the eaves and palm fronds scratched at her window like a family dog seeking shelter.

She checked her alarm clock and saw she had a few minutes until she had to get up – time to think, as if she hadn't done enough of that. Dimitri was coming to town today and this time she knew he wanted an answer. But she still didn't have one to give him.

She closed her eyes and images of the summer tumbled through her mind in a series of golden vignettes. Dimitri dominated each one.

He had returned to Monterey a month after their first meeting, invited her to dinner again and this time she had accepted. They ate at a fisherman's hangout near the wharves where the calamari was so fresh that it still had the briny taste of the sea.

He had spoken of his family, of growing up in Santorini, with a warmth that made her envious.

She repeated the story she had told Tiny, of parents who died unexpectedly and the hard economic times that followed.

When she finished, Dimitri took her hand. His warmth and strength seemed to seep into her bones. 'It must have been very hard – to find yourself alone at so young an age.'

'I got by,' she replied, so touched by his concern that she made no attempt to pull away.

To her surprise, she found herself saying that their deaths had written *finis* to her dream of attending the Chicago Art Institute. It was as close as she dared come to the truth.

Dimitri won her friendship and trust by offering to give her art lessons whenever he came to town. 'There are no strings attached,' he'd said. 'I hope you will come to Big Sur and model for me someday because I would love to sculpt you, but I don't want to feel you owe me anything. Teaching you will sharpen my own skills.'

The lessons had begun the next day. Dimitri had driven into the hills, parked when he found a place with a view of the city, and set up his easel.

'Draw, show me what you learned from the portrait painter.'

'I'm not very good at landscapes,' she replied.

'Doing landscapes helps an artist learn about spatial relationships. I'm not going to give you a grade. This is a chance to learn, nothing more.'

He stood behind her, speaking softly while she worked. 'Loosen up. Stop trying to control the charcoal. What you see must flow from your eyes to the paper with nothing to impede it.'

It had taken hours before she was able to do as he asked. When the lesson ended she had taken a giant step forward as an artist.

Dimitri had appeared at the boarding house unexpectedly three weeks later, carrying a bouquet of flowers he had picked outside his cabin. She didn't mind that they hadn't come from a florist or that the heat had wilted them. They meant more to her than the white orchids her father had given her for her debut.

After another lesson, they had dinner at the Konstantines' and she had seen an entirely different side of Dimitri. An only child, she didn't know how to relate to children. However Dimitri knew exactly what to say and do. He rough-housed with the boy until Elena complained they were going to wreck the furniture.

The playful man Glory saw that evening was as appealing as the artist and teacher. There seemed to be so many facets to Dimitri's personality that she wondered if she would ever get to know them all.

On his next visit, he raised the issue of her moving to Big Sur to live with him again.

'Maybe,' she had replied.

But she couldn't go on saying maybe for ever.

Dimitri spent the morning cleaning his cabin, a job he seldom bothered to do. But he would do that and a great deal more for Rouge. Somewhere between the birth of desire and his attempts at seduction, he had fallen hopelessly in love with her.

Now he meant all the empty promises he had made to Tiny at the beginning of the summer. He would sooner die than hurt Rouge. But surely loving her, taking her to his bed and making her his woman wouldn't cause her pain – at least not the sort he couldn't kiss away.

With his help she could have a career in art someday too. Nothing to equal his, though. However she would have no trouble selling the sort of paintings he thought of as decorator-art.

She needed his help and he would gladly give it. Why was she hesitating? Although they'd become close, he sensed an inner core he had yet to touch. Hell. He hadn't touched the outer one yet either.

He had just put the broom and the mop away when he heard a knock on the door. 'It's open,' he called out.

Leah Pomerance walked in wearing a peasant blouse and a dirndl skirt that emphasised the square lines of her body rather than concealing them.

'You've cleaned,' she said as she gazed around. 'You should have asked me to help.'

'Didn't I do a good enough job?'

'You should have waxed the floor after mopping it, and it wouldn't hurt to straighten up when you dust rather than just move things around. What's the occasion?'

'I may be bringing someone back from Monterey with me.'

Leah ignored the acidic burst of jealousy that soured her stomach. 'A new model, I presume.'

He looked startled. 'How did you know?'

'I know you. This stew should come in handy when you get back. There's enough here for two,' she said, offering the bowl she was carrying.

He smiled and she felt it clear through her body. He had the most beautiful smile she had ever seen.

'You're a true friend, and that husband of yours is a very lucky man.'

She longed to tell Dimitri her husband was also the biggest fool, a rotten poet, a lousy lay, and a ne'er do well who would long since have squandered the fortune he had inherited if she hadn't been there to rein him in. But telling the truth was a double-edged sword that would expose her as a fortune hunter who had married for money rather than love – and she wouldn't do anything to lower Dimitri's opinion of her.

Although he'd brought a succession of models home in the four years since she and Court had sold him their guest house, the relationships hadn't been serious. She could put up with another one.

He fucked them – and sculpted them – but she was the one he confided in.

'Speaking of Court,' Dimitri said, 'where is Big Sur's poet laureate today?'

She let go a laugh at hearing Dimitri use the honorific Court had bestowed on himself. 'The poet laureate is somewhere in the forest staring at a redwood and waiting for his muse to hit him over the head. Yesterday he wrote, *Love is like a flower and friendship like a tree.* He was smitten with himself, until I told him Coleridge had written it better a hundred years ago.'

Dimitri burst out laughing. 'Having a well-read wife must be hell for a poet.'

'There are certain compensations,' she said, giving him an arch look, then pointed at the bowl in his hands. 'And I don't mean my cooking. You had better put that in the icebox.'

'Talking with you has a way of distracting me.' Dimitri gave her another dazzling smile, then carried the bowl off to the kitchen.

She turned what he'd said over in her mind. It was happening. Yes – it was finally happening. Little by little, she was making herself as indispensable to Dimitri as she was to Court.

She had grown up knowing she wasn't pretty and had early on decided to sharpen all her other talents. A woman could get by without a pretty face if she had a brain and knew how to use it.

Her intelligence had got her Court. While he may not have been the prize she once thought, he certainly had changed her standard of living for the better.

Now she wanted Dimitri – and she would stop at nothing to get him.

'Tell me about this new model,' she asked him when he returned.

'Rouge is much more than a potential model.'

'Don't tell me she has agreed to do some housekeeping in addition to posing for you and warming your bed.'

'I'd rather you didn't talk about her that way, Leah. Rouge will need a friend when she gets here. I was hoping you would be it.'

Leah felt her cheeks colour. Dimitri had never spoken to her so sharply before. Who the hell was this Rouge, and what kind of a hold did she have on him?

'I didn't mean to offend you, and I certainly won't offend your –' she hesitated, searching for just the right word, 'your new friend.'

Dimitri's scowl faded. 'I'm the one who should apologise. I didn't mean to bark at you. In any case, Rouge may not come back with me.'

'But you want her to.'

'Very much.'

Damn. His heart was in his eyes. He'd been so moody lately, so dependent on her company that she'd been sure she would be able to coax him into her bed soon. Now she realised nothing could be further from the truth. He'd been mooning over some damn whore with the improbable name of Rouge.

'I hope she comes – for both our sakes. I would love having a woman nearby. In case you hadn't noticed, it is rather lonely up here.'

Dimitri's eyes warmed. 'Then I can count on you?'

'For anything.'

Leah knew better than to linger on stage after a good exit line. She also knew Dimitri. He didn't have it in him to be faithful to one woman. This Rouge was no more than a passing fancy and when she passed, Leah's time would come.

Although Tiny had made sandwiches from last night's roast, Glory didn't have any appetite. She took a couple of bites, then pushed her plate aside.

'Is something wrong?' Tiny asked, pulling the plate towards her.

'Not with the food.'

'Why are you acting so blue? I thought Dimitri was coming to town today.'

'He is. He should be here in a couple of hours.'

'Don't tell me the romance is over,' Tiny said between mouthfuls. 'Has that man been giving you a hard time?'

'He is getting impatient with me – not that I blame him.'

'I gather you still haven't made up your mind about moving up to Big Sur.' Tiny swallowed the last bite of Glory's sandwich, took a cigarette from the pack on the table and lit it.

'If I don't give him an answer this time I don't think he'll be back,' Glory said. It was a relief to voice her fears.

Tiny settled her girth more comfortably in the narrow kitchen chair. 'I was slim and pretty like you once but I sure as hell don't yearn for the good old days. You couldn't pay me to go through them

145

again. I'd much rather enjoy my food than make myself sick over some man – even the best of them.'

'Does that mean you wouldn't go up to Big Sur if you were me?'

'Did I say that?'

'I think so. You're confusing me.'

'I was talking about men in general, kid. They love giving ultimatums. It goes with having testicles. They don't mean half of what they say, though. Dimitri has the hots for you. He may stay away longer the next time but he'll be come panting back. You can count on it.'

'Perhaps. But I can't keep the two of us in limbo for ever.'

'So what's the problem. Is it marriage? Because if it is, I can tell you straight out Dimitri isn't the marrying kind.'

Glory nodded. 'He thinks marriage is *bourgeois*. He says people who love each other don't need a piece of paper to hold them together – and people who don't shouldn't be forced to stay together because of one.'

'If marriage isn't an issue, what's the problem? Dimitri is crazy about you. He's willing to do almost anything to make you happy, including taking time from his own work to give you art lessons. And I bet he's no slouch in the sack either.'

Glory stared down at the table. 'We haven't made love yet.'

'You're kidding?'

Still staring at the top of the table so she wouldn't have to meet Tiny's gaze, Glory shook her head.

'If that don't tie the tail on the donkey. Who would have figured?'

'Why are you so surprised?'

'Surprised doesn't cut it. Lord, that man must really love you.'

'I don't understand.'

'Dimitri is used to – well, he's used to having sex. After all, honey, he is thirty years old and attractive as hell. A man only holds off from jumping a woman's bones when he loves her enough to put her feelings ahead of his needs.'

Glory finally looked up to see the quizzical look on Tiny's face. 'I was raised to believe a gentleman would never demand sex before marriage.'

Tiny burst out laughing. 'Honey, I don't mean to speak ill of the dead, but it sounds like your parents didn't know a damn thing about the real world. The question is, how do you feel about Dimitri? Are you in love with him?'

'I think about him all the time when we're apart and count the days until I'll see him again. He's the most fascinating man I've ever met, and I think he's a genius—'

'But?'

'Why do you think there's a but?'

'I hear it in your voice, honey.'

'Maybe I'm hopelessly old-fashioned but I don't see myself as a fallen woman. My father warned me it might happen if I got involved in the art world. If I go to Big Sur with Dimitri I can never go home.' The minute she said it, she realised she'd made a mistake.

'Home? I thought your parents were dead.'

'I meant go home in a theoretical sense. I certainly wouldn't be the same person.'

'Losing a piece of tissue won't change you that much. And it really isn't that painful if that's what you're worried about.'

Glory knew she could never make Tiny understand unless she told her about Noble and Anna. And it was much too late for that. 'I used to think I'd be so happy when I was old enough to make my own decisions. Now I realise it's not that simple.'

'Nothing's ever as simple as we want – or as complex as we think. You can't dot all the I's and cross all the T's before you get to them. In the end all a woman can do is follow her heart – and you've got a good one. Don't be afraid to go where it leads you.'

'What if I make a mistake?'

'We all make mistakes. Hopefully we learn from them. If Dimitri turns out to be a mistake you'll always have a home here so don't give another thought to that fallen woman stuff. I never told you but I always wanted a daughter. You're as close as I'm likely to come. I would never advise you to do something I wouldn't do myself and believe you me, if I wanted to be an artist as much as you do and a man like Dimitri was willing to help me, I'd have gone up to Big Sur long before this.'

Tiny had said all the things Glory needed to hear. 'Oh, Tiny, you're so good to me. I don't know what I'd do without you.'

'From the look on your face, you'll soon find out. You're going to say yes, aren't you?'

*

While Glory went about her work she paused every few minutes to listen for the sound of Dimitri's Ford coming up the drive. Now her decision was made, she could hardly wait to tell him. She was in the parlour working lemon oil into the mahogany tables when he drove up. By the time he parked the car, she had run out the front door and down the porch steps.

'Yes, the answer is yes,' she called out before she lost her nerve.

Dimitri turned to face her. Surprise and happiness mingled on his face as he caught her in his arms. 'You just made me the happiest man in the world. *Agapao esee*. That means I love you.'

'I love you too,' she told him for the first time.

'I can't wait to take you home. Let's leave today.'

'So soon?' She needed a couple of weeks to get used to the idea of going before she actually did.

'Why not?'

'I haven't even given Tiny notice. She's been so good to me – to both of us. Surely you wouldn't want me to leave her in the lurch.'

'Tiny would be the first to tell you to go. Are you sure there isn't some other reason? Are you having second thoughts already?'

Please, she silently cried out, if you love me don't pressure me. But she couldn't say the words. She freed herself from his arms, stepped back and gazed into his eyes.

'You just got here. You haven't picked up your supplies or visited the Konstantines yet. What's the hurry?'

Glory didn't realise Tiny had joined them until she heard Tiny ask, 'How are you two love bugs?'

'Glory just accepted my invitation to move up to Big Sur,' Dimitri replied. 'I want to go home today but she's worried about you not having help.'

'Pshaw. I wouldn't dream of standing in the way of your happiness. I can manage for a few days.'

'You won't have to. My oldest niece has been talking about getting a job. If you're willing to give her a chance, she could be here tomorrow.'

Tiny beamed at him. 'Dimitri, I can see you've thought of everything.'

'I always do,' he replied.

And so Glory found herself bidding farewell to Tiny an hour later. 'I'll really miss you,' she said, struggling to hold back her tears.

'I'll miss you too. Remember what I said about having a home.'

'Of course she has a home – with me,' Dimitri declared. He gave Tiny an exuberant kiss, then helped Glory into the Ford.

He seemed so happy, so sure of himself. Glory wished the emotions were contagious. However a sense of loss weighed her down as they drove away. She looked back and waved at Tiny until they turned a corner and the boarding house disappeared from sight.

'I can't wait to show you my studio. I bought the cabin from the Pomerances and it needs a woman's touch but I built the studio myself. It's perfect in every way.'

'Tell me about the Pomerances,' she said, preferring the steady drone of Dimitri's voice to her own anxious thoughts.

'Did I tell you my cabin used to be their guesthouse?'

She nodded. 'You mentioned something about it.'

'The property belonged to Court's parents. They used the big house for a summer place and put guests up in the cabin. After they died Court sold their estate in Los Angeles and moved to Big Sur with his wife.'

'What's she like?'

'Leah's one in a million. She's a superb manager. A marvellous cook. The most sensible woman I've ever known. She was the Pomerances' housekeeper before Court married her. He's a poet of sorts – a dreamer rather than a doer. He couldn't get by without Leah. I asked her to help you get settled.'

'Were you so sure I'd say yes?'

Dimitri reached across the front seat and pulled her close. 'I wasn't sure at all. In fact I never even mentioned you to Leah until yesterday for fear of making a fool of myself.'

The admission melted Glory's reserve. She hadn't realised he had insecurities too. Perhaps they weren't so dissimilar, she thought, snuggling closer.

Glory had seen pictures of the redwood forest but photographs hadn't prepared her for reality. As the road climbed into the coastal range the trees soaring overhead created tenebrous shadows at ground level. The air felt thick, damp, and cold. It smelled of decaying vegetation and mould.

'This is it,' Dimitri said as he slowed the Ford and turned onto a rough path carpeted with pine needles.

She peered ahead. In the gathering darkness she could barely discern a log cabin huddled under the trees. It reminded her of a mushroom.

She glanced at Dimitri.

He beamed back.

'That's your new home,' he answered, setting the brake and bounding out of the car.

He hurried to her door, opened it and helped her down, then pulled her into his arms and kissed her more forcefully than he ever had before. Her lips parted under the bruising pressure. His tongue invaded her mouth. He pressed her hips against the hardness in his trousers.

She had imagined a languorous seduction, not this – this assault. Gasping, she jerked free. 'You hurt me.'

'I'm sorry,' he said. 'It's just that I want you so much, I can't wait. But I ought to show you the cabin first and give you a chance to settle in. We have lots of time for love making now you're here.'

He took her hand, tugged her towards the front door, flung it wide and switched on a light, illuminating what she supposed was the parlour. Peeled logs formed the walls. The ceiling and floor were pine too, dark with age and in bad need of wax. The furniture looked even shabbier than the furniture in the Blackstones' parlour.

'I told you it needed a woman's touch,' Dimitri said cheerfully. 'Now you're here I'm sure you'll set things right in no time. Let me show you the rest of the place.'

She followed him into a dingy kitchen with a wood-burning stove and an icebox, then on to a bedroom dominated by a lumpy looking double bed.

'I'll bring in your things and warm supper while you unpack,' Dimitri said as she gazed around.

Dear God, she thought as his footsteps receded, what had she got herself into?

CHAPTER FIFTEEN

Dimitri ate so quickly, he barely tasted Leah's savoury stew. A fever of impatience possessed him as he watched Glory dawdle over her food. He couldn't wait to get her into bed.

'Leave the dishes on the table,' he said when she finished.

'They'll be twice as hard to clean in the morning,' she replied, carrying their plates to the sink. 'It won't take long to wash them.'

He came up behind her, put his arms around her waist and pressed his erection into the cleft of her buttocks. He'd been turgid when they reached the cabin. Now he was so hard he ached.

'Two minutes would be too long. Come to bed, Rouge. I want to make love to you.'

He nibbled at her neck, then thrust his tongue into her ear. She trembled, arousing him even more. She liked it, he thought. He would do other things to her she would like even more.

'Please, Dimitri. I hate waking up to a mess like this.'

'You won't have to. I'll get up first thing and do the dishes.'

At that moment he would have promised anything to get her into bed, including licking the damn plates clean. 'Let me show you how much I want you.' He pressed his erection into her even more forcefully. 'Can't you tell? Take pity on me. I've been like this far too long as it is.'

Words of protest died in Glory's throat. She couldn't tell Dimitri what she felt – couldn't explain the mingled longing and fear that prickled her skin. She wanted his kisses, his embrace, his tenderness – but did she want the thing he pressed so insistently into her back?

It felt so big. She shivered at the thought of him putting it inside her. The act of love couldn't have been less romantic to contemplate. She knew what he expected of her tonight – knew she would have to lie on her back and open her legs to receive him. She had no choice in the matter. Sex was an unspoken part of the bargain she had made with Dimitri.

She followed him to the bedroom like a Christian martyr walking into the Colosseum, prepared to do her duty but dreading it. While unpacking she had opened the window to air out the room, but she hadn't had time to change the sheets.

'Let me make the bed,' she said, stalling for time.

'It is made.'

'How long is it since you changed the sheets?'

'What's this talk of making beds and doing dishes. I would have thought you had enough of such work at Tiny's.' He reached for her again. 'I want to kiss you here,' he said throatily, touching her breast, 'and here,' he added, palming her sex.

Her body yearned for affection even as her mind quailed at their joining.

'Are you nervous?' he asked.

'Very. I want to please you – but I don't know how.'

He smiled at her. 'Having you here pleases me. Being with you pleases me. Knowing I'll wake up by your side pleases me. The rest will take care of itself in time. No matter how much we want each other, we both know sex will be better after we've done it a while.'

She wanted to tell him she knew no such thing. Shame kept her silent. If Dimitri assumed she was a woman of the world, she had no intention of disillusioning him.

'Why so quiet?' he asked as he unbuttoned his shirt. 'You haven't put a dozen words together since we got here.'

'I thought men didn't like a talkative woman,' she replied, hoping she sounded nonchalant.

The shirt slid from his shoulders revealing a chest so well muscled and tanned that it might have been hewn from mahogany. The power implicit in his bare torso would have intimidated a far more experienced woman. It sent a tremor from Glory's head to her toes.

His eyes sought hers. 'Aren't you going to undress? Or are you waiting for me to help?'

'I'll do it myself,' she replied, fumbling at her buttons.

Despite her best effort to look anywhere else, her gaze was riveted first by his bare chest and then by the rampant bulge in his trousers. She forgot all about undressing as his trousers fell to the floor. He wasn't wearing anything underneath them except his own proud masculine flesh.

The curly black hair that covered his torso narrowed as it ran down his abdomen, then bunched in a nest between his powerful thighs. His penis looked nothing like the ones on Greek statues, she realised with alarm.

It stood straight out from his body like a warrior's lance. In the shadow beneath, she could just make out the round shape of his testicles.

She didn't realise she was staring until he said, 'Do you like what you see?'

Unable to raise enough spit to lubricate her tongue, she could only nod.

He came closer and lifted his manhood as though offering it for close inspection. 'I'm told I'm a bit broader than other men. What do you think?'

Although she had no basis for comparison, she nodded again. He looked huge.

'Have you ever seen an uncircumcised man?'

'No,' she said truthfully. Or a circumcised one either, she silently added, wondering what the difference was.

'The way you're staring, I thought as much.' He pushed the skin back at the tip of his penis. 'I've never understood why a man would submit to losing even a fraction of an inch of his manhood. But I suppose male babies in this country aren't given any choice. Thank God I was born in Greece.'

He released his penis and reached for the buttons on her blouse. 'Now Rouge, you've seen what's in store for you tonight. It's my turn to see what you have for me.'

His large fingers fumbled with the tiny pearl buttons for what seemed an eternity before he was able to pull the blouse open. The night air raised goose bumps on her bare skin.

'God, how many layers of clothes do you wear?' he asked, taking in her chemise and brassière.

He tugged both sets of straps down until they would go no further, then growled in frustration.

'Please, don't tear anything,' she said, finally finding her tongue.

His hands dropped to his sides. 'I'm not used to undressing my women.'

'Your women?'

'You know you aren't my first – any more than I'm yours.'

153

Again, pride kept her from confessing her virginity – and from begging him to slow down, to be gentle.

'Take those things off. I want to see your breasts,' he commanded.

When she removed her chemise and bra, Dimitri's gaze was so intent she could almost feel it crawling over her skin.

'I like big nipples,' he said huskily. 'It means a woman is passionate.'

Passionate didn't fit what she was feeling. Terrified did.

He took both breasts in his hands, testing them for weight and firmness as though they were tomatoes. Then he pinched her nipples. They crested in response as though they had a mind of their own.

'Do you like having them sucked?' Without giving her a chance to reply, he bent and took one in his mouth. A shiver ran through her, as much from fear as pleasure. Did women really like this – or did they just pretend?

She reached for the light and turned it off. She had seen all she wanted for one night.

'I want to look at you,' he protested.

'No lights, not this time,' she replied as she finished removing her clothes.

With a primal moan, he pushed her now naked body onto the bed. He kissed her with punishing force, prying her mouth open, his greedy lips demanding more than she was ready to give as his passion far outraced hers.

His hands and tongue seemed to be everywhere at once, touching and then tasting places she never imagined.

'Oh God,' he rasped, 'I waited so long, I can't wait another minute. This first time is for me, Rouge. The second will be for you – for your pleasure.'

She had no idea what he meant – and no experience by which to judge his love-making. She only knew she wanted it to be slower, sweeter, more affectionate.

She had dreamed of tenderness and sighs. Instead a sex-crazed stallion of a man pried her thighs apart and positioned himself above her.

'Heaven here I come,' he said.

Heaven didn't last long.

'Damn, you're still dry,' he muttered, then spit-wet two fingers before thrusting them inside her.

She jerked involuntarily at the intrusion.

'Easy girl,' he said as though she were a mare.

He poised above her again. His penis poked at her centre. Resting on one elbow, he took hold of his organ and guided it into her body. She cried out as pain knifed through her. For a second, he held his quivering torso motionless.

'Why the hell didn't you tell me you were a virgin?' he demanded in a tone she had never heard him use before.

'I – I don't know.'

'I would never have been in such a hurry if I'd known. Now it's too damn late. You're in for it, Rouge.'

She felt his body tense. Then with a single powerful push he rammed past her maidenhead, burying himself deep inside her.

'Christ. *Merde.* Shit,' he muttered. The words punctuated thrusts that seemed to reach high into her abdomen. Her body jolted with each one as he pinioned her to the bed like a butterfly to a specimen board.

Her mind spiralled away from the onslaught. This couldn't be making love, she thought. It was more like making war. Dimitri continued to curse and groan in a mixture of pleasure and anger, entering and withdrawing with ever-increasing speed. The wet-fish sound of his flesh slapping into hers added to her mortification.

Their coupling ended with a triumphant shout on his part, immediately followed by a tremor that shook his powerful frame. Then he collapsed on top of her, his breath coming in gasps as though he'd run a race.

She struggled to shove him away. But Dimitri was as immovable as a mountain. He didn't move until his deflated penis slid out of her. Only then did he roll onto his back.

'God, that was good,' he declared, 'but it would have been a hell of a lot better if I had known you were a virgin.'

'Well you know now,' she quavered.

He smiled into the darkness. Indeed he did, he mused as his body and mind returned from *le petit mort* – the little death as the French so aptly called orgasm.

He had never taken a virgin before, had never understood why other men boasted of it. Ever since his initiation with the fisherman's lonely wife, he had preferred experienced partners who knew how they wanted to be pleasured and how to pleasure him in return.

Now though, remembering how tightly Rouge had sheathed him made him reconsider. He had never felt anything quite like it, or experienced as primitive a thrill as the one he'd known when he broke her hymen. No wonder men talked of being where no man had been.

Now he knew why Rouge had been so silent during dinner, and so modest about undressing in front of him. No wonder she had stared at his genitals in wide-eyed awe. She had never seen a naked man before.

Who the hell was this Rouge of his? How did a woman who looked so sexual stay so sublimely innocent? What other secrets hid behind her grey eyes? She lay rigid beside him as though she didn't dare breathe for fear he'd be at her again. The poor kid. She'd had one hell of an initiation into sex.

'Did I hurt you?' he asked, deliberately gentling his voice.

'Yes,' she replied.

'I'm truly sorry, Rouge. I wanted tonight to be perfect for you. I hoped to make you want me as much as I wanted you. And in time, I swear you will. I'll teach you about your body – and mine.'

His words were so loving and he kissed her so tenderly that Glory almost forgot the throbbing ache between her legs. 'I'm not angry. I should have told you the truth.'

'I hurt you when I only wanted to love you. Stay here and rest, *chèrie*. I'll get something to make you feel better.'

Dimitri was gone so long that Glory almost got up to look for him. But that would have meant turning on the light – and she couldn't face the reality of the bedroom and what had happened to her in it.

Instead she closed her eyes and tried to shut out all feeling. The next thing she knew, a cologne scented cloth covered her brow and another caressed her thighs. Awareness returned with a rush – and with it, embarrassment.

'I can do that,' she said, trying to capture Dimitri's hand.

'I know you can. But I hurt you down there and I will be the one to make the hurt go away.'

He washed her gently, pausing to dip the cloth in a basin he must have brought with him until all trace of the sticky fluid on her private parts had been washed away. Then to her horror, he put his fingers inside her again. This time though, they slid in easily.

'Don't be afraid. I'm using Vaseline. I thought it would make you more comfortable,' he said. 'I keep it in the studio to lubricate moulds. That's why I was gone so long. Were you worried?'

'A little,' she replied in a small voice.

He finished between her legs, rinsed his hand, then took the scented cloth from her brow and cleansed the rest of her body. 'Better?' he asked.

'Much better.'

He leaned over and kissed her cheek, then cradled her in his arms. 'I swear to you, Rouge – on my life and my talent – I'll never hurt or frighten you again. Do you trust me enough to let me sleep with you?'

Soothed by his ministrations, comforted by his vow, she moved over and made room for him on the bed. He lay down and held her while she drifted off to sleep.

In the middle of the night she woke to feel him by her side and pressed closer to him for comfort. He mumbled her name, then caressed her with the gentleness she had longed for earlier, stroking and soothing until she vibrated with pleasure.

She found herself fondling him in a gentle give and take that was as different from their previous love-making as vinegar from honey.

Dimitri seemed determined to fulfil her every desire as he asked if she liked to be touched here and then there. Their foreplay went on and on until Glory urged him to take her. This time she was warm and wet and ready.

Her cries of pleasure mingled with his as they climbed the mountain of mutual desire and slid ever so gently down the other side.

Glory had all but forgotten the sybaritic delight of lounging in bed after the sun rose while someone else prepared breakfast.

'The bacon and eggs are done,' Dimitri called from the kitchen. 'Do you want to eat in the kitchen or in bed?'

'In bed,' she replied.

'Then be advised, breakfast won't be the only thing you'll get,' he answered boastfully.

She chuckled. They had made love again before Dimitri got up. There might be no end to his sexual appetite but she was starved for food. Besides, she wanted to see the house in daylight and then visit his studio.

'I'll be right there,' she answered.

Her natural modesty reasserted itself as she climbed naked from the bed. She had put her chenille robe in the armoire last night. She took it out and put it on, belting it tight at her waist. Her body ached all over – but it was a delicious ache.

She followed the rich aroma of bacon and fresh coffee to its source. Dimitri gave her a welcoming hug, then helped her into a chair.

'You've served me so often, I thought it was time I served you. But don't get too used to it. I'm usually in my studio by now,' he said as he put a laden platter in front of her.

'I can't wait to see it,' she answered between hurried bites.

'I see making love was good for your appetite.'

'I hope you have lots of food in the house,' she teased, feeling confident in her femininity, 'because I expect to be hungry all the time.'

Last night she had crossed over an invisible threshold from childhood to womanhood and now she couldn't help wondering why it had taken her so long.

Because you were waiting for Dimitri, an inner voice was quick to answer.

'What do you have planned for today?' she asked.

'I want you to sit for me. I have a commission for a sculpture of Aphrodite.'

She almost choked on a mouthful of bacon. 'Me? Aphrodite? You must be kidding.'

'Why not? You have a magnificent body. At least I think you do from what I could feel last night.'

'But I have so much to do today.'

'Like what?' he challenged.

She gazed around. 'Clean the house. Do laundry. Cook dinner.'

'Rouge, my love, you're not living in a *bourgeois* boarding house any more. You're living with an artist and art must always come first.' He grinned impudently. 'Except for making love.'

He was right, she thought, forgetting all about her own plans. She would pose for a couple of hours and then insist on an art lesson.

*

The studio was everything Dimitri had promised and more, Glory thought as he opened the door. Except for photographs, she had never seen his sculpture before. Her pulse accelerated as she took in a dozen pieces in various stages of completion, some on tables, others on pedestals.

Dimitri's drawings had acquainted her with his talent. The sculptures revealed the full extent of his genius. She walked from one to another, experiencing a reverence she had never known in church. The work reflected Dimitri's classical training and yet it was as modern as tomorrow.

There were several finished bronze of nudes, a carved male torso in a dark wood she couldn't identify, a couple of marbles, waxes on armatures, and fired terracottas.

'What do you think?' Dimitri asked.

'Are you serious? Can there be any doubt?' she enthused. 'I think you're a genius. I love your work.'

His eyes darkened with emotion. 'And I love you, Rouge. I've never said that to another woman.'

She grinned at him. 'You're my first lover – and I'm your first love. I'd say that makes us even.'

'I didn't know you were keeping score.' He put an arm around her waist. 'Let me show you around and tell you what everything is for.'

He had built the studio twenty feet from the house. The floor was concrete, painted and varnished to a deep amber. The redwood walls had been left in their natural state and were beginning to silver. A huge skylight let in so much light that they might have been outdoors.

Windows covered one wall and a stone fireplace, the other. Dimitri told her of shaping the granite himself. Shelves holding art supplies of every description, for every conceivable use, took up the other two sides of the room.

Fascinated, she followed him around while he pointed out and explained the tools of his arcane trade – armatures for the waxes from which bronze sculptures were cast – chunks of stone in varying sizes and colours that he described as marble, alabaster and travertine – and pieces of cherry, walnut and oak which he used for both sculptures and sculpture bases.

Metal turntables held works in progress. Dimitri sent them spinning slowly while he explained using them so he could view pieces from all sides. A cheval mirror served the same purpose for pieces too large to put on a turntable.

In addition there were drawing pads in several sizes, pastels, conte pencils and charcoals by the box, tubes of paints, cans of turpentine and linseed oil and an oversize container of Vaseline that brought a flush to her cheeks, remembering the use they had had for it last night.

A kilim tapestry suspended on a rope screened one corner of the room. Tables covered with tools for carving stone and wood as well as for working in clay took up another corner. A chair, a high stool, and a chaise looked out of place in such rugged surroundings.

'What are those for?' she asked.

'For models like you. We've wasted enough time, Rouge. I have to get to work.' He pointed at the kilim tapestry. 'You can undress behind the screen. There are a couple of hooks on the wall to hang up your clothes. By the time you're ready to pose, I'll have a fire going to keep you warm.'

'Undress?'

'I told you I had a commission to do a sculpture of Aphrodite. Surely you don't expect me to sculpt the goddess of love in modern street clothes.'

It was one thing to make love in the dark, she decided as she reluctantly took off her clothes, and quite another to walk into the middle of a room stark naked.

'What's taking so long?' he called out a few minutes later.

'I'll be right out,' she answered, looking down and taking a hasty inventory of her body. She had never seen another woman completely nude – not even Cal – and had no basis for comparison. Her skin looked preternaturally white in the shadowy corner created by the hanging tapestry. Her breasts were too large, her nipples swollen and cherry red from Dimitri's attentions last night.

While Rouge undressed, Dimitri put a large sketch-pad on his easel, then placed the stool in easy view. He planned to pose Rouge on it and do several preliminary sketches before working in wax. He had just finished draping the stool with fabric that would translate easily into the bronze when Rouge walked out from behind the screen.

'Mother of God,' he gasped.

'Is something wrong?'

'Wrong? I knew you were beautiful last night. I felt it with my hands. But I had no idea you were this beautiful. You don't need to pretend to be Aphrodite. You *are* Aphrodite.'

His avid gaze trailed from her head to her feet, then made the heart-stopping journey again more slowly, ravishing her with his eyes the way he had last night with his hands, mouth and tongue.

She had marvellous shoulders and slender arms. Her collarbones were so deeply carved that they created places for shadows to pool. Her breasts, dear God, would he ever be able to do them justice? They rode her rib cage so proud, high and deep that his hands ached to touch them.

Her stomach rounded nicely beneath a surprisingly small waist. She was slender enough to give her pubic mound an erotic prominence that drew his gaze and then held it. Her pubic hair, untouched by sunshine, was a deeper red than the hair on her head. Her labia, swollen from last night's lusty usage, peeped out from that erotic bush. Her legs were long, slender, and lightly muscled from all the trips she had made up and down the boarding house stairs.

'Turn around,' he commanded in a strangled growl.

She did as he ordered, displaying a back whose perfection culminated in the most marvellous buttocks he had ever seen.

Everything that made him a man urged him to throw her down and take her then and there.

The talent that made him a great artist ordered him to his easel.

The artist in him won.

'You can turn back around,' he managed to say in a more normal voice.

'Do you really think I'll be a good model for Aphrodite?'

Other women – some smiling coyly, others flouting their feminine charms – had asked him the same question. He had heard false modesty in all their voices. Not in Rouge's, though. She truly didn't know what a magnificent piece of work she was.

'You'll do,' he replied with uncharacteristic understatement.

He pointed at the stool. 'Sit there.'

She followed his instructions. 'I'm afraid of losing my balance.'

'Put your hands behind you and hold the edge of the seat. It will help.'

Again, she did as he asked. He stepped back and eyed the pose critically, doing his level best to bury his libido. The way Rouge sat

Alexandra Thorne

thrust her breasts out nicely and showed the curve of her rib cage to advantage.

So far, so good, he thought. 'Now, cross your legs at the ankle.'
'Like this?'
'Just like that – and twist your shoulders so that your spine curves.'
'Wonderful,' he exclaimed when she finished.
'Uncomfortable is more like it.'
'I wanted to create tension in your spine – and then have it released in your hips. Tension and the release of tension has been used by sculptors since Polykleitos. It's called *contraposto*.'

He walked over to the easel, picked up a conte pencil, and squinted at her, the better to see the play of light and shadow on her body. At that moment he stopped thinking of her as a fuckable female. Her breasts and buttocks became geometric shapes rather than objects of desire.

As magnificent as she was, his sculpture would be better.

CHAPTER SIXTEEN

Leah stood at her kitchen window staring at the smoke pluming from Dimitri's studio chimney. She hadn't expected him back so soon. Had the woman he called Rouge come with him?

She finished shoving slivers of garlic into the rib roast she intended to cook for supper, gave it a liberal sprinkling of coarse pepper, put it in a pan and set the pan down on the kitchen counter. Then she stripped her apron off and went to find Court.

He was in the study, a pen poised over a blank pad of paper on his lap, sucking at the stem of his pipe like a piglet on a sow's tit.

'Tonight's roast is big enough for four,' she said without preamble. 'Why don't we invite Dimitri and his new model to share it with us?'

Court started at the sound of her voice. 'I wish you wouldn't sneak up on me like that. I was getting the glimmerings of an idea for a poem and now you've driven it away.'

He unfolded his six feet four inches from the chair and glowered down at her, his lower lips protruding in a childish pout. She no longer remembered why she had ever thought him attractive – except, of course, for the money.

The money had meant everything to her before she realised it couldn't compensate for Court's shortcomings. No matter how well she fed him there wasn't enough meat on his bones to make a decent soup. Baldness made him look far older than his thirty-four years. His watery blue eyes peered out from behind the ridiculous affectation of steel rimmed half glasses that hadn't been in fashion since Benjamin Franklin's day. And he was bone lazy, a dilettante rather than a doer.

All in all, he was a poor excuse for a man, she mused, making certain her expression didn't give her thoughts away. 'I'm so sorry, dear. If I'd known you were inspired, I wouldn't have intruded. I thought you were resting.'

His shoulders hunched. 'I fear my muse has deserted me. I wait for afflatus and you come in with your talk of roasts. You have no

163

idea how elusive free verse can be. One minute you think you have it and the next, it's gone.' He flung an arm wide for emphasis, spilling tobacco on the newly vacuumed carpet. She could have killed him.

'Perhaps you've been working too hard, darling,' she soothed although he didn't know the first thing about hard work – either mental or physical. He was lucky to publish an occasional poem in obscure quarterly reviews that no one read.

'Do you really think I've been pushing myself too hard?' Court asked.

He wanted reassurance. She had her own agenda. 'I certainly do. A diversion might be just what you need.'

'Diversion?'

'Before he left, Dimitri mentioned he might bring a new model back with him. He returned last night. Let's go on over to the studio and invite him for supper tonight, and the model too if she's there.'

'I do enjoy talking with Dimitri and God knows, he's crazy about your cooking,' Court's expression brightened. His cheeks flushed. 'What's this about Dimitri having a new model?'

Court couldn't be more predictable. He'd got a vicarious thrill from the parade of models who passed through Dimitri's studio and Dimitri's bed. 'He told me about her yesterday when I took over the stew.'

'What stew?' The details of their daily life didn't linger any longer in Court's mind than his so-called muse.

'The stew we had for dinner two nights ago. You had two helpings,' she reminded him.

While working for Court's parents, Leah had heard his mother refer to him fondly as a dreamer. His father had contradicted her, saying Court was an impractical asshole who would need a keeper if anything ever happened to them.

His father had been right. She was as much Court's keeper as his wife.

Taking his hand, she led him from the room.

Glory found posing far less onerous than she had feared. Dimitri's conversation was so fascinating that she forgot all about her cramped muscles and the kink in her neck.

'The rise of democracy put an end to the days when artists could rely on the patronage of the nobility,' he told her. 'Now artists have to deal with gallery owners. And no two are alike. Artists have to please them all as well as the collectors and the critics. I have to keep careful records of where my work is and how it's priced. And I don't make a penny until a piece sells.'

'That doesn't sound fair. Don't dealers ever pay on delivery?'

'Not if they can help it. They like to tell you about the high cost of doing business and never want to hear about what it costs you. They pay once a month, deduct their thirty per cent commission and send the artist what's left.'

In her naïveté Glory had imagined she only needed art lessons to become a success. Now she realised she would have to be a business-woman too. 'How do artists get dealers to show their work?'

'Dealers are always on the lookout for new talent, someone they can promote to stardom. Occasionally a dealer visits a studio or an out of town gallery or hears about an artist from a collector. I got my start when a New York dealer visited the Paris atelier where I was studying. He offered to give me a show in New York. After that, one thing led to another.'

'You make it sound easy.'

He shrugged. 'Spoken like a true naive. Believe me, Rouge, it's not an easy life. I live from month to month. My materials don't come cheap and there have been times when I starved to pay for them. That's why I work in so many mediums. In the old days when I couldn't afford to buy a block of marble or pay to have a wax piece cast in bronze, I sculpted in wood or clay. I still do when I want a change of pace.'

'Which one is your favourite?'

He looked thoughtful. 'Marble. I know it so well, I can tell what design best suits a block by looking at it. I love the feel of it, the sense of coaxing a sculpture from the living stone. I like working from the outside in rather than from the inside out, the way you do with the wax or clay.'

Finally she had the nerve to ask the most important question of all. 'Do you really think I have talent?'

He came around the easel. 'I wouldn't have offered to teach you if I didn't. But you'd be wise not to be too ambitious. You have a nice gift. Given enough training and hard work, you may even make a living selling your paintings. But you'd do well to remember that female artists have small careers at best. There are no Michel-angelinas to match Michelangelo.'

Glory's cheeks flamed. Listening to Dimitri, posing for him, breath-ing the air in his studio, made her feel as if she had been admitted to the most exclusive organisation in the world – one based on talent rather than money or social status. Now she felt as though the doors to that club had been rudely slammed shut in her face.

She never expected a true Bohemian like Dimitri Konstantine to espouse the very ideas her father had held. Next Dimitri would undoubtedly tell her she was fortunate to have a chance to model for him and share his bed – that a woman could have no higher calling.

Did all men think gender defined talent – or only the men she loved? She hadn't walked away from a life of luxury and worked her fingers to the bone in a boarding house to have a *little career*.

Someone knocked at the door before she could voice the thought.

'Dimitri, it's Leah and Court,' a female voice called out.

Glory covered her breasts with her hands and squeezed her thighs together. 'I'm not dressed. Tell them to go away.'

'The Pomerances have seen my models before. Put your hands back where they were. I'm not finished sketching,' Dimitri said from behind the easel.

Aghast, embarrassed, and more than a little angry, Glory resumed her pose as the studio door swung wide to admit the most mis-matched couple she had ever seen.

He was tall. She was short. His body was thin and attenuated. Hers was heavy and squat.

'You must be Rouge,' she said, coming towards Glory with her hand held out. 'Dimitri told me all about you. I'm Leah Pomerance and this is my husband.' She beckoned the scarecrow with a jerk of her head. 'Court, darling, come on over and meet our new neighbour.'

Leah took a quick inventory of the girl's assets while shaking her hand. She had to give the bitch her due. Rouge had a stunning figure – one Dimitri had enjoyed to the hilt if the girl's swollen nipples meant anything. And she was a natural redhead too.

'Dimitri told me about you too,' the model answered, colouring prettily as though being naked in front of strangers embarrassed her.

Fat chance, Leah mused. A woman with a body like hers had undoubtedly taken every opportunity to show it off.

'I apologise for barging in on you like this, Rouge,' Court said, his eyes fixed on the girl's breasts as though he'd never seen a pair before.

Leah let go a guttural laugh. 'It's perfectly obvious you're not sorry at all, Court. Stop staring at Rouge's nipples and get out of the way so Dimitri can continue working.'

She tugged Court over to the chaise, pulled him down beside her, then turned her attention to the sculptor. 'You're back early.'

'After Rouge agreed to return with me I didn't see any reason to stay in Monterey. I couldn't wait to get her back here. Now you've met her I'm sure you can see why.'

Court gave Dimitri a conspirator's wink. 'I sure can. I'm amazed you have the energy to sketch today after the workout you must have had last night.'

'Making love may tire other men. It energises me,' Dimitri replied with a wicked grin. As if to reinforce what he was saying, he kept right on sketching.

Leah resented their male camaraderie. She didn't want anyone else to be close to Dimitri – especially not her husband. 'We didn't mean to interrupt,' she said. 'Court and I came over to welcome Rouge and to ask the two of you to have supper with us tonight.'

Dimitri turned to Rouge. 'You're in for a treat. The Pomerance house is a marvellous example of the Craftsmen style of architecture, and Leah is a fabulous cook.'

'You're very kind,' the girl said to Leah but she looked as though she'd taken a bite out of a lemon.

Leah got up and headed for the door, confident that Court would trot at her heels. 'Dinner's at seven,' she said.

Glory waited until the door shut, then left her perch to confront Dimitri. 'How could you embarrass me like that?'

'What are you talking about?'

'You know very well what I mean. Maybe your other models didn't object to being naked when they met your friends for the first time. I do.'

'You knew I wanted a nude model when you left Monterey.'

'I didn't realise your neighbours would wander in and out of the studio. How many more should I expect today?'

To her consternation, Dimitri burst out laughing. 'I know it's a cliché but you really are beautiful when you're angry. You should see the way it makes your eyes sparkle.'

'I'm not angry. I'm furious.' She stamped a foot for emphasis.

'Do that again,' he said.

'Why?'

'It makes your breasts shake.'

'You are impossible.'

'*Au contraire* my dear Rouge, it's you who are being impossible. And childish too. If you truly want to be an artist you're going to have to rid yourself of your middle-class ideas. There is nothing shameful about the human body. It's beautiful – and yours is more beautiful than most.'

'If there's nothing to be ashamed of, why don't you take your clothes off and pose for me?'

'Will that make you happy?'

Glory hadn't expected him to agree. However she was too stubborn to back down. 'Absolutely.'

She pointed at the kilim rug, deliberately mimicking what he'd said to her a couple of hours ago. 'You can undress behind the screen. There are a couple of hooks for your clothes.'

His dark eyes gleamed dangerously. 'I'll pose for you on one condition. You can draw me to your heart's content provided you don't get dressed.'

'Of all the ridiculous—'

'I need a nude model – but you aren't comfortable posing for me. That leaves us two choices. I can take you back to Monterey – or you can try getting over your inhibitions. I'm suggesting a way to help you do it.'

'Aren't you the thoughtful one.'

'You may not realise it but I am. An artist can't afford to have a shop-keeper mentality. Go to any museum and what do you see? Nudes painted by the world's greatest artists. Someone posed for those paintings and other people were in the room with them.'

Glory couldn't refute his logic. Museums were full of paintings and sculptures of nudes – and they had never bothered her. She had admired them, had even sketched them. 'All right. We'll do it your way.'

She expected Dimitri to undress behind the screen. Instead he stripped where he stood and let his clothes fall at his feet. He was a magnificent male animal. Although her stomach clenched and her mouth dried at the sight of him, she was determined to not to show it.

'How would you like me to pose?' he asked meekly.

'Sit on the stool, then turn your shoulders to create – what did you call it – *contraposto*.'

He grinned at her. 'You're a quick learner, Rouge.'

She grinned back. 'I had better be if I hope to keep up with you.'

He talked while she sketched, pouring out his knowledge in disjointed and often unrelated sentences.

Sculpture began in the Neolithic with so-called Venus figures.

Egyptians created the first monumental sculpture.

Greek artists were the first to know enough about anatomy and perspective to portray the human form in fluid motion.

Greeks invented classical sculpture.

The Kouros or standing youth is a traditional Greek art form, one that Michelangelo and Rodin adapted to their own use in portraying David and Balzac.

The human body consists of a series of geometrically linked shapes. So-called modern artists like Picasso disassemble and reassemble those pieces at will.

A sculptor should use the human body to play with light and shadow the way Van Gogh and Cézanne used landscapes.

Positive and negative space define all three-dimensional forms.

Sculpture must never be static.

Dimitri left his perch from time to time to stretch and assess her work. Never once did Glory think about nudity – his or hers. She was much too busy trying to remember everything he said. She lost all track of time and was surprised when he suggested a quick lunch break.

She put the conte pencil down and headed for the screen to put on her clothes.

'Don't bother to dress,' Dimitri said. 'We'll eat here in front of the fire. Afterwards you can pose for me again. I've decided to do a maquette in clay next.' He added a log to the blaze, then piled pillows on the floor in front of the hearth.

Lunch consisted of cheese, salami, crackers and wine that he kept in a cupboard in anticipation of the days when he was too absorbed in work to return to the cabin.

The crackers were stale, the cheese and salami dry, and the wine totally lacking in subtlety. It was the crudest meal Glory had ever eaten, consumed in the strangest circumstances, but it tasted marvellous. Although the day had begun badly, she had never been happier.

CHAPTER SEVENTEEN

Leah prepared for Dimitri and Rouge as though they were royalty. She cleaned the already immaculate house, changed the linen in the guest bathroom, filled vases with flowers, polished the silver and washed the good china and crystal just as she had when Court's parents had a party. While she worked she thought about the evening ahead, planning how she would show Rouge up for a two-bit whore.

Court was oblivious to the commotion. He retired to the library to await afflatus – his favourite word – an occupation that seemed to require closed eyes and loud snores. Not that she gave a damn. He could spend the rest of his life pretending to be a poet for all she cared.

She woke him at six and told him it was time to dress. Looking a bit befuddled from his long nap, he followed her upstairs to their bedroom as obediently as an old lap dog.

'What did you think of Rouge?' she asked as she took a stylish bias-cut navy crêpe dress from the armoire.

'I don't know her well enough to think anything,' Court replied, stripping off his shirt.

'You did everything but drool on her. I thought you were going to foam at the mouth.'

'I may be a poet, Leah, but I'm a man too. Any man would be affected, seeing a naked woman with a body like hers.'

Leah lay the dress out on the bed, stripped off her blouse and skirt, took her cologne from the dressing table and sprayed herself liberally. 'Would you like to go to bed with Rouge?'

Court's eyes bugged out. 'What kind of question is that? I'm in love with you and only you.'

He was lying through his teeth. She had seen the pack of lewd French cards he hid in his desk, the ones that showed every conceivable sex act. And she had watched impassively while he leered at

171

Dimitri's models. She suspected he would have done a great deal more than look if he'd had the chance.

She would love to catch Court in an adulterous affair so she could divorce him and keep his money. If only she were free and financially able to offer Dimitri some meaningful help instead of just an occasional dinner, she thought with a sigh.

She knew she couldn't compete with Rouge when it came to looks. However there were other ways to beat the model at whatever game she was playing. Leah intended to get to know her well enough tonight to learn her weaknesses – and then use them against her.

The thought made her smile. She patted Court's cheek, took a fresh shirt from the dresser and handed it to him. 'You're so sweet. But you said it yourself. You are a man – and a very sexy one.'

'Oh, very well, Leah. Since you insist on knowing, Rouge is quite enticing on a purely physical level. In fact I've been playing with an idea for a poem about her. *Rouge*, he intoned, *the colour of lips and life and blood.*' He looked to Leah for approval. 'That's as far as I got. Do you like it?'

'It's—' she paused, searching for words to describe that particular piece of pedestrian poetic shit, 'it's very interesting.'

He knew her too well. 'You don't like it.'

'It's too soon to tell.'

'It doesn't matter. Rouge may be a looker but it's my experience that beautiful woman are terrible bores.'

Leah devoutly hoped so. Dimitri would soon tire of a bore.

She finished with her make-up, put on her dress and helped Court tie his Ascot in the loose knot that hid his scrawny neck. Then she led the way downstairs and went around the parlour plumping pillows while Court fixed a shaker of Martinis. It was the one talent he could truly boast about. No one made them crisper or drier.

The doorbell rang and she hurried to answer it. Her welcoming smile froze on her lips. The woman on Dimitri's arm looked as different from the naked model in his studio as a queen from a whore.

Rouge wore a dress whose every stitch shrieked money. The white georgette had fine pleats at the bosom and thigh that emphasised her magnificent figure. Where had she got a dress like that?

'It was so kind of you to invite us to dinner on my first night here.' Rouge sounded like a lady to the manner born. 'Dimitri kept me in the studio until dark. But for you we'd be eating sandwiches.'

'I'm delighted to have you. Now you're here I won't have to listen to male conversation the way I used to.'

'I could listen to Dimitri talk about art all day,' Rouge enthused. 'In fact I did just that today and I loved every minute.'

Seeing Dimitri flush with pleasure, Leah realised she had underestimated the girl. There was a clever mind behind the pretty face – a mind that knew how to flatter a man.

'You're just in time for Martinis,' Court called out.

'Go ahead and join Court,' Leah told Dimitri. 'It's Rouge's first visit and I want to give her the grand tour.'

There had been a time when Leah loved showing the house to visitors, when living there as its mistress had seemed like a miraculous achievement. Now though, the only pleasure she took from the house was having Dimitri for a neighbour.

'Did Dimitri tell you anything about the house?' she asked as she preceded Rouge down the hall.

'Only that it had been in Court's family.'

'It's a local landmark, one of the first examples of the Craftsmen style in all California. Are you interested in architecture?'

'A little. But I'm much more interested in art.'

'I suppose that's only natural since you're living with a sculptor and modelling for him.'

'I'm not a professional model.' Rouge smiled shyly. Damn. The girl was a good actress. 'In fact I was mortified when you and your husband walked into the studio this morning. Dimitri and I argued about it after you left.'

Leah came to a halt and gave the girl what she hoped was a sympathetic look. 'You should have said something. We certainly didn't intend to embarrass you. We assumed it was all right since we'd been to the studio dozens of times when other models were there.' She put her hand to her mouth, pretending chagrin. 'Oh dear, I hope I didn't let the cat out of the bag.'

Leah's revelation didn't have the desired effect. Rouge didn't so much as blink before she replied, 'You didn't. I know Dimitri lived with other women before me.'

'The two of you must be very close for him to have told you.'

'We are. Very. He's the most fascinating man I've ever known, the most talented, and the most generous. I always wanted to be an artist. Dimitri is making it possible.'

Bile rose up Leah's throat. Rouge was going to be a formidable adversary.

'You were right about Leah being a marvellous cook,' Glory said when she and Dimitri returned to the cabin later that night, arm in arm. 'She's a very nice woman too.'

'I hoped the two of you would get along.'

'I'm sure we will. We have something in common.'

'What's that?'

'We're both very fond of you.'

He opened the front door and turned on the lights. 'Fond of me? Is that all?'

'I can't speak for Leah.'

'Speak for yourself.'

'I'm crazy about you.' She giggled. 'I enjoyed the dinner and the conversation but I couldn't stop thinking about coming back here and being alone with you.'

The howl of a coyote woke Glory in the middle of the night. A coda of other animal cries filled the darkness. The sounds were unfamiliar and exhilarating to her.

Dimitri had given her the chance to begin her life anew. She loved him for that, and for so many other things. Glory Girard had been banished for ever. A woman called Rouge had taken her place.

Too exhilarated to go back to sleep, she slid from the bed, dressed and tiptoed from the room. Like iron filings attracted by a magnetic force, she made her way to the studio and let herself in.

At first she was content to just inhale the air in greedy gulps as though she could inhale Dimitri's talent and knowledge with it. His sculptures loomed on their stands like mystical beings waiting for the spark of life. She walked from one to another in a trance, silently communing with the man who had created them.

She built a fire, then sat on the pillows where she and Dimitri had eaten lunch. He had been so patient with her today, so giving. She wanted to make him proud – to show him his efforts weren't wasted. The question was how?

The answer came to her with breathtaking clarity. The best way to show her appreciation was to do a sculpture of him. She bolted to her feet, turned on the lights and went to the shelves where Dimitri kept his supplies.

Armatures in varying sizes and shapes were there for the taking. She chose one Dimitri had told her he used for torsos and carried it over to his work table. Then she went to the big barrel where he kept clay covered with wet burlap.

The terracotta felt cold, clammy, and slightly grainy as she dug into it with her bare hands and carried a load back to the table. She returned to the barrel several times until she thought she had enough clay for the piece she had in mind. Last, she chose a number of tools that looked as though they might be useful and carried them back to the table.

She set to work, twisting the armature this way and that until she felt certain the finished sculpture would have all the *contraposta* anyone could want. An hour later she had succeeded in roughing in a broad-shouldered, slender-hipped male body.

She had spent years learning to draw and had never been satisfied with her efforts. But her hands seemed to know how to sculpt as if they had a knowledge of their own. As she worked she pictured Dimitri's heavily muscled torso and reproduced it by feel as much as by sight.

The months she had spent working for Tiny gave her the upper body strength she needed to manipulate the clay. She added bits and pieces, pushing them into place with her fingers, knuckles and nails when she couldn't find a tool that fit her needs.

She dipped and swayed, dancing with the piece in a graceful adagio as her interior vision sprang to full-bodied life.

The sun woke Dimitri. He had been dreaming about Rouge. God, it was wonderful to have a woman in his bed again, he thought as he rolled over and reached for her.

It took his sleep-sodden brain a moment to realise she wasn't there. He opened his eyes and gazed at her side of the bed. The pillow still bore the impression of her head and her scent rose from the sheets.

'Rouge,' he called out.

He called her name louder, waited a second, then got out of bed. What game was she playing? he fretted as he made his way through the parlour to the kitchen. He had hoped to find her there making breakfast.

The room was empty, the stove as cold as a worn out love affair. His emotions seesawed between anger and concern as he hurried back to the bedroom to dress. Where the hell was she? Could she have gone for a walk? Had she gone to Leah's for coffee? Or was she even now hitching a ride back to Monterey?

Merde, he swore under his breath. There'd be hell to pay if – no, make that *when* he found her. He had always been the one to end an affair. No women had walked out on him before.

He shrugged into a sweater, pulled on a pair of trousers, shoved his bare feet into boots, returned to the parlour and yanked the front door open. The Pomerances' house was fifty yards away. He sprinted the distance and pounded on their front door.

Leah opened it in her nightgown. 'Dimitri, what's wrong?' she asked.

'Is Rouge here?'

'Not that I know. I just got up myself.'

'She's gone,' he blurted out.

Leah gazed towards the cabin. 'She can't have gotten far. Your car is still there.'

'She doesn't know how to drive.'

'Have you checked the studio?'

'No. It never occurred to me.'

'It should have been the first place you looked. I'm sure she's fond of you in her way, but it's obvious that being an artist is far more important to her than you are.' Leah touched his face, smoothing the frown line between his brows. 'Don't look so worried. Girls like Rouge are born knowing how to take care of themselves. Would you like me to go to the studio with you?'

'I appreciate the offer but it won't be necessary.'

'You will let me know if you need me?'

'You've already been a help.'

Leah caught his arm before he could walk away. 'I hope you don't mind a little advice from an old friend. Rouge is a very headstrong young woman. When you find her you had better make certain she knows you're the boss. If you don't lay down the law she'll lead you a merry chase.'

He shook his head. He didn't see Rouge that way. Perhaps it took a woman to know a woman.

'I'll keep that in mind,' he replied.

When he'd made his way to the Pomerances', the cabin had concealed the studio from view. Now as he circled the cabin he saw lights burning inside the studio and smoke coming from the chimney. Leah had been right, he thought, yanking the door open.

Was Leah right about everything else?

What he saw inside the studio answered his question. Rouge stood in front of his work table, so caught up in whatever she was doing that she didn't realise she wasn't alone.

What game was she playing? He hated feeling uncertain and off balance – and for the briefest instant, he hated the woman who made him feel that way.

'What the hell are you doing?' he demanded.

She spun around. 'You startled me. I didn't hear you come in.'

'That's obvious.'

'I have something to show you. I couldn't sleep last night so I came here to work. I hope you don't mind.'

Mind? He could have strangled her. 'This is my studio. I don't want anyone in it when I'm not here.'

She made a seductive moue. 'Not even me?'

He refused to be distracted. 'Not even you. Now show me what you've been doing,' he commanded.

She stepped aside to reveal a sculpture.

His breath caught in his throat. She had sculpted his torso, cock and all. It was good. Damn good.

'Do you like it?'

'You told me you had never sculpted.'

'I haven't.'

He grabbed her arm. She was so tall that they stood eye to eye. 'Don't lie, Rouge. I won't let any woman make a fool of me – not even you.'

'I swear it's the truth.'

'Then how—?' He didn't bother to finish the question. He already knew the answer. Rouge was one of those rare artists who had been born to work in three dimensions. Sculpture was her *métier* – just as it was his.

'I wanted to show you what a good teacher you are. I wanted to please you.'

'I woke up alone this morning without so much as a note to tell me where you'd gone. Do you really think that pleased me?'

'You're not being fair. I didn't do anything wrong. You didn't tell me the studio was off limits.'

He couldn't help admiring her courage. She had nerve, and talent too – far more talent than he had imagined.

'Fair? I ran over to the Pomerances' and made a complete ass of myself because I was worried about you.'

'I'm sorry. I didn't mean to upset you. I just wanted to see if I could sculpt.'

He didn't give her the satisfaction of telling her she could. She would figure that out for herself soon enough. God, had Leah been right about her? Had Rouge given him her body in exchange for his knowledge?

'I want your promise that you won't come over here and use my materials without permission – and that you won't go off again without telling me first.'

'I won't do anything that makes you unhappy. I love you too much.'

Damn. He couldn't stay angry when she looked at him that way. 'I didn't mean to growl at you. Come here,' he said opening his arms wide.

She walked into them and held him close. 'Are you still angry with me?'

'A little. Just enough to really enjoy making up.'

Leah stayed in the doorway watching Dimitri walk away, wondering if her wish could have come true so quickly. Had Rouge really gone? Five minutes passed, then ten. Oblivious to the cold, she waited and wondered, calculating the odds.

She bit her lips and clenched her hands. She couldn't stand not knowing what was happening in the studio. After all, Dimitri was her friend. If Rouge had cut and run, he would need her. She damn well intended to be there for him. It might be the very opportunity she'd been waiting for.

She snatched a sweater from the hall stand, slung it around her shoulders, shut the front door and followed the path Dimitri had taken minutes before. Her breath vapourised in the chill air. Her heart pounded. At the last second, she lost her nerve. Instead of knocking on the door she tiptoed around the back of the building to the windows. If Dimitri and Rouge were together, she would leave unseen.

She pressed against the logs and peered inside. Her heart stuttered to a stop as she saw Dimitri standing near the fireplace as naked as the day he'd been born.

She gasped, then clapped her hand over her mouth to smother the sound. The sight of his fully engorged phallus mesmerised her. It was as thick as a pepper mill. And then she saw Rouge spread-eagled on the floor waiting for him.

Leah had assumed that voyeurism was a purely male pleasure. Now though, she couldn't tear herself away. She gazed raptly while Dimitri mounted Rouge. When he thrust his penis between Rouge's thighs, Leah imagined herself in the girl's place.

Her body trembled as though she were the recipient of each powerful thrust. She felt her clitoris swell and squeezed her legs together in response. Court had never satisfied her. She had but to look to know Dimitri would.

She moaned softly, then pressed a hand to her mouth to stifle the sound as Rouge's hips lifted to meet his thrusts. Dizzied by the sight, sick with jealousy, Leah staggered away.

Dimitri wouldn't soon tire of sex like that, she thought as she returned to her front door. It would take all her wits to separate him from Rouge.

She would have to continue to sow seeds of distrust between them just as she had this morning. In time the poison plant would grow large enough to bear bitter fruit.

PART FOUR

Rouge

Jealousy is always born of love,
but does not always die with it.
La Rouchfoucauld – *Maxims*, 1665

CHAPTER EIGHTEEN

San Francisco, 1929

The sight of the empty art gallery sent pain spearing through Dimitri's stomach. He felt as though a hidden opponent had punched him in the gut. Where the hell were all the people Don Correy had said he had invited?

This time last year Dimitri's annual one-man exhibition had been a triumph. Admirers eager to buy his work had crowded wall to wall. Two hours after the doors opened red stickers marked every piece as sold. Dimitri had been so confident of his talent, so certain of a rosy future that he'd gone out the next day and bought a new car.

Tonight's failure had shattered that confidence. The few collectors who put in an appearance hadn't lingered. They spoke in the muted tones people used at funerals, looking at everything but his work as they talked not of art but of the stock market's collapse.

Now as Dimitri gazed around the exhibition, his unsold sculptures seemed to rebuke him like children whose parents have abandoned them.

'It's a damn shame,' Don Correy interrupted Dimitri's unhappy reverie.

The art dealer was an urbane, well-dressed man with a full head of silver hair and an ever ready supply of *bons mots*. Tonight, however, his glib tongue seemed to have deserted him. *Damn shame* didn't begin to cover the devastation Dimitri was experiencing.

'Don't take the débâcle personally,' Correy said. 'I don't think collectors would have bought anything less than a genuine Michelangelo after what happened last week.'

Dimitri shrugged. Correy could say what he liked. His work – the product of his heart and soul – had been consigned to ignominy.

Dimitri felt less of a man. How could he carry this failure home to Rouge?

The dealer held out a bottle of Kristal and two glasses. 'I bought this to toast you tonight. It's a damn shame to let good wine go to waste,' he said, filling a glass and handing it to Dimitri.

Dimitri would have preferred hemlock but he drank the wine down.

'Rotten luck, my scheduling your show one week after Black Friday,' Correy said.

Dimitri felt as though he was strangling. He unknotted his black bow tie and undid his collar button. 'You couldn't have known what was going to happen.'

Correy accepted Dimitri's absolution with a perceptible straightening of his spine. 'Thank God we sold one of your Rouge pieces. It will cover the cost of printing and mailing the invitations.'

'I'd appreciate the cheque as soon as possible.'

'I'll write it before you leave tonight.' Correy strolled over to Rouge's bronze likeness. 'It's a magnificent piece. But then I imagine she's a magnificent woman. I have the strangest feeling that I've seen her somewhere. It's probably just wishful thinking, though.'

Dimitri choked down his jealousy. He had attacked a collector in this very room when the man offered a small fortune to spend a single night with the living breathing woman after buying a Rouge sculpture. It had taken Correy and two bystanders to keep him from beating the man senseless. Strangely enough, the buyer still insisted on having the piece.

'I had hoped Rouge would come tonight. I would have enjoyed meeting her,' Correy said.

'She never attends my openings.'

'Perhaps if you had done a few more Rouge pieces—' Correy's voice trailed off.

'Working with the same model all the time is too limiting,' Dimitri answered.

The pieces Rouge posed for had been so popular with collectors that Dimitri wondered if they were motivated to buy her likeness – the innocent eroticism that pervaded the pieces – rather than his work. On his darkest days he pictured a parade of faceless millionaires stroking Rouge's bronze breasts and buttocks. It had driven him to sculpt other models – hard-muscled loggers with craggy faces, their less than lovely wives, even Leah.

Correy refilled their glasses, took a pack of French cigarettes from his elegantly tailored evening jacket and offered one to Dimitri. The Gauloises brought back memories of Dimitri's student days in Paris. A sense of loss accompanied his first deep drag.

What he wouldn't give to be young and full of hope again – to believe his talent would conquer the world. Having watched his talent collide with events beyond his control made him feel far older than thirty-three and utterly impotent.

'I suppose there's no point in scheduling next year's show,' he said, hoping his tone didn't betray his anxiety.

'You suppose right.' Regret roughened Correy's voice. 'And not because my best customers lost all their money. Savvy businessmen got out of the stock market months ago. But doubt and fear are as infectious as measles. You saw them tonight. They're frightened. Not that I blame them. So am I. People buy art with disposable income and after this week my customers don't think they have any. It looks as though the art market is going to be deader than the proverbial dodo for the foreseeable future.'

Dimitri had been so busy getting ready for the show that he had barely listened to Court's rambling discourses about the volatile stock market. The enormity of the crash hadn't hit Dimitri until he got to the gallery three hours ago, expecting the usual well-heeled opening night crowd.

Correy was walking from sculpture to sculpture, shaking his head in patent disbelief. 'If only I'd scheduled the opening a month ago, it would have been a sell out. This is the best work you've ever done.'

Dimitri followed Correy from piece to piece, trying to recapture the visceral pleasure he'd known while creating the collection. The thrill of seeing something in his mind's eye and then bringing it to three dimensional life was as close to being God as a mortal man could get.

Correy stubbed out his cigarette and immediately lit another. 'I hope President Hoover was right when he said the country's business is fundamentally sound.'

'You don't sound convinced.'

Correy shook his head. 'Only fools believe in a politician's pronouncements. I'm afraid the worst is yet to come. Have you put a little money aside for a rainy day?'

Damn little, Dimitri thought as he nodded yes. The uncertain

185

future log-jammed in his mind. He couldn't see around it or past it. Rejection by the buying public was a bitter pill no matter the cause.

Tonight's débâcle diminished him in ways he hadn't thought possible. If he hadn't felt his balls between his legs he would have reached down to make sure they were still there.

'I'll be all right. How about you? Will you stay open?'

Dimitri couldn't believe he had asked that question of the most successful art dealer in San Francisco. But then he'd never imagined a country as prosperous as America could be brought to its economic knees overnight.

'I'll certainly try. I've got a five year lease on the building. Will you stay in Big Sur?'

'I haven't had time to think about it.'

'You still have family in Greece, don't you?'

'A whole tribe. Mother, father, sisters, brothers, cousins.'

'If I were you I'd forget all about America for a while and pay them a visit – a long visit. I hear it's a lot cheaper to live there.'

Glory hated to admit she did her best work during Dimitri's absences. Deep down, though, she knew it was true. Alone in the studio, she could let her imagination soar and express herself without worrying about him looking over her shoulder.

When she began sculpting three years ago his critiques had been dispassionate and helpful. Now there were times when she thought them unnecessarily harsh. It seemed the more she excelled, the more he found fault. And not just with her work in the studio. He complained about the way she kept the house, the way she cooked, even the way she posed.

How could two people argue all day and still want each other each and every night? Despite their differences in temperament and personality the three years they'd lived together hadn't diminished their passion.

Dimitri had kept the promise he made the first time they made love. He had taught her all about her body and his. She had done things with him and to him that made her blush in the light of day. Was it sexual obsession that bound them together rather than love?

'Yoohoo, is anybody home?' came the sound of Leah's voice. Not waiting for a reply, she opened the studio door and marched in. 'I hope you don't mind me dropping by. The way Court is carrying on about the stock market is driving me crazy. I needed to get out of the house for a while. Besides, I thought you might be lonely with Dimitri away.'

'Did Court lose a lot of money in the crash?' Glory asked out of *politesse* rather than genuine interest.

'I told him to sell out months ago and he always follows my advice,' Leah replied with a self-assured smile. 'But you know his penchant for drama. Court has made a career of turning molehills into mountains.'

The way Leah ran Court down made Glory uncomfortable, especially on those occasions when Leah encouraged Glory to talk about Dimitri the same way.

'Have you heard from Dimitri since he got to San Francisco?' Leah asked in one of the lightning changes of topic that characterised so many of their conversations.

'No. I didn't expect to.'

'Not even a postcard?'

'He's busy.'

'I'm sure he is,' Leah answered with a knowing smile. 'You know how men act when they're out of town. But then, I suppose true Bohemians like you and Dimitri don't look at fidelity the way Court and I do. After all, it's not as though you're really married.'

'I trust Dimitri,' Glory replied, struggling to maintain her equanimity and keep on working. Sometimes Leah's company was as nerve wracking as the sound of chalk on a blackboard.

Leah plopped down on the chaise, tucked her legs under her and leaned back as if she intended to be there quite a while. 'If I were in love with someone as attractive as Dimitri I wouldn't let him out of my sight for a minute. I imagine the society women who attend his openings are mad for him.' She paused as though she expected Glory to comment, then continued, 'I've never understood why you don't go with him, especially since you've posed for so many of his pieces. I certainly wouldn't pass up a chance to go to San Francisco or New York.'

'We've been over this before.'

'Then you shouldn't mind going over it again.'

Glory couldn't tell Leah she didn't travel with Dimitri because she didn't want to risk running into someone she knew. 'My answer hasn't changed. The openings are Dimitri's time to shine. I wouldn't want to do anything to get in his way.'

'I don't mean to talk out of turn but we both know Dimitri is highly sexed. I imagine he's a bear after being celibate for a week or two. Assuming he has been celibate.'

'Actually he's more of a stallion than a bear when he comes home,' Glory replied with a sweet smile. She seldom played Leah's game but when she did, she played to win. 'Does Court know where you are?' she asked, hoping to speed Leah on her way.

'You may not worry about what Dimitri does or where he goes, but my Court worries about me. He always knows where I am.' Leah uncoiled her body and got to her feet. 'I can see you're not in the mood for visitors. Don't bother to see me out. Tah, tah.'

Now what was that all about? Glory mused as Leah shut the door. The woman had a way of popping in unexpectedly and starting aimless conversations. Glory had tried to like her for Dimitri's sake. Now she kept up the pretence of friendship for the same reason.

Dimitri had planned on spending a couple of days in San Francisco after the opening, visiting collectors, helping them choose the perfect place to display his work in their homes.

He hated that part of being an artist. Shaking hands, making small talk, explaining pieces whose meaning should have been obvious to a blind person, weren't his style.

Tonight though, he would gladly have done all that and more. However there hadn't been any hands to shake except Correy's, he thought grimly as he walked to his car. He slid behind the wheel, wondering what to do next. The thought of spending another night in an expensive hotel room wasn't appealing or sensible.

He still couldn't assimilate the changes in his life. Damn America for shattering his dreams, he thought angrily as he pounded an impotent fist against the steering wheel. Perhaps Don Correy had been right. Perhaps he should go to Greece for a while.

He drove back to the hotel, stayed long enough to pack his bag and pay his bill, then headed out of town. He was anxious to get back to Rouge and to the forgetfulness he found in her arms.

Rouge. He hadn't considered how what had happened would affect her. Common sense told him he didn't need another mouth to feed during the hard times ahead.

An hour later Dimitri had made all his choices. He'd ask the Pomerances to buy the cabin back, sell the car, give Rouge the proceeds and send her back to Tiny's. It was the logical thing to do, he told himself.

Sure, he'd miss her. He'd never felt about a woman the way he did about her. She challenged him in the studio and left him weak in bed. The combination was captivating, mesmerising – and maddening. God knew, he could do without the maddening part. But he would sure as hell miss the sex. A week at most and he'd be on the way to Santorini.

He reached the cabin during the small hours of the night when the spirit is at its lowest ebb and courage deserts the bravest man. A rush of nostalgia enveloped him as he opened the front door. He would miss this place. Most of all, he would miss Rouge.

He had already said his mental goodbye. Now he would say a physical one. He hurried to the bedroom, undressing on the way. She was sleeping on her back with her hair fanned across the pillow, her lips parted as though she expected his kiss.

She had cast a spell over him, he thought as he pulled the sheet down. Moonlight silvered her body, transforming it into a mysterious and unknown territory he ached to explore. He lay down beside her and pulled her close.

Her body fitted against his so perfectly that they might have been made for one another. There were times when he resented her burgeoning talent, when he felt as though she had cannibalised his genius and made it her own, but he never stopped wanting her.

He trembled in expectation of what was to come. He must have been mad, thinking he could leave her behind. A premonition of disaster lurked at the edge of his mind but he forced it away.

For good or ill, he loved Rouge.

CHAPTER NINETEEN

Monterey, 1931

Glory never imagined she would spend two years of her life on Santorini. It had been a time of sun-drenched pleasure – bathing on black sand beaches, investigating the ancient ruins of Akotiri and Thera, long walks in the hills, picnics of bread, cheese and olives on the cliffs overlooking the Sea of Crete.

But it had been a dream and, like all dreams, it didn't last. One day out of the blue, Dimitri announced the time had come to return to America. She had been as helpless to resist the decree as the tide is to resist the pull of the moon.

Now as a taxi left her in front of Tiny Czernik's boarding house, Glory felt as though she had spent the last four years wandering in a circle only to return to the place where she had started. She paid the driver, picked up her luggage and headed up the path. How sad to think the bits and pieces of her life fitted inside two suitcases.

She narrowed her eyes against the blazing sun and gazed at the riotous pink Victorian house while memories flooded her mind. She could almost see the girl she had been coming out in the night to meet her fate in the form of a Greek sculptor.

She had fallen in love with Dimitri on Tiny's porch with the bitter-sweet aroma of geraniums hanging in the air. So much had happened in the time since, that their first meeting seemed like ancient history.

She paused at the door and decided not to ring the bell. Tiny would be in the kitchen at this hour, putting finishing touches to supper. Glory couldn't wait to see her. She left her bags by the front door and walked into the entry.

The smell of pot roast and apple pie overwhelmed her. She pressed a hand against her mouth as bile rushed up her throat. God, she was so sick of feeling sick. It had been going on for weeks now. At first she had attributed it to something she ate or drank. Once she and Dimitri were aboard the ship that brought them to New York, she concluded it was *mal de mer*. Now she didn't know what ailed her.

When the nausea passed she continued down the passage, through the swinging doors and on into the kitchen. Tiny sat at the table, her back to the door, her feet propped up on a chair, taking a cigarette break.

Glory tiptoed up behind Tiny and covered her eyes. 'Guess who,' she said.

'Glory, is that you?' Tiny heaved to her feet with surprising speed and spun around, her fat rolls quivering. 'Land a goshen, girl, you scared the hell out of me. I wasn't expecting you and Dimitri so soon. Where is the handsome devil?'

Glory held up both hands in mock surrender. 'One question at a time. Dimitri is in New York.'

'Why didn't you stay with him?'

'I wasn't feeling well. I was sea sick all the way from Athens to New York. And I still don't seem to have my land legs.'

Instantly solicitous, Tiny pulled out a chair. 'You do look a bit peaked. Take a load off while I fix some camomile tea. It's guaranteed to settle your stomach.' She cut a sharp glance at Glory. 'I guess all that Greek food didn't agree with you.'

It felt wonderful to have Tiny fussing over her. 'The food was wonderful and so were the Konstantines. They treated me like a member of the family.'

Tiny lifted one brow. 'Are you?'

'Is that your way of asking if Dimitri and I got married in Greece?' Tiny nodded.

'The answer is no. If we ever do, though, you'll be the first to know.'

Tiny returned to the table a few minutes later with two steaming cups of fragrant tea and a plate of oatmeal cookies. 'Was Santorini as pretty as the pictures you sent?'

'Prettier. The quality of light was quite extraordinary.'

'Only you would talk about the damn light. Tell me where you went and what you did.'

Glory rummaged through her memories, wondering which ones Tiny would enjoy the most. Food came to mind. 'We stopped in

Athens on our way to the island and Dimitri gave me a grand tour of the Acropolis and the Plaka. That's the old part of town at the foot of the Acropolis. We dined in a different *taverna* every night. The food was inexpensive and very good. We ate things like lemon soup, sluvaki, stuffed grape leaves, yoghurt, and the most wonderful salads.' Glory paused long enough to sip the tea, hoping it would work as advertised. No wonder Dimitri had seemed relieved when she told him she wanted to leave New York. What man would want to spend time with a woman who threw up all the time?

'If I want a travelogue I'll go to the picture show,' Tiny said. 'How are things between you and Dimitri? Is he treating you right?'

'Things couldn't have been better on Santorini. You've seen him with his nieces and nephews here. He's a different man around children and there are lots of them in the family.'

'You keep on talking about Dimitri. What about you? Were you able to do any of that sculpture you're so crazy about?'

'Dimitri didn't want to go to the expense of setting up a studio.'

'Why not? Surely he needed to go on with his work.'

'It just seemed like a lot of trouble since he could sculpt in his father's workshop.'

'What about you?'

Tiny looked so indignant on her behalf that Glory couldn't help smiling. 'I wasn't welcome there. *O pateras* believes that carving stone is man's work. He's old-fashioned but very kind. He's so proud of Dimitri. He convinced a quarry owner to buy a couple of Dimitri's sculptures every year, provided they were done in marble from the quarry. The quarry owner persuaded the National Gallery to take one of the pieces into their permanent collection. Dimitri was in seventh heaven.'

'Glory, Glory,' Tiny said on a sigh, 'you certainly have changed.'

'In what way?'

'Before you left you talked about the work you were doing. Now it's Dimitri this and Dimitri that. I know you're proud of him but you have as much talent as he does, maybe more.'

'Sometimes an artist is best served by taking time out to think. I put my career on hold for a while, that's all.' The tea had settled Glory's stomach. She felt better than she had in weeks. 'Dimitri's happy when he's doing good work and he went from strength to strength on Santorini. A London dealer saw some of his pieces in Athens and asked to represent him.'

'It sounds as though Dimitri is having the success he's always wanted. I hope that means your money problems are over.'

'Dimitri doesn't talk about money. For all his liberal ideas, he's quite old-fashioned about some things.'

'I would never have guessed he'd be the keep-them-barefoot-and-pregnant type. Since Dimitri's career is back on track and you loved Santorini, what brought you back to the States?'

'Dimitri made up his mind not to exhibit in America for the time being. He's much more at home in Europe.'

'Where will you live?'

'In Paris. He's arranging to have his unsold pieces shipped to a gallery there.'

Tiny's brows lifted. 'What about the cabin?'

'He hopes to talk the Pomerances into buying it back.'

'I thought he tried that before you left.'

'He did. But the market had just crashed and Leah was worried about their finances.'

'What makes you think she'll change her mind now?'

'Leah corresponded with Dimitri once a week while we were away. From what she wrote, Court is still a wealthy man.'

'A lucky one too if he hung onto his money.' Tiny lit another cigarette and inhaled deeply, her expression sober and contemplative. 'You should see the soup lines and the poor men who are reduced to selling apples on street corners. Whole families are living in cardboard boxes under bridges. It's enough to break your heart. President Hoover doesn't do anything about it except to tell folks things aren't as bad as they think.'

Tiny could have gone on about the government for days. But there was no sense burdening Glory. She'd find out how things stood soon enough. Besides it was obvious the girl had problems of her own. She looked worn out. Thin too.

'How have you been doing?' Glory asked.

'All the rooms are rented but for the two where you and Dimitri used to stay. I lowered my prices a year ago.' She shrugged at the inadequacy of words to convey the anxiety that permeated the house and all who lived in it. 'I've never found a maid as good as you and my feet hurt like crazy. But we can talk about me later. I want to hear more about you. Why do you look like something the cat dragged in?'

'I don't know. I wasn't sea sick once on the trip to Athens but I couldn't keep a thing down on the way home. I guess I'd better see a doctor before I head up to Big Sur.'

Tiny took a long hard look at Glory. The girl's head was so full of Dimitri's coming and goings that she probably didn't know what ailed her. 'How long has it been since you had your monthlies?'

'I don't keep track. I've never been regular and with all the travelling—'

'I can save you the cost of a doctor's visit, honey,' Tiny interrupted. 'You're pregnant.'

Glory paled even more. 'That's impossible.'

'Are you telling me you and Dimitri haven't been sharing a bed?'

'No, but—'

'But what? It doesn't take an MD to put two and two together. You've been having regular sex. You can't remember the last time you fell off the roof. And you've been tossing your cookies for weeks. It's called morning sickness, honey.'

To Tiny's dismay, Glory burst into tears.

'I can't be pregnant,' Glory sobbed. 'It's one thing to live with a man. I made that choice and I'm not ashamed of it. It's another to bring a bastard into the world. I can't do that a child.'

'If I'm right, it's too late for that sort of talk.'

'If you're right, Dimitri Konstantine is going to have to marry me!'

Leah shook Court awake at one in the morning. 'Someone's in Dimitri's cabin,' she said.

Court blinked owlishly. 'How do you know?'

'Your snoring woke me. I couldn't get back to sleep so I went down to the kitchen for a glass of milk. That's when I saw the lights.'

'What lights?'

Leah repressed the urge to slap her husband. 'The lights in the cabin.' She handed him his robe and slippers. 'Put these on and get the gun.'

Leah had been in a heady state of anticipation since learning of Dimitri's imminent return. Although she'd kept the cabin and studio clean in his absence, she'd taken extra pains with both last week, waxing the floors, polishing the furniture, washing all the linen so it would smell sweet and fresh. It had been a labour of love and she'd be damned if some dirty drifter looking for a place to sleep was going to ruin her hard work. Everything had to be perfect for Dimitri.

Still yawning, Court took his revolver from the bedside table drawer and followed her downstairs. 'Shouldn't we call the police?' he asked.

'The Carmel police? God knows when they'd get here.'

She led the way through the door and along the path to the cabin. A strange car was parked at the front. 'You go in first,' she whispered, fitting the key in the lock.

'Why me?' Court whispered back.

'Because you have the gun.' She gave Court a shove. He stumbled into the cabin with her at his heels.

'Who the hell are you?' an overweight woman demanded as though she had every right to be there. Apparently the gun in Court's hand didn't intimidate her.

'I'm Leah Pomerance. Who are you and what are you doing here?' Leah shot back.

The fat woman walked towards them with her hand held out. 'Rouge told me about you. My name's Tina Czernik.'

Leah had no trouble placing the name. She remembered everything Dimitri had ever told her about his life. 'I presume you drove up from Monterey to ready the cabin for Dimitri. As you can see, though, you didn't need to bother.'

Before the woman could answer, Rouge walked in from the kitchen. 'Tiny didn't drive up to Big Sur to clean. She brought me.'

Seeing Rouge startled Leah. 'We weren't expecting you.'

'I can see that,' Rouge replied, her eyes going to the gun in Court's hand. 'Court, please put that away before you shoot someone.'

'Why didn't Dimitri bring you?' Leah demanded. If Rouge had done something to keep Dimitri away she'd strangle her – and smile while doing it.

'He had business to take care of,' Rouge replied. 'He should be here in a week or two.'

Rouge looked pale, thin and tired, Leah noted, and she sounded less than sure of herself. It wasn't hard to figure out why. For all her show of independence, Rouge wouldn't have travelled across the country by herself unless she and Dimitri weren't getting along.

Yes, indeed, Leah thought, there was trouble in paradise. 'Welcome home, Rouge,' she said with a satisfied smile.

When Dimitri returned to Big Sur two weeks later he found Rouge hard at work in the studio.

'I'm home,' he called out as he came through the door.

She turned and gave him a wan smile. 'I missed you.'

'Really?'

His gaze traversed the new terracotta sculptures drying on a shelf. They represented a new phase in Rouge's artistic development. Her work had often seemed a pale shadow of his. But these had an originality, a stunning vitality that made him envious. Glory had taken everything he'd taught her and added a new element.

On Santorini, when she hadn't made a scene about not working in his father's shop, he assumed she accepted the fact that her sculpture would always be second-rate. After months went by he concluded she had given up sculpture for good. Now he knew she had been playing a waiting game.

'It looks like you were too busy to miss anyone,' he said. 'You must be feeling better.'

She had the strangest look in her eyes – one he couldn't begin to decipher. 'I'm not better yet – but the doctor told me I will be soon.'

Thank God for small favours. He'd had enough of her puking to last a lifetime. 'Did he know what's been making you sick?'

She nodded. 'Perhaps you should sit down before I tell you.'

She sounded so serious that a tremor ran through him. There had been times here, in this studio, when he had come close to hating her. She'd been so insistent on having lessons and doing her own work at the expense of the things women were supposed to do, like cooking and cleaning and catering to their man. But all that had changed on Santorini. He'd attributed it to his family's influence and loved Rouge all the more for her willingness to change.

'What's wrong with you? Is it serious?'

Tears shimmered in her eyes. 'I'm carrying your child.'

'You're what?'

'I'm three months pregnant.'

He was so stunned, he didn't know what to say. When they first began sleeping together he considered using condoms. But he couldn't deny himself the pleasure of flesh to flesh contact. When month after month went by without Rouge becoming pregnant, he'd concluded she was one of those unfortunate women who couldn't conceive. He'd even felt a little sorry for her.

'Are you sure?' he asked.

'Absolutely. The rabbit died.' She stared at him so hard it made him uneasy. 'What are you thinking?'

Rouge made the question sound like an accusation. If ever there had been a time to speak the truth between them, this was it. 'I'm thinking I hadn't planned on this. The timing is all wrong. A child is a huge responsibility. But I'm also remembering how much I love my nieces and nephews. I've thought about having a child someday when I'm financially secure. I didn't expect someday to be six months away.'

'Do you hate the idea?' she asked.

'Sweet Rouge, I don't hate it at all. The truth is, I'm thrilled. I like knowing I planted a baby inside you. Come here, *chérie*.'

She walked into his arms and lowered her head to his shoulder. 'I'm so glad you feel that way. I'd like to get married as soon as possible.'

He jumped away from her so suddenly that she wobbled. 'Married? Where the hell did that come from? I didn't say anything about getting married.'

Colour flared on her pale cheeks. 'I just assumed, since you're happy about the baby—' her voice trailed off. Her tears dried up. She didn't look heartbroken. She looked angry. 'I don't want to bring a bastard into the world.'

'I thought you'd forgotten all your middle-class ideas. I don't have to put a ring on your finger to prove how much you mean to me. I show it every day with every breath I take. I'm your teacher, your provider, your mentor, as well as your lover. And now I'm going to be the father of your child – a child I truly want. I can't do more than that for you. I don't have it in me.'

CHAPTER TWENTY

Glory reached past her swollen belly to put the final touches to a clay sculpture. With the baby due in just two weeks, she wouldn't have the time or energy to begin another piece.

Tomorrow she and Dimitri planned to drive down to Monterey to await the birth at Tiny's. God only knew when she would find time to sculpt afterwards.

Her work complete, she gazed out at the dour autumnal day. The noon sun hadn't been able to pierce a wall of fog so thick that it hid the forest from view and muffled all sound. The gloomy weather reflected her mood. She felt as though she would never see the sun again.

Her pregnancy had been an emotional roller-coaster ride. None of it pleasant. The nausea lingered long after the doctor said it would end. Her ankles swelled. Her breasts ballooned. Her body felt so heavy, it seemed to weigh down her soul. She was expectant all right – but not of a blessed event. She had the ominous feeling that something terrible was about to happen.

Despite Dimitri's protestations of affection, the bigger she got, the more distant he became. He spent more time in Leah's kitchen these days than he did in the studio. Glory felt certain she knew why.

Her bloated body disgusted him. They hadn't made love since her fourth month – but who was counting?

Damn it, she was, she answered herself as she began to clean up the studio. Sex had been the glue that held them together. It had been the way they made up after an argument. It wasn't the act she missed as much as the afterglow, the sense of oneness that lingered on into the daylight.

She craved their lost intimacy – the feeling that they belonged to one another – the way an alcoholic craves a drink.

Dimitri had even taken to sleeping on the sofa in the parlour, saying their bed wasn't big enough for three and he wanted her to be as comfortable as possible. But that was just an excuse. He simply didn't love her any more.

If he had, he would have married her.

She choked back a sob. If only she had listened to her father when he warned her about the artistic life, she wouldn't be in this fix. She could almost hear her mother saying *as you sow, so shall you reap*. No matter what she achieved or how successful she became, she could never go home to Noble and Anna with a bastard clinging to her skirts.

Home. Now there was a word. A meaningless one in her case. Dimitri made her feel as though she lived in the Big Sur cabin on sufferance.

Glory knew her feelings were getting the better of her, but she was powerless to control them. She disliked self-pity and yet here she was wallowing in it. She felt more alone now with the child crowding her body than she had the day she left San Francisco.

Lately she couldn't stop thinking about her mother – and wondering if she hadn't inherited some of Anna's less desirable traits, including her melancholia. No matter how Glory tried she couldn't love the baby she was carrying any more than Anna had ever loved her.

The admission added to her sense of impending doom. She shook her head as if doing so could dispel her misery, then tried for a different perspective. The last six months hadn't been all bad, she reminded herself. She had spent them creating the sort of sculpture she envisioned on Santorini.

Her ability had grown in tandem with her belly. Twenty terracotta pieces and four waxes destined to be cast in bronze sat on the studio shelves. All but three of the terracottas had been fired, finished, and mounted on bases.

When they sold she would have the money to take the waxes to a foundry where they would be replicated in bronze. She intended to oversee the entire process from the making of the first mould, to the pouring of the molten metal, to applying the patina, even if she had to do it with the baby strapped to her back like a papoose. Somehow, she promised herself, she would find a way to be both an artist and a mother.

*

Dimitri enjoyed watching Leah cook. She wasn't beautiful like Rouge but in the kitchen, flushed from the heat of the stove, Leah radiated an earthy femininity that reminded him of the women in his family.

While Leah cored, peeled and sliced apples for a pie, he had talked to her about anything and everything except what was really on his mind.

However Leah had a way of seeing right through him. 'You're still upset with Rouge, aren't you?' she asked out of the blue.

He nodded. 'You were right about her all along. She cares more about her sculpture than she does about the baby or me.'

'You don't mean that,' Leah answered, taking dough from a bowl and rolling out a crust. 'Rouge may not be very domestically minded – but it would take a monster not to care about her unborn child.'

'I know you and Rouge are good friends but please don't make excuses for her. Her doctor told her to take it easy, to make sure she ate a balanced diet. Instead she spends day after day in the studio and half the time, she forgets to eat. It can't be good for the baby. If anything's wrong with the kid it will be her fault. I swear I'll never forgive her.'

He couldn't bring himself to confess that the excellence of Rouge's work upset him even more than the time she devoted to it. When he'd offered to give her art lessons he hadn't anticipated her becoming a sculptor who rivalled him.

Leah put the pie in the oven, walked over to him and laid a comforting hand on his shoulder. She was as easy to be around as Rouge was difficult.

'I hate seeing you so upset. I know it's interfering with your creativity.'

'I can't stand spending time in the studio with Rouge any more. I know it sounds insane, but sometimes I think she's a succubus who has drained away my talent.'

'I warned you about Rouge when she first came to live with you. She's very ambitious.'

'I wish I had listened.'

'So do I,' Leah replied, giving his shoulder a little squeeze.

Grateful for her concern, he turned and brushed her hand with his lips. It smelled of the spices she'd put in the pie. 'But for Rouge's pregnancy, I'd be in Paris now, readying for an exhibition, strolling the boulevards with my peers instead of being stuck here.'

'You've been so good, standing by Rouge the way you have.'

When the doctor told Rouge not to undertake the long trip to Paris until the baby was three months old, Leah had exulted in silence while commiserating with Dimitri out loud. His repugnance towards the physical aspects of Rouge's condition had been an unexpected bonus, Leah mused with a secretive smile. She and Dimitri had never been closer.

'I've never dared ask you this before but I can't help wondering—' Her voice trailed off as she waited for him to take the bait.

'Wondering what?'

'If you're certain the baby is yours?' Leah didn't dare look at Dimitri. She kept busy at the sink.

'Of course it's mine. Rouge has lots of flaws but screwing around isn't one of them.'

Leah stayed at the sink so Dimitri couldn't see the merry gleam in her eyes as she drove another verbal nail into Rouge's coffin. 'I'm glad to hear that for your sake. I would hate to think of the sacrifices you've made the last few months—' Again she let her voice fade away.

Experience had taught her to be wary of pushing Dimitri too far. She had succeeded in driving a wedge between the sculptor and his whore when they returned from Greece. She was widening that breach every day, innuendo by innuendo. In time it would gape so wide that not even a child would bridge it. And when that happened Dimitri would be hers.

'I don't know what I'd do if I didn't have you to talk to,' Dimitri said.

'You'll never have to find out. I'll always be here for you. You know that.'

She looked up from her work, gazed out the window, and saw Rouge heading from the studio to the cabin. Suddenly Rouge staggered, then stopped and clutched her belly as if she were in pain. What was the bitch up to now? If her act was a ploy for sympathy, she'd get none in this house.

Ignoring what she'd seen, Leah returned to peeling vegetables for supper. If she knew Rouge, the whore would soon come knocking on the door.

The severity of the second pain took Glory by surprise. It was so much stronger than the cramp she'd felt in the studio. She thought the first one had been brought on by spending too many hours on her feet sculpting – and that all she needed was rest. She couldn't ignore this one, though. Her labour had begun.

As the sensation eased she changed direction and headed for the Pomerances' house to fetch Dimitri. She'd been concerned about giving birth and relieved that it would take place in a hospital in Monterey. She and Dimitri would have to leave immediately or they wouldn't get there in time.

The pain came again as she knocked on the Pomerances' door. She felt as though a giant hand was squeezing her abdomen. The doctor had assured her that first babies took a long time being born. Hers seemed to be in a hurry.

Court opened the door and peered at her over the rim of his reading glasses. As usual, he was completely self-absorbed and oblivious to her plight.

'Oh dear,' he said, 'I just had an idea for the most fabulous rhyme and now you've driven it away.'

'Please get Dimitri,' Glory said with a gasp.

'Isn't he with you?'

'For God's sake, Court, you must know he spends most of his time in your kitchen with Leah. Just get him.'

'My, aren't we grumpy today.' Court ambled off with no assurance that he would do as Glory asked.

Glory had never felt at home in Leah's house. Under ordinary circumstances she would have waited in the hall until Dimitri came. But the circumstances were far from ordinary today. Walking with infinite care so as not to bring on another contraction, she made her way to the kitchen.

Dimitri sat at the table with his back towards the door. Leah was refilling his coffee cup. They looked as comfortable with one another as an old married couple.

'Have you decided what you're going to do?' Leah asked Dimitri.

Do about what? Glory wondered. She didn't wait for Dimitri's answer. 'It's time to go to the hospital,' she said.

He bolted from the chair and wheeled to face her. 'If that's your idea of a joke it's not funny.'

'I didn't mean it to be. I'm in labour.'

'The baby isn't due for a couple of weeks,' Dimitri protested.

'Apparently the baby doesn't know that.'

'How long have you been having contractions?' Leah asked.

'I'm not sure. I had a backache all morning but I didn't pay attention until I finished the sculpture I was working on.'

'How far apart are the pains?' Leah barked out the question like a drill sergeant with a recalcitrant recruit.

'About five minutes, I think.' Glory turned her attention back to Dimitri. 'We really should get going.'

'Are you out of your mind?' he burst out, sounding less sure of himself than usual. 'What if you have the baby on the way?'

'That isn't the only problem,' Leah interjected. 'It could be a dangerous trip in the fog.'

'We don't have any choice. I'm not going to have the baby here.'

'Rouge, how could you do this to me?' Dimitri demanded as the fight that had been shimmering between them for months threatened to boil over.

'Do what?' she shot back. 'Get pregnant. As I recall you're the one who didn't want to use a French safe.' Before she could say more, another pain enveloped her.

'You damn well know what I mean. If you had followed the doctor's orders you wouldn't be giving premature birth. If anything happens to the child, I'll—'

'You'll what? Leave me?' The questions emerged from between Glory's clenched jaws. 'You already have in every way that matters.'

'Now, now, you two,' Leah intervened. 'This isn't the time or place to air your grievances. I had better call the doctor and see what he advises. In the meantime, Dimitri, help Rouge into a chair.' Leah went to the wall phone, dialled the operator and asked for the doctor's office.

Dimitri came over to Glory and attempted to put his arm around her heaving sides. Still angry, she pushed him away, sat down unaided and buried her head in her hands. Was Dimitri right? Had she brought on a premature delivery? Perhaps the doctor had been wrong about the due date? Certainly, she hadn't been any help when it came to pinpointing the time of conception. Dimitri had made hot, hungry love to her every night on Santorini like a man who, having starved once, could never get enough to eat.

Leah put the phone back in its cradle, sat down beside Glory and

203

took her hand. Dimitri's anger hadn't undone Glory. Leah's unexpected kindness almost did.

'What did the doctor say?' Glory asked, swallowing the lump in her throat.

'I'm afraid he wasn't much help. The fog is even worse in Carmel and there's been a terrible automobile accident. He'll be tied up for hours. But he told me what to do.'

'Have you ever delivered a baby?' Glory asked.

Leah shook her head. 'I'm sure you'll be all right, though. Lots of women give birth without any help. You're a strong, healthy young woman.'

'I've seen goats, sheep and dogs give birth,' Dimitri offered, his voice devoid of anger as though he had finally taken in the seriousness of the situation.

'I'm sure that will be a big help,' Glory replied sarcastically. She turned to the woman who had been her nemesis and now seemed her only hope. 'What do we do now?'

'Get you to bed.'

'Will you help me back to the cabin?'

'Not the cabin. Here. In our guest room,' Leah replied. 'You know how helpless Court is. I can't leave him.'

Within an hour Dimitri knew his experiences with animals in labour were not applicable to childbirth. Seeing Rouge in pain made him feel helpless – and feeling helpless made him angry. He blamed Rouge for their predicament and in the next breath prayed for her safe delivery.

When he couldn't deal with his conflicted emotions another minute he went downstairs to the library and asked Court to make a Martini. But all the gin in the world couldn't inure him to the sound of Rouge's anguished cries.

His increasingly frantic calls to the doctor produced no results. An impatient nurse told Dimitri the doctor was in surgery, sewing up accident victims and setting bones.

Just before midnight Dimitri was on his way back upstairs, having finished his fifth Martini, when Leah called for him. 'The baby is coming Dimitri. Get the hell in here. I need your help.'

The summons banished his alcohol-induced fog. He arrived in the room to find Rouge sitting up, her face distorted with effort, clutching the bed posts, her legs wide spread. Her pubic mound was so distorted that it bore no resemblance to the place he had tongued with so much pleasure. He stood transfixed, watching the distortion enlarge. Suddenly he saw a mop of sticky wet black hair.

'Oh my God, it's the baby,' he gasped. 'What should I do?'

Leah shoved a towel into his hands. 'Catch the baby as soon as it comes out and I'll cut the umbilical cord.'

Dimitri's knees shook as he positioned himself like a catcher at a baseball game. Afraid the child would be malformed, he closed his eyes.

'You'd better look!' Leah told him with a real edge in her voice.

Repelled yet fascinated, he watched the child emerge from between Rouge's heaving thighs. First the head, then the neck and shoulders and finally, the entire baby was revealed to his view.

A girl, a perfect girl, he thought as Leah cut the umbilical cord that attached the child to Rouge. At that moment, holding the infant between his own strong hands, feeling its frailty and utter dependence, he experienced an upwelling of love so powerful that it brought tears to his eyes.

No one had to tell him to turn the child over and slap its buttocks, or to towel away the signs of its passage down the birth canal. He felt as though he'd been waiting his whole life for this moment. The baby's first wail blended with his own triumphant cry.

'Is the baby all right?' Rouge asked in a hoarse voice.

'Fine? She's magnificent,' Dimitri exulted. He held the child up, not to show to Rouge but to see her better himself. 'By heaven, with that black hair she's a Konstantine through and through. She looks just like me.'

Although he hadn't given any thought to a name during the months of Rouge's pregnancy, the perfect one came to him now. 'I'm going to call her Ariadne. It means the divine one,' he announced, cradling his tiny daughter against his broad chest.

Glory was too weary to argue with Dimitri's choice. She had imagined she would feel exultant at the first sight of her infant. Instead she'd been too exhausted to take a good look. The pain of bringing her into the world was too recent to be forgotten. Glory felt as if her joints had been prised apart. Her muscles ached and the child had torn the tender tissue of her mons.

She was vaguely aware of Leah stripping away the soiled linen beneath her hips. When Leah finished, she pulled the covers up over Glory. 'Would you like to hold the baby now?'

'Yes, please,' Glory replied. Her throat was hoarse from the screams she hadn't been able to hold back.

'Give the baby to Rouge for a minute,' Leah told Dimitri.

He brought it over and put the child in Glory's arms. She held it a moment, waiting for the feeling of fulfilment and happiness she'd been told to expect. Instead all she felt was a bone-deep weariness and an echo of sorrow, like a distant voice calling to her.

'I just want to rest,' she said.

Dimitri immediately snatched the baby back up and carried it from the room. Leah, with her arms full of linen, trotted at his heels. But Glory didn't see them go. She had already drifted away on the wine dark sea of sleep.

There had been a time after marrying Court when Leah wanted children. However after realising what a child he was she'd been glad she didn't conceive. Having reached her forty-first year, she'd closed that particular door.

Until tonight.

Leah had never done anything more thrilling than delivering Rouge's child. Leah loved Ariadne already. And not just because she was Dimitri's, although she would have loved any child of his blood.

She loved this one even more because she had helped bring her into the world.

'What now?' Dimitri asked when they reached the bottom of the stairs.

Leah put the bedclothes down on a chair and held out her hands. 'Give me the baby so you can go to the cabin and bring her things back with you.'

'I planned to spend what's left of the night in my own bed.'

'Don't be silly. The doctor said Glory will need two weeks of total rest and you certainly can't take care of her. The three of you are more than welcome here.'

'Shouldn't you ask Court?'

'You know how he is. He'll agree with anything I want.'

While Dimitri returned to the cabin Leah took Ariadne to the kitchen to give her a sponge bath. On the way she passed Court in the library, loudly sleeping off what appeared to be a monumental drunk if the empty gin bottle was any indication.

The miracle of birth had taken place under Court's roof but he neither knew nor cared. The man has no soul, Leah thought, then dismissed him from her mind as she pressed the baby to her bosom.

Little Ariadne chirped during her bath like a baby bird. Leah revelled in the sound. She really was a beautiful child, the image of her handsome father, Leah decided as she wrapped the infant in a fresh towel.

She held Ariadne with one arm, picked up the phone and asked the operator to connect her with the doctor again. This time he actually came to the phone.

She filled him in on the birth and he assured her that it had been perfectly normal and that he'd get up to see the mother and child as soon as he could.

'What should I feed the baby?' she asked when he finished.

'Her mother's milk is the best thing in the world for her,' the doctor replied.

'What if the mother doesn't have enough milk or she doesn't want to nurse. What do I do then?'

The doctor told Leah how to prepare a formula, then added, 'Don't be in a hurry to give the child a bottle. New-borns do quite well for hours without being fed.'

'Oh I won't,' Leah said earnestly.

'Won't what?' Dimitri asked, walking into the kitchen with a suitcase in one hand and a couple of baby bottles in the other.

Leah hushed him with a gesture, then said goodbye to the doctor before answering. 'The doctor told me not to let Ariadne go hungry while Glory is sleeping. Why don't you hold her while I make up her bottles.'

An hour later, dressed in a gown and swaddled in a blanket, her tummy full of milk, Leah and Dimitri put Ariadne to sleep in the second guest room. They stood side by side, gazing down at the infant in her makeshift laundry basket crib.

'I don't know how to thank you for everything you did tonight,' Dimitri told Leah, then turned and gently kissed her lips.

She swore she could hear the triumphant blare of trumpets. Dimitri was as good as hers – and Ariadne along with him. She was going to have it all, the man of her dreams and the child too. She controlled the urge to deepen the kiss. All in due time, she told herself.

She walked to the bedroom door, then turned to Dimitri. 'You don't need to thank me. Taking care of you and little Ariadne is going to be pure joy.'

CHAPTER TWENTY-ONE

Six weeks after Ariadne's birth Glory lay on her bed enduring the daily rest Leah insisted she take. She could hear Leah moving around the cabin doing the chores that were properly hers – and undoubtedly doing them better.

Little by little Leah had usurped her place and now Glory didn't know what to do about it. She didn't want to seem like an ingrate but she wanted her life back. Only she wasn't sure she had the strength to wrest it away from Leah.

She had read articles in women's magazines about the joys of motherhood. Nothing had prepared her for the tribulations. The authors had been far too delicate to mention the fact that urinating burned a new mother's private parts, that her bowels didn't function the way they used to, that her breasts ached with excess milk, and that the simple act of sitting in a chair would make her wince.

Glory could have happily endured all of it, though, if only Ariadne had welcomed her mother. But the baby fussed and fretted and turned away from Glory's breast every time she tried to nurse her. Watching Leah bottle-feed Ariadne, seeing the contented baby go to sleep in Leah's arms, had hurt most of all.

She could hardly wait to leave Leah behind when she, Ariadne and Dimitri moved to Paris. The trip would give her a second chance to be a mother. It was her last hope, she mused, as tears spurted in her eyes.

God, what was the matter with her? She had cried more in the last few weeks than she had in her entire life. Could the baby sense her depression, her uncertainty? Was that why Ariadne preferred Leah just as she had preferred Ellen over Anna? Had she inherited Anna's melancholia?

The question raced through Glory's brain like an electric current, jolting her into action. She would rather die than live the way her mother had, she thought as she swung her legs over the side of the

209

bed and got up. She squared her shoulders and marched into the living room.

Leah was seated in the rocker, swaying back and forth while Ariadne cooed and gurgled in her lap.

'What are you doing up?' Leah demanded. 'You're supposed to rest for thirty more minutes.'

'I'm finished with naps,' Glory declared – and finished doing what Leah told her, she silently added.

'But the doctor—'

'Never mind the damn doctor. I know how I feel.'

'Really, Rouge. There's no need to get all worked up.'

Leah looked so wounded that for a moment, Glory almost apologised. 'I appreciate everything you've done for us but I'm sure Court misses you and needs you at home.'

'Court is fine as long as he gets three meals a day.'

Glory walked over to the rocker and held her hands out. 'I'd like to hold my daughter.'

'I'll get up and you can take my place.' Leah's tone was placating but Glory felt certain she saw something implacable and cold in her gaze.

Leah would just have to get over her misplaced motherly feelings, Glory thought as she settled in the rocker and gazed down at her daughter. For once Ariadne didn't fuss at her. She had Dimitri's dark hair but the dimple in her chin clearly marked her as Glory's child. Her eyes were dark blue, her nose perfectly formed.

Sweet, sweet, baby, I'm going to take care of you from now on, Glory vowed. She glanced up to see Leah hovering nearby as if she didn't trust Glory with the baby.

'You can go home now,' Glory said.

'I'm afraid that's not your decision. Dimitri asked me to take care of Ariadne. I'll go home when he tells me to and not a minute sooner.'

Glory knew a declaration of war when she heard one. Holding Ariadne tight, she got to her feet. 'Since you feel that way we had better talk to him now.'

Just then, the doorbell rang.

'If that's Court he's going to get a piece of my mind. I've told him and told him the bell wakes the baby,' Leah said, hurrying to answer it.

She yanked the door open to reveal a stranger.

'You must be Mrs Konstantine,' the man said, doffing his hat at Leah. He wore a flamboyant white suit, a white on white shirt that matched his perfect white teeth and set off a terrific tan.

'I'm Leah Pomerance, a close friend of Mr Konstantine's,' Leah replied.

The stranger advanced into the room without being invited. 'Then you must be Mrs Konstantine,' he said to Glory.

Embarrassment flamed on her cheeks. She could hardly tell this stranger she was Dimitri's lover. 'There is no Mrs Konstantine.'

The man came closer. 'Have we met before? You look very familiar.' Before she could answer, he exclaimed, 'You must be Rouge. I've seen several sculptures you posed for. But the bronzes didn't do you justice.'

Glory felt her blush intensify. 'And who might you be?'

He held out his hand, displaying a perfect manicure and an enormous diamond. 'Maurie Golden of the Golden Gallery in Los Angeles at your service. I was in the area. I'm a great fan of Mr Konstantine's so I thought I'd take a chance on his being here.'

'Pleased to meet you, Mr Golden,' Glory replied.

'Is the great one at home?' Golden asked.

It took Glory a moment to realise he meant Dimitri. 'He's in the studio.'

'Even better.' Golden rubbed his hands together like a man about to sit down to a feast. 'Seeing him at work would be an honour and a privilege.'

'Dimitri doesn't permit strangers inside the studio.'

'He won't mind me,' Golden replied, moving to the door. 'In a manner of speaking we're old acquaintances.'

Glory searched her memory for some recollection of Golden's name, then glanced at Leah, hoping for reinforcement.

Instead Leah said, 'You can leave the baby with me while you take Mr Golden to the studio.'

Glory had no choice but to give Ariadne to Leah and follow the dealer.

'When did you meet Dimitri?' she asked, leading the way to the studio.

'I haven't. But I do know his work.' Golden gave her an impish grin. 'The art world is a small one. I'd have run into Mr Konstantine sooner or later. This way it's sooner.'

211

Glory knocked on the studio door, then opened it and preceded Golden inside. Dimitri was nailing the cover on a crate. Perspiration stained his shirt. Scraps of wood and particles of sawdust littered the floor. He had packed his sculptures himself to save money.

'What do you want?' he asked, not bothering to look up.

'There's someone here to see you.'

'Get rid of whoever it is.'

'Dimitri, he's here with me.'

Golden didn't appear to have heard the exchange. He had walked over to the shelves that held her terracotta sculptures. 'Marvellous, simply marvellous,' he said.

'Mr Golden is a Los Angeles art dealer. He drove up here especially to meet you.' Glory hoped the implied compliment would defuse the anger she saw on Dimitri's face.

Golden finally tore his gaze from her work and turned to Dimitri. 'I can't tell you how pleased I am to meet you at long last, sir.'

Dimitri ignored the hand Golden held out. 'As you can see I'm busy.'

'Of course you are, sir. An artist of your stature is always busy. I'll just take a moment of your time. I've told your – ah – your friend, Miss Rouge, how much I admire your work. I couldn't pass up the opportunity to see more of it.' His raisin dark eyes returned to the terracottas. 'Do I detect a change in your style?'

Dimitri ignored the question. 'You should have called first. If you had you would have been told I no longer show in American galleries.'

Golden's eyes widened. 'Surely you don't plan to leave those magnificent terracottas behind?'

'They're not mine.'

'If you didn't do them who did? I drove up from Carmel to discuss exhibiting your work in my gallery. Since you're not available I'd like to talk to this other sculptor.'

'They're mine,' Glory burst out.

She had been sick at leaving her best work, the fruit of months of hard work, behind because Dimitri didn't think they were worth the cost of shipping. Perhaps this Maurie Golden had an alternative in mind. She didn't even care if he wanted to give them away – as long as he wouldn't throw them out.

'Where did you get them?'

'I didn't get them. I created them. They're my work.'

'Well – if that doesn't beat all!' Golden declared.

Dimitri had quite enough of both the dealer and Rouge. 'As I said, Mr Golden, you're interrupting my work.'

Neither Golden or Rouge appeared to have heard him. They were staring at one another as though they'd discovered the holy grail.

'Do you really like my sculpture?' Rouge asked.

'Like it? Dear lady, I love it. You could make quite an impact on the LA art scene. Movie people are so conscious of beauty. They'd fall over themselves to buy your work.'

Dimitri wasn't accustomed to being ignored by art dealers, especially not in his own studio. 'Just what do you have in mind?' he demanded of Golden.

'Are you Miss Rouge's agent?' Golden shot back.

'She doesn't need an agent. Her work isn't ready for the gallery scene.'

'I beg to differ with you. Perhaps you're too close to the situation to see her talent as clearly as I do.'

'I'm not so close that I don't know a con artist when I see and hear one.'

Golden's chest puffed up. His eyes narrowed. 'You can check my bona fides with anyone. Call Goldwyn or Chaplin or Garbo. They all buy from me.'

Dimitri never went to movies. The names of famous stars didn't impress him. 'Rouge is a novice. I'm not. So don't bother making empty promises. The American art market fell apart along with the American stock market.'

Golden held up a hand in protest. 'I beg to differ. The American art market is taking a breather. That's all. In any case it doesn't apply to LA. The movie business has thrived like no other since the crash. The public is hungry for fantasy and Hollywood pumps it out day after day, reel after reel.'

'What the hell does that have to do with art?'

'The majority of my clients are in the motion picture business. They have more money than they can possibly spend. They're enthusiastic if uneducated collectors and many of them rely on me to tell them what to buy.'

The little man sounded so convincing that Dimitri couldn't help wondering if he'd been wrong to write Golden off as a con artist. At the very least he was one hell of a salesman. If he was being truthful

213

his gallery represented a *golden* opportunity in more ways than one.

Before Dimitri could say anything, Golden had turned back to Rouge. 'Do you show in any other galleries?'

'No, but I have sold a few pieces on my own.'

'Better and better,' Golden replied. The little man practically danced with enthusiasm. 'You're the answer to my prayers.'

'And what prayers are those?' Dimitri asked sourly, wondering if Golden's enthusiasm had more to do with the bedroom than the gallery.

'Every dealer dreams of discovering a genius like your – ah – friend, Miss Rouge,' Golden replied without hesitation.

Dimitri shook his head. He couldn't deny Rouge's work had improved since the hiatus she took in Santorini, however he wouldn't have called her a genius. Far from it. He saw more to criticise in her new pieces than he ever had in the old ones.

What the hell was going on here? Golden had come to see him, not Rouge. Golden had wanted to represent him, not Rouge. How had things become so twisted?

'I'd love to be in your gallery,' Rouge was saying with a butter-wouldn't-melt-in-her-mouth smile. 'I've dreamed something like this would happen someday. I didn't think it would happen so soon.'

'Why not? You're more than ready,' Golden replied. 'Your work is mature, well conceived and your execution is flawless.'

Rouge glanced sidelong at Dimitri and he swore he read triumph in her eyes. To hell with her, he thought with mounting fury. She'd soon see how rough it was in the marketplace.

She turned back to Golden. 'It's nice to hear those things from someone like you.'

'You'll soon be hearing them from collectors.' Golden struck his forehead with the heel of his palm. 'I've just had a brainstorm. I'm holding a show for a renowned painter in a few months. April the tenth to be exact. I could use some sculpture to round out the exhibition. Would you be interested?'

'Are you serious?' Rouge's eyes shone like a child's on Christmas morning.

'Of course.'

'Then I accept.'

Dimitri's temper snapped. 'The hell you will. We'll be in Paris by then.'

Rouge gave him a blank look as if she didn't know what he was talking about.

'Damn it, Rouge,' he said, his voice rising with every word, 'how can you be so selfish? I put the move off because of your pregnancy. I won't do it again. I'm going to Paris with Ariadne and I expect you to go with us.'

After Rouge and Golden left, Leah put Ariadne down for a nap. Anxious for an excuse to find out what was happening in the studio she made a pot of coffee, filled a plate with biscuits and put them on a tray. She heard Dimitri shouting before she opened the studio door and walked in.

'What's this about putting the Paris trip off again?' she asked, looking from Dimitri to Rouge and Golden and then back again.

'This man,' Dimitri jerked his head at Golden, 'wants Rouge to do a show in his gallery in April.'

'How exciting for Rouge,' Leah replied.

Smiling sweetly, she put the tray down on the nearest table, then walked over to Dimitri and put a hand on his arm. Instinct told her this might be the moment she'd been waiting for – a tailor-made opportunity to drive a final wedge between Rouge and Dimitri.

'In case you've forgotten, Rouge is supposed to be in Paris with me and our daughter in April.'

Leah had known Dimitri was jealous of Rouge's burgeoning artistic ability and had played on his resentment. Now fate had handed her the *coup de grâce*. 'Rouge shouldn't pass up such a marvellous opportunity. I think I can come up with a way to make all of you happy, to say nothing of myself,' she told Dimitri.

'What the hell might that be?'

'I could go to Paris in Rouge's place – to care for the baby. I've been dying to go abroad but Court is such a stick in the mud that he has yet to take me.'

Rouge looked as surprised as a pole-axed steer. 'Leah, would you really do that for me?'

Leah choked down a laugh. Rouge thought she was going to catch the brass ring when in fact the true prize would soon belong to Leah. Both of them!

'We've shared a very special bond these last six weeks, my dear, and you know I adore Ariadne. I couldn't love her more if she were

215

my own. I've been dreading saying goodbye. If you and Dimitri accept my offer I won't have to for a while.'

'What about Court?' Rouge asked.

'Once I'm in Paris he'll be sure to follow. The two of you could even travel together.'

Dimitri had the strangest look in his eyes. 'Are you sure you wouldn't mind?'

She squeezed his arm. 'There's nothing in the world I'd rather do. The trip would be the answer to my prayers.'

Golden spoke up. 'I must say Mrs Pomerance, you are one in a million.'

Leah accepted his compliment with a gracious nod. 'I brought coffee for four. However you and Rouge have things to discuss and I don't like leaving the baby alone even though she is napping. Dimitri, why don't you walk back to the cabin with me?'

'What the hell was that all about?' Dimitri asked once they were alone in the parlour. 'It isn't like you to interfere.'

'That was about solving your problems and mine,' Leah answered serenely.

Dimitri's gaze probed hers. 'What do you mean?'

Leah had spent years laying the groundwork for what she said next. 'I think it's time we were honest with each other. We're too close for you to pretend. You're much too honourable to complain about Rouge but I know how you feel. I've seen it in your eyes when you look at her. The truth is I feel the same way about Court.'

'What way is that?'

'We don't wish them any harm but our lives would be so much easier without them. Isn't that so, dearest?'

'You certainly know how to lay it on the line.'

'Am I wrong?'

'You would have been yesterday. After what just happened in the studio the answer is no. You were right years ago when you told me Rouge cared more about art than she did about me. I never imagined it would extend to our child. But you heard her. She doesn't give a damn about leaving Ariadne.'

'I hate to see you so unhappy,' Leah said.

'I'm not unhappy. I'm angry. I don't understand Rouge and I'm sick of trying. I need to concentrate on my work and I can't with her around.'

Leah put an arm around his waist. 'She's not worth it. There's no reason to let her make your life miserable.'

'What else can I do? We have a child together.'

'You already said she doesn't care about Ariadne. She's ambitious. She wants a career first and a family second – if she wants one at all.'

'What do you mean?'

'Women like Rouge like to be footloose and fancy free.'

'You're wrong about that.' Dimitri sounded uncertain.

No matter how angry he was at the moment, he needed one more push. 'Haven't you ever noticed the way she acts around Court? He's mad about her and she knows it. The two of them will probably have a very good time once we're out of the picture.'

Dimitri looked startled. 'Do you really think so?'

'I know so. Court is a very wealthy man. Rouge is a beautiful woman. You know what they say about the mouse playing once the cat's away. I doubt the two of them will ever follow us to Paris.'

'And if they do, what then?'

'My dear Dimitri, between the two of us I'm sure we can find a way to keep that from happening.'

Glory couldn't believe her good luck – although Maurie Golden said it wasn't luck at all. She looked out of the train window as it climbed the coastal range to Big Sur but she didn't see the rolling hills. Instead she saw the fashionable crowd that had filled the Golden Gallery two days ago, buying up her work as if it were the best thing since sliced bread. For the first time in her life she had felt like a real artist rather than a postulant.

'I knew you'd hit it big!' Maurie declared after closing time. 'Did you hear the way Claudette Colbert carried on when she was trying to decide which piece to buy? You're going to get one hell of a cheque at the end of the month.'

Apparently Maurie Golden had never heard that the most a woman artist could hope for was a small career, Glory thought, as she settled herself more comfortably for the long ride. The money didn't mean as much to her as the affirmation of her talent and the decision she had made when she left San Francisco five years ago.

She had hated being away from Ariadne for even one day, let alone the weeks it had taken to get ready for the show. It had broken her heart to wave goodbye to her baby girl the day Dimitri and Leah left. For a second Dimitri had looked even more upset, so much so that she'd had the fleeting idea he might cancel the trip and wait for her. His parting words had been peculiar too.

'No matter what happens, promise me you'll take care of yourself,' he'd said.

'Don't worry about Glory,' Leah had interjected. 'She can look out for herself if anyone can – and Court too.'

In the weeks since Dimitri's departure with Ariadne, Glory had made herself face the unhappy truth. Dimitri had never returned to her bed after Ariadne's birth and he wasn't the sort of man to go without a woman for ever. One of these days another one was bound to catch his eye and she and Ariadne would have to move on.

Doing the show for Mr Golden had launched her career and given her a measure of financial independence at a time when she needed it most – for Ariadne's sake as well as her own.

Court had been in a muddle since Leah left with Dimitri and the baby seven weeks earlier. He hadn't understood why he couldn't travel to Paris with them until Leah explained that it wouldn't be right for Rouge to make the trip by herself. He rather fancied himself in the role of Rouge's protector.

He could hardly wait for her to get back from Los Angeles today so the two of them could set off for Gay Paree. Today? Yes, it was today he decided as he looked down at the rubber band on his finger.

He'd put it there to remind himself to pick her up at the train station at noon. There was no trick to remembering important things if you had a system, he reassured himself as he settled in the study with pencil and paper.

The one good thing about being alone was having all the time in the world to write. He knocked the dottle from his pipe, refilled it, took a contented puff and closed his eyes. The smell of something burning woke him some time later. He looked down and realised the something was his woollen vest.

His pipe must have fallen onto his chest when he was asleep, he thought as he flailed at the smouldering wool. He had succeeded in putting the last ember out and taking the vest off when the doorbell rang.

He checked his watch, saw it was one in the afternoon and hurried to answer the summons, thinking he would find a disgruntled Rouge waiting on his doorstep.

'Are you Mr Court Pomerance?' a strange man asked when Court opened the door.

'I'm not certain,' Court replied, grinning at his own joke.

'I have a telegram for Mr Pomerance,' the man said, holding out a yellow envelope.

'I'm he,' Court replied, smiling happily. 'My wife is in Paris, France. It must be from her.'

Leah wasn't much of a letter writer. He hadn't expected to hear from her. She must miss him. Pleasure coursed through him at the thought. Dear Leah wasn't as independent as she pretended to be.

When the man continued to stand there with his hand held out, Court realised he was waiting for a tip. He reached in his pocket for a handful of change and dropped it in the man's palm. He was so anxious to read what Leah had to say that he didn't even bother to count it.

'Thanks a lot,' the man said, tipping his cap. 'I hope it's good news.'

Court shut the door and hurried to the library. He put on the glasses he'd left there and tore the envelope open. A thin sheet of yellow paper lay inside.

Dear Court, Leah's message read, *I have very bad news.*

Court read the typed words three times over before their meaning sank in. When he finally understood what had happened, he put his head in his hands and wept.

Glory was so happy to be home that she wasn't upset when Court didn't pick her up at the train station, even though she had called to remind him last night. Leah had told her Court was a seasoned traveller who would look after her on the way to Paris. But she had always suspected the opposite. She would have to watch out for him.

She walked to the post office to see if she could get a lift from someone who'd come to get their mail. A logger's wife was happy to oblige.

When they pulled up in front of the cabin the curtains were closed just as Glory had left them. The place looked deserted already.

'Do you want me to come in with you?' the logger's wife asked as Glory lifted her bag from behind the front seat.

'I'll be fine,' Glory replied, sending the woman off with a jaunty wave.

More than fine, she added to herself. In three days she'd be on her way to Ariadne. She put the key in the lock and opened the door.

The parlour was so dark that she almost missed the telegram someone had shoved under the door. Suddenly, for no reason, her heart lurched. She put her bag down, tore the envelope open and turned on the light.

Ridiculous the way her hands were shaking, she told herself. She had no reason to feel fearful. Dimitri had promised to wire the address as soon as he rented an apartment and yet she couldn't control the dread that iced her blood.

Dear Glory, the message began, *I'm sorry to have to tell you that Ariadne died of diphtheria three days ago. We buried her this morning. Dimitri is so distraught that he asked me to send this telegram in his place. I have tried to reason with him but he blames you for not being here. He doesn't want to see you again, now or in the future. Please don't attempt to contact him. It will only make things worse. Leah.*

Tears poured down Glory's face. She screamed Ariadne's name over and over as if she could call her back from a foreign grave. She'd been so healthy. She couldn't be gone.

The thought of her dying alone without her mother to hold her, to comfort her, to love her, was too terrible to contemplate. Glory wished she could die but her heart kept right on beating.

She continued crying out Ariadne's name for hours. Birds in the trees flew away at the sound and forest creatures hid in their burrows. At sunset no light showed in the cabin window, no fire warmed the hearth.

Glory had travelled beyond grief to a place deep inside her brain the pain couldn't reach.

PART FIVE

Glory

What a man *is* begins to betray itself when his
talent decreases – when he stops showing what he
can do. Talent, too, is finery; finery, too, is a
hiding place.
Nietzsche – *Beyond Good and Evil*, 1886

CHAPTER TWENTY-TWO

San Francisco, 1932

Saul Steiner had such memorable turquoise eyes that women thought him handsome despite his scimitar nose. Freckles looked incongruous on so imposing a beak yet there they were, dotting the bridge and spreading onto Saul's cheeks with the punctilious pointillism of a Seurat painting. The freckles coupled with wiry strawberry blond hair to make him look younger than his forty-five years.

Saul's mother believed his magnificent eyes were wasted on a man. His wife Rose disagreed. She had fallen in love with the beauty of her husband's eyes – and then with the intellect shining in them.

Saul Steiner was that rarest of individuals who, despite having inherited a fortune, refused to sit back and rest on his ancestors' laurels. Born into San Francisco's *haute monde*, he'd endured years of hardship as a medical student, intern and resident, to become a psychiatrist of note.

Although he had a large and lucrative practice the greatest challenge to his skill and humanity came from his *pro bono* work at the Atwood State Hospital, where he had a well-earned reputation for helping the most intransigent cases.

This morning he sat in the director's office discussing the imminent release of one of his patients. 'I'm glad he responded to psychotherapy,' Saul said. 'I've read Manfred Sakel's claims for insulin shock, however in view of the physical trauma, I'm reluctant to use it at this experimental stage.'

'But you would – use it that is,' the director pressed.

'Only as a last resort,' Saul replied.

The director took a file from the top of his desk and passed it to Saul. 'You may have to in this case.'

Saul opened the file and looked through the slim contents. 'There's certainly not much to go on in here,' he said when he finished. 'Can you fill in any of the blanks?'

'Not really. The patient was brought in by a neighbour six months ago.'

'Surely he knew her name.'

'Only the first one, and even that sounds more like a nickname. The admitting nurse said he seemed quite vague. He told her the patient hadn't said a word since learning her baby had died. Apparently the baby's father was somewhere abroad. Rouge had no money, no family that the neighbour knew of.' The director shrugged, then gazed out the window. 'We've had several cases like this one since the crash, poor demented people who wander the streets until the police or some Samaritan brings them to us. Sometimes I think I can actually smell the anxiety out there.' He shrugged again as though to shake off the tragedies he dealt with every day. 'Frankly I don't hold out much hope for this particular woman. I'd like you to take a look at her anyway.'

'I'd be happy to,' Saul replied, checking his watch as he got to his feet. He had a little time before his regular office hours, enough to see this Rouge. 'Can you have her brought to the first floor visiting room?'

The director nodded and picked up the phone as Saul left the office.

Saul could have seen his new patient in one of the examining rooms or in the small office the director had assigned to him, but he preferred using the visiting room because it more closely resembled the world patients had left behind. From what he saw in the file, this Rouge hadn't had a single visitor since being admitted. The change of scene might do her good.

He found her standing in the middle of the waiting room floor, her hands hanging slack at her sides, her expression a cipher. He had seen vacant stares like hers many times. Did any emotion hide behind that inward turning gaze? Or could catatonics shut off their minds so completely that they existed in a different reality?

A flash of memory transported him from the visiting room to the University of Pennsylvania medical school where he'd first dissected a cadaver, sawing through the cranium to reveal the brain crammed in the skull like the pithy pulp of a pumpkin. *In these furrowed passages lies the soul,* he'd told himself. He'd never quite got over a sense of awe at the mysteries contained in that grey mass.

A female attendant's voice brought him back to the present. 'I've got other duties, Doctor Steiner. If it's all right I'll leave you alone. You won't need me.' A dip of the attendant's head indicated the patient. 'She's harmless.'

'Fine,' Saul replied, evaluating his new charge.

She was tall, slender – too slender he thought. However if she put a few pounds on her bones, she would have a good figure. Her hair was dark red, her eyes the colour of a stormy sky. Her features had the porcelain perfection of a china figurine and the same lack of expression.

'Good afternoon, Rouge,' he said, taking her hand guiding her to a sofa. 'I'm Saul Steiner, your new doctor.'

She didn't acknowledge his presence by so much as the flicker of an eyelash, following him to the sofa and sitting next to him as docilely as a dog follows a trusted master. He kept up a soothing patter, watching her all the while for any reaction.

Her face remained still and calm. Who are you, he mused, and what happened to you? So much of his work depended on knowing a patient's background, their family history, the events immediately preceding their admittance to Atwood. He couldn't begin therapy without that knowledge.

The strange thing was he had the distinct feeling he did know this woman – had seen her before. Was it *déjà vu*?

She wasn't catatonic in the purest sense of the word. Her file said she dressed and fed herself and followed directions. He suspected she suffered from severe neurotic depression caused by a personal tragedy like the loss of the child the director had mentioned.

Suddenly he realised why she looked so familiar. 'You know,' he said, taking her hand again to get her attention, 'you look a lot like a girl I used to know. Her name was Glory Girard.'

Did the patient's eyes widen? He thought so.

'My wife and I went to Glory's coming out party back in – I think it was twenty-four. I heard she went to Europe and never came home again. She'd be twenty-six now. Are you twenty-six, Rouge?'

God, was that a spark of life in her dead eyes?

'Glory's father, Noble Girard, has been quite ill the last few years.

He's had several strokes. I'm sure it would mean the world to him to have his daughter come home.'

To Saul's amazement a single tear rolled down the patient's face. Could his wild guess have come near the truth? It didn't seem possible. He continued talking, describing the debutante ball, the dress Glory Girard had worn, the way the mansion had been decorated, even the gift of diamond earrings his own wife had envied. But once again he might as well have been talking to himself.

Half an hour later, baffled and frustrated, he sent Rouge back to the ward. After she'd gone he cursed silently at the waste of such a lovely woman. Chances were nothing could help her. God knew, he didn't have many weapons in his arsenal.

Still, he had to try.

He stayed on the sofa with only the ticking of a wall clock for company, deciding on a course of action. The key to her recovery would be knowing her true identity. He opened the file and removed the photograph that had been taken when she was admitted.

Noble Girard sat in his wheelchair in the solarium, the frantic scurrying of his brain hidden by the incapacitating stroke that had stolen his ability to verbalise anything but the simplest ideas. Damnation! Why hadn't the last stroke killed him instead of making him a drooling prisoner of his own infirmity?

'Fucking bastard. Fuck, fuck, fuck,' he bellowed, hoping Anna was in earshot.

The doctor had assured her his swearing was involuntary – something all stroke victims did when they lost the power of speech. But the idiot doctor didn't live inside Noble's body. He couldn't imagine the pleasure Noble got from venting his frustration – and from seeing Anna's reaction.

True to form, she appeared in the solarium's arched entrance, her complexion even greener than usual. 'Is something wrong, dear? Are you in pain?'

'Fucking bastard. Shit,' Noble replied, wishing he could tell her to take her phony solicitude and shove it up her ass.

'Jesus forgives you for saying such things,' she said, holding fast to her rosary beads, 'and so do I. We know you can't help yourself. That's why I never left. My soul is at peace.'

'Asshole,' Noble snarled in reply.

Any day now he expected Anna to have had enough of him. If he was lucky she'd leave for good. If he wasn't, she'd wash his mouth out with soap while saying a prayer for his bedevilled soul.

He turned away from her and gazed out of the window to see a car coming up the drive. Strange. Other than the doctor coming to check his vital signs and Jeremy Montclair reporting on the business, they never had visitors any more. Lifting his good hand, he grunted and pointed at the car.

'Don't worry, dear,' Anna said. 'Clarence will send whoever it is away.'

From the ensuing noise in the entry hall, Clarence wasn't having much success.

'I must see the Girards,' a forceful male voice insisted.

'They aren't receiving,' Clarence answered with equal purpose.

A second later Noble heard two sets of footsteps hurrying towards the solarium.

Noble smiled with the half of his face that wasn't paralysed. He'd been bored. A diversion would be amusing, he thought, using his feet to propel his chair towards the door. Just then Saul Steiner burst into the room with Clarence at his heels. Noble had done business with Saul's father's bank and had never understood why Saul hadn't followed in his father's footsteps.

'I'm sorry for the annoyance, sir,' Clarence said. 'I told the doctor you didn't want to be disturbed but he wouldn't listen.'

'Noble, Anna,' Steiner inclined his head in their direction, 'please excuse my barging in like this. I wouldn't bother you if it weren't a matter of some importance.'

Noble couldn't initiate words but he was able to repeat them. 'Matter of importance,' he said, nodding to show he understood.

'Really, doctor, I resent this intrusion,' Anna declared in the brittle tone that indicated extreme displeasure. 'My husband isn't a well man.'

Noble propelled his wheelchair closer to Steiner. 'Matter of importance,' he said again.

'I think I may have found your daughter,' Steiner announced with breathtaking abruptness.

Noble felt as though he'd suffered a hammer blow to his chest. His ailing heart raced. He gasped for breath. Yet he managed to smile.

'That's impossible. Glory is in Europe,' Anna burst out. She had held fast to the lie for years like a tick clinging to a dog.

'Fucking bitch,' Noble said.

Anna shot him a venomous look, then turned back to Steiner. 'Pay no attention to my husband. He can't help himself.'

Steiner didn't need her explanation. He'd worked with stroke victims in the past, helping them overcome their initial depression. 'How long is it since you last heard from your daughter?'

'You know how young people are. They don't care how we parents worry over their welfare,' she replied.

'How long?' Steiner persisted.

'We got a card from her just last year.'

Noble shook his head, then held up eight fingers. He might not be able to speak but clearly he understood every word. Poor bastard.

'That long?' Saul addressed the question to Noble.

Noble nodded. A tear trickled down his face. Like most stroke victims, he couldn't keep from revealing his emotions. It must be hell on him. He had been a proud man with an iron-clad will.

Saul continued to ignore Anna, choosing instead to keep his gaze fixed on Noble. 'Mr Girard, I do a great deal of charity work at the Atwood State Mental Hospital. A female patient was brought to my attention yesterday. I have a picture of her here.' He took the photograph from his coat pocket. 'I know it's the longest of long shots, but I thought she might be your daughter.'

'If anything happens to my husband – if he has another stroke because of your meddling, I'll hold you responsible,' Anna warned Steiner.

Noble took the photograph in his good hand and held it up to the light, expecting to see someone who looked a little like Glory. But the woman in the picture didn't just resemble his daughter in a few superficial ways. By God, he'd have known that face anywhere. It was his Glory.

A hundred times a day he thought about what he wanted to say. The words always seemed to be on the tip of his tongue but they emerged as unintelligible grunts. This time, miraculously, his thought came out intact.

'My Glory,' he shouted in triumph. 'My Glory!'

Anna snatched the photograph so precipitously that one of the corners tore. 'Don't be ridiculous,' she cried out, giving the picture

a cursory glance. 'This woman may have a vague similarity to Glory
– but that's all.'

Why the dichotomy between husband and wife? Saul wondered.
Why was Anna hell-bent on denial?

'May I have a look?' Clarence asked.

The question took Saul by surprise. 'Did you know Glory well?'
he asked.

'From the day Mr Girard brought her home,' Clarence explained.

Saul took the picture from Anna and handed it to Clarence. The
butler studied it, the furrows of his brow deepening. 'I can't believe
it. Our Glory in the state hospital? But it does look just like her.'

'Would you be willing to come to the hospital tomorrow to identify
her in person?' Saul asked.

'Of course,' Clarence replied.

'You will do no such thing,' Anna interjected, glaring at Clarence
as if she'd happily cut out his tongue.

Saul had heard his parents talking about the Girards, sometimes
in envy but most often with pity. If his new patient was indeed Glory
Girard, she couldn't have had a very happy childhood in this house.

To effect a cure he would have to find out a great deal more about
her early years. Obviously neither Anna nor Noble would serve as
a source of information. Perhaps Clarence Ashton could be of help.

'Tomorrow is my day off,' Clarence said to Anna. 'I can do what
I like.'

Good man, Noble thought, nodding yes and smiling his approval.
He had never resented his illness more. What he wouldn't give to
be able to go to Glory himself. The thought of his daughter alone in
some damn state run institution tore at his innards. She needed him
and he was powerless to help her.

'If you go to the hospital, don't bother coming back,' Anna told
Clarence. Her tone was so icy that Noble wouldn't have been surprised if it had splintered into visible shards. 'You and your wife
won't have jobs here any more.'

'Fucking bitch,' Noble said.

The expletive seemed to encourage Clarence. 'Mrs Girard, that
would be just fine with me. But for Mr Girard, Ellen and I would
have retired long ago. He hired us and he's the only one who can
fire us.'

Noble forced his lips to obey his brain. 'No fire.'

Clarence turned to Steiner. 'Ellen and I can meet you at the hospital any time.'

'Make it ten in the morning,' Steiner replied, 'and thank you.'

Clarence finally verbalised the question that had been thundering through Noble's mind. 'What's wrong with Miss Glory?'

'She's in a very depressed state. She hasn't said a word since she was admitted to Atwood six months ago. I hope that seeing someone familiar will break through the mental barrier she's built between herself and the rest of the world.'

'Mental barrier,' Noble parroted and pointed at his own head.

'It's not the same as a stroke,' Steiner explained. 'With a little luck and a lot of love, the patient has a chance to recover completely.'

'Go. Go,' Noble said.

Fortunately Steiner seemed to intuit Noble's meaning. 'I don't think it would be wise for you to see each other now. But if this woman is your daughter I promise the two of you will be reunited.'

'Over my dead body,' Anna muttered.

'Over dead body,' Noble said, nodding yes all the while. If wishes were bullets, Anna wouldn't have lived another second.

Saul Steiner rarely spent time on the wards. He made an exception this morning to prepare Rouge – or was it Glory? – for her visitors.

He found her sitting on the edge of her bed, staring off into nothingness.

'Good morning, Glory,' he said.

Her gaze lifted.

'Clarence and Ellen Ashton are coming to see you. I wanted to be sure you were ready.'

He could swear the patient's eyes lit up from within.

'Do you remember them?'

She didn't respond.

He motioned for an attendant to come over. 'I'd like you to brush her hair and help her with make-up. When you're finished bring her down to the visiting room.'

The Ashtons were already there when he walked in. The two of them looked pale and nervous but resolute. Clarence held a gift-wrapped package. Ellen clutched flowers.

'Doctor Steiner,' Ellen said, 'I pray we haven't got our hopes up for nothing. I've never forgiven myself for letting Glory go.'

'I don't understand. I thought she went to Europe with her father immediately after her debut.'

Ellen's face flushed. 'Oh dear, I shouldn't have talked out of turn.'

'It's not out of turn if there's the smallest chance it will help my patient,' Saul assured her. 'I know that's what Mr Girard would want. We have a few minutes before the young lady joins us. Won't you tell me what happened?'

'It was the night of Miss Glory's debut,' Ellen began in a halting voice.

As she spoke her husband occasionally chimed in so that their words tumbled into each other like bowling pins. Their story didn't surprise Saul. He had seen a number of rebellious youngsters over the years. There had been nothing wrong with them that growing up a little more wouldn't cure.

'I don't understand why Mr Girard was opposed to letting Glory go to art school,' Saul said when the Ashtons finally ran out of words.

'There's lots goes on in that house that's been kept secret all these years,' Ellen replied cryptically.

Before Saul could ask what she meant the patient arrived. He would never forget what happened next.

Glory stood in the visiting room door for a long while, her gaze fixed on the Ashtons. Then, one halting step at a time, she walked up to Ellen.

Utter silence held the room in thrall as the two women stared at each other. Saul watched while Glory's dead eyes slowly came back to life. She looked as frightened as a lost child, yet her upright posture evidenced courage and determination. She would need both to get well.

Tears oozed from Ellen's eyes and she swallowed convulsively. Clarence stood behind her, a supportive hand under her elbow.

'Glory, is it really you?' Ellen asked softly as if she feared a loud sound would make Glory disappear.

'It's me,' Glory replied. Her voice sounded as rusty as a neglected tool. 'Don't cry, Ellen.'

'I'm crying because I'm so happy. I thought I'd never see you again.'

And then the two of them were in each other's arms, hugging and weeping while Saul and Clarence gazed at one another over their heads. It was as magical a moment as any Saul had seen while he studied the mind-body medicine practised by the Navajos.

Glory Girard was on her way to recovery. The road would be hard, but thanks to Ellen Ashton, she had taken the first step. For a moment, Saul felt left out and a bit useless. All his knowledge couldn't have accomplished what this reunion had just done.

He often marvelled at the sisterhood of women, their ability to communicate verbally and physically, and wished men had a similar gift. He suspected that more wounded souls had been healed at coffee mornings than on psychiatrists' couches.

CHAPTER TWENTY-THREE

Cal and Jeremy Montclair, Clarence and Ellen Ashton, and Saul and Rose Steiner were assembled in the Montclairs' parlour waiting for Glory to come downstairs. The elegant art deco decor was a far cry from the tatterdemalion hand-me-downs in Professor Blackstone's house. However Cal took no satisfaction in her prosperity today. She was too worried about Glory.

On the surface Glory seemed to have taken Noble's sudden death in her stride. Cal worried about what lay beneath the surface. What a lousy break for Glory, she thought, then grimaced – recalling it had been an even lousier break for Noble. At least he didn't have to look at Anna's sanctimonious, holier than thou pickle puss any more.

How could that woman spend so much time on her knees praying and treat her only child the way she had? Cal would never know. Talk about unnatural mothers. Unnatural fathers too, as far as Cal was concerned.

The night of Glory's debut, it hadn't taken a genius to figure out Noble had hand-picked Jeremy as Glory's future husband. Cal had watched him watching them and picked up on his intention as though she had a pipeline straight to Noble's mind.

She hadn't told Glory the day Glory left San Francisco and she hadn't told Jeremy when they started dating. By then there seemed no reason to muddy the waters. But she had never trusted Noble any further than she could throw him. Anna either, for that matter.

Glory had come such a long way in the four months since the Ashtons had identified her at the hospital. Would she have the strength to complete the journey? Or would today write *finis* to her remarkable recovery?

Cal shifted in her chair so that she had a better view of Saul. 'Are you sure Glory is strong enough to go to the funeral?'

'I wouldn't let her if I didn't think she was,' Saul replied. He had a wonderfully soothing voice that must have been a real asset with patients. 'If Anna had permitted Glory see Noble while he was alive, I might have advised Glory to stay at home today. She needs to say goodbye, to close the door on her childhood. It's called closure.'

'You can call it by any fancy name you like,' Ellen Ashton interjected. 'As far as I'm concerned wakes and funerals are just plain heartbreaking. I put a couple of extra handkerchiefs in my purse for those that forgot. Between us, I'd like to use one to strangle Anna Girard.'

Cal repressed a giggle. She couldn't have agreed more.

'Mrs Girard loved Noble in her own way,' Jeremy said.

'Mrs Girard is a sick bitch,' Rose Steiner declared. 'She made Noble's life miserable.'

Jeremy quickly came to Anna's defence. 'Anna told me she had planned to join a Catholic order but she stayed with Noble instead, because he needed her.'

'I doubt the decision was completely selfless,' Rose said. 'Noble was a very rich man. Would you like to bet his entire estate goes to Anna.'

'If it does, she deserves it. He was a hard man to be around the last few years.'

Cal glanced across the room to where Jeremy stood by the fireplace. He was so much nicer a person than she was. How many men would have agreed to let Glory come to live with them?

Jeremy had a talent for seeing the best in people and situations. Everyone liked him. More importantly, they trusted him. Those qualities had undoubtedly contributed to his rapid advance at the Girard Company.

Last year when Noble suffered his final incapacitating stroke, Jeremy had been his second in command. Jeremy had done a splendid job in the months which followed. What would happen to him and his job – to Glory and the Ashtons too – now that Noble was gone?

The sound of Glory's steps on the stairs brought Cal's meditation to an abrupt halt. Glory needed her today. Cal could worry about everything and everyone else tomorrow.

The seven of them rode to Saint Mary's in the Steiners' Pierce Arrow limousine. Ellen and Cal sat on the back seat on either side of Glory. Jeremy and Saul were on the jump seats while Clarence rode next to the chauffeur.

The day was appropriately overcast as they arrived for the funeral

Mass. The men helped the women out of the car, then surrounded Glory in an almost military phalanx as they walked into the church and down the aisle.

Glory did her best to ignore the curious stares that came her way. Cal had told her San Francisco society was a-buzz with stories of her return. Let them talk, she thought. Nothing they said had the power to hurt her. She had stopped caring about so-called polite society. Memories of her father filled her mind.

She looked down the aisle to the dais where he lay in an open casket with his head on a satin pillow. He had towered over her childhood like a giant. Now he seemed shrunken, as though death had finally cut him down to size. She had a hard time equating his waxen features, garish in make-up the undertaker had applied, with the handsome man she remembered.

It had been much easier to come to terms with his death than it had been with Ariadne's. Her father had lived a full life but her daughter's had been over before it had begun. Glory hadn't attended the funeral or visited the grave. Thank heaven she could do that much for Noble.

Caught up in her thoughts, she didn't see her mother until Anna was just a few feet away.

'I'm so sorry,' she said, reaching for Anna's hand. 'I know how hard this must be on you.'

Anna shrank from her touch. 'How dare you come here?'

It was the last thing Glory had expected Anna to say. The bitterness between them had to end. They had no one but each other now. 'I wanted to say goodbye to my father.'

'You did that when you walked out of his life.'

'I didn't meant to hurt him – or you.'

An irrational light burned in Anna's eyes. 'I know why you came back when you did – why you're here today. You think you're going to inherit a fortune, don't you?'

'I don't want Daddy's money.'

'Then you won't be upset to learn he left every last cent to me.'

'If it makes you feel better, Mother, I'm glad,' Glory replied, hoping to placate Anna and put an end to the dreadful scene.

'Don't you dare call me mother,' Anna shrilled so loudly that people at the back of the church looked their way. 'You're not my daughter.'

'Control yourself, Mrs Girard,' Saul commanded in the authoritarian voice that made nurses and orderlies jump to do his bidding. 'I know you're upset but that doesn't excuse you making irresponsible accusations.'

The awful light in Anna's eyes burned brighter. 'You think you're so smart but you don't know everything. Noble found Glory out on the street like so much trash. She isn't my daughter any more than she was his. I don't want her here.'

Glory didn't wait to hear more. Blinded by tears, she raced up the aisle and out of the church. Like mother like daughter, she thought, choking down a groan. They were both crazy as loons.

Cal and Jeremy were always telling her how good she looked, how well she seemed. She thanked them and smiled to hide the emptiness inside her where grief, guilt, pain and anger had dwelled before her so-called cure.

She felt a hand on her arm and looked up to see that Cal had joined her. 'I always thought your mother was a monster but she outdid herself today.'

'Why? Why does she hate me?' Glory's heart spasmed as she remembered her own sorry attempts at motherhood. She wasn't in any position to judge Anna.

'Your mother doesn't hate you,' Saul said, puffing a little as he joined them. 'She hates herself. I've never seen her professionally and I'm not given to snap diagnoses but I'd be willing to bet she's a manic-depressive with a real persecution complex. She thinks everyone is out to hurt her.'

Glory had been feeling the same way herself. 'Is that what's wrong with me?' she burst out. 'Have I inherited her mental illness?'

'Count yourself lucky that you couldn't inherit anything from Anna Girard,' Ellen said vehemently. She put an arm around Glory's waist as if to say, lean on me.

Just as she had years ago, Glory took comfort from Ellen's solid body. 'I don't understand. Do you know what Anna meant about my not being her daughter?'

'She was raving like a lunatic,' Cal said fiercely, then blanched at her use of a word that could just as easily have been applied to Glory.

The arrival of the limousine brought a temporary halt to the unhappy colloquy.

'What did you mean about my not inheriting anything from Anna?'

Glory asked Ellen as soon as they were settled in the back seat.

'It's the truth,' Ellen answered, 'and if I were in your shoes I'd be happy for it.'

'Ellen, it's not your place to tell her,' Clarence warned from the front seat.

'Then whose place is it? Now Mr Girard is gone we're the only ones who know what happened.'

'Tell me what? What did my mother mean about my father finding me on the pavement?' Glory's throat felt so tight that she could hardly get the words out.

'Leave it to Mrs Girard to put things in the worst possible light,' Ellen harumphed.

'Then it's true?'

'In a manner of speaking. Perhaps I had better begin at the beginning. It was the day of the great quake. The mayor had asked your father to tour parts of the city and give him a detailed report on what he found. You remember him talking about it?'

Glory nodded. 'He was proud of serving on the mayor's emergency committee.'

'Your father was a proud man. But he had a special reason for being proud of what he did that day. He was driving up Taylor Street when he saw a crib on the pavement. Something made him stop to look inside it. That's when he found you. He saved your life.'

Glory felt as though the earth had shifted beneath her feet, just as it must have the day of the great quake.

'How old was I?'

'Newborn. Your umbilical cord hadn't dried up yet.'

'What happened to my parents? Did Noble find them too?'

'I'm afraid they died in the quake. But they loved you very much.'

'How do you know?'

'You were in a handmade crib – and a fine piece of work it was too. And your blankets were hand-stitched. Anyone with eyes could see the love in the workmanship.'

The information didn't help. 'If I'm not Glory Girard, who am I?'

'I'm not sure Mr Girard ever knew,' Ellen replied. 'What with the fires and all the injured people and everyone running this way and that trying to escape, the city was in total chaos the day he found you. When Mr Girard walked into the kitchen with you it seemed like a good omen. I remember telling him he was responsible for your life. I think he fell in love with you then and there.'

'What about the rest of the staff? Would he have told any of them?'

'He sent them away and swore Clarence and me to secrecy. He didn't want anyone to know you were adopted. I wouldn't have told you even now if your mother hadn't blurted out part of the story.'

Mother. Father. How little meaning those words had to Glory now. At last she knew why she had never truly felt she belonged in the mansion on Nob Hill – why there had been times when she felt like a stranger inside her own skin.

The Ashtons hadn't given Anna a chance to fire them. They quit their jobs the day Noble died. A new butler came to the door when Glory rang the bell. It felt strange to see someone in Clarence's place – but not half as strange as it did to stand in the hall knowing what Glory now knew.

'Please tell my mother – that is tell Mrs Girard that Miss Girard is here to see her.'

The new butler lacked Clarence's *sang froid*. His gaping mouth betrayed his surprise at her name. He left her standing under the glass roof that had come down the day of the quake – the day her father had found her. Only he hadn't been her father. She would have to stop thinking of him that way.

When the new butler returned she half expected to be sent away. Instead he ushered her into the parlour. The curtains were closed, the mirrors covered, the room dark but for pinpoints of electric light that cast eerie shadows on the walls and floor.

Anna materialised out of the gloom like Banquo's ghost. 'Father Tremaine told me I should have been kinder to you at the funeral yesterday,' she said.

Glory looked beyond Anna to see the cleric behind her. His dark robe and the cross on his chest invested him with the authority of the Church. However Glory didn't believe in God any more. He struck her as a pleasant looking man just past his youth, wearing a ridiculous costume.

Glory wasted no time on an exchange of pleasantries. She hadn't come to chit chat. 'The Ashtons told me how Father – that is how Noble found me. I came to ask you who I am – who my parents were.'

238

'I haven't the vaguest idea,' Anna replied with a dismissive wave of her hand.

'Now Mrs Girard, what did we just discuss?' Father Tremaine interjected.

'You asked me to be more charitable towards Glory,' Anna replied as though she were guilty of nothing more than a breach of manners. Her dark gaze returned to Glory's face. 'I don't know who you are. I never did. Noble hired a Pinkerton detective to look into your background but the man was utterly incompetent. All I can tell you is that Taylor Street was a working class neighbourhood in those days.' She gave the words an ugly emphasis, like a judge pronouncing a sentence.

'Is that why you never loved me – because you didn't think I was worthy of being a Girard?'

'You aren't. Just look at you. Noble should have known he couldn't make a silk purse from a sow's ear.'

'Now, Mrs Girard, there's no call to talk that way,' Father Tremaine said. 'Glory, I'm truly sorry you had to learn the truth this way. If you want to know more you'll have to check with the Pinkertons.'

Anna appeared not to have heard him. Her gaze had turned inward to a vision only she could see. 'Noble used my grief against me to make me take you in. He knew I never got over Isabel's death.'

'Who was Isabel?' Glory asked, wondering what new cruelty Anna had devised.

'My *real* daughter. She died in her crib before her first birthday. Noble convinced me you could take her place. Of course being what you are and who you are, that was impossible. Isabel was so refined, so well behaved—' Anna's voice trailed off. The click of the rosary beads running through her hands sounded like castanets in the quiet room.

'Why wasn't I ever told about Isabel?'

'Noble didn't want you to know. Perhaps he thought it would make you feel sorry for me. He didn't want you to care about anyone but him.'

Glory knew what Anna had been through because she had endured the same loss. It had twisted Anna's heart and mind, leaving her as crippled as any amputee returning from war. Glory was determined not to let that happen to her.

Saul had told her she had suffered from post partum depression

239

after Ariadne's birth. The tragedy of Ariadne's death had heightened her depression, compelling her to seek relief in a total withdrawal from the world. But she had no excuse for a breakdown now. She was well again and she intended to stay that way.

'I'm terribly sorry for your loss,' she said, then leaned forward and brushed her lips against Anna's cheek for the last time.

Glory walked away from the mansion without a backward glance and headed down California Street towards the waterfront, deep in thought. When she reached Fisherman's Wharf the salty scent of the sea and the oily odour of fish brought back memories of Monterey – of meeting Dimitri the day she went to sketch the Konstantines' cannery.

Had they ever loved each other – or had the years they'd spent together been a hideous cosmic joke resulting from a collision of time, place, and opportunity? Had she mistaken a sick sexual obsession for something deeper and more ennobling?

She had lost everything – her home, her parents, her lover and child, even her identity. In a way hitting rock bottom was comforting. She couldn't imagine how things could get any worse.

She had made gains too, an inner voice reminded her. She knew herself as never before. She had wonderful friends who wanted to help her. And she had her talent.

It was enough. It had to be.

Once again, six people had gathered in the Montclairs' parlour to wait for Glory – and once again a common concern united them.

'Where can Glory be?' Cal didn't address her question to anyone in particular and she certainly didn't expect an answer. 'She's been gone for hours.'

'Perhaps it's time to call the police,' Rose Steiner suggested for the third or fourth time. She had been pacing the floor like a mother hen who lost a chick. 'How can you be so complacent?' she demanded of Saul.

'I'm not complacent. I just have more faith in Glory than the rest of you.'

'If you have so much faith,' Rose shot back, 'why did you leave an office full of patients to come running over here?'

In reply Saul simply lifted his shoulders so high that he looked like a turtle shrinking into his shell. It was the most eloquent shrug Cal had ever seen.

'I think we could all use a drink,' Jeremy said.

'I'll get them,' Clarence offered. 'Just point me in the right direction.'

'You don't need to wait on us,' Jeremy replied. 'You're not a servant in this house. I'll do it.'

Before either man could move Cal heard the front door open and close. She jumped to her feet and ran into the hall to see Glory calmly taking off her coat.

'Hi there,' Glory said as if she hadn't been gone all day without a word of explanation.

'Where in the world have you been?' Cal demanded. 'I've been worried sick. So have the Steiners and the Ashtons. They're here with me. I called them when I realised you were missing.'

Cal's agitation reinforced the decision Glory had made. She loved her friends too much to have them worry every time she did something the least bit unusual.

'I'm sorry. I guess I lost track of the time. I went to see Anna to find out if she knew who my parents were.'

'Did she tell you?'

'I honestly don't think she knows – except she's sure I came from a lower class than the Girards.'

'Lower class my foot. You're head and shoulders above her.'

'I felt sorry for her. She seemed so lost and alone.'

'Save your sympathy for someone who deserves it. Seeing her couldn't take more than an hour. What then?'

'I went to the Pinkerton Detective Agency.'

'What do the Pinkertons have to do with it?'

'Anna told me Noble hired them to find out who I was. I'm afraid she was mistaken, though. Their files go back to 1906 but there's no record of such an investigation.'

'So you still don't know who you are,' Cal said a little more calmly.

'I don't know my parents' identity. However I do know who I am. That's why I was gone so long. It took me a while to figure it out.'

Cal frowned. 'You're not making sense.'

'Please don't look so worried. I'm not going to have another breakdown. I'm an artist, Cal, and a damn good one. It's time I started acting like one.'

Glory took Cal's hand and walked into the parlour where the others repeated all the questions Cal had already asked plus a few new ones Cal hadn't thought of. Glory retold her story again, going into more detail this time. 'So you see,' she concluded, 'I'm fine. I love you all for worrying about me but it can't go on. I'm twenty-seven – not two. It's time I resumed my career. I telephoned Maurie Golden this afternoon to ask him if he was still interested in representing me. Not only does he want to, he said he owes me quite a bit of money.'

Glory smiled, recalling Maurie Golden's enthusiasm. 'After I disappeared he had my bronzes recast to meet the demand for my work. Apparently the editions of fifteen sold out too. I can afford my own place complete with a studio.'

'Surely you aren't thinking of going back to Big Sur?' Cal said.

Glory gave her a fond smile. 'I'm not that brave. But I don't want to stay here either. I need to begin my life again and I can't do that with all of you fussing over me.'

'Do you have any idea where you'll go?' the ever practical Jeremy asked.

'Not yet.'

'Have you ever been to New Mexico?' Saul asked out of the blue.

'No. I hear the light there is fantastic, though. And I've read about the artists' colonies in Santa Fe and Taos.'

Rose looked at her husband. 'Are you thinking what I'm thinking?' she asked in the shorthand communication that Glory had heard them use before.

Saul nodded. 'Would you like to do the honours, my dear?'

Rose beamed. 'I'll leave that to you.'

Glory looked from one to the other. 'What are you two talking about?'

'I spent a year in New Mexico after I completed my residency,' Saul told her, 'studying shamanistic healing traditions in the Navajo and Pueblo tribes. I fell in love with the area, bought twenty acres outside of Taos and built an adobe house there. Rose and I spent our honeymoon in it. We'd be happy to lend it to you.'

'I couldn't let you do that,' Glory replied.

'It's not a gift,' Rose said. 'In return for the first year's rent, I'd like you to do a bronze bust of Saul.'

'I've never done a portrait before,' Glory demurred.

Despite her protest she found herself looking at Saul and wondering if she could convey the essence of the man without the use of pigment. A thrill ran through her as she realised she was thinking like an artist again.

'You'd be doing us a favour,' Rose insisted. 'Saul and I love the place in Taos but we haven't got there as often as we hoped. We do have an Indian caretaker on the premises but I'd feel so much better if someone we knew lived there.'

Glory did some quick mental calculations. The money Maurie owed her should cover her expenses for a year. Surely by then he'd have sold even more of her work.

'How big is the place?' she asked.

'About two thousand square feet,' Saul answered. 'There are three good sized bedrooms, two bathrooms, a big living room. Beehive fireplaces in every room. A good solid garage at the back. You could use it as a studio until you could afford to build one.'

'Don't forget the view of the mountains,' Rose chimed in.

Glory sighed. 'It sounds like heaven.'

'It sounds like the middle of nowhere,' Cal objected. 'I hate to think of you going so far away all by yourself.'

'She wouldn't be by herself if Clarence and I went with her,' Ellen burst out. She looked at her husband and when he nodded, went on with what she'd been saying. 'We were going to buy our own place when we retired. But now Mr Girard is gone I don't see any reason why it has to be here.' Her eyes misted as she looked at Glory. 'You're as close to kin as we've got. Would you mind so very much if we moved with you?'

Glory hadn't yet decided to accept the Steiners' largesse. Now she realised it would be foolish to refuse. 'Are you sure all of you know what you're doing?' she asked, pushing the words past the lump in her throat.

Saul, Rose, and the Ashtons nodded in unison.

'Jeremy and I can help too,' Cal said. 'We can call Lawrence Wyant and ask him to show your work in his New York gallery. You remember him, don't you, Glory?'

Glory remembered him all too well. Lawrence Wyant was one complication her life didn't need. 'I appreciate the offer but it wouldn't be fair to Mr Wyant or me. He might hate my work. And it's important to me to succeed on my own.'

Cal sighed. 'Have it your way for now. The offer is open any time you want to take us up on it.'

Glory felt tears pooling in her eyes – happy tears. When she left the house on Nob Hill this morning she'd felt alone in the world. How wrong she'd been, she thought as she went to embrace her friends one by one.

She may not have found out who she was today but something equally important had taken place. She wasn't angry any more – at Noble or Anna or herself. From this moment forward she vowed her every step would lead her away from the darkness and into the light.

CHAPTER TWENTY-FOUR

New Mexico, 1934

Lawrence Wyant always felt guilty when he went out of town on business trips, perhaps because he enjoyed the solo excursions so much. He loved his wife and God knew he felt desperately sorry for her, but he had long since learned that pity and passion made uneasy bed mates. If Beth's multiple sclerosis had been diagnosed before their engagement, he might not have proposed.

He would never forget the afternoon when she told him she was ill. He had returned to New York days before, his doctoral degree in hand, eager to take on a man's responsibilities. Sensing something was on Beth's mind beside their wedding plans, he'd suggested brunch at the Plaza followed by a leisurely stroll in Central Park.

It had been such an average summer day, the day that changed the course of his life. He remembered the heat rising from the pavements, the exact blue shade of the sky, the feel of the sun on his face and arms, the earthy scent of growing things, the way Beth's tears glistened like ice crystals before he took her in his arms and told her the diagnosis didn't matter.

Beth had done the honourable thing by telling him before they said their vows. In return he could do no less. Mistaking compassion for passion, he'd gone through with the marriage.

That had been eight years ago – eight long years of hoping Beth's latest remission would continue – eight years of watching his wife lose stamina and muscle control – of praying for a medical miracle while the joy slowly leached from their lives; eight years of envying other men their children and knowing he and Beth would never have any because the doctor had said pregnancy might exacerbate her disease.

Hard as it had been for him, it had been ten times harder for Beth. Business trips gave him a chance to escape. There was no escape for her.

Oh yes, he thought as he walked through the lobby of Santa Fe's La Fonda hotel, he relished his business trips. He looked forward to them more than he cared to admit. He blessed art for the beauty it brought into his life each and every day – and for the excuse it gave him to leave home when his frustration and sorrow became too great to bear.

He had arrived after dark last night, had eaten a light supper in La Fonda's half empty dining room, then gone straight to bed with a guide book for company. Now as he strode through the lobby the pueblo architecture and southwestern decor made him feel he had travelled much further away from Manhattan than the two night train trip had taken him.

He opened the street door, blinking in the bright March sunlight as he took a moment to orientate himself. La Fonda sat at the northern terminus of the famous Santa Fe trail, facing a plaza that had been old long before the cowboy era.

An odd *mélange* of Victorian and pueblo style buildings lined the square. An ornate white bandstand served as its centrepiece. The guide book had told him the three hundred year old Governor's Palace on the north side of the plaza held a museum devoted to the city's history. The chapel of Loretto with its miraculous winding staircase was a block to the south, and the oldest continuously inhabited house in America could be reached in a short walk.

However he hadn't come to play tourist. He'd come to look at art. The writings of Willa Cather, Oliver LaFarge and Carl Sandburg had popularised the southwest. The Indian Tribal Arts Exposition in New York in 1931 had whetted the public's appetite for native American arts and crafts. And Georgia O'Keefe's oils and John Sloan's watercolours had imbued the work of southwestern artists with new prestige.

He'd made the trip from Manhattan in the hope of discovering unknown artists of equal talent. Such discoveries would burnish his growing reputation as one of the most innovative and farseeing dealers in New York. He had three days to find what he'd come for before heading back to the gallery – and Beth.

Expectancy lightened his step as he headed across the square to the art museum. The light was quite marvellous, he thought, looking up at the turquoise sky. No wonder artists were drawn here.

His gaze returned to the museum, his thoughts to the connection between the city and its most talented citizens. In an extraordinary leap of communal faith, the city fathers had built the museum in 1917 at a time when the entire population of Santa Fe had numbered less than seven thousand – and only fifteen of them claimed to be full-time painters.

From opening day the museum had been noted for giving local artists a voice in policy as well as offering them free exhibition space. The result had been a flourishing of art that led to the formation of groups like Los Cinco Pintores and the Taos Ten. Between them they had created a whole new artistic genre.

The museum's twin bell towers reminded him of the pueblo churches whose pictures he'd seen in the guide book. The entry gallery displayed marvellous examples of Indian crafts. At any other time he would have lingered long enough to enjoy them. Given the brevity of his stay he gave them a cursory inspection before moving on. He'd come to see the east wing, devoted to the work of local artists.

He spent the next hour wandering through the exhibition. It was a far cry from the carefully thought out shows he mounted in Manhattan – a hodge-podge of cubicles arranged by individual artists rather than a powerful show defined by a single unifying vision. And yet the vivid art held his attention.

He had just jotted down the name of a painter whose work interested him when he turned a corner into yet another small exhibition space – and stopped dead in his tracks. His pulse elevated, his heart pounded, his mouth dried. The experience was akin to falling in love.

He had no trouble discerning genius when he had the rare good fortune to be in its presence. He was now.

He had been looking for an exceptional sculptor for years, someone with a unique vision and the technical ability to carry it off. His physical response told him he'd finally found one.

There were twelve pieces divided between bronzes and terra-cottas. The subjects, Indian women in traditional garb, an old man resting on a bench, children at play, were so lifelike that he wouldn't have been startled to hear one of them speak. And yet the artist had taken a giant leap beyond mere photo-realism. The work's textural finish and elongated lines reminded him of Rodin.

Excitement rolled through him like a stream in flood as he wondered what sort of man had created the pieces. Someone mature, he felt certain, someone who had loved and suffered, perhaps a father or even a grandfather given the impassioned renderings of both youth and old age.

Although his eyes were jaded from seeing so much art he actually found himself looking at the work like a collector trying to decide which one to buy. He would happily have packed up any or all of them to take home. If the sculpture had that effect on him he knew it would on the dilettantes who frequented his gallery.,

He bent down to read their creator's name at the base of a sculpture. G. Girard. It seemed strangely familiar and yet he knew he'd never seen the work until today. Where the hell had he heard that name before?

In a flash memory transported him back a decade or more to San Francisco and a memorable tango with a beautiful debutante named Glory Girard.

It had to be a coincidence, he told himself. Girard wasn't that rare a name. There was even a Girard Street station on the Philadelphia subway. G undoubtedly stood for George, Gilbert or Gerald.

Glory always took a walk after lunch. Sometimes she headed a mile down a dirt road to visit the Ashtons in their new home. Other days, when the work was going well, she never made it past the letter box.

This was one of those days. The piece she'd started that morning promised to be one of her best. She had gulped down a cup of tea and a dish of cold refried beans and then quick-stepped down the drive with Laredo at her heels.

When she stopped at the box the shaggy dog whined as if to say he wanted a longer excursion.

'Not today,' she told him as she sorted through the post.

'Wuff,' Laredo replied, wagging his tail.

She had found him – hungry, dirty and forlorn – wandering along the road to Taos pueblo the week after the Ashtons moved into their own house. Hoping he'd be a good guard dog she'd brought him home. But the only thing Laredo watched was her. She often woke in the middle of the night, unnerved by the feeling of being spied on, to find Laredo gazing at her like a lop-eared love slave.

Unable to ignore the dog's unconditional affection, she took a moment to scratch him behind the ears before heading back to the house. The main structure, a rosy beige adobe in an L shape, had been built by the Steiners. Six months ago she'd felt financially secure enough to add a studio so that the whole now formed a U surrounding a courtyard.

She still felt a thrill of ownership every time she looked at her property – hers, that is, except for the mortgage held by the bank. Thinking about that gave her an altogether less pleasant sort of thrill. She'd never realised how insecure Dimitri must have felt until the weight of paying for a house rested on her own shoulders.

She no longer blamed him for Ariadne's death – any more than she blamed herself. But she couldn't get past the brutal way he'd let her know about it. Saul had urged her to forgive him for her own mental health. God knew she had tried – and failed.

Enemy and rival, that's what Dimitri was to her now. The desire to outclass him, to have a huge career that surpassed his, drove her harder than she could ever have driven herself. Time lost all shape and dimension when she was sculpting.

Today was no exception. The sun was hanging low in a blood red western sky when she heard a car pull up in front of the house. Mabel Dodge Luhan often stopped by in the afternoon, bearing a bottle of the best bootleg Scotch money could buy and the latest local gossip.

The fortyish Mabel was a law unto herself – and Glory admired her for it. Mabel had divorced a wealthy Easterner to marry Tony Luhan, a man of importance in Taos pueblo but certainly not in the Anglo world.

She had flouted all the unspoken laws of his tribe and hers – and made people accept her for who she was rather than who they thought she should be. Glory enjoyed Mabel's lay-your-cards-on-the-table personality, her conversation, her *joie de vivre* – and her Scotch.

She smiled as she opened the door, expecting to see Mabel. Instead a stranger stood beneath the *latillas* sheltering the veranda. His back faced her as he gazed at the nearby Sangre De Christo mountains. His dress coat and Homburg clearly defined him as a city man. The trail of dust on the drive told her a car had dropped him off.

Mabel was given to pranks. If this stranger was one of them—

Glory never finished the thought. The stranger turned around and she recognised him at once. 'Did Cal send you?' she asked accusingly.

'Cal?' Lawrence Wyant looked surprised. 'I haven't talked to her in a couple of years.'

Either he was a superb actor or he really hadn't expected to see her. She looked him up and down while memories of him merged with the present.

This older Lawrence was far more imposing than the man who had attended her debut. His shoulders were broader, his torso more powerful. He had the easy stance of a natural athlete and the proud carriage of a man of consequence. He wore his years well.

Remembering her manners, she said, 'Come on in, Lawrence. It's been a long time.'

His sudden smile reminded her of how handsome she'd thought him at the ball. He appeared urbane, sophisticated and debonair while she was uncomfortably conscious of her *déshabillé*. Sculpting was dirty work and she dressed accordingly in jeans, boots, and a faded man's workshirt. Today clay streaked all three.

'What brings you to Taos?' she asked as he followed her through the open door.

'I'm looking for new talent for my gallery. The Santa Fe Art Museum was my first stop this morning. I saw the most marvellous sculpture there, done by a G. Girard. You wouldn't happen to have married someone named George?'

He smiled again and this time she felt it in the pit of her stomach.

'I haven't married anyone.' A quick glance at his left hand told her he had. Good, she thought. If he were single she might be tempted – and the last thing she needed or wanted in her life was a man to screw it up.

'How did you find me?'

'I made a pest of myself until someone on the museum staff gave me your address. I hired a car to bring me here. The driver didn't speak English very well. He didn't realise I wanted him to wait. I'm afraid I'm stranded.'

'Stranded?' she repeated like an idiot. She wasn't over the shock of seeing him on her doorstep.

'I was counting on G. Girard giving me a ride back to Santa Fe after we talked. I thought he, that is you were a man.'

'That's why I sign my work that way.' She looked askance at him. 'I guess you didn't know it was a three hour drive when you started out.'

He chuckled. 'Over some of the worst roads in the world too. I didn't come all this way to discuss my travel arrangements. I want to talk about you and your work.'

'Then you really did like it?'

'When you said you wanted to study art at your coming out party I had no idea you were so talented.'

She laughed. 'Neither did I.'

He smiled again and this time Glory's knees went weak. 'I hope you aren't already showing in New York. I'd like to sign you to an exclusive contract.'

'Are you sure the altitude hasn't deprived you of your senses?'

'I've never been more serious in my life.'

Glory had been a beautiful girl. Now she was a magnificent looking woman. Although Lawrence had come to talk about her art he couldn't help responding to the lush figure her clothes failed to conceal. With the riot of red hair haloing her face, the sparkle in her eyes, and the flush on her cheeks, she seemed more vital and alive than anyone he'd ever known.

'Let me take your hat and coat,' she said, holding out her arms.

For a long moment they just looked at each other. Then she burst out laughing. 'I'm not usually this tongue-tied. It's just that you're the last person I expected to see.'

She gestured for him to take a seat. He gazed around the parlour, enjoying the superbly balanced juxtaposition of comfortable furniture, *objets d'art*, paintings and sculpture that only the most gifted interior decorators achieved.

Something told him Glory would never submit herself to anyone else's taste. The room bore the stamp of her personality.

'From what I see, you've done very well for yourself. I can't help wondering why I've never come across your work before.'

'I have an exclusive deal with the Golden Gallery west of the Mississippi.'

'And east of the Mississippi?'

'I'm uncommitted.'

'Leave it to Maurie to come up with a talent like yours and keep it to himself.'

'You know him?'

'Everyone in the business knows him. He's quite a character and he has a terrific eye. How long have you been with him?'

'A few years.'

'I assume you finally talked your father into art lessons. Where did you study?'

What had he said wrong? Lawrence wondered at Glory's suddenly wary expression.

'Here and there,' she replied.

Most artists loved having a chance to parade their credentials. Why didn't she? Since the question had made her uneasy, he changed the subject. 'How is your father? Does he still have that fabulous art collection?'

Her gaze lowered. She clutched the arms of her chair. 'He died a couple of years ago. We were estranged at the time.'

Lawrence could have kicked himself. Jeremy had sent him a brief note about it.

'I'm sorry on both counts,' he replied, determined not to put his foot in his mouth again.

He wanted to make a good impression on Glory Girard – and not just because he hoped to introduce her work to the New York art world. He had walked away from her years ago for Beth's sake. He had a damn good reason to stay now for his own. What remained of his poise kept him from staring at her. She was as stunning a piece of work as any of her sculptures.

'I'm over the loss,' she said. Her words belied the pain in her eyes.

The thought of her in pain – emotional or physical – bothered him. A lot. He couldn't remember the last time he'd been as aware of a woman.

No, that was a lie. He could remember. He'd felt the same way the first time they met.

This time his reaction had to be due to her extraordinary talent.

'I really do want to talk business. I wish I had taken you seriously years ago when you told me you wanted to be an artist.'

'Why?'

'Knowing what I know now, I would have signed you to a contract then and there.'

She shook her head, setting her Titian hair in motion. For a second he surrendered to a vision of the way it would look spread across a pillow. His pillow. His bed.

'What difference would it have made?' Glory asked, suspicion evident in her tone.

Either she didn't trust art dealers – or she didn't trust men. He suspected the latter. Considering her beauty he doubted if she had spent the last ten years alone. What had she done since he last saw her and who had she done it with? He looked around for any sign she shared her home with a man, and felt relieved when he failed to find one.

'I would have liked to discover you myself. I suppose the honour belongs to Maurie.'

'If you can call it one,' she answered modestly in view of her genius.

Lawrence could hardly equate the stunning debutante he'd known with the talented artist who sat by his side. She had worn a couturier gown then. It didn't do any more for her than her trousers and shirt. She would be beautiful in anything. When he realised he was about to undress her with his eyes, he forced himself to look away.

'This is a lovely place. How in the world did you find it?' he asked, taking in the cream coloured walls and bright Navajo rugs scattered over the Mexican tiled floor. It was a comfortable room rather than an ostentatious one like the drawing room in his Manhattan duplex.

'It belonged to some friends of mine. I leased it from them for a year and then worked out a way to buy it.'

'You're lucky to have friends like that,' he replied, envying the people who had helped her.

A woman like this one just naturally made a man wish he could give her the world. A frisson chilled his blood as the setting sun gleamed on his wedding ring. What the hell was the matter with him? He had no right to think of Glory as anything more than an artist, albeit a very talented one.

'It's getting late,' Glory said.

He hoped her comment wasn't a signal for him to leave. 'We still have a lot to talk about.'

'Would you like to stay for supper? I'm a truly abysmal cook but

I can usually produce an edible steak. I'm dying to chat with someone who knows what's going on in the art world.'

He would gladly have swallowed ground glass if it came from her kitchen. 'I'd love to stay if it isn't too much trouble.'

She got to her feet. 'Would you like something to drink first?'

'A glass of wine would be nice.'

He tried not to stare as she walked across the floor and took a bottle and a couple of glasses from the top of a low chest.

It proved to be an impossibility. Unless he was very much mistaken, Glory wasn't wearing anything under her jeans. The thought sizzled through his mind like a power surge. Don't have an erection, he warned himself.

'Did you mean what you said about wanting to represent me?' she asked, returning to the sofa and handing him a glass of wine.

The question was a welcome distraction. Considering her prodigious talent she didn't sound very sure of herself. The art world could be a cruel place for female artists. He had a sixth sense it had been especially cruel to G. Girard.

'It isn't something I'd joke about.'

She sipped her wine, then smiled at him. 'I'm awfully glad you're here. I'd been planning to go to New York to look into gallery representation. I won't have to now.'

He ignored the voice in his head telling him to leave. He'd done that once in the name of honour and duty. He wouldn't make the same mistake twice.

In any case, it was much too late. G. Girard could rip his heart out of his chest and play ball with it and he'd smile at her as he died.

CHAPTER TWENTY-FIVE

Glory had never been more critical about her sculpture. She wanted the pieces she did for the Wyant Gallery to be her best work. Time and again she roughed in a piece, twisted an armature into an interesting pose and covered it with sculpting work, only to destroy it after deciding the results failed to meet her high standards.

No matter the time and effort, the missed meals and sleepless nights, she was determined to make every single piece as near perfection as her imagination and technique allowed. She told herself Manhattan was the toughest market she would ever encounter and her career would benefit from a *success d'estime* as much as her bank account would benefit from increased sales.

In the quiet hours of the night when she lay alone in her bed, she admitted the truth. She wanted Lawrence to be proud of her – and not Lawrence Wyant, the art dealer either. She wanted to make an enduring impression on the man.

At the end of October she arranged for shippers to crate the new work and put it on a New York bound train. At the last minute she decided to go to New York with them.

'It's really good business,' she told Clarence and Ellen Ashton when they came to take Laredo home. 'An artist should always visit the gallery where their work is being shown.'

'I'm sure you're right, dear,' Ellen answered although Glory read doubt in her eyes. 'It's just that the trip is so sudden. Are you sure nothing's wrong? Because we're here for you if it is. I could call Saul—'

'Please don't worry about me,' Glory interrupted. 'I love you for it but I've never been happier.'

Clarence took his wife's hand. 'Leave be, Mrs Ashton. Glory's a grown woman – and a successful one too. If she thinks it's important to see the Wyant Gallery then that's the end of it.' He softened his words with a smile before turning back to Glory. 'You don't need to worry about a thing while you're gone. We'll take good care of Laredo and I'll check on the house every day when I pick up your post.'

'I'll be back before you know it,' Glory answered as they got up to leave.

She would have to buy them something special in New York to thank them – although come to think of it there wasn't anything special enough to repay the debt she owed the Ashtons.

'Are you sure you don't want us to drive you to the train station?' Ellen asked. 'It wouldn't be any trouble.'

'I've already imposed on you far too much.'

'Pish, tosh, young lady. We love doing for you – always have, always will,' Ellen replied.

The next day Glory was glad she had refused Ellen's offer. She was too enervated to make conversation with anyone. While she waited for the train she had the odd sensation of being suspended between two worlds – the one she had made her own in Taos and the unknown one in New York.

She had thought a great deal about Lawrence Wyant in the six months since his visit. She resented him for having the power to remind her she was a woman with a woman's needs – and yet she couldn't wait to see him.

For two days and nights her pulse kept pace with the clatter of the train's wheels as the scenery outside her compartment window metamorphosed from the craggy mountains of New Mexico, to the flat land of the plains states, to the undulating Appalachians bordering the East coast.

She had grown accustomed to the profound peace of the Sangre De Christos. From the moment she left the train in Grand Central Station, Manhattan assaulted her senses. The exhaust fumes of countless taxis added a noxious aroma to the gritty air. A cacophony of multi-lingual voices rose above the grinding of gears and the blaring of horns. An ever changing kaleidoscope of sights filled her eyes.

It had been years since she paid attention to fashion. As she taxied to the Waldorf past pavements crowded with chic women, she wondered when they had started wearing suits and dresses with padded shoulders and well-defined waists. And what in the world would she wear when she went to the gallery? The age-old female question hounded her all the way to the hotel.

Jeans and over-size shirt might be *de rigeur* in her studio and the remnant of her once magnificent wardrobe might still pass for style in a backwater like Taos, but neither would do in New York. She didn't want to see Lawrence again, let alone meet his undoubtedly chic wife, looking like Robinson Crusoe's Man Friday.

Glory's new sculpture had surpassed all his expectations, Lawrence thought as his staff uncrated the last of them.

'Wow!' one of the salesmen said. 'Now I know why you were so excited when you came back from New Mexico. Girard's work is going to sell itself.'

'Wow, indeed,' Lawrence replied, silently compiling a list of important collectors to contact and offer an exclusive first look at the best pieces. Although from a cursory inspection, they were all *best pieces*. Glory had outdone herself. He wished he believed she had done it for him.

'Where do you plan to display them?' a member of the staff asked.

Lawrence pointed at a superb bronze of an Olla maiden. 'I think this one should go in the front window. I want four more pieces placed where they can be seen from the street. And I want to choose the paintings behind them myself.'

'That will mean rehanging half the gallery,' the first salesman said, then grinned. 'Not that I'm complaining. Girard's work is worth the effort.'

Lawrence nodded his agreement. Although he usually consigned the work of artists who were new to the gallery to less prominent display in the back rooms, Glory's sculpture deserved no less than star treatment.

A top gallery didn't depend on walk-in traffic to generate sales. Dealers used their mailing lists to send photographs of new work to major collectors, including birthday and anniversary cards with them if the timing was right, inviting valued customers to have champagne and special showings in the private viewing room. But instinct told him he'd sell several of Glory's pieces to first time customers who had seen them from the street.

Unlike many Manhattan art dealers who rented whatever space they could afford – often in brownstones converted to commercial usage – the Wyant Gallery had been designed and built with one purpose, to display art to the best possible advantage.

Daylight from the ceiling to floor windows facing Fifth Avenue was augmented by a multitude of overhead spotlights. Decor had been kept to a minimum so as not to distract from the art. The pale grey walls matched both the carpeting and the upholstered benches that invited visitors to linger.

The second floor was devoted to offices, a frame shop, an art library, a storage area, and the private viewing room. Lawrence's well-trained staff enhanced the elegant ambiance. He had taught them to inform and educate rather than sell and he paid well enough to attract the best in the business.

His client list, gathered over the thirty years the gallery had been open, was a *Who's Who* ranging from old Eastern money like the Astors and Rockefellers to the most glittering show business stars. His openings – famous for blending good art, good wine, and good conversation – played to standing room crowds.

Now as he looked at Glory's sculpture he realised he should have broken his self-imposed rule of waiting until an artist proved themselves before offering a show. If he had trusted his instincts the invitations would have gone out weeks ago and Glory would be on her way. It might be months before he saw her again and much as he loved her work, it couldn't stand in for the woman.

Four hours later after placing the last sculpture to his satisfaction, Lawrence looked up from his labours to see a well-dressed woman making a grand entrance through the gallery's bevelled glass doors. She wore red from head to toe as though the colour had been invented just for her.

Lawrence was admiring her style when he realised it was Glory – reinvented and redefined yet again. Gone was the bohemian, clay-smudged artist of Taos. A breathtaking woman of the world had taken her place.

'As you can see, I'm at your feet,' he said, commanding his racing heart to slow down. 'I was just going to telephone you. You've saved me the trouble of dealing with a long distance operator.'

There was so much more he wanted to say and didn't dare – things a married man had no right to say to anyone but his wife.

'Why were you going to call? Didn't you like the pieces I sent?'

'Like them? Dear Glory, they're magnificent.'

At that moment nothing short of a command from God, accompanied by a bolt of light to prove its authenticity, could have kept Lawrence from giving physical expression to his emotions. He closed the distance between them in a few brisk steps, opened his arms and pulled her into them.

The second he touched her, he knew he'd never be the same. It wasn't a cliche about time standing still after all. The room seemed to implode and fall in on itself until he was only aware of Glory – the beat of her heart, the fragrance of her skin, her body's curves that fitted so well against him.

He only meant to offer her a congratulatory hug but he couldn't seem to let her go. 'Surely you know how good your work is. The staff has been raving about it since we opened the first crate.'

She gently disengaged from his embrace. 'I hoped you would react that way. It's so hard for me to be objective. I can't really tell if my reach and my grasp are anywhere near each other.'

'That's one of my jobs as your dealer,' he said, then checked his watch. 'It's almost closing time. I'd love to take you to supper. Now you're here I intend to monopolise your time. I want to introduce you to collectors and set up interviews with local art critics. We can talk about your schedule while we eat.'

'What about your wife? Isn't she expecting you home?'

'Beth is used to last minute changes in my plans.'

'Will she join us?'

The last thing he wanted was to spend the evening trapped between loyalty to Beth and his burgeoning love for Glory. 'I'm not even going to ask her. She might feel obliged to come and Beth has already heard all the art talk she needs in one lifetime.'

Lawrence considered taking Glory to some place like 21 where he knew the *maître d'* well enough to be assured of getting a good table without a reservation – and quickly decided against. He didn't want to dine somewhere so public that table-hopping acquaintances would report his every move to Beth.

Instead he chose a relatively unknown uptown trattoria with an intimate atmosphere, a small but adequate wine list, and the best northern Italian cuisine this side of Florence. He excused himself long enough to call Beth and say he wouldn't be home due to the unexpected arrival of an important out-of-town client and not to wait up for him.

It wasn't a lie, he reassured himself, as he returned to the table. Glory's arrival had been unexpected, she was from out of town, and very important to him.

The dinner was an unqualified success, the conversation even better than the food, although he later realised he'd done most of the talking. Glory was the best listener in the world. Her gaze never left his face as he discussed the ever shifting sands of the art world, the growing importance of publicity and public relations, the way hype could make or break an artist.

'I know it must sound naive but I always thought talent was the only thing that mattered,' Glory commented.

'I have the feeling that's exactly what Vincent Van Gogh told his brother. Theo Van Gogh was a respected art dealer but he didn't have the clout to help Vincent.' Lawrence grinned. 'Fortunately I'm in a much better position.'

'What you're talking about takes money.'

'Don't worry. I don't believe in throwing mine away. An artist of your calibre is worth every penny. Maurie has done a terrific job for you on the West coast. I want to do the same thing here and then go beyond that.'

'What do you mean?'

'If things go the way I anticipate you'll have a national reputation in a few years. I won't be satisfied, though, until you're an auctionable artist with an international following like Lipschitz, Archipenko, or Boccioni.'

'But they're all men, and modernists too.'

'Haven't you heard that beauty is in the eye of the beholder? I've been in the business long enough to know you can't measure your style against anyone else's. You've got the ability to become a *force majeure* in the art world, and I have the know how to make it happen. I'd say that makes us a winning combination.'

'I'm thrilled—' she hesitated, 'but I don't understand. Why do you want to do all that for me?'

He couldn't tell her he had fallen in love with her. He couldn't give her the things a man longs to give the woman he loves – his name, a home, children – but he would help to make her a famous and wealthy artist.

Since he couldn't say any of those things, he replied, 'It's good business. The more money you make, the more I make. The bigger your reputation gets, the bigger mine does too. Maurie discovered you. I want to be the dealer who promotes you to international recognition.'

'It sounds like an impossible dream,' Glory responded with a catch in her voice.

'Is it your dream?'

'It's every artist's dream.'

Grinning, he crossed his heart. 'In that case G. Girard, I solemnly swear to make it come true.'

He beckoned the waiter and ordered a bottle of the restaurant's best champagne. Minutes later he offered her a toast.

'To the two of us,' he said. And to love, he silently added.

'To the two of us,' Glory echoed.

Lawrence looked upon the vow he'd given her as an unbreakable trust. Before he was done she would be one of the world's leading artists. He only needed to give her a showcase. Her talent would do the rest.

He wanted the evening to last until sunrise. Mindful of Beth waiting at home he paid for dinner, helped Glory into her coat, escorted her outside and flagged down a cab before ten.

'Aren't you going to ride with me?' she asked as he handed her in.

'I thought I'd walk supper off,' he replied, already counting the hours until he saw her again. 'Don't make any plans for tomorrow until you hear from me. I'll be in touch as soon as I've had a chance to talk to a few collectors.'

He watched until the taxi rounded a corner, then headed up the street, walking slowly to put off the time when he would face his wife. He had never betrayed Beth before by thought or deed. But dear God, how he wished he could spend this night in Glory's arms.

He missed her already. How could that be? What insanity had taken hold of him? He'd always been a supremely rational man. He'd looked long and hard before he leaped, examining situations from every possible angle. Had that been his downfall?

As Manhattan traffic whizzed by he wondered what would have happened if he had lingered at her debutante party and insisted on a second dance. Would they be married now? Would he go home each night to her arms? He groaned aloud at the thought.

He felt guilty as hell and gloriously alive for the first time in years. He wanted to dance down the street and bay at the moon.

'I'm in love with Glory Girard,' he shouted, heedless of the peculiar looks other pedestrians sent his way.

*

261

The next three days passed in a whirlwind of appointments, lunches with collectors, cocktails with art critics, dinners with museum people – and Glory loved every minute of it. Her new clothes did double and then triple duty as she went from one occasion to the next on Lawrence's arm.

Although she hadn't been in society for years he made her feel so at ease it might have been yesterday she stood in the receiving line at her coming out party.

The days she spent with him were another sort of coming out for her – this time as a rising star in the art world. She was so happy that she didn't once think about the past. She lived in the present, wringing every last drop of joy from each and every moment as the clock of her stay slowly ran down.

Her fourth and last full day in town the phone rang in her room as she was drying herself after a long and luxurious soak. She picked up the receiver expecting to hear Lawrence on the other end of the line.

Instead a strange female voice said, 'May I speak with Miss Girard?'

'You are,' Glory replied, sitting down on the edge of the bed.

'I'm so glad I caught you before you went out. This is Beth Wyant. I know my husband has kept you on the go but I hoped you could save a little time for me today. Could we meet for tea in the Palm Court at three?'

Glory ran the day's schedule through her mind. It would be close but she could make it. 'I'd love to if you're sure it won't be too much trouble.'

'It won't be any trouble at all. I shall look forward to it. Oh, there is one more thing. I'd appreciate it if you didn't mention our meeting to Lawrence. You may not realise it but he's very proprietorial about his artists and his gallery. I wouldn't want him to think I was interfering in any way.'

Although the request puzzled Glory, she had no reason not to agree. She arrived at the Palm Court at the appointed time. When the *maître d'* escorted her to Beth's table, she saw a fragile looking blonde whose natural prettiness was almost overwhelmed by brittle chic.

'I'm Glory Girard,' she said, holding out her hand. It almost swallowed Beth's much smaller one.

'And I'm Beth Wyant.' Beth's voice and her grip were much stronger than Glory would have imagined. 'Won't you sit down?'

'Your waiter will be right with you,' the *maître d'* said as he helped Glory into a chair.

Beth's casual nod of dismissal told Glory that she too had grown up in a house full of servants.

'I would have recognised you anywhere,' Beth said in a well-modulated voice. 'Lawrence told me Titian would have loved to paint you. Now I know what he meant.'

Glory didn't know how to respond to a compliment uttered in such a judgmental tone. To mask her discomfort, she picked up the menu and hid behind it.

'Would you like tea?' Beth asked, breaking the silence before it grew uncomfortably long.

'I'd prefer something stronger.'

Beth's answering smile didn't warm. It emphasised her glacial good looks. 'So would I. Thank heaven Prohibition is over. I used to hate squeezing a flask into an evening bag. I like dry Martinis. How about you?'

'A Martini is just what I need. To tell you the truth I'm a little nervous about meeting you this way.'

Beth's blue-eyed gaze drilled Glory. 'Oh, really? Whatever for?'

Glory sensed a hidden agenda behind Beth's finishing school manners. 'I was a little baffled when you asked me to keep our meeting a secret.'

Beth lit a cigarette and blew out a thin stream of smoke. 'I love a little intrigue, don't you? It keeps life interesting. Since mine may be somewhat truncated, you can understand why I try to make it amusing.'

She had been right to be on guard, Glory mused. For all her gracious manners Beth Wyant was a riddle wrapped inside an enigma. 'I don't know what you mean.'

'Has my husband mentioned my illness?' Beth asked.

'Should you be out if you're feeling sick?'

Beth let go a silvery peal of laughter. 'Your naivete is quite refreshing. The truth is I've been sick every day for the last decade. I have multiple sclerosis. I'm surprised Lawrence didn't tell you. The two of you certainly have spent enough time together the last few days.'

263

'For business, Beth.'

'Oh? I thought you and my husband were very much closer. Lawrence told me he'd met you years ago and that your best friend Cal, was married to his best friend, Jeremy Montclair. That plus showing your work in our gallery almost makes you family. By the way, how are Cal and Jeremy doing these days?'

The question didn't relax Glory. Beth was on a fishing expedition. She had merely changed the bait. 'Wonderfully well. Did you know they're expecting their first child in a couple of months?'

Beth shook her head. 'Lawrence didn't mention it. But then he makes a point of not talking about our friends' offspring since we're unable to have any of our own. He is so thoughtful about things like that. Any man can remember the big things like anniversaries and birthdays. My Lawrence is the rare man who never forgets the small things. So he doesn't talk about children. He wouldn't willingly hurt me in any way.'

Glory wanted to ask why Beth felt a compulsion to divulge so many things that should have remained private. However that was one Pandora's box Glory didn't dare open. 'I'm not sure what you want me to say.'

'Whatever is in your heart of hearts will do.'

'That's easy. You have my sympathy.'

'When you live with a disease like mine life becomes a series of losses. Being married to a man like Lawrence makes it all worthwhile, though. Did he tell you we were childhood friends?'

'It must be wonderful to live with someone you know that well,' Glory replied.

'My dear, I don't just *live* with him. We're very much married in every way,' Beth replied.

'So I see.' Glory didn't blame Beth for erecting a verbal hands-off sign where Lawrence was concerned. She would do the same thing in Beth's shoes. Under other circumstances they might have been friends. Unfortunately in this case the tie that bound was Beth's husband.

No indeed, Glory didn't dislike Beth. She was terrified of her.

'An attractive man like Lawrence,' Beth continued in a conspirator's low tone, 'has lots of opportunities to stray. He once told me about a wealthy young widow who asked him to come to her duplex to help rehang her deceased husband's collection. As it turned out

264

the only thing the widow was interested in seeing well-hung was Lawrence. After that he turned over all such requests to his employees. Lawrence is loyal, devoted and honourable. He would never succumb to a casual roll in the hay.'

'Why are you telling me all this? I already have the greatest admiration for your husband.'

'I was just making conversation. I think it's a funny story, don't you?'

'You're very lucky to have married a man like Lawrence,' Glory said, wondering how soon she could politely make her escape.

'Tell me about you,' Beth replied smoothly. 'Is there a special man in your life?'

'Two,' Glory replied with a smile. 'A Hollywood art dealer named Maurie Golden and a dog named Laredo. The first keeps me solvent and the second keeps me warm at night. Is there anything more you want to know?'

'Where does my husband fit in?' Beth asked with a boldness that took Glory by surprise.

'He's a fine dealer and I'm honoured to be in his gallery. But then I'm sure you've heard similar remarks from the other artists he represents.'

Glory was glad the waiter's arrival interrupted the conversation again. In need of a little Dutch courage, she took a sip of her Martini.

'In the ten years Lawrence and I have been married, I've never heard him carry on so with – that is *about* a woman artist.'

'We aren't carrying on,' Glory said. 'Our relationship is professional – nothing more.'

'Oh dear, you've misunderstood me and that's the last thing I want. I don't know you very well, my dear, but I do know my husband. Lawrence is a very upright man with the highest moral standards. Under the circumstances – that is in view of my health, he would feel like such a heel if he had an affair. If you knew him as well as I do you would realise he would never forgive himself. Ultimately he would come to hate the woman who had tempted him.' Beth gave her the poorest excuse for a smile that Glory had ever seen. 'But the question is moot, isn't it?'

'Very,' Glory replied forcefully.

She had never expressed her feelings to Lawrence and after this talk with Beth, she knew she never could.

CHAPTER TWENTY-SIX

New York, 1938

Memories. Bits and pieces of experience that accumulated to shape a character just as Glory created a sculpture from clay. Memories. The best of them of Lawrence, she thought as she gazed at him across the dinner table the evening before her third annual show at the Wyant Gallery.

The art business had dominated their conversation. The thoughts and feelings she had never expressed reverberated through their silences. She was so aware of him that her breathing kept pace with his. She longed to touch his face, to memorise the feel of him with her hands.

He took a last sip of coffee, then paid their bill. 'Would you like to take a walk in Central Park?'

'I'd love to stretch my legs,' she replied.

He came around the table, helped her out of her chair and his touch ran through her like quicksilver. 'Ready?' he asked, offering her his elbow.

'More than ready.'

They had dined at Rumpelmayers. He kept his hand firmly on her elbow as he guided her across Fifty-ninth into the green shield of shrubbery surrounding the park. Finding a quiet path, they walked in silence.

Although Glory loved her work and was able to lose herself in it, she never felt fully alive until she was with Lawrence. His visits to Santa Fe and hers to New York defined her calendar more clearly than any holiday. His trips to New Mexico felt like Christmas and New Year rolled into one. Hers to New York had the explosive excitement of a Fourth of July fireworks. Not that they came anywhere near those dates. However that's how they made her feel.

She had faithfully kept the promise she made to herself after meeting Beth though it grew more difficult with every passing year. She never revealed her love for Lawrence by word or deed but her thoughts were her own – and they were all of the man by her side.

Sometimes when she was working it almost seemed she could see her sculpture through his eyes rather than her own. She envisioned the lift of his brow when he first looked at a piece, the quiet moment of withheld judgement that was invariably followed by a smile of pure delight.

She lived for those moments when she knew her work pleased him. They were an affirmation of the long lonely hours she spent in the studio struggling with materials that defied her efforts like stubborn children.

Her art was not performed in public like a concerto or a ballet. She practised it in solitude. The discipline she brought to the daily struggle, the willpower that made it possible to turn away from distraction, helped her to keep her emotions in check now.

'You're awfully quiet tonight. Is something on your mind?' he asked.

'I guess I'm just a little nervous about the opening.'

He tightened his grip on her arm. 'After all these years surely you realise you have nothing to be nervous about. I expect a sell-out tomorrow night.'

She loved the concern in his voice. To be honest she loved everything about him – except for the ring on the fourth finger of his left hand. Few men wore a wedding band. Why did he have to be one of them? As if she needed any reminder of Beth!

Such reminders came in the mail far too often in the form of birthday cards and Christmas messages signed in both Beth and Lawrence's names. Either Beth didn't know or she deliberately chose to ignore the fact that Lawrence sent more personal messages himself.

Then there were the notes on Beth's personal stationery with Mrs Lawrence Wyant engraved in a bold scroll across the top, asking if they could get together the next time Glory came to New York. Martinis in the Palm Court with Beth had become as much a part of her stays in New York as the time she spent with Lawrence.

True to her word, she never told Lawrence about any of it. Her relationship with Beth was the only illicit one in the bizarre triangularity of their lives.

The sound of his voice interrupted her introspection. 'You haven't heard a word I said, have you?'

She shook her head. 'I'm afraid not.'

'You seem preoccupied tonight. If something's troubling you I'd like to help.'

'There's nothing you can do.' Except divorce Beth, she thought. Brightening her voice, she said, 'What were you talking about?'

'You. Your career. You've gone further faster than I dared hope four years ago. You've got a solid national reputation. I think it's time to move on to an international one.'

'What do you have in mind?' Glory made a moue as they strolled arm in arm past the Gapstow bridge. At this hour the park belonged to lovers. Yet here she was with the man she adored – talking business.

'I'd like you to go to Europe with me sometime soon. I have close relationships with several dealers on the Continent – dealers who would accept your work on my word alone. But I don't want mere acceptance. I want them to launch you properly and that means face to face meetings with me doing the negotiating while you charm them out of their socks.'

Glory was about to say yes when she remembered Dimitri and Leah lived in Paris. There had been a time when the thought of doing them bodily harm, of raking Leah's face with her nails or jamming her knee into Dimitri's crotch, had been as Shakespeare put it, a consummation devoutly to be wished. Thanks to Saul she had transferred her anger and hostility to a new venue. She wanted to triumph over Dimitri as an artist. But was she ready to do battle on his home turf?

'I'm not sure that's a very good idea.'

'It's the next logical step for your career.'

'It's just that Europe is so unsettled these days. I don't like what I know about Hitler.'

'I don't either. But now the Munich Pact has been signed, I don't think we're going to war with him.'

He paused in mid-stride, took both her arms and turned her to face him. The nearby street sounds seemed to fade away as she looked into his eyes.

'I want you to go with me. I want more than a few stolen hours with you.'

She reached up to silence him with her hand. 'You mustn't say another word.'

He caught her hand and kissed her fingertips. She felt the warmth of his lips through her glove. 'I can't go on living like this, being with you and yet not really with you, pretending you're just another artist when you're my heart. I've fought against telling you how I feel for years. I'm ready to accept defeat. I love you. I have from our very first dance. To my eternal regret, I ran away from my feelings then. Our lives would have been so different if—'

Dear God, she thought, don't let him say another word – and don't let me. She tried to pull her hand free but Lawrence held it tight.

She had dreamed this moment would come, wanted it and dreaded it in equal measure. Her soul reached out to his even as her brain clamoured for caution.

'You have a wife,' she said in a shaky voice that bore no resemblance to her normal husky tone.

'Don't you think I know that?' he burst out, his face so filled with anguish that she longed to take him in her arms. She didn't dare, though. Desire burned far too bright inside her already.

'If I were free—' He never finished the thought. Instead he embraced her and told her how he felt with his lips, his arms, his body. And, God help her, she responded in kind. Her mouth opened, her tongue tasted his, her fingers tangled in his hair, her breasts and hips pressed into him so firmly that she could feel his manhood through the layers of clothing they wore.

One kiss, she told herself – one kiss can't do any lasting harm. But she couldn't have been more wrong. When they finally parted with the heat of unleashed desire pulsing between them like a living thing, everything had changed.

Lawrence returned home to a quiet apartment at ten. Moving as soundlessly as a cat burglar he made his way to the bedroom he shared with Beth, undressed and slid into the icy embrace of the single bed across from hers.

Before they married her doctor had insisted on twin beds so Beth could sleep undisturbed. Lawrence had objected at the time. Now though, he was glad he had obeyed the decree. He couldn't have got in bed with his wife while the taste of Glory's kisses lingered on his lips.

Beth stirred once but her slow exhalations told him he hadn't wakened her. At least one of them would get a good night's sleep, he thought with uncharacteristic self-pity. He had left Glory with nothing resolved between them except the realisation that she loved him too – a helpless, hopeless love she had told him, one they must never acknowledge or act on again.

Her words tolled in his mind like medieval church bells calling sinners to repent. But deep down, he didn't feel like a sinner. Love like his could never be a sin.

That it was love he had no doubt. He was no stranger to lust, had felt it rising in his loins often enough in the presence of an attractive and obviously available woman. He was no better than any other man. An unexpected glimpse of cleavage or thigh could send warmth spiralling to his groin.

However those feelings had always been transient, those moments as ephemeral in the greater scheme of things as soap bubbles. What he felt for Glory had withstood the twin tests of time and separation.

Yes, he wanted her. The joining of their bodies was long overdue considering the joining of their souls and minds. However friendship, respect and infinite admiration were inextricably entwined with physical longing.

Glory's talent absorbed him as much as her beauty. He had put all the gallery's resources behind her career and the effort had paid off handsomely for them both. Now he wanted so much more for them than material success. He wanted to wake beside her every morning. He wanted her face to be the last thing he saw before he went to sleep at night.

He wanted.

Dear God, how much he wanted – and could never have.

Rolling onto his side, he gazed at Beth. She slept with one hand under her cheek, her hair artfully draped over her brow as though she knew he was looking at her and had taken a flattering pose so he would see her at her best. She appeared so frail – her hold on life so tenuous. Yet here he was wishing her away.

How could he consider himself to be an honourable – even a good man?

Dear God, did a monster lurk deep inside him, a self-serving demon that thought only of gratification? The question sent a frisson across his skin. He couldn't imagine adding to the burdens Beth already carried – and yet he couldn't abide the thought of being tied to her for the rest of his life.

When she returned to her room at the Waldorf, Glory felt as though the world had taken on a new topography, one that doomed her to stumble across the strange terrain of requited but unconsummated love.

Feeling more uncertain and confused than she had in years, she picked up the phone to call the one person whose advice and understanding she had always been able to count on. The long distance call went through with surprising speed.

'Is Cal there?' she asked when someone picked up the phone.

'Who the hell else would be answering the phone in my boudoir at eight? I was freshening up for my hubby. What are you doing back so early? I thought you were having dinner with Lawrence.'

'We had a little disagreement.'

'You sound really down. Are you sure you shouldn't be talking to Saul instead of me?'

Glory let go a brittle laugh. Although Saul had long ago pronounced her well, she supposed it was only natural for Cal to think she might have a relapse. 'There's nothing wrong with my mind. The problem is my heart.'

'It's Lawrence,' Cal declared with one of the intuitive mental leaps that made her such a superb confidante.

'How did you know? Is it that obvious?'

'Sure – to someone who has known you since first grade and who just happens to have married Lawrence's best friend. Frankly darling, Jeremy and I have been wondering when you and Lawrence would take time out from art to smell the roses. What happened?'

'He kissed me and I kissed him back.'

'And?'

'I told him never to do it again.'

'Now I know you should be talking to Saul.'

Cal had never given up on her penchant for drama. At the moment she was doing a superb take-off of Bette Davis in one of her life's-a-bitch-and-so-am-I roles.

'You don't understand. There are other people to consider.'

'I suppose you mean Beth. In her quiet way she makes damn certain no one forgets her. Jeremy thinks she trapped Lawrence into marriage as surely as if she had roped and tied him.'

'That's not true. She told me she was sick.'

'Ah yes, the great confession. Noble Beth and all that crap.'

'It's not like you to be unkind.'

'Wake up, Glory. If he had walked away from her after she told him about her illness his parents would have never forgiven him. He might even have been out of the job he trained for all his life.'

'I doubt that,' Glory replied.

'I'm just repeating what Jeremy told me. Beth and Lawrence's parents have always been thicker than thieves. They even have adjoining summer places on Fire Island, for God's sake. It would have been hard enough to break their engagement if she had been healthy as a horse. She knew he wouldn't after she told him she was sick.'

Cal's revelations made Glory see Beth in a new light. She had always pitied the woman. Now she realised she could learn to hate her.

'If Beth really loved Lawrence,' Cal continued, 'she wouldn't have tied him to a woman who couldn't give him children. She would have broken off the engagement herself. So don't waste too many tears on her. She's had him for years. All you're asking for is an occasional weekend here and there.'

'You make it sound so cut and dried. How would you feel if someone went after Jeremy?'

'Lots of someones have already tried. He doesn't care about them and neither do I. But Lawrence is crazy in love with you. He deserves a little happiness. And so do you. *Carpe diem* as my daddy would say. Seize the day, Glory – or perhaps I should say seize the night.'

'You certainly are a superb devil's advocate. I expected you to defend the sanctity of marriage.'

'There's nothing sanctified about what Beth did. Where I come from, we call it manipulation. You haven't said it yet but I assume you do love Lawrence.'

'Yes, I do,' Glory answered, taking comfort from speaking the words out loud.

'And he feels the same way?'

'So he says.'

Cal chuckled. 'Then what are you waiting for? Good God, you haven't been with a man for so long that you've probably grown a new cherry by now. You may be the only woman in the world to lose her virginity twice.'

'You could have come up with a more romantic image.'

'I'm just trying to help you put things in perspective. I know how bad Dimitri burned you. But Lawrence isn't Dimitri. He's a deeply caring man – and you've got so much to give him if you'd just once let go. The two of you need each other.'

Cal stopped talking and let out a little grunt.

'Are you all right?' Glory asked.

'The baby just kicked me under my right boob. The little booger is going to grow up to be a soccer player.'

'I can't wait to see him – or her,' Glory replied, envying Cal as much as Cal must have once envied her.

Cal had everything she talked about wanting years ago – a successful husband, a beautiful house, and a baby on the way. Glory only had her career – and it wasn't enough.

'I hope you're in the mood to celebrate,' Lawrence said to Glory as the gallery doors closed on what had been a sell-out show. 'I made reservations at the Stork Club.'

Although Glory would have preferred a less public setting, she knew that being seen was an important part of the art business. 'Will anyone be coming with us?'

'Not bloody likely,' he replied. 'You and I have unfinished business.'

'It had better be art business,' she was quick to say.

She had battled her emotions last night and lost badly. If he kissed her again she might surrender without any fight at all. Perhaps a public place like the Stork Club wasn't such a bad idea after all.

Half an hour later Glory followed the *maître d'* to a choice banquette table. Howard Hughes cut across her path, reached for her hand and pressed it against his lips.

'If you weren't such a damn fine artist,' Hughes said, 'I'd take you to Hollywood with me and make you a star.'

Glory managed a smile although she considered his remark an insult. She would never be able to accept the fact that most men set a higher value on her looks than her talent.

She and Lawrence were barely seated when a short squarely built man headed over to their table. He strutted rather than walked and his eyes gleamed like a bird of prey.

'Mr Winchell, how nice to see you again,' Lawrence said, getting to his feet.

'Is this the girl you've been telling me about?' Winchell jerked his head at Glory.

'This is the sculptor, Glory Girard,' Lawrence said to Winchell.

'You mean sculptress, don't you?' Winchell turned his enquiring gaze on Glory. 'I hear Hughes bought one of your pieces tonight. It must have been something to get a skin-flint like Hughes to part with his money.'

'I'll take that as a compliment,' Glory replied warily.

Winchell's gaze left her to traverse the room. 'I've been told there's another sculptor here tonight, a fellow by the name of Dimitri Konstantine. You wouldn't happen to know him, would you? I hear he's as famous in Europe as you are in the States.'

Glory's heart stopped. Her stomach knotted. Her skin went hot, then cold. Dimitri here? It was her worst nightmare come true. Was Winchell hot on the heels of a story, one that would reveal her scandalous past?

Fortunately Winchell didn't appear to expect an answer from her. He kept up a staccato stream of comments, asking and answering his own questions as though he had no interest in any opinion but his own.

Glory let Lawrence handle the columnist while she searched the room for Dimitri. He was sitting alone with his back towards her but she would have known the breadth of those shoulders and the shape of that head anywhere. She watched – as helpless as a butterfly pinned to a board – while Dimitri turned to beckon a waiter and saw her.

Their gazes met, then held. An affable smile froze on his face. There was nothing affable, though, about the look Glory sent his way. If looks could kill he would have perished on the spot. Apparently he got the message. He jumped to his feet and hurried for the exit.

She pushed the table away so abruptly that it hit Winchell.

'What the hell,' she heard the columnist say as she raced past him and headed after Dimitri.

Lawrence's first thought was to follow Glory. But he couldn't leave Winchell standing there. He had hoped Glory would get a favourable mention in Winchell's column. She couldn't have picked a worse time to be rude.

'What the fuck was that all about?' the columnist asked, rubbing his thigh where the table had bumped it.

Lawrence could only shake his head. 'I don't know. Believe me, it's not like her.'

To Lawrence's relief, Winchell laughed. 'Who the hell knows what gives with broads? Maybe she's on the rag. But she sure is a looker.' Winchell gave Lawrence a man-to-man wink. 'You'd better go after her.'

Lawrence didn't have to be told twice. He pulled a ten dollar bill from his wallet, dropped it on the table and left at once. He found Glory in front of the restaurant, a look of utter despair on her face as she gazed up and down the crowded street.

'He's gone,' she said.

'Who do you mean?'

'Dimitri. I followed him but I couldn't catch him.'

'Are you talking about Dimitri Konstantine?'

'Yes.' She continued to gaze down the street as though she expected Konstantine to return.

'I didn't realise you knew him.'

Before she could reply a cab pulled up to the kerb and disgorged a load of well-dressed passengers. Lawrence quickly helped Glory into it, then sat down beside her and took her hand. It felt ice cold.

'Where to?' the cabby asked.

'Just drive around the park for now,' Lawrence replied, then turned his full attention on Glory. He had never seen such a lost look in her eyes. 'Can't you tell me what's wrong?'

'Oh God, it's such a long story, one I should have told you long before this.'

Lawrence had always respected the no trespassing sign she'd erected around her past. Now a sixth sense told him Dimitri had been a part of it. 'The first time I saw you in Taos I asked you where you had studied art but you wouldn't answer. I know Konstantine lived in Big Sur. It's not far from Monterey. Did he give you a few lessons?'

'How did you know he lived at Big Sur?'

'I was taking a doctorate in art history at a nearby university. I made it my business to know. Am I right – about Konstantine? Was he your teacher?'

To Lawrence's horror, Glory let go a low moan. The sound seemed to come from the depths of her soul. Bewildered, he could only take her in his arms as shudder after shudder racked her body.

'For God's sake, talk to me. Let me help,' he said urgently. 'Why did seeing Konstantine upset you?'

'I hate him.'

Her voice was so low that at first he wasn't sure he had heard her right. 'Why?' he asked, continuing to hold her tight. 'What did he do to you?'

'Do to me?' Her voice sounded as thin as tissue paper. 'God, where do I begin? He taught me to sculpt, to make love, and finally, he taught me how to hate.'

'Why didn't you tell me about him before? Didn't you trust me?'

'It's not you I don't trust. It's myself. I didn't want to relive what happened. But I'm ready now.'

As the taxi rolled through the night, Glory finally confessed how she had spent the years from their first meeting in San Francisco to their second one in Taos.

Lawrence ached for her, suffered with her as she spoke of the daughter who had died and the mental breakdown that followed. By the time she finished, resolve had hardened in his heart like newly forged steel. He wasn't a violent man but somehow, some way, he would see to it that Konstantine paid for what he had done to Glory.

'Do you hate me?' Glory asked.

'How could you even think that? I told you I loved you last night. I have for years. Nothing's going to change that. Ever,' he said emphatically.

'I wouldn't blame you if you did. I have a great deal to be ashamed of, not the least of which is not telling you about my past long ago.'

'You didn't do anything wrong – then or now. You had a chance to do something with your life and you took it. That's not a sin. I'm so sorry about your little girl. I hate the thought of you going through something like that alone. But you're not alone now.'

Lawrence's arms tightened around her until he could feel the beat of her heart against his chest. He couldn't pinpoint the exact moment when compassion became passion. Gentle kisses grew more urgent, soothing touches more intimate. By the time the cab pulled up in front of the hotel he wanted to make love to her more than he had ever wanted anything. He thought she felt the same way but he gave her one chance to refuse.

'Do you want me to come up to your room?' he asked when they reached the bank of lifts.

'Yes. I've never been more sure of anything in my life,' she replied.

They rode the lift in silence, communicating with their eyes. Glory's hand shook when she gave him her room key. His shook when he opened the door. A trail of clothing marked their path to the bed. They met at its edge, clinging together, lay down to meet their fate.

CHAPTER TWENTY-SEVEN

San Francisco – 1939

Months of accumulated tension slowly seeped away as Glory sat in Cal's parlour, sipping her second Manhattan. She'd been troubled about so many things – specific ones like the impossibility of a future with Lawrence and general ones like the possibility of another world war. Alone in Taos, her mind leapt from one to the other with barely a respite in between.

Being with Cal helped her put things in perspective. An after dinner calm had settled on the house. Jeremy was working late, Cal's baby was tucked in for the night, and the servants had gone to their rooms, leaving Cal and Glory alone for the first time since Glory had arrived from Los Angeles earlier that day.

'I've missed you,' Glory said, letting her breath out in a sigh as she gazed about the room. From the cheerful fire in the hearth to the family photographs on the tables to the playpen in the middle of the floor, everything evoked an idyllic family life. Lucky Cal. She deserved all the happiness in the world.

'*Moi aussi,*' Cal replied. 'The nights are lonely since Jeremy began putting in such long hours.'

'How long has that been going on?'

'A few months. Roosevelt can talk all he likes about America being neutral, but Jeremy is convinced we'll soon be at war with Japan if not Germany. When the time comes he wants the Girard Shipping Company to be ready to do its part.' Cal's voice faltered. Her lashes fluttered as rapidly as a pigeon's wings. A flush crimsoned her cheeks. 'I feel so awkward every time I talk about your father's company – even though Jeremy does run it now.'

'It doesn't bother me one bit. You're proud of Jeremy, as well you should be.'

'But you're the one who should be getting rich from the Girard Company. Not us.'

'Are you forgetting I'm a Girard in name only? If I knew my real name I'd use it. Besides, thanks to Lawrence and Maurie I'm doing well. I'm even thinking of adding a guest wing to the house so there'll be more room for you and the Steiners.'

Cal took a sip from her cocktail and tucked her legs beneath her. 'If you do I'll be there to christen it. We're going to need each other more than ever in the years ahead.'

'You sound awfully gloomy.'

'Our parents had to deal with a world war. I'm afraid it's our turn.'

'Just so long as it doesn't start before Lawrence gets back from Europe,' Glory said with a shiver of foreboding. It had been difficult enough to get through each day when half a continent separated them.

'I still can't believe he took Beth. I thought the two of you were going together.'

'We were.'

'So? What happened?'

'Beth wanted a second honeymoon.'

'Bitch,' Cal muttered. 'I never have liked that woman.'

Glory grinned. 'That's because you're my friend. Lawrence was anxious to make the trip ever since he heard Hitler had ordered the German Nationale Gallerie to dispose of all the so-called degenerate art in its collection.'

'What's degenerate art?'

'Anything painted by Jews. Anything that isn't representational. Would you believe they've already sold a Kandinsky for a hundred dollars and a Klee for three hundred? But I suppose that's better than burning them.'

'Where's the auction?'

'Lucerne.'

'I imagine Lawrence will make a killing reselling whatever he buys when he gets back.'

'I'd rather you didn't talk about killing under the circumstances. I don't like the thought of him dealing with the German government.'

Cal got up, took the silver cocktail shaker from the tray on the coffee table and refreshed their drinks. 'When will you see Lawrence again?'

'Not until my next show. Unless I go to Europe when he makes his next trip.'

'Why in the world would he want to go back?'

'You've got me. I know it sounds crazy but I can't help wondering if he isn't some sort of spy.'

Cal burst out laughing. 'Glory, you always did have one hell of an imagination. Why in heaven's name would the government enlist an art dealer as a spy?'

'It's not all that crazy. Hitler and Goering are rabid art collectors. They're clever enough to realise art can be a great propaganda tool. That's the whole point behind this business about degenerate art – most of which was created by Jewish artists. First they get rid of the art. Then they get rid of the artists.'

'But that's crazy.'

'Is it? I'm just being realistic. The most dangerous despot since Genghis Khan is loose in Europe and he has his eye on art. So don't tell me an expert like Lawrence is an unlikely spy.'

'There's nothing quite like the Ritz,' Beth said to Lawrence as they walked to the registration desk arm-in-arm. 'I'm so happy to be here with you.'

'I'm glad you were well enough to travel,' he told her, although nothing could have been further from the truth.

He had hoped to be with Glory. She would have enjoyed doing things with him, going to museums, walking in the Bois, climbing to the top of the Eiffel Tower at sunrise, having coffee and brioche at a sidewalk cafe and feeding the crumbs to the pigeons. Beth planned to spend her days at the couturiers and her evenings dining at the best restaurants. At least she wouldn't get in his way.

A frantic energy seemed to pulse through the lobby as men and women came together, then parted, the vivid colours the women wore contrasting with the sombre hues of the men's suits and uniforms. And not just French uniforms either. Lawrence saw as many German ones, Wehrmacht and SS. So much for *peace in our time*, he thought.

What he saw confirmed the letters he'd been getting from European gallery owners, telling him war was inevitable. They had enlisted his aid in helping Jewish collectors get their art out of the country.

It had sounded like a simple enough plan the first time he heard it. Using bogus bills of sale, he would take their favourite canvases back to the United States along with the pieces he bought legitimately in Lucerne. When the owners reached America – if they ever did, given the low immigration quotas imposed by Congress – they could either take the works back or authorise him to sell for them. If war started before they escaped, Lawrence had promised to hold the work in trust for the owners or their heirs.

In view of the severe limitations on money and personal possessions that Jewish *émigrés* could take with them when they left the continent, it had seemed like a risk-free way to ensure they had some capital when they arrived in America. Seeing all the German uniforms, Lawrence realised there were risks involved.

Beth reclaimed his attention. 'I'm going to the ladies room. Don't forget to ask for the room we had on our honeymoon.'

'I'll do my best.'

By the time she returned, two bellboys were waiting to take the luggage up to their room.

'Did you get the room we wanted?' she asked.

'The manager told me it was taken by a German officer.'

Beth made a moue. 'Did you offer to make it worth the manager's time?'

'Apparently a German uniform means more than the American dollar in Paris these days.'

Beth slipped her hand in the crook of his elbow and gave him an intimate smile. 'I'm sure we'll have a wonderful time no matter what bed we sleep in. I can't wait to go shopping. Daddy gave me something extra to have fun with.'

Beth's parents spoiled her even more now than they had when she was small. Not that he blamed them. He couldn't imagine anything worse than losing a child – except never having one to lose.

Beth squeezed his arm. 'A little extra money never hurt a girl – especially since I'm going to Chanel tomorrow. Coco's prices are insane.'

'Are you sure you feel up to it?'

'I feel almost as good as I did on our honeymoon. And that, my darling, is saying something. This is probably my last trip to Paris.

I don't want anything to spoil it, including a worry wart of a husband.'

The next morning Lawrence dropped Beth off in front of Chanel's, secure in the knowledge that she would be busy for hours. He told the taxi driver to take him to an address on the Left Bank.

A few minutes later he got out in front of a fine looking apartment building on a quiet side street near the Seine. He rode a groaning antique lift to the fifth floor and knocked on the only door at that level.

It opened to reveal a heavy-set man in his late thirties or early forties. He wore a loose shirt open halfway to his waist, a red scarf, worn corduroy trousers and sabots. Lawrence studied him, wondering what Glory had seen in him.

'Make it fast,' the man said in accented French. 'I'm working.'

Inhospitable bastard, Lawrence thought. 'Are you Dimitri Konstantine?' he asked in English.

'Yes. Who the hell are you?'

Lawrence offered one of his business cards, wondering if his name would ring a bell. If Konstantine read American art magazines he might realise Lawrence represented Glory.

Konstantine read the card without any sign of recognition, then put it in his pocket. 'So you're an art dealer. What brings you to my door, Mr Wyant?'

'I've heard a great deal about you,' none of it good, Lawrence silently added.

Konstantine smiled at what he must have perceived as a compliment. 'Please forgive my lack of hospitality. Do come in. I keep a bottle of Calvados in my studio. Will you join me in a drink?'

In view of his reason for being there, Lawrence preferred the brusque Dimitri to the affable one. 'I'd like that.'

'How is art selling in New York these days? I've been thinking about showing in your country again,' Dimitri said, leading the way through a high-ceilinged apartment that seemed to take up the entire fifth floor.

The studio was as fine as any Lawrence had seen. Well-organised and flooded with light, it offered an over-the-roof-tops view of Notre Dame on the Île de la Cité.

'I have some interesting pieces in progress. Would you like to see them?' Konstantine asked, joining Lawrence with two filled tumblers in hand. He offered one to Lawrence. 'À votre santé,' he said.

Just then a little girl burst into the room.

'Daddy,' she cried out, 'I can't find Matilda.'

Konstantine's broad smile made him look younger. 'Matilda is my daughter's favourite doll,' he explained to Lawrence, then turned back to the child. 'I think you'll find her on the breakfast table where you left her.'

'Thank you, Daddy,' the girl trilled and was gone as quickly as she came.

Lawrence had the peculiar feeling he'd seen her before.

'Please excuse the interruption,' Dimitri said. 'My housekeeper has the day off and there's no one to look after my little girl but me.'

'She's a beautiful child. You and your wife must be very proud.'

'My wife died of cancer two years ago. I've raised Ariadne by myself since then.'

The name burned in Lawrence's brain. Was Konstantine ghoulish enough to name a living child after one who had just died? 'Did you say Ariadne?'

The sculptor nodded. 'It's Greek. Do you like it?'

'Oh, I find it fascinating.'

'Is something wrong?' Konstantine asked. 'You've gone quite white, as though you've seen a ghost.'

'Perhaps I have,' Lawrence replied.

He had come here with one thing in mind – to make Konstantine regret the brutal way he had left Glory. Now a different purpose demanded to be served. Lawrence spent a moment deciding on an approach and then chose the most direct one.

'Does the name Glory Girard mean anything to you, Mr Konstantine?'

Konstantine shook his head.

'Perhaps the name Rouge rings a bell?'

Konstantine glared at him. 'Who the hell are you and what are you doing here?'

'You know who I am. You've seen my card. What you don't know is that I represent Glory Girard.'

'Are you her *avocat* – her lawyer?'

'I'm her art dealer. She told me all about you.'

'You took me by surprise. I'd forgotten Rouge was Glory Girard. She'd be so insulted. You must accept my apology on her behalf.'

Konstantine seemed determined to bluff his way out of what he undoubtedly saw as no more than an awkward situation. 'I can see that I haven't made myself clear,' Lawrence began in a deceptively mild tone. 'In addition to carrying Glory's work in my gallery, we are friends. I know all about her past including the death of her daughter, Ariadne. Seeing Ariadne alive and well today is enough to make me believe in miracles.'

The sculptor's bombastic expression crumpled like a papier mâché mask. 'I never meant to hurt Rouge. I loved her.'

'You had a damn peculiar way of showing it.'

'I did love her. You must believe me. She was the only woman I've ever loved.' The words seemed to have been torn from his gut.

Lawrence had no doubt Konstantine was telling the truth as he saw it. 'If you loved Glory as you say, how could you tell her Ariadne was dead and then compound the pain by saying you never wanted to see her again? Do you have any idea what that did to her?'

Konstantine crossed the room, poured himself another Calvados and drank it straight down. 'I wrote to tell Rouge the truth a few weeks after Leah sent the telegram. When the letter came back marked *address unknown – return to sender*, Leah convinced me that Rouge had gone on her way, that she never cared about Ariadne or me.'

'So you blame Leah for everything.'

Konstantine collapsed into the nearest chair and buried his face in his hands. 'Of course I don't blame her. I blame myself. I was crazy, jealous of Rouge's talent. I thought she was using me to get ahead. All I knew was I had to get away from her.'

'So you took her child and then made her think the child was dead.'

'You don't understand. You weren't there. She was a terrible mother.'

'From what she told me, neither you nor Leah gave her a chance to be a good one.'

'I didn't think she cared about the child the way I did. When that Los Angeles art dealer came to the house and offered her a show, she jumped at it even though—'

Konstantine let go an anguished sob. It took him a moment to regain control. '*Merde.* There is no excuse for what Leah and I did. When Leah got cancer I thought it was God's way of punishing her. I wondered when he would finally get around to punishing me. Now you're here I don't have to wonder any more.'

Lawrence hadn't expected the sculptor to capitulate so quickly. He'd come in the name of revenge. Instead he'd learned a truth that had been hidden for years. 'You're right about one thing. There isn't any excuse for what you did. The woman you describe as a disinterested mother, the woman you say you loved, went through a living hell after she got that telegram. She spent a year of her life in an asylum trying to get over what you did to her. She still bears the mental and emotional scars from the experience. And all the while Ariadne was alive and you were playing Daddy.'

'I didn't know. When that letter came back, Leah convinced me it meant—' Konstantine's voice trailed off. 'I can't blame Leah. It was me. I was Glory's lover and Ariadne's father. I knew I was doing a terrible thing. I hated myself for it. But I couldn't stop myself.' He finally looked up and met Lawrence's gaze. 'I was out of my mind with jealousy of her talent. I'd hit a dry spell in my work and I blamed her for it.'

Lawrence knew the man was facing up to the truth – perhaps for the first time. However he was incapable of feeling any sympathy for him. It was all he could do not to beat the shit out of Konstantine. 'How did you explain things to Ariadne?'

'She was much too little when we left California to remember Glory. She grew up thinking Leah was her mother. And now she believes her mother is dead.'

Lawrence could only shake his head at the man's audacity. He had hurt Glory and his daughter beyond imagining. 'You made her a victim too, then.'

'Nothing could be further from the truth. You saw her. She's a happy little girl. Leah was a wonderful mother and I've always done my best to be a good father.'

'A good father wouldn't turn his child's life into an endless lie.'

'I've tried to explain what happened.' Konstantine jumped to his feet. 'Why the hell are you here anyway? Did Glory send you?'

'Glory knows nothing about my visit. I came because I wanted you to realise what you'd done to her. I wanted you to take responsibility for your actions and feel some guilt. I had no idea what you had really done.'

Relief washed over the sculptor's face. 'Thank God she doesn't know. There isn't a day goes by that I don't regret what I did. I've written to Glory more times than I can count to tell her the truth.

But I could never bring myself to post those letters. How the hell do you tell a woman you stole her child?'

'That's a good question, one you're going to have to answer before I leave. And I assure you, I have a very different view of what happened than you do.'

Konstantine started to pace the floor. 'What you think of me doesn't matter. My only concern is my daughter's happiness. I won't put it at risk.'

'You don't have any choice. Besides, what makes you think she won't be thrilled to find out her real mother is alive?'

'What makes you think Glory will want her?' Konstantine shot back.

Lawrence clenched his hands, fighting the desire to use his fists on Konstantine. 'She never stopped wanting her.'

'I don't care what you think of me. I'm asking you to put your emotions aside and think of Ariadne. She loves and respects me. If I tell her the truth it may scar her for life. I'm all she has.'

'You should have thought of that a long time ago.'

'I suppose there's no way I can convince you to walk away and forget you were ever here.'

'You suppose right.'

'What do you intend to do?'

'I'm not sure – except that Glory needs to know the truth and so does Ariadne.'

Konstantine pressed his fingertips against his temple. 'You think you know Glory but I knew her too. She was as driven as any artist I have ever known. She may not want a child in her life.'

'That's absurd.'

'Absurd or not, the decision to tell Ariadne should be Glory's. Will you at least agree to that much?'

Reluctantly, Lawrence nodded even though he would have liked to take Ariadne then and there and book passage on the first ship to the States.

'Can you stay the rest of the afternoon?'

'Good God, what for?'

'Because I need time to write Glory a long letter. And you need to see more of Ariadne so that you can give Glory a full report. I swear you will see a happy, well-adjusted little girl who loves her father almost as much as he loves her. I want Glory to hear that from your lips before she comes to any decision.'

'You ask a great deal.'

'I'm not asking for myself. It's for my daughter. And for Glory too. I want you to deliver the letter in person. She shouldn't be alone when she learns the truth. I assume your being with her won't be a hardship.'

'What the hell is that supposed to mean?'

'I can't imagine any art dealer going to the lengths you have today – unless a personal relationship were involved. You're in love with Glory, aren't you?'

Konstantine was astute, Lawrence thought. He'd give him that much credit. 'My feelings have nothing to do with the matter at hand.'

The sculptor accepted the rebuke with surprising equanimity. 'You're right. Only two people matter now – Ariadne and Glory. You know the one. It's time you got to know the other.'

CHAPTER TWENTY-EIGHT

The September air had a real chill as Glory returned from her daily walk with Laredo at her heels. Autumn came early in Taos. The aspens were shedding their leaves. A few more weeks and snow would dust the Sangre De Christos' highest peaks.

It had been a lonely summer. The Steiners had been unable to make their annual pilgrimage. Cal, pregnant again and suffering from morning, afternoon and evening sickness, had stayed at home too. Most of all, Glory had missed Lawrence.

He had called a few times since returning from Europe but she sensed a reserve in his voice she had never heard before – and wondered if Beth's latest relapse had caused it. She had tried to get him to tell her what was bothering him and each time he changed the subject.

Throughout the summer she fought the feeling that something dreadful was going to happen – a feeling the headlines bolstered. Congress's repeal of the 1937 Neutrality Act made another world war seem like an eventuality. The turmoil abroad enhanced her foreboding.

She picked up her pace as though she could leave her worries behind. Ever faithful Laredo trotted at her side, watching her every step. It was wrong to refer to men as dogs, she decided. Canines were far superior.

By the time she reached her driveway, sweat had plastered her blouse to her skin and Laredo panted at her knee like a steam engine. She took her post from the box and looked through it, hoping to find a letter from Lawrence.

'I was afraid you were gone for the day,' she heard him say.

Had her imagination conjured him up? Was he a chimera or a flesh and blood man? She was almost afraid to find out.

'I hoped for a more enthusiastic welcome,' he said.

She looked towards the house and the letters spilled from her hands. 'I was just thinking about you,' she cried out, racing into his open arms. He certainly wasn't a mirage, she thought, as she felt his body against hers.

'Good thoughts, I hope,' he murmured against her mouth.

'Lonely thoughts. I've missed you so. How long have you been here?'

He silenced her questions with a long kiss that left her breathless.

'I've dreamed about doing that for months,' he said when he finally let her go.

'Me too.'

She unlocked the front door and led the way into the house, then tilted her face to his. 'Are those kisses rationed?'

'Not for you,' he replied huskily.

Glory clung to him, willing the moment to last forever. She could happily have spent the rest of the afternoon reacquainting herself with his mouth. She had been desperate for the sight, the touch, the taste of him and now she couldn't get enough.

He groaned, then let her go so abruptly that she almost lost her balance.

'I must smell like a draught horse after my walk,' she said, thinking that was the reason he'd ended their embrace.

'You smell of sunshine, fresh air and pure you. I wish I could bottle it and take it home with me.'

The word *home*, with all it implied, brought her back to earth. 'How long can you stay?'

'Just tonight.'

'Why bother to come at all?' she sputtered.

It wasn't enough time. God. They never had enough time. She could feel tears at the back of her eyes and refused to give in to them.

'I had to see you.'

What did he mean by that? she fretted – and was half afraid to know the answer. 'What about Beth? I thought she was in the hospital.'

'She was released last week. She's staying with her parents.'

The polite chit chat was driving Glory crazy. She had the distinct feeling that Lawrence had something on his mind and, from his frown, she doubted if it would be good news. 'Why is she staying with her parents? Does she know about us? Did she leave you?'

'Beth was ready to leave the hospital but she still needs a lot of care. We decided it was best she stay with her family.'

We speared into Glory's heart. *We*, she thought sadly would always mean Lawrence and Beth – never Lawrence and Glory. Movies always portrayed the other woman as a glamorous creature. But there was no glamour in being jealous, uncertain and perpetually lonely.

Sometimes Glory wondered if the brief moments of happiness were worth the grief of loving a man who belonged to another woman.

Lawrence took her hand, led her to the sofa and pulled her down beside him. 'Beth has a lot of adjusting to do. She lost the sight in her left eye.'

'Is the loss permanent?'

'I'm afraid so. She's being very brave about it, talking about getting all sorts of coloured eye patches to match her wardrobe.'

'I don't get it. Why did you come here if Beth is still sick?'

'Beth is always sick to one degree or another. We've learned to live with it. But I didn't travel all this way to talk about Beth. I have something important to tell you.'

Here it comes, Glory thought, this is where he says he's made a terrible mistake and that he really loves his wife. She braced to hear the words. No matter what, she promised herself she wouldn't cry. She had walked into the relationship with her eyes wide open. She would walk out with her head held high.

'You sound so serious,' she said.

'I am.' He took an envelope from his jacket pocket and held it out. 'This is for you.'

The tightness in her chest eased. He wouldn't have travelled two thousand miles to give her a Dear John letter. 'Is it from one of those European art dealers you wanted me to meet?'

He continued to hold onto the letter as though he were reluctant to let her have it. 'No, it isn't.'

'It's not like you to be so mysterious.'

'I don't mean to be. It's just that I don't know how to prepare you for what's inside this envelope – except to warn you it's from Dimitri Konstantine.'

Now she was truly frightened. 'You told me you didn't know him.'

'I didn't until I went to see him in Paris,' Lawrence said calmly as though visiting a man he didn't know – a man Glory thought of as her enemy – made perfect sense.

Glory barely managed to control her anger. 'What in the world possessed you to do that?'

'I wanted to see him face to face and tell him what I thought of him.'

'I don't need you to defend me.'

'I did it because I love you.'

'You're just like Dimitri. Every time he hurt me, he said he did it because he loved me.' It was the cruellest thing she had ever said to Lawrence but at the moment she didn't care.

'Believe it or not, he was more upset when I was with him than you are now.' Lawrence put the letter in her hand. 'Read it. Then we'll talk.'

Glory was so furious that she almost tore the letter up unread. She felt betrayed by the one man she thought she could count on. She'd read the damn letter and then she'd tell Lawrence she never wanted to see him again.

She opened the envelope, then unfolded the paper inside it. *Dear Rouge*, the letter began.

She gritted her teeth at the sight of the familiar scrawl. Damn Dimitri. She hadn't been Rouge for a long time.

I can't tell you how many sleepless nights I've spent imagining myself writing this letter. I've lost count of the times I actually did.

If Dimitri was hoping for sympathy, he'd written to the wrong woman, she thought. After what he'd done to her she didn't care if he ever slept again.

I never posted any of them though, the letter went on. *I was too big a coward. Now Lawrence Wyant has given me no choice. I have to tell you of the terrible wrong I did you years ago. I don't know how to say this except to say it.*

Ariadne is alive.

Glory reread the last line a couple of times, then closed her eyes and pressed a hand to her mouth. It couldn't be true. Ariadne had died of diphtheria. Why was Dimitri torturing her this way? And why had Lawrence let him do it?

'Do you know what's in this letter?'

'I do.'

Her eyes opened and she looked at him long and hard. 'How could you be a part of this – this monstrous sham? Are you crazy – or am I?'

She felt Lawrence's hand on her arm. 'Neither of us is. Dimitri is telling the truth.'

Glory began to tremble. Dimitri might lie. Lawrence wouldn't.

'Are you all right? Can I get you anything? A drink, perhaps.'

Lawrence's voice seemed to come from a great distance. She continued reading, unaware that she had bitten her lips hard enough to draw blood.

The telegram Leah sent years ago was a lie, a cruel hoax whose sole purpose was to get you out of my life and keep Ariadne in it. Not a day passes when I don't regret doing it. I couldn't forget you no matter how hard I tried. Ariadne has your eyes and a miniature dimple in her chin just like the one in yours.

I don't expect you to forgive me. I haven't been able to forgive myself. I did what I did because I was jealous of your talent. I wanted you out of my life – and yet, I never stopped loving you. I've come to realise hatred and love are two sides of the same coin. God knows I hated you when I left Big Sur.

Leah played a part in what I did and God Almighty punished her for it. She died a cruel death from cancer two years ago. I know I will have to pay a price one day too.

As I said, I can't ask you to forgive me and yet you must try for Ariadne's sake. I have not told her that her real mother is alive and I won't until I hear from you.

If your life has moved on, if there is no place in it for a young girl, I will understand. To be honest I hope that is the case. If not I will do my best to ensure that our daughter blames me and only me for keeping the two of you apart.

I have asked your Mister Wyant to deliver this letter in person to answer all your questions about Ariadne. He spent an afternoon with us and can attest to her happiness. Her fate and mine are in your hands. I pray that wisdom and love will guide your decision.

Glory didn't realise she'd been holding her breath until her oxygen-starved lungs clamoured for air.

'Dear God, how could he,' she wailed, 'how could he do something so terrible? I almost lost my mind when I thought Ariadne was dead but Dimitri must have lost his long before. When I think of the months I spent in Atwood, the years I've lived without my daughter.'

She didn't realise Lawrence had left her side until he returned to the sofa and handed her a glass. 'It's brandy. Drink it down. You'll feel better.'

She sprang to her feet abruptly, not caring that she knocked the glass from his hand. 'Feel better? It's going to take a hell of a lot more than a brandy to do that. I won't feel better until I'm holding my baby in my arms.'

'She's not a baby, Glory. She's a seven year old girl with a mind of her own, just like you.'

Glory's anger deflated as quickly as a pricked balloon. A bone-deep sadness replaced it. 'I have a daughter I don't know. I missed her first step, her first words. I never got to hear her call me mother. I never saw her go off to school. I never had the chance to love her. Nothing can make up for that. You've known about her for weeks and you never said a word. You betrayed me too.'

She knew she was near hysteria but she couldn't control her emotions. She didn't even want to try. Her body didn't seem strong enough to contain the conflicting feelings that roared through her like a fire in dry timber. One second she was angry enough to kill Dimitri with her bare hands. The next she felt like weeping. No wonder the miserable bastard had run from her at the Stork Club.

Laredo sensed her upheaval but he didn't correctly identify the reason for it. The world's most harmless pooch bared his teeth at Lawrence and growled deep in his throat. It brought Glory to her senses.

'It's all right,' she said, dropping to her knees and wrapping her arms around Laredo's shaggy head. 'Don't bite Lawrence. He's not the enemy.'

Laredo responded by wiggling in canine ecstasy.

'If I wiggle like that, will you hug me too?' Lawrence asked.

She let go of the dog, sat down on the sofa, and reached for him. The tears she'd held back poured down her face. Her daughter was alive. Nothing else mattered.

'Tell me about Ariadne,' she said when she could finally speak.

'She's tall like you – all arms and legs and enchantingly awkward.' He grinned. 'I think she's going to be as beautiful as her mother some day, but right now with her second teeth coming in she looks like a cross between a colt and a chipmunk.'

He let her go long enough to take a few photographs from his

293

jacket and hand them over. 'Glory, meet your daughter,' he said.

She gazed at the pictures through a haze of tears. One was a formal studio portrait. It showed a solemn looking child with enormous eyes – her eyes, just as Dimitri had written. But Ariadne had Dimitri's black curls and his full lips. Her appearance said she belonged to both of them.

Glory studied her daughter's face, desperately trying to equate the *jeune fille* with her memories of a three month old infant. Not even her skilled artist's eye could make that great a mental leap.

What would Ariadne say when she learned she had a mother? Would she want to see Glory – or would she choose to stay with her father? Glory ached to hold her daughter in her arms, to perform the thousand and one tasks of motherhood. Would she ever have the chance?

She put the portrait aside and looked at the snapshots. One showed Ariadne on a pony looking immensely pleased with herself. In another she was sitting at a miniature table serving tea to a doll.

'That's Matilda, Ariadne's favourite doll,' Lawrence said from over Glory's shoulder.

Glory couldn't take her gaze from the photograph. 'What's Ariadne like?'

'I'm no expert when it comes to children but she seems very intelligent and poised for her age. She speaks French, English and Greek fluently.'

'Does she have everything she needs? Is she happy?'

'From what I could see in one afternoon, the answer is yes to both questions. At the risk of upsetting you even more, you need to know Ariadne and Dimitri are very close. He really loves her.'

'He always did,' Glory replied, remembering the joy on his face the first time he held his daughter. 'He just didn't love me.'

'I don't think that's true. If anything he loved you so much that it scared him almost as much as your talent did. I went to his apartment expecting to dislike him but his honesty impressed me. He told me how insecure he felt as an artist in those days. Did you know he stopped showing his work in America because of one failed show at the beginning of the Depression?'

'He never mentioned it,' she replied, recalling their precipitous trip to Greece. 'None of it makes sense.'

'When it comes to things he cares about, his career, his daughter, even you, he's not the most rational person in the world.'

'That doesn't excuse what he did.'

'I don't think he's looking for excuses. Understanding is another matter. Try to put yourself in his shoes, to imagine what it must have been like to fall in love with a beautiful woman and then learn she was a better artist.'

'Who says I'm better?'

'I do. I think Dimitri knows it too.'

'That's ridiculous. Art doesn't lend itself to that sort of qualitative comparison. Besides, you're prejudiced.' Glory frowned. 'I don't want to talk about who is the better sculptor. Time and the critics will make that decision. I want to talk about my daughter. How soon can I see her?'

'Whoa. You're getting ahead of yourself. First Dimitri has to tell her about you. She'll probably need a little time to adjust to the idea that Leah wasn't her mother before you burst into her life.'

'Time? I've already lost seven years. I can't stand the thought of losing another minute.'

'Dimitri won't tell Ariadne until he's sure you want her.'

Glory let go of Lawrence's hand. 'Much as I hate the thought of hearing Dimitri's voice, I'm going to call him right now.'

Lawrence checked his watch. 'It's midnight in Paris.'

'If you're suggesting I wait until morning, forget it. I don't care if he loses a little sleep.'

She hurried to the phone, got the operator on the line and told her she wanted to talk to Dimitri Konstantine in Paris, France and yes, she knew it would take time to put the call through, and no, she didn't mind what time the operator got back to her.

While she waited for the phone to ring, she quizzed Lawrence about every detail of the afternoon he had spent in Dimitri's apartment. She didn't relent until she had a clear picture of the layout and the furnishings. From what Lawrence remembered, Dimitri had created a comfortable home, one with enough nooks and crannies to delight a child.

Apparently Ariadne had everything a little girl could want – everything that is except a mother. Glory couldn't wait to remedy that situation. It didn't matter if it took Ariadne a while to learn to love her. For the time being she had enough love for them both.

The call came through at sunset. Glory listened impatiently while her own operator in Taos talked to one in New York who talked to another one in Paris. Suddenly, before she was ready, Dimitri came on the line.

'Glory is that you?' His voice sounded as clear as though he were in the next room. 'Are you all right? Is Lawrence there with you?'

Hypocrite. How dare he pretend to care about her. 'It's a little late to worry about me, don't you think?'

'I never stopped.'

'You had a strange way of showing it. But I didn't call to talk about the past. When can I see Ariadne?' Her heart pounded so hard that she pressed a hand to her chest.

'Be reasonable, Rouge. She doesn't even know you exist.'

'Whose fault is that, you bastard?'

'Mine. I could spend the rest of my life apologising and it wouldn't be enough. We have to try and get along for our daughter's sake.'

'When will you tell her the truth?'

'First thing in the morning.'

'I want you to call me after you do. I don't care what time it is here. I want to talk to my daughter. She needs to know I love her and want her here with me.'

'You're right. She does. I can't promise you'll see her soon, though. She may not want to make the trip.'

'I imagine her reaction will depend on what you tell her.'

'Don't worry on that account. I plan to take the blame for everything.'

'If you expect me to thank you, think again. You *were* to blame.'

'There are no words to tell you how much I regret my actions.'

She thought she heard tears in his voice. However they didn't impress her. 'Sure. Now you've been found out, I imagine you do.'

'I regretted it long before Wyant knocked on my door. Even more so after he told me you'd been ill.'

Although she hadn't talked to Dimitri in years she recognised the sincerity in his voice. It came too late – much too late. But she would have to be civil for Ariadne's sake.

'Are you well?' he asked.

'I'm not crazy if that's what you mean. You won't be able to use that excuse to keep me from seeing Ariadne.'

'I don't plan to use any excuse. Frankly your friend Wyant couldn't have shown up at a more opportune time.'

'What do you mean? Is something wrong with Ariadne?'

'She's fine. I was referring to the political situation. The Boche are getting more arrogant all the time. I'm afraid they'll come marching down the Champs Elysées in full force one of these days. I was going to send Ariadne to my family in Greece but there's no guarantee she'd be safe there. I'd much rather send her to you.'

It was the last thing Glory expected him to say. 'Do you really mean it?'

'Absolutely. Paris is no place for a child these days. Besides, she needs a mother now she's getting older. She needs to live in a world where—'

'Where what?'

'Where children can stay children. I'm afraid Europe is in for a terrible time. I'd just as soon have Ariadne on her way before it gets here.'

'What can I do to help? Do you need money?'

'That won't be a problem. However she does need an American passport. She travelled to France on mine. You can get one for her much faster than I can.'

'You make it sound urgent.'

'I don't know how much time we have to arrange things. Do your best, Glory. With any luck Ariadne will be on her way to you before you know it.'

CHAPTER TWENTY-NINE

New Mexico, 1939

'I can't take much more,' Glory said, tossing the morning paper down on the Ashtons' breakfast table.

She had picked the paper up in her driveway minutes before, read the headline about Great Britain and France declaring war on Germany, and headed straight for their house. 'I spent the last year trying to get Ariadne out of Europe. It took weeks to get her passport, months to book her passage and then the steamship company wouldn't let her travel alone so I had to find someone who would agree to be responsible for her.' Her voice rose with every word. 'And now this. I just can't take it.'

'You can and you will,' Ellen said firmly. 'Stop shouting, sit down and I'll pour you a cup of coffee. After you calm down we'll talk about what to do next.'

'I don't want coffee. I want my daughter,' Glory wailed.

Ellen got up from her place, walked over to Glory and pushed her into a chair. 'I know you do and I know you've moved heaven and earth to get her here. But you can't help her if you fall apart.'

'I'm sorry. I don't mean to sound like a spoiled brat.' Glory gazed at Ellen and Clarence, thinking how much they had aged and wondering how she would ever manage without them.

'I'm glad you came,' Clarence said. 'Once Ellen read the news, she'd have insisted on going straight to your house anyway. You saved us the trip.'

'I didn't save you anything. I've brought my troubles to you since I was a little girl. It's time I handled them myself.'

Ellen put a cup of coffee in front of Glory, then sat down beside her and took her hand. 'You have the peculiar notion that people aren't supposed to ask for help under any circumstances. I suppose we can blame Mr Girard for that. But he was wrong and so are you. We're your family, Clarence and I, and families lean on each other.'

'I don't know what to say – except thank you.'

'Have you tried to call Dimitri?'

Glory shook her head. 'I came right here.'

'Things might not be as bad as you think. The experts say Germany will have a hard time getting past the Maginot Line. Besides, we're not at war and Ariadne does have an American passport. There's no reason she can't make the trip the way you planned. Drink your coffee and when you've finished put in a call to Dimitri and see what he says.'

'I will as soon as I get home,' Glory replied, thinking overseas calls weren't on the Ashtons' retirement budget.

She spent fifteen more minutes with them, then hurried back to her house. The phone was ringing when she walked in. Please let that be Dimitri, she prayed as she ran to answer it.

'I've been trying to get you for half an hour,' Lawrence said at once. 'Are you all right?'

'I'm calm now. But I was a mess when I heard the news about the war.'

'That's why I called. I talked to a friend who is fairly high up in the State Department this morning and he assured me we're not going to get involved. I thought you'd want to know. So you see, there's no reason to change Ariadne's travel plans.'

The familiar timbre of Lawrence's voice soothed her as much as what he said. It was so like him to call just when she needed to hear from him. 'That's what Ellen said too. I was just going to put in a call to Dimitri to talk about it.'

'I won't hold you up. Just remember I love you and my thoughts are with you.'

'I wish it was more than your thoughts,' Glory replied. 'Take care, darling. I couldn't stand it if anything happened to you.'

She said goodbye and immediately tried to place a call to Paris. The Taos operator got back to her an hour later to report that the overseas phone lines were jammed but she would keep on trying.

Glory stayed up all night hoping the operator would finally get through to Dimitri. Red-eyed, she walked down the drive the next morning to pick up the paper – and her dream of being reunited with Ariadne came crashing down as she read the latest news.

Thirty Americans had died at sea when a German U-boat sank a British passenger liner. Secretary of State Hull was advising Americans to travel only under *imperative necessity.*

Imperative necessity. What did that mean? Was it imperative to get her daughter out of France when the Germans were making war on civilian ships? Or would Ariadne be better off in Paris?

By noon she knew the answer. She drove to the Western Union office and cabled Dimitri at once.

His reply came in the mail four weeks later. *By now you must be out of your mind with worry,* he wrote. *I'm happy to be able to tell you that Ariadne is safe and well. The fall of France was relatively bloodless. The new Vichy government seems determined to keep the peace and most Parisians are going along.*

In view of the circumstances you were right to cancel her trip. I will do my best to look after and keep her safe until these terrible times are over.

Glory wept as she read the rest of the letter. She had lost her daughter before. This time hurt even more than the first because her hopes had been so high. When she had control of her emotions and could hold her hand steady enough to write, she answered Dimitri's letter.

I shall pray for Ariadne every day, and you too of course. Perhaps things will change in the near future. Americans don't want to go to war. Once it becomes clear to Herr Hitler, travel may again be possible.

Glory's last hope was shattered when Japan bombed Pearl Harbor and the United States declared war on both Japan and Germany.

From that 7 December on, her days had too many hours, the weeks too many days, the years too many months – and all of them passed with agonising slowness. Not even her work could fill them. Sculpting made the daylight endurable. Nothing could comfort her at night.

She slept fitfully, only to wake in the small hours of the morning when the mind and spirit are at their lowest ebb, knowing she wouldn't sleep again. As she waited for the dawn her thoughts invariably turned to Ariadne.

She became an avid reader of newspapers, a fanatic moviegoer who cared nothing for the feature film as long as a newsreel preceded the show. When Japan overran the Philippines and Germany appeared to be on the brink of bombing Great Britain into rubble she thought the war was lost. But Churchill rallied England by sheer strength of will, Hitler divided his forces to attack Russia, the American war machine went into high gear and the tide began to turn.

Every time Glory heard people complain about hardships like rationing it was all she could do not to tell them to go to the hell. Although dairy products, meat and sugar were in short supply and the best of everything went to the troops, no one went hungry.

Were they hungry in Paris? Or cold? The thought of her daughter doing without necessities was truly unbearable. She would have given her soul to be able to change places.

The realisation that other mothers had sons and daughters at risk helped a little. But Lawrence was the lifeline that held Glory's sanity in place. He had an uncanny way of knowing when she had reached a low ebb. A card, a letter or a phone call always came on those days.

In 1943 German forces surrendered in Africa and American troops landed in Italy. Glory ached for every parent who lost a son in battle, yet each sacrifice brought the day when she would know her daughter's fate that much closer. By 1944 it appeared the United States, Great Britain and France would eventually win the war. The only question was when.

While she waited Glory did more than her share for the war effort, planting a huge victory garden, spearheading salvage drives for paper and metal and donating blood with a profligacy that left her feeling as drained as though she had been victimised by a vampire rather than helping the Red Cross.

The more she did, the greater her personal sacrifice, the better her sculpture became, as if anguish and artistic excellence were opposite ends of the same equation. Just as Lawrence had promised a decade earlier, she was one of the best known, most successful artists in the country. However fame had lots its evanescence. She would have given it up in a heartbeat in exchange for having Ariadne by her side.

On 6 June the Taos paper splashed news of the invasion of Normandy across its masthead in two inch high letters. Too exhilarated to sculpt, Glory spent the morning weeding her vegetable garden. She was ankle deep in manure and mud when she heard a car coming up the drive. She reached the front of the house in time to see Lawrence getting out of a taxi.

'Why didn't you let me know you were coming?' she called out, wiping her grimy hands on her shorts. 'I must look a mess.'

'You look fine to me,' he replied with a grin that made her feel more like an eighteen year old than a care worn woman of thirty-three.

Forgetting her *déshabillé*, she marched straight into his arms, gave him a quick kiss and then leaned back to get a better look at his dearly loved face.

'Is that all I get after travelling two thousand miles?' he asked.

'That and a cup of coffee,' she replied, leading the way into the house. 'Dinner and a bed too.'

'Your bed I hope?'

'Of course.'

'In that case forget the coffee and dinner.'

This time he claimed her lips so fiercely that he bruised her lips. Not that she minded. Undoubtedly she had bruised his too. She wanted him with an endless need that swept all else before it. The minutes spun away unheeded as she kissed his mouth, his eyes, the tip of his nose, and then his mouth again.

Momentarily sated, she stepped back and looked at him. 'Is there any reason you don't want to answer my question?' she asked.

'What question?' he murmured, nuzzling her neck.

'Why didn't you let me know you were coming?'

'I'm not coming yet,' he replied with a husky chuckle.

She enjoyed his teasing almost as much as his caresses. However she knew him well enough to realise he was avoiding something.

She took a couple of steps backwards and gave him a stern look. 'Lawrence Wyant, answer me.'

'I didn't telephone because I wasn't sure of getting a seat on the train until I got to Grand Central.'

'Why didn't you mention the possibility of the trip in your last letter? It's not like you. The only time you surprised me was when—' Her voice trailed off. The last time he arrived unannounced, he came to tell her about Ariadne.

In that uncanny way he had of reading her mind, he said, 'Don't worry, darling. I don't have bad news about Ariadne. I don't have good news either – but that may change sooner than you think.'

Was that a sheepish grin on his face – or a grimace? 'Why are you being so mysterious? Do you have military connections like the one you have in the State Department?'

'In a manner of speaking,' he replied cryptically.

'Will you please tell me what's going on?'

'I do have a military connection who may be able to track Ariadne down.'

'Who is it and how can I thank him?'

'Another kiss might do it.'

'That's not funny.'

'I didn't mean it to be. I'll be going to France soon.'

'Have you forgotten there's a war on?'

'I'm going into the service, Glory.'

'I thought Beth's illness and your age exempted you.'

'From the draft, yes. But not from service.'

The air seemed to have become so much colder that she glanced out to see if the weather had changed. She should have been prepared for the news. She knew Lawrence viewed himself as a slacker or worse for staying at home while other men went off to war. She couldn't fault him for wanting to do his part and yet she felt as though her heart was in free fall.

It finally stopped in the vicinity of her knees. 'Oh Lawrence, what have you done?' she whispered. 'You're a forty-two year old man with a sick wife. You have no business in uniform.'

'I've been asked to do a job – one that demands unique qualifications.' He looked as thrilled as a boy getting behind the wheel of a car for the first time.

It scared her to death. 'I can't believe Beth approves.'

'She didn't at first. I made my peace with her. I came to make my peace with you.'

'What did you do? Twist Beth's arm?' Glory blurted out, willing to use fair means or foul to keep Lawrence from risking his life in a war everyone said would soon be over.

'Of course not,' he answered, sounding like a parent addressing a dim-witted child. 'Beth understands why I have to do this. I hope you will too.'

Extolling Beth's virtues was the last straw. Damn him, Glory thought. By comparing her to the saintly Beth he had played his trump card. 'What is this job only you can do?'

'I got a call from a friend in the OSS a month ago asking me to come to Washington to discuss working for them.'

Before the war Cal had scoffed at the idea of Lawrence being a spy. But the OSS was a counter-intelligence agency. 'What do they want from you?'

'It's pretty simple,' he began. 'Remember when I went to Lucerne before the war?'

'Yes.' How could she forget? The trip had been a second honeymoon for him and Beth.

'While I was there, dealers and collectors talked about their joint fear that Germany would loot Europe's finest art.'

'What does that have to do with your going into the OSS now?'

'Germany outdid everyone's worst case scenario. Hitler systematically stole masterpieces from museums, private collections, even churches all over the Continent. The list is endless.'

'How do you know?'

'I can't tell you that.' His gaze locked with hers. 'I've said what I have in confidence so you'll understand why they need me.'

'What do they want you to do? Parachute into Berlin, track Hitler down, put a gun to his head and say *your art or your life.*'

'I wish it was that simple. Important paintings are an easily transported asset like fine jewels. The OSS wants to keep the Nazis from sending stolen art work to countries who remain on good terms with the Nazi regime.'

'Even if a few misguided nations were stupid enough to deal with those monsters, I don't see what that has to do with you.'

'You know the value of a Rembrandt or a Titian as well as I do. Masterpieces like that could finance a rebirth of Nazism after the Third Reich is defeated.'

'You still haven't answered my question. Why does the OSS need you? You're not a soldier.'

'They don't want soldiers. They're looking for art historians. I have the credentials and I'm not exactly ready for a wheelchair. I enjoyed good relationships with major European art dealers and museum directors before the war. I've been told that many of them tried to hide their collections. If they will trust anyone to reveal the locations, they'll trust me. The OSS wants me on the scene as soon as possible.'

The enormity of what he was going to do made Glory sick to her stomach. 'That could be dangerous.'

'Perhaps. That's why I had to tell you in person. I wanted to hold you when I said goodbye.'

'Goodbye sounds awfully final.'

'I don't expect to die. Believe me I'm no hero. But I've been asked to do a job, one I think is important. The Germans have taken pieces of culture and history that belong to the entire world. They can't be permitted to get away with it.'

'I just wish you weren't the one to try and stop it.'

'There's a famous quote that goes, if not me, who? If not now, when?'

Seeing the determination on his face, Glory forgot all about her own fears. He was her man – the love of her life – and he was going to war. She wouldn't send him off with questions and recriminations ringing in his ears.

'You're right,' she said.

'About taking on the job?'

'About forgetting coffee and dinner.'

There had always been urgency in their love making, a need to take and be taken until their weary bodies demanded a respite. This time desperation added to the urgency, heightening both hunger and passion. Knowing they might be spending their last hours together intensified every kiss, every caress.

Glory gave herself with total abandon, arching her back to display her breasts, parting her legs to reveal her sex. He responded by kissing, then tonguing her everywhere until she thought she would die from sheer pleasure. When she could take no more, she begged him to enter her. Their joining transported her beyond rapture to a new realm for which she had no words.

The morning came far too quickly. As she dressed her eyes kept straying to the clock. They had so little time left. There were so many things she wanted to say, so many I love yous and thank yous for all he had done for her, for being a part of her life. The best part. Always.

He had given her so much. She was determined to give him a serene and peaceful goodbye. She could and would cry her eyes out after he left. But not now.

'I was wrong about you being too old to serve your country,' she said with a smile as she dressed.

'What changed your mind?' he asked, buttoning his shirt.

'Last night.'

'What about last night?'

'You acted more like a twenty year old than a man past forty. I worked up quite an appetite. How would you like your eggs?'

'Cooked any way except by you,' he teased. 'I'll do them if you'll take care of the toast.'

The thought of putting anything in her stomach sent a rush of bile into her throat. How could she eat when her heart was breaking?

This might be the last morning they spent together, the last time they talked, the last time they kissed. She wanted to throw herself in his arms and beg him to stay.

Instead, gathering the remnants of her courage, she replied, 'Toast coming right up.'

'If you have some cheese, I'll make omelettes,' he said as he followed her to the kitchen.

She walked over to the refrigerator and took out a wedge of Cheddar. 'Will this do?'

'Perfectly. You don't happen to have any scallions in there?' '

How could he talk about food at such a time? Sunlight streamed through the windows. Laredo woofed to be let out. The scent of coffee filled the air. It was an ordinary morning in every way but one. Her beloved Lawrence was going in harm's way to save a few paintings for posterity.

For the first time in her life art meant nothing to her. She would gladly burn her studio to the ground and never sculpt again if by doing so she could keep him safe.

She reined in her own fears, managed to make toast without burning it and even choked down a little omelette.

'When will you leave for France?' she asked over coffee.

'I can't tell you. But one of these days I expect to be in Paris. When I get there I'll do everything in my power to find Ariadne.'

Guilt churned in Glory's already uneasy stomach. She hadn't given a thought to her daughter since hearing Lawrence's news. It had been a hell of a price to pay for a brief respite from that particular worry.

'Do you think you can? Find her that is. It's been so long since I heard from Dimitri that I don't even know if they're still in Paris.'

'Anything is possible if you want it badly enough, Glory. You of all people should know that. I've failed you in so many ways. If it's in my power I won't fail you in this one.'

'You've never failed me,' she said, taking his hand. 'The only happiness I've known has been with you.'

'You are my happiness,' he answered, then getting to his feet, pulled her into his arms.

'I'll write you every day,' she said, clinging to him.

'I will too if I can,' he replied.

But his letters proved to be few and far between and so carefully worded that she had no idea where he was or what he was doing. She read each one over and over until the tissue-thin paper threatened to disintegrate.

The anxious days became frantic weeks. The Allied armies rolled into Paris and on to Germany and still he made no mention of Ariadne in his letters. When a telegram came in November, Glory feared the worst.

Mothers and wives often learned of a loved one's death that way. She closed the door on the delivery boy and slid to the floor on legs too weak to stand. Her hands shook as she opened the envelope.

She read the first line through a blur of tears, expecting it to say, *we regret to inform you.*

CHAPTER THIRTY

Glory clutched Lawrence's telegram like a talisman as she taxied from the Waldorf to the Wyant Gallery. She had long since memorised the brief message.

Meet me in the gallery at noon December second. Have news of Ariadne. Love, Lawrence.

Although the taxi heater blasted hot air into the interior, a frisson ran through Glory's body. What did the cryptic message mean? She had spent the last few days seesawing between elation and despair, convinced one minute that Ariadne was alive and well – and fearful the next she would never be reunited with her daughter.

'Can't you go any faster?' she asked the driver when snarled traffic slowed the cab to a crawl.

'Lady, this cab can't fly,' he replied.

She read the meter, took a dollar from her wallet, handed it over and got out of the taxi without another word. Her daily walks in Taos stood her in good stead as she jogged the remaining blocks to the gallery.

On her way she paid no attention to the holiday displays in the windows. Christmas had no meaning if Ariadne was lost to her forever. When she reached the gallery she looked inside, hoping to catch a glimpse of Lawrence. She recognised him at once even though he stood with his back to the street.

She ran up to the bevelled glass doors and shoved them open. The next thing she knew she was in Lawrence's arms, clinging to him with all her strength as though he'd disappear otherwise. Thank God he was home. And now so was she.

His heart beat against hers. His breath stirred her hair. His scent filled her nostrils. She didn't dare kiss him for fear one of his employees would walk in but dear Lord, how she wanted to.

Her heart said *I love you.* Her lips didn't dare. 'When did you get back?' she asked breathlessly.

He gave her such an intimate smile that she felt the heat of it deep in her abdomen. 'Late last night.'

'I wish I had known. You could have come to the hotel.'

'That wouldn't have been wise,' he answered under his breath, then raised his voice. 'You're right on time.'

At that moment, wanting to be held, to be kissed, to say the things with her body that language was inadequate to express, she resented the charade that forced her to act as though he were no more than an old and dear friend.

Looking away to mask her chagrin, she saw a couple standing at the opposite end of the gallery's front room, studying one of her sculptures. European refugees, she thought, noting the way they were dressed. Poor ones from their threadbare coats. The man's hair was white – the woman's the inky black of a raven's wing. There was something vaguely familiar about the breadth of the man's shoulders and the shape of his head.

Lawrence's voice reclaimed her attention. 'I have a surprise for you.'

At the sound, the man turned to face her. He looked like Dimitri's father. But that was ridiculous. Dimitri's father would be in his eighties if he were alive.

'Glory, is that really you?' the man said, coming towards her.

He sounded like Dimitri. He moved like him too. But Dimitri was in his late forties and this man looked much older. The woman with him turned around just then – only she wasn't a woman yet. She was a girl – a very tall one who gazed back at Glory with the very eyes Glory saw every time she looked in the mirror.

Glory's vision narrowed. Her throat tightened. She swayed on her feet. 'Ariadne?'

'Is that you, Mother?' the girl replied.

Mother – no one had ever called Glory mother before. How sweet the word sounded. She had imagined this meeting a thousand times – tried to put herself in Ariadne's place and anticipate her reaction. She had supposed Ariadne would be hesitant, even a little shy.

She had been wrong. The instant she nodded yes, Ariadne flung herself into Glory's arms, crying and laughing like the woman-child she was.

'Daddy told me you were beautiful. He didn't tell me you were so young.'

'I'm not young at all.'

How mundane, Glory thought as she met Dimitri's eyes over her daughter's shoulder. But there weren't words in the English language to express what she felt – the awe, the joy, the surprise.

Her recollection of the infant Ariadne merged with the pictures Dimitri had sent, then metamorphosed into the teenager in her arms. Ariadne was tall for her age just as she had been. Glory could discern the beginning of womanly curves beneath her ill-fitting coat.

'You're beautiful too,' Glory said.

'Just like her mother,' Dimitri commented as though he and Glory had parted on the best of terms a few days earlier. 'It's a long time since I saw anything or anyone so lovely. A very long time. I'd begun to think there was no beauty left in the world.'

Ariadne looked at her father with concern. 'Are you all right, Daddy?'

'I'm fine,' he was quick to reassure her.

But he was far from fine, Glory soon realised. The hand he held out to her in greeting was hideously misshapen, the nailless fingers twisted and bent. It was all she could do not to gasp in horror.

'Don't worry,' he said, tracking her gaze. 'It doesn't hurt any more.'

'What happened to you?'

'Daddy was a member of the Resistance,' Ariadne answered, her eyes shining with pride. 'The last few weeks of the Occupation the Maquis couldn't wait for the Americans to rid Paris of the Nazis. They fought for Paris themselves. Daddy was one of their leaders. He was captured during the street fighting.'

Ariadne's matter-of-fact recounting riveted Glory. War had robbed her of her childhood. Glory longed to give it back – if it wasn't already too late.

'What happened to you?' she asked Dimitri.

He gave her a bleak smile. 'I was questioned for days. They wanted the names of the leaders of the revolt. They knew I was a sculptor. They knew what would hurt me most.' He paused and squared his shoulders. 'I didn't tell them anything.'

His simple declaration conveyed more than screaming and shouting could. His mutilated hands attested to the torture he had endured. Sympathy flickered to life in her heart, banishing the last vestiges of resentment and ill-will. Dimitri had paid the price he had mentioned in his very first letter – and it had been a terrible one.

'Will your hands get better?'

He held them both of them up. His gaze was almost dispassionate as he looked them over. 'They are better.'

'They sure are,' Ariadne interjected. 'You should have seen them when he was released from prison. He couldn't even feed himself.'

'Ariadne, we didn't travel all the way to New York to dwell on my misfortune. We came so you could be with your mother.'

'I have so many questions for the two of you,' Glory said. 'How did you escape France in the middle of a war?'

'You can thank Lawrence for that,' Dimitri replied. 'He tracked us down, persuaded an American Army doctor to treat my hands and wangled a couple of extra seats on a plane to London and then on to New York. The fact that Ariadne is an American citizen helped. But we'd still be in Paris if he hadn't found us.'

In the excitement of seeing her daughter, Glory had all but forgotten Lawrence. From the way he was beaming though, he didn't mind. To think he had once talked about failing her.

'How in the world can I thank you?'

'By being happy,' he replied.

'Happy doesn't begin to cover it.'

'I can see. You're glowing.'

She felt torn between the desire to be alone with him and the need to spend time with her daughter. 'How did all this happen? I wasn't expecting you back for months.'

'Beth's health is worse. I was released from service ahead of time for compassionate reasons.'

'I'm so sorry. Is there anything I can do?'

He shook his head. 'You and Ariadne have a lot of catching up to do and Beth is expecting me at home. You've waited a long time for today. Enjoy it.' He took her hand and kissed her palm. The intimate touch was all too brief. 'I've got to go.'

'Thank you, *mon ami*,' Dimitri said huskily. 'I wish you and your wife the best. We will meet again soon I hope.'

Lawrence nodded, turned with military precision and marched to the door, opening it far more softly than Glory had minutes before.

In the past, seeing him leave, Glory would have been overcome by loneliness. Now though, joy far outshone any other emotion.

'Let's go somewhere special for lunch,' she said gaily, wanting to celebrate. She looked from Dimitri to Ariadne and noted their shabby clothes. They would have to do for lunch. 'Afterwards we had better see about getting you both a new wardrobe.'

'Could we really?' Ariadne asked as though she wasn't certain she could trust her good fortune.

Glory headed for the door with Ariadne in tow but Dimitri planted his feet like a baulky mule. 'Ariadne, need I remind you we don't have any money except what Mr Wyant loaned us. Our funds, what's left of them, are in a bank in Paris.'

'I can well afford whatever you need,' Glory replied, enjoying a long overdue moment of supremacy. 'I've waited twelve years to spoil Ariadne.'

Glory used the gallery's telephone to call the Waldorf and ask that her things be moved from a single room to a suite. Then she treated Ariadne and Dimitri to a late lunch. After they hungrily devoured every morsel of a meal that included soup, salad and an entree, she insisted on ordering dessert and was rewarded by Ariadne's enchanting smile.

The child gobbled up a huge piece of chocolate cake topped with vanilla ice cream. Clearly she had been starved for sweets along with more nourishing food. Before going back to the hotel for the night, Glory made up her mind to buy lots of candy – not the sort of chocolates an adult would enjoy either. Ariadne would undoubtedly relish something sinfully sweet and gooey.

'How long do you plan to stay in New York?' Dimitri asked over coffee.

'I hadn't really thought about it. There's so much I want to show Ariadne. How about you? Have you made any plans?'

'I haven't had time. Of course I have lots of friends to look up. Since you know my financial situation I hope you will permit me to stay in your suite – if you have room.'

He looked so miserable at asking for her largesse. 'I stayed with you once. Turn about is fair play.'

Glory had all but forgotten what it felt like to be happy, to wake up every morning with the anticipation that something wonderful lay ahead. She spent the days with Ariadne, squeezing the last drop of pleasure from excursions that other more fortunate mothers and daughters took for granted.

They took a carriage ride around Central Park, visited the Bronx Zoo, rode a ferry to the Statue of Liberty, went skating at Rockefeller Center, strolled through the Metropolitan Museum and the Museum of Natural History, and saw a Broadway musical.

Dimitri left them alone, an act of grace for which Glory was eternally grateful. He excused himself from their outings, saying he had people to see and places to go. But Glory wasn't sure he went out. She invariably found him in the suite when she and Ariadne returned to the hotel at night.

'I'm worried about Daddy,' Ariadne confided to Glory over lunch on their sixth afternoon together.

'You shouldn't be, honey. He's very capable of looking after himself.'

Ariadne pushed a half eaten piece of pie aside, a sure sign of the depth of her concern. 'He used to be – before his hands were ruined. Now I don't know. Haven't you noticed how sad he looks when he thinks no one is watching. It makes me want to cry.'

Glory's heart ached for Ariadne. She was trying so hard to be grown up. 'How can I help?'

'I know you want me to come to live in New Mexico – but I can't leave Daddy. He needs me.'

So that was it, Glory thought. She wished every problem she had encountered in her life could be so easily resolved.

'I never expected you to. I've been waiting for the right time to ask your father to go with us. He says his hands are better but losing the ability to sculpt has to have been a terrible blow. He needs time to get used to it – and to decide what he wants to do with the rest of his life.'

Ariadne jumped up with coltish grace and gave Glory a huge hug. 'You were certainly worth waiting for. You're the best mother in the whole world!'

'That's the nicest thing anyone ever said to me,' Glory replied, fighting back tears.

Dimitri sat in the living room of Glory's Waldorf suite, contemplating a future made bleaker by the knowledge that he would soon lose his daughter. That singular loss would be even more painful than what the Germans had done to his hands.

He finally knew the full extent of the bereavement Glory had

313

suffered years ago. But he couldn't and wouldn't get in the way of his daughter's happiness. Or Glory's either. Love had blossomed between them as quickly as a hothouse flower.

They adored each other.

He was happy for them – and miserable for himself. And not just because he would soon say goodbye to Ariadne or because he couldn't sculpt any more. He had learned to live with the latter and he would deal with the former.

The truth was he adored Glory too.

He hadn't meant to fall in love with her a second time. Hell, be honest, a voice at the back of his brain commanded him. *He had never stopped loving her.*

He had been out of his mind when he let Leah persuade him to go along with the plan she had concocted. Jealousy of Glory's talent had destroyed everything good in his character. He had wanted to hurt her as much as he imagined she had hurt him. In the end though, he had punished himself.

In time he had come to realise that his Rouge pieces were the crowning achievement of his career and that Glory hadn't cannibalised his talent – she had elevated it to new heights.

He would have given anything to change the past, to mould it in a different form just as he used to mould a sculpture. Alone in the luxurious suite while the cloak of night enveloped the city, he conjured up a life that could have been – a life filled with triumph instead of regret.

If he hadn't been such a fool he and Glory would have had a life together. Ariadne might have had brothers and sisters. She might even have been spared living through the war.

Instead he had consigned his beloved daughter to a childhood made bleak by privation and fear. He had doomed Glory to a mental breakdown and himself to a remorse so deep that it had seared his soul. His mistake had ruined all their lives.

Day after day while Glory and Ariadne enjoyed the sights of New York, he sat alone in the suite struggling to put the past to rest and face the unknown future. He dreaded the moment when his daughter and the woman he loved would return and yet he couldn't wait to see them again.

He was standing by a window, pretending to be absorbed in the view when Glory and Ariadne burst into the parlour, bringing the scent of the outdoors with them.

'What have you got there?' he asked as Glory began emptying a couple of paper bags.

'It's our supper,' Ariadne said.

Dimitri made a great pretence of groaning. 'Oh no. Your mother is a terrible cook.'

Ariadne giggled. 'So she said. We stopped at a delicatessen on the way back. I've never seen so much food.'

'Are you tired of eating in restaurants so soon, *ma chère?*'

'Mother and I think it's time we had a family conference so we decided to eat in. I hope you're hungry. We bought enough for an army.'

Undoubtedly Glory and Ariadne were going to tell him they were returning to New Mexico. Dimitri's jaws clenched at the thought. Ariadne must never know how he dreaded their separation.

'Would you like a drink before we eat? You look a little pale,' Glory said as she unpacked the contents of the bags.

'I'm fine. What do the two of you want to tell me?'

Glory handed him a plate loaded with food. 'It's time Ariadne and I returned to Taos. She should start school after the Christmas holiday and I have to get back to work.'

Dear God, he'd been right. 'Of course. I understand perfectly.'

'No you don't, Daddy,' Ariadne burst out gleefully. 'Mother wants you to go with us.'

He almost dropped the plate. His eyes sought Glory's. 'Is this Ariadne's idea – or yours?'

'I suggested it. You need more time to recuperate.'

The last thing he wanted from her was pity. 'Nonsense. I'm fine.'

'No you're not, Dimitri. You're too thin, you have a terrible cough, and you aren't in any shape to work at anything. Aside from that, Ariadne has already endured far too many changes for a girl her age. She needs your support while she settles into her new life.'

'Please Daddy, say you'll go with us,' Ariadne urged. 'It would mean so much to me.'

He took a minute to consider his options. Lawrence had offered him a job in the gallery, but Dimitri only needed to hold up his ruined hands to know he would frighten customers away.

He had no money and no way to earn it. Glory had been right

about him needing time to recover. His participation in the Maquis had been far too rigorous for a man who had spent four years on the knife edge of starvation so his daughter would have a little more to eat.

'Well, what do you say?' Glory prompted.

'You're very kind.' The thought of spending a few quiet months with Glory and Ariadne seemed too good to be true. Had God given him a second chance? Could the three of them be a real family? Glory had loved him once. Could she learn to love him again?

He turned to face her. 'Are you sure it won't be an imposition?'

'I have more than enough room if that's what you're worried about. The main house has three bedrooms and two bathrooms and I built a separate guest wing with two more bedrooms and bathrooms a few years ago.'

Glory knew she was babbling. She couldn't seem to stop, though. The thought of living under the same roof with Dimitri made her uncomfortable. But she couldn't deny her daughter anything, including Dimitri's presence.

'I have a lot of company,' she continued. 'Do you remember Tiny Czernik? She comes to visit once a year. And then there are people you don't know – the Montclairs and the Steiners. And the Ashtons. I mustn't forget them. They came to Taos with me but they have their own house now.'

Mercifully, Ariadne interrupted before Glory ran through the list of every single acquaintance. 'Mother told me her house looks out on a mountain, and that real Indians live nearby. She has a dog and she said I could get one too. And a horse if I want. Oh Daddy, doesn't it sound wonderful?'

'How soon do you plan to go?' Dimitri asked.

'As soon as we can get space on a train,' Glory replied.

Dimitri gave her a grave smile. 'I would be delighted to go with you.'

Ariadne bubbled over with excitement all through supper, asking so many questions about Taos that Glory didn't have time to think about the consequences of her generosity until she was alone in her room.

What would Lawrence say when she told him she had asked Dimitri, the man she professed to hate, to live with her?

CHAPTER THIRTY-ONE

Taos – 1945

Although Easter was just a few weeks away a blizzard sent a wall of snow hissing and swirling around Glory's sturdy adobe home. Bad weather made the house seem that much cosier, she mused.

A bone-deep contentment brought a smile to her face as she watched Dimitri rise from the armchair across from hers to put another log on the fire. He'd returned to robust health in the months he'd spent in Taos, a tribute to the peace and quiet – and to his cooking.

His corduroy trousers and flannel shirt made him appear very much the country gentleman. With the startling shock of white hair framing his tanned features, he looked even more handsome than he had when they were lovers – and certainly more distinguished. Time had tamed the lion. Now she knew him for a lamb.

She looked down at the letter she'd been writing to Lawrence and picked up her pen. *I never thought I'd feel so at ease with Dimitri,* she wrote. *To my surprise, we've become very good friends. He used to be so demanding. Now he always asks what he can do for me.*

His being here has been a Godsend for Ariadne. The three of us get along so well, a stranger might think we'd always been a family.

Being the mother of a beautiful teenage girl takes more time, energy and thought than I imagined. But I love all of it. I don't miss the hours I used to spend alone in my studio – although to tell the truth I'm not alone even when I'm working.

Dimitri will never be able to sculpt but he still likes puttering around a studio. I had forgotten what a wonderful teacher he is. His comments have been invaluable. I think you'll see the difference when my new pieces arrive.

At the moment the three of us are in the living room, sitting around a fire. Make that four. As usual, Laredo is sleeping at my feet. Dimitri is reading A Bell For Adano, laughing and getting a little teary-eyed just the way I did when I read it. Ariadne is doing algebra homework. I can't believe she's in the ninth grade, even though that's where her test scores put her. She is a grade A student. English composition is her favourite class. She says she wants to be a writer.

My concern that she wouldn't fit in with Americans her age was totally unfounded. Although my brilliant daughter is a year younger than the others in her class she is very popular. Dimitri is threatening to buy a shotgun the first time she asks permission to go on a date. Considering her interest in the opposite sex and theirs in her, that won't be long.

Glory held her pen poised in mid-air as she searched for something else to say. It seemed strange to write about her own happiness when Lawrence had been going through hell with Beth. Although he hadn't loved Beth passionately, he had been devoted to her and now, despite the doctor's best efforts, she seemed to be slipping away.

'If that's a letter to Lawrence, give him my best,' Dimitri said.

'Mine too,' Ariadne added, closing her books with a thud. 'I've finished my homework. The way it's snowing I bet school is closed tomorrow. If it is, can I go sleighing?'

Glory put her letter aside to finish later. Her daughter might look like a young lady but underneath, she was still a child. 'We'll see. Would you like some hot chocolate before you go to bed?'

'I'd love it, especially if you put lots of gooey marshmallows on top.'

'You make it, honey,' Dimitri said to Ariadne. 'I want to talk to your mother.'

With a little frown, Ariadne headed for the kitchen.

'Is something wrong?' Glory asked as soon as she was sure Ariadne was out of hearing.

Dimitri put his book down and gazed at her. 'On the contrary, I've never been happier. I never thought I'd feel that way again. When the Germans finished with me, I thought my life was over. You've made me see that life still has infinite possibilities. But I can't mooch off you forever. It's time I got back to work.'

She smiled at his use of slang. Although he'd lived in America for years, he had never sounded like an American before. 'Do you have an idea what you want to do?'

'Thanks to you, yes. I'm going to teach art.'

'Privately here in town?'

He shook his head. 'Remember what I told you about private art teachers when we first met?'

'How could I forget? You made me feel like an idiot.'

He leaned towards her. 'I'm sorry for all the things I said that hurt you. If I could, I'd take every one back.'

'That's all behind us. Where do you plan to teach?'

'I applied for professorships at several colleges. I've already heard back from the chairman of the art department at Columbia University. He offered me a professorship beginning in the autumn term.'

He had taken her by surprise and not just because he'd acted without telling her. His life was his own. But she hadn't expected to feel such a sense of loss. 'You'll be a marvellous teacher. No one knows that better than I do.'

'Do you ever think about our days together in Big Sur?'

'Of course. You taught me to sculpt. You made the life I have now possible. How could I forget that?'

'I won't be leaving for New York for a few more months. Can you put up with me that much longer?' He looked so solemn, she almost laughed.

'Put up with you? Are you serious? I've loved having you here. I'm going to miss you.' She was so fond of him now that there were times when she forgot how she used to hate him. Their past seemed like something that had happened to two other people.

He rose, walked up behind her and put his hands on her shoulders. 'I'd like to believe you mean that.'

She reached up and covered his broken hands with her own. 'I do. We've come a long way, you and I.'

'Not far enough,' he answered huskily. 'I wish—'

Before he could finish, Ariadne reappeared carrying a tray laden with steaming cups and a platter of biscuits she and her father had made when she got home from school.

'Did I interrupt anything?' she asked, her bright gaze going from Dimitri to Glory.

'No, dear,' Glory replied.

However that wasn't quite true. Glory had no idea what would have happened if Ariadne hadn't walked in. She had enjoyed the weight of Dimitri's hand on her shoulder, the feeling of closeness, of sharing her life with another adult. Only not just any adult. This one had fathered her child. Parenting Ariadne had bonded them.

'How's the cocoa, Mother?' Ariadne asked. A chocolate moustache adorned her upper lip. She looked utterly adorable.

'It's delicious.'

Glory tried to concentrate on Ariadne's and Dimitri's conversation but her thoughts kept skittering away like a high-strung horse. She had long ago learned to rein in her memories of the time she spent in Big Sur. Now those memories broke free.

She had loved Dimitri so in those days. And the sex had been, well, memorable to say the least. She had lived and breathed only for him. Now every time he did something just to make her happy, every hour he spent in the studio, every time she looked at Ariadne, she was reminded of that love. Living with him had taught her that a love like theirs never died completely. It had come back in a new and better form that gave comfort rather than pain.

The chiming of the clock brought Glory back to the present. 'It's ten,' Dimitri was saying to Ariadne. 'Time for bed.'

'My friends don't go to bed this early,' Ariadne declared, looking at Glory as though she expected to be reprieved. 'Why do I have to?'

Glory repressed a grin at the normalcy of Ariadne's complaint. After all she had been through it was wonderful to see her acting like her peers. 'Because your father told you to – and I agree with him. As for your class mates, don't forget you're a year younger than they are.'

Ariadne flounced out of the room like the injured party in a civil suit, leaving Glory alone with Dimitri. She grinned at him. 'I wonder if all children are born knowing how to divide and conquer their parents.'

'Thanks for backing me up.'

'Why wouldn't I? You're a wonderful father.'

'And you're a wonderful mother.'

'That's what I call a mutual admiration society,' Glory replied as she piled their cups and saucers on the tray. Just then the telephone rang.

'It's probably for you,' Dimitri said. 'I'll do the dishes.'

320

'Thanks.' His willingness to do what he used to regard as woman's work still surprised her. She picked up the phone while he carried the tray to the kitchen.

'I have a person to person call for Glory Girard from a Mr Wyant in New York,' an operator said.

'This is Miss Girard.' It was midnight in New York. Why would Lawrence call so late, she wondered. 'Are you there, Lawrence?' she asked as a burst of static filled her ear.

'Yes. Did I wake you up?' His voice had a thin quality the long distance line didn't fully explain.

'Dimitri and I were just going to bed.' Too late, she realised how that must sound.

'I'm sorry to disturb you.'

'You didn't. You never could. What's wrong, darling? You sound so strange.'

'Beth died an hour ago.'

Her hand tightened on the phone. 'Oh God, I'm so sorry. Are you all right? Would you like me to come to New York?'

'I doubt Dimitri can spare you.'

She wished she could reach through the phone and put her arms around Lawrence. 'Don't you mean Ariadne?'

'I said what I meant.' He sounded so hurt. Angry too. Surely he couldn't be jealous – of Dimitri of all men.

'I hate to think of you going through the funeral alone. I could be in Manhattan in a few days.'

'I won't be alone. Beth's parents will be with me.' He paused, then said, 'I have to go now.'

He hung up so abruptly that Glory didn't even have a chance to say goodbye – or to tell him how much she loved him and grieved for him.

She didn't realise she was crying until Dimitri came into the room. He hurried to her side and handed her a handkerchief.

'What's the matter?'

'Lawrence called to tell me his wife had died.'

'I didn't realise you knew her.'

'We used to have Martinis at the Palm Court when I went to New York. She was so young, I can't believe she's gone.' Or that I wanted it so much, she added to herself. Guilt compounded her sorrow.

Dimitri took her in his arms. 'Cry it out. You'll feel better.'

Glory didn't feel like crying, though. She didn't know what she felt. She had wanted Lawrence for herself, had imagined him coming to her. But her life had changed from the days when she used to dream of marrying him. She had a daughter to think of – and her daughter had a father.

Dimitri pulled her closer. His scent, the muscled wall of his chest brought back sensory memories of other times when he had held her. He was warm and comforting. Most of all, he was here for her while Lawrence had never seemed further away. She didn't object when he bent to kiss her.

There had been a time when he could set her blood to bubbling like champagne with a kiss. When their lips met she expected to feel the inward spiralling warmth of sexual arousal. Instead she felt embarrassed. The magic was gone.

When Dimitri took Glory in his arms he intended to soothe her. That's all. He should have known he couldn't get close to her without wanting more.

He poured a decade and a half of pent up passion into his kiss, hoping to awaken the fiery response he remembered so well. Love me, he silently implored. Love me, Glory, as I love you.

She didn't respond by so much as a muscle twitch. She didn't fight his kiss. She didn't return it either.

Her lack of enthusiasm finally reached his befuddled brain. She didn't want him. Reluctantly, ever so gently, he set her free. 'I'm sorry. I had no right to do that. It won't happen again. Please forgive me.'

'I already have.'

She looked so desolate, so lonely, it was all he could do not to gather her up again. Instinct told him she wanted a man to hold her – but the man wasn't him.

'Tell me why you're so upset.'

'I thought I did,' she said shakily.

'You told me Beth died. What you didn't tell me is how you feel about it.'

'Sad, I guess. Lawrence sounded dreadful. I'm worried sick about him.'

'I've never asked you before – I didn't think it was any of my business – but I have to know. Are you in love with him?'

She nodded. 'I thought you knew. I have been for years.'

'I assume he returns your feelings?'

'I used to think he did. Tonight I'm not so sure. I don't expect him to be glad his wife is dead but—'

'But what? Surely you didn't expect him to rush straight from her deathbed to your arms.'

'You're a man, Dimitri, so you must have some idea how a man would feel under the circumstances. Do you think I should go to New York?'

He used to be the only man where she was concerned, he thought with infinite regret, then buried the thought as deep as he could. Glory had a lover in Lawrence. She needed a friend. He wanted to be the best one she had ever had. 'I know you don't like me talking about Leah. Hell, neither do I for lots of reasons you will never know. But I married her and, when she died, I mourned her. Lawrence may not have loved Beth the way he does you – but he cared for her enough to marry her. He needs time to mourn too.'

Glory never mailed the cheerful letter she wrote that night. She sent a condolence card instead along with a spray of roses for Beth's funeral. She waited a few weeks, then called Lawrence at home only to be told he'd left town for a while.

She could understand his need to get away. She couldn't understand his not telling her about it. As the weeks passed without any word from him it became more and more difficult to pretend everything was all right in front of Ariadne. Fortunately she didn't have to pretend with Dimitri. He had assumed Cal's old role as her confidant, advising her to a patience she didn't seem to possess.

When her thirty-ninth birthday passed without so much as a card from Lawrence the childlike part of her that still believed in happy endings shrivelled up. She looked in the mirror and was surprised not to see a wizened face looking back.

She had assumed she and Lawrence would be together someday. What a fool she'd been.

Lawrence took the contract the lawyer held out and signed it without reading the contents. He knew what the document said. He had sold the gallery for a fabulous price. He ought to be thrilled.

'I wish I was sure you knew what you were doing,' the lawyer said.

Lawrence laughed but there was no humour in the sound. 'It's too late now.'

The lawyer put the papers in a manila folder, then looked back up at Lawrence. 'The new owners have asked me to try one last time to convince you to stay on at the gallery as a consultant – at least for a couple of months. They're prepared to pay a handsome fee for your services.'

Lawrence pulled a pack of Lucky Strikes from his pocket, lit one and inhaled deeply. He had stopped smoking when Beth complained that the smell bothered her. Now the nicotine soothed him. 'I don't need the money. If the new owners keep their promise to retain the staff they won't need me.'

'Can I buy you a drink?'

'Thanks but no. I want to go back to the gallery and box up the last of my things.'

The lawyer got to his feet. 'As you requested, the money from the sale will be deposited directly in your account before the close of the business day.'

'You've been very helpful.' Lawrence stubbed out his cigarette to shake the lawyer's hand.

When he reached the street he lit up again before heading back to the gallery, moving at such a fast pace with such a glower on his face that other pedestrians stepped aside. He had decided to sell the business a few weeks after Beth's death. A buyer with cash in hand had come along faster than he had anticipated. For the first time in his life he had no obligations to anyone.

His parents and Beth were gone and, in a different yet equally final way, so was Glory. He was free to go anywhere – do anything. He had always wanted to visit exotic places and had never had the time. There was nothing to stop him now. He could walk into the nearest travel agency and book a ticket anywhere in the world. He ought to be on cloud nine.

Instead he felt as though he'd just come from his own funeral. The Lawrence Wyant he'd known, the man who wanted to bring beauty to the world, had been buried along with Beth – and he had Glory to thank for it. One of these days he might let her know.

He had been startled when she told him she had asked Dimitri to stay with her and Ariadne in New Mexico. The letters that followed, describing how she and Dimitri had been able to put the past behind them, had been hell to read.

Although Glory never admitted it in so many words, he had no trouble reading between the lines. She had fallen in love with Konstantine all over again. End of story. End of everything that mattered to him.

He reached the gallery, tossed his cigarette in the gutter and hurried inside through a gauntlet of employees who wished him well and wanted to shake his hand. It was a relief to reach his office and close the door on his staff.

Only he wasn't alone. Speak of the devil, Dimitri Konstantine stood not ten feet away, looking considerably better than he had the last time they were together. Tender loving care had a way of doing that for a man.

'What's this I hear about you selling the gallery?' Dimitri demanded without so much as a hello. 'Why the hell didn't you let Glory know about it?'

'Don't you dare lecture me on what she does or doesn't have a right to know. What are you doing here anyway?'

Lawrence walked over to a credenza, took a bottle and a glass from a tray on its top and poured himself two fingers of Scotch without asking Konstantine if he wanted a drink.

'You're not very hospitable,' Dimitri said drily. 'I had hoped we might be friends.'

'Not bloody likely. You got the girl. I got the shaft.'

'I'm not following you.'

'It didn't take a genius to figure out what was happening in Taos. Every other line Glory wrote to me was about you.'

'That's only natural. I'm Ariadne's father. Glory and I were trying to make our daughter feel she had a family.'

'And she does, doesn't she? The three of you are one big bundle of love.' Lawrence downed his drink. He knew he was being an ass but he didn't care what Konstantine thought of him. 'Don't bother to send me an invitation to the wedding. I don't plan to leave a forwarding address.'

To Lawrence's amazement, Dimitri burst out laughing in a series of basso profundo chortles that would have been contagious under other circumstances. 'Wedding? Is that why you've kept your distance, why you haven't written?'

'Don't tell me I've got it all wrong.'

'That's exactly what I'm telling you. Yes, Glory and I did become friends. And it's a damn good thing we were able to for our daughter's sake. Glory will always be very special to me, as I hope I will be to her. You don't forget the people you love. That doesn't mean you can't move on. And that's what I'm doing. I've accepted a job at Columbia University teaching art at the graduate level. It's my first night in town and I thought we could have dinner together.'

Lawrence stared at the empty glass and then at the bottle. Could he be drunk and hallucinating? 'Dinner. You want to have dinner with me?'

'That's what I said.'

'Where's Glory?'

'At home in Taos, pretending she's happy for Ariadne's sake although nothing could be further from the truth. Your silence has broken her heart.'

'If you're so worried about her why did you leave?'

'Because I'm not the man she wants. She wants you. Why, I'll never know.'

'Sure. And pigs can fly.'

'It's true, my friend, Glory loves you or I'd still be in Taos. She likes me. We're friends. That's all. She's a wonderful woman, a strong one too, but she's given up hope where you're concerned.'

So had he, Lawrence thought, feeling his facial muscles reassemble themselves. It felt strange to smile again. 'Are you saying what I think?'

'Ah, at last I seem to have penetrated your thick skull. Let me repeat, Glory is in love with you. If she felt that way about me I'd be on the next train to New Mexico.' Dimitri spoke slowly, emphasising each word as though Lawrence had a hearing problem.

Lawrence took a last look around, then headed for the door.

'How about that dinner?' Dimitri said.

'I'll take a rain check,' Lawrence replied. At the last minute he turned and grinned at Dimitri. 'I owe you one.'

Lawrence followed Dimitri's suggestion to the letter, not even stopping at his apartment to pack a bag on his way to Grand Central Station. A West coast bound train was leaving in forty minutes, just time for him to buy a toothbrush, toothpaste, a change of underwear and a couple of shirts.

He arrived in Taos two days later without enough money to pay for a cab. It was a long walk to Glory's house. He swore he floated all the way. The smell of something burning came from the kitchen when he arrived. Glory must be cooking, he thought, then burst out laughing. When they were married he'd hire a chef.

He walked in without bothering to knock, caught Glory's arm, spun her around and said, 'We've wasted enough precious time. Will you marry me today?'

She brandished a potato masher in his face as though it were a sword. 'How dare you march in with a question like that when I haven't heard a word from you for months?'

'I dare because I love you and I think you love me. You've got the daughter you always wanted. It's time you had a husband too.'

The expression in her eyes went from anger to confusion. 'Do you mean it?'

'I never meant anything more.'

'Prove it,' she challenged.

'How?'

'Get down on your knees and propose properly.'

Lawrence didn't have to be told twice. He dropped to his knees with an audible thunk but his smile never faltered. He was where he wanted to be, about to do what he had dreamed of doing for the last twenty-one years. It made him feel young and incredibly happy.

'Miss Girard, I've travelled two thousand miles and two decades to be here with you. I have loved you my entire adult life. You are the only woman in the world for me. I'll perish on the spot if you say no.' He knew he was laying it on with a trowel but he meant every word.

'Go on,' she urged.

'You're the most talented artist I've ever known and the most beguiling woman. If I were a poet I'd sing your praises in iambic pentameter. But I'm just a humble man, down on his knees begging you to marry me.'

She uttered the one word he'd come all that way to hear.

'Yes.'

'Can I get off my knees now? They're killing me.'

Laughing, Glory helped him to his feet. They had a lot to talk about but at that moment he settled for a kiss.

327

CHAPTER THIRTY-TWO

Taos – 1947

Although Glory and Lawrence had been married for two and a half years the sight of him across the breakfast table still gladdened her. They made a practice of lingering over a second cup of coffee after Ariadne left for school. It was a rare quiet time in their busy lives.

Although Lawrence had officially retired when he sold the gallery he kept busy managing Glory's booming career, heading up the Taos Art Council, raising private funds to support the school of Indian Art in Santa Fe, and acting as a buffer between Ariadne and Glory now that Ariadne's teens had settled in with a vengeance.

Thank heaven Ariadne didn't resent Lawrence the way so many children resented their step parents. She never forgot how he had appeared in Paris with his pockets bulging with soap and sweets, and helped her and her father escape from Europe.

'You look so far away,' Lawrence said. 'What's on your mind?'

'I was just thinking how lucky I am. Thanks to you, all my dreams have come true.'

'Shucks ma'am. It weren't anything.'

Glory giggled. 'You may be wearing cowboy boots and a bolo tie but you haven't lost your eastern accent.'

The ringing of the doorbell interrupted their badinage. 'Finish your coffee,' Lawrence said. 'I'll answer the door.'

He returned a minute later carrying a wrapped package. 'It's special delivery for you from a Monsignor Tremaine.'

Glory started. 'I haven't heard that name for years.'

'He probably wants you to donate a sculpture for a church fund raising.'

Glory ignored the goose bumps crawling across her skin. 'I don't think so. The Monsignor was my mother's personal confessor.'

'Perhaps he wants to take you to task for not attending her funeral.'

'I doubt it. If anyone could understand my reasons for not being there, he would. Besides, she died six months ago.'

'Glory dearest, we can spend the rest of the morning speculating about what's in the package, or you can open it now.'

'I'm a little afraid to. I just finished telling you how happy I was. I don't want anything to spoil what we have.'

'It's probably some minor business to do with your mother's estate.'

What Lawrence said made perfect sense. However Glory's hands trembled as she tore the wrapping paper open. A musty scent, redolent of age and mildew rose from beneath it. Inside, a letter bearing the Monsignor's letterhead lay on top of a folder.

She showed it to Lawrence. 'Will you read it out loud? If it's bad news it will sound better coming from you.'

'Of course,' he replied, taking the letter from her hand.

He put on his reading glasses. *Dear Glory, I hope you don't mind my addressing you that way. Although you are a married woman and a world famous artist, I still remember the rebellious teenager who didn't want to waste her time on the widows' and orphans' clothing drive.*

Lawrence paused and looked at Glory. 'So that's where Ariadne gets her seditious inclinations. And you told me you were such an obedient child.'

Glory knew he was trying to lighten the moment but she was too anxious to be teased. 'Please, just read it.'

His gaze returned to Tremaine's letter. *You must be wondering why I'm writing after all these years, perhaps feeling a little anxious. That is not my intention. You have no cause for concern. I think the contents of the enclosed folder will put your mind at ease.*

As you undoubtedly know from your friend, Jeremy Montclair, your mother left her entire estate to the Church with the proviso that I act as a trustee. Yesterday when workmen were tearing down the Girard Company's old building to make room for a commercial development, one of them came across the folder hidden in the floor of your father's office. It's the long-lost Pinkerton report and it will tell you a great deal about your natural parents. I pray the truth will bring you a measure of peace and happiness. God bless and keep you.

Lawrence's voice came to a halt, he took off his reading glasses and gazed at her with so much love that she felt as though he'd wrapped her in his arms. 'I told you it wasn't bad news.'

'What if I'm the daughter of an axe murderer?'

'I love you and I always will. That's the bottom line for me. But there's no reason to anticipate the worst. You could be about to get some very good news.'

Glory had never stopped wondering who she was. The question had taken on even greater importance after Ariadne came to live with her.

She opened the folder to find a page covered with her father's graceful Spencerian script. Seeing it, she felt the tug of memory pulling her back into the past. Noble's saturnine features rose before her as she read what he had written years ago.

My dearest daughter, the fact you are holding this letter means I am dead and someone far wiser than I came across the secret cache in my office and gave the folder to you.

I have no doubt Anna has already told you about your adoption. She swore she would do it before I was in the ground. You are probably wondering about your birth parents. Aside from a long dead Pinkerton detective, I alone knew who they were.

I found you the day of the 1906 quake. I was touring a part of the city at the mayor's request when I came upon your crib. At first, I only meant to save your life. When I took you back to the house and held you in my arms I knew I could never let you go.

The Pinkerton detective I hired to look into your background told me your grandparents were looking for you. I bribed him to lie to them. My only excuse is that I loved you not wisely but too well.

When she finished the letter she stared into space while her emotions took a roller coaster ride. Noble had given her a privileged childhood but he had deprived her of the one thing everyone had a right to know – her identity. How could he? Furious, she pounded the table so hard her cup fell over.

'What is it?' Lawrence asked.

She passed the second letter to him, then opened the file. An old-fashioned photograph of a woman lay on top. But for her dark hair, Glory might have been looking at a picture of herself. The inscription on the back identified the woman as Rebecca Hersh O'Meara.

'My God,' Glory whispered.

'Are you all right?' Lawrence asked, coming to her side.

Glory showed him the photograph. 'I think she's my mother.'

Lawrence studied the picture for a moment. 'You look just like her. So does Ariadne.'

Eager to know the full truth at long last, Glory read the Pinkerton report while Lawrence stood at her shoulder reading too. She learned how and where her parents met and why they eloped. She learned how Noble had kept her grandparents from finding her.

While she read fragments of her past appeared before her eyes. She saw herself as a girl of nine, sitting cross-legged on a chair while she copied the Raphael. Then she was in the gazebo sketching. She felt the heat from the fire when she bent to rescue the Chicago Art Institute catalogue from the flames. She watched herself leave home on the twenty-three-year journey that had brought her to this time and place.

And now she knew why. Art had been a part of her inheritance.

'How do you feel?' Lawrence asked when she put the last page down.

'Dazed. This answers so many questions, not just who I am but why Noble and Anna treated me the way they did. No wonder he didn't want me to go to the Chicago Art Institute. My grandparents were probably alive then.'

'What are you going to do now?' Lawrence asked.

'I'm going to Chicago,' she replied at once. 'I want to walk in my parents' footsteps – breathe the air they breathed – see the place where they met and fell in love.'

'I'd do the same thing in your place. When do you plan to go?'

'As soon as possible.'

'It will take a while to find someone to look after Ariadne.'

Glory reached for his hand. 'I hope you can understand this is one trip I have to take by myself.'

Three days later Glory checked into the Blackstone Hotel in Chicago. She followed the bellboy to her room, gave him a generous tip and unpacked quickly, anxious to get out and explore the city that had been her parents' home.

331

When she finished she freshened up and headed towards the door, guide book in hand. At the last minute she took the phone book from the nightstand and paged through it until she came to the H's.

It was a longshot, she realised as she scanned the listings for Saul Hersh. Her mother had been twenty when she was born. She was forty-one herself. Her grandfather would be a very old man if he was alive.

She wasn't surprised at not finding his name. However there was a listing for a Miriam Hersh. Glory's heart stuttered when she read the name. Could it be her grandmother? She jotted down the Lakeshore Drive address, then headed for the door.

By the time the lift had carried her down to reception she'd made up her mind to go and see Miriam Hersh before she did anything else. If they weren't related, she had lost nothing but a little time. If they were . . . ?

Glory didn't finish the thought. It was too much to hope for. She stopped at the desk for directions to the Hersh house, then left the hotel. It would be a long walk. She hoped the exercise would settle her rattled nerves.

A stiff breeze caught at her skirts as she turned onto Lakeshore Drive a few minutes later. It was an imposing avenue filled with luxury stores and handsome buildings. She walked past them, wondering if her mother had walked the pavement too.

Up ahead, she saw a break in the skyline created by a stone mansion sitting on what appeared to be several acres. It was the only private residence on the busy street.

The name Hersh, spelled out on the wrought iron gates, told Glory she had reached her destination. Could it possibly be the house her mother had left years ago? She followed a short driveway to the front door. Her pulse pounded in her ears as she used the brass knocker to announce her arrival.

Moments later an elderly woman opened the door. She was far too well dressed to be a servant, Glory thought, taking in a pale mauve suit that looked as though it had been designed by Dior himself.

Glory wore a similar suit although hers was nowhere as expensive. Fashion experts had dubbed the new longer skirts and nipped in waists 'the New Look'.

'Is Miriam Hersh home?'

'You've found her. What do you want?'

Not exactly an auspicious beginning, Glory mused. 'Could we discuss it inside?'

'If you're here to try and sell me something, I'm not interested,' Miriam Hersh said. She moved to shut the door.

'Please don't go. I'm Rebecca's daughter,' Glory burst out.

Miriam Hersh blanched. 'That can't be. Rebecca died in an earthquake before her baby was born.'

A second woman, as elderly as Miriam Hersh but nowhere near as well dressed, walked into the hall.

'I'm sorry I didn't answer the door,' the woman said to Miriam. 'You know my hearing isn't what it used to be. Can I fix tea for you and your visitor?'

A little colour had seeped back into Miriam's face. 'Forget the tea, Harriet. I don't know about my visitor but I could use two fingers of whisky.'

'I could use some too,' Glory replied.

'We'll be in the drawing room,' Miriam told Harriet. 'Follow me,' she said to Glory, 'and we'll get to the bottom of this. But I warn you, if you're a fortune hunter who thinks I'm going to be an easy mark for a sob story, think again.'

She preceded Glory into a room whose enormous proportions were set off by a well thought out furniture arrangement that included two seating areas divided by a grand piano.

'Do you play?' Miriam asked, leading the way to the closest grouping.

'A little,' Glory replied.

'Rebecca did too,' Miriam answered in a tone that clearly said she thought Glory was a charlatan. 'She was so talented. She painted too.'

'I know. I'm an artist myself.'

Miriam perched on the edge of the edge of a chair and motioned for Glory to take a seat. She didn't look like an elderly woman who'd just had the shock of a lifetime. She looked very much in charge. 'I didn't catch your name.'

'It's Glory Girard Wyant. But I was born Joy O'Meara.'

Miriam's only response was a slight widening of her eyes. 'You certainly do have the right answers, Miss Wyant.'

'Won't you call me Glory?'

'We'll see about that.'

Harriet tottered in with two Waterford shot glasses and a matching decanter.

'Go lay down before you fall down,' Miriam told the elderly maid.

When Harriet was gone Miriam half-filled both glasses and handed one to Glory. Although it was the middle of the day she went around the room turning on all the lights, then approached Glory again.

'Between Harriet's hearing and my eyes, we barely add up to one functioning human being,' she said. She motioned Glory closer. 'The last time I saw Rebecca she was eighteen years old but I think she would have looked very much like you if she had lived long enough. How old are you, Miss Wyant?'

'I'm forty-one. I was born in San Francisco in 1906 the day of the quake.'

'How do you know so much, Miss Wyant? Who coached you?'

Glory wished she could hug the feisty old woman. 'No one coached me. And it's not Miss. It's Mrs. I have a Pinkerton report in my hotel room that proves I'm your granddaughter. Since I was foolish enough not to bring it with me I had better tell you what's in it.'

Miriam took a man-sized swallow of Scotch, then cocked her head as if to say, give it your best shot.

Not to be outdone, Glory took a healthy swallow of Scotch too. Then she launched into the story she had so recently learned herself. Miriam listened intently throughout, her expression going from disbelief to exultation.

When Glory finished, Miriam got to her feet and said, 'Follow me.'

She led the way back through the echoing hall and beyond to a cheerful room furnished with flowered chintzes. Raising one arm, she pointed at an almost life-sized oil painting of a young woman hanging on the far wall.

'Glory, I'd like you to meet your mother, Rebecca,' Miriam declared with a sense of drama Cal would have envied. Then abandoning restraint, she threw her arms around Glory and gave her a surprisingly strong hug.

Glory hugged her back a little more carefully in view of her age. When she let go she wasn't surprised to see tears in her grandmother's eyes. She felt them pooling in hers too.

'I can't believe you're really here,' Miriam said. 'After we got that dreadful Pinkerton report I promised myself I wouldn't give up hope.

Every time the doorbell rang I rushed to answer it praying it would be Rebecca. My husband, your grandfather Saul, tried to convince me Rebecca was dead but I refused to believe him. You have no idea how terrible it is to lose a child. When Saul died ten years ago I didn't feel near as bad.'

'I do know how it feels to lose a child and how wonderful it is to get one back,' Glory replied. 'Grandmother, you and I have a lot of years to catch up on. But first I've got to get a better look at that painting. Is it a Sargeant?'

She walked up to the portrait, as smitten with the artistic skill it had taken to produce it as she was with the subject matter.

'It's a marvellous painting, isn't it?' Miriam said merrily.

'I've seldom seen its equal. The brush work, the colour, the composition are the work of a master. Why isn't it signed?'

'It's not signed because Saul wouldn't have let it in the house if he had known your father, Sean O'Meara, painted it. He gave it to your mother for a birthday present. She had to leave it behind when they eloped.'

Glory felt so elated, she could have danced around the room. 'My father painted that?'

'I always thought he was a genius. So did Rebecca. Unfortunately Saul couldn't see past the name O'Meara. You said you were an artist. Do you paint like your mother and father did?'

'No. I'm a sculptor.'

Miriam gasped. 'I feel like an old fool. I've seen pictures of you and your work in art magazines. I just didn't put two and two together when I heard your name. But you did take me by surprise.'

'I surprised the two of us, Grandmother. I hope you don't mind me calling you that.'

'Mind? I can't hear it enough. Now you've found me, I want you to stay here in your mother's room. I redecorated the rest of the house years ago but I didn't change a thing in there. It's exactly the way she left it. There's a collection of her work on the walls. Would you like to see it?'

'I'd love to.'

How inadequately words expressed her feelings, Glory thought as she followed her grandmother upstairs and down a hall. Miriam stopped at a door, pushed it open and time drifted back to another era. Glory could almost feel her mother's presence as she walked into the bedroom.

The walls were covered with art, delicate pen and ink drawings, pastels as bright as spring, watercolours that evoked a hint of the Orient. An unfinished oil sat on an easel near the window. Her mother's work had a unique style that was, in its own way, every bit as good as her father's.

'What do you think?' Miriam asked.

Glory sighed. 'I don't know if I can find the words to tell you. When I learned about my adoption I felt disconnected, as though I didn't belong anywhere. I have a wonderful husband now and a daughter I love more than life itself but finding you and being in this room, all I can say is I feel as if I'm home.'

'You are, Glory. You are.' Miriam gave Glory a shaky smile. 'Unless you relish the thought of seeing an old woman crying her eyes out, we had better go back downstairs and have another drink. I want to hear all about that husband of yours, and your daughter too. Good heavens, I'm a great grandmother. That will be something to tell the ladies at the next Mahjong game.'

It will indeed, Glory thought. As she followed at her grandmother's heels she felt at peace with herself and the universe. An infant named Joy O'Meara, a girl called Rouge, and a woman known as Glory Girard Wyant, were finally one.

EPILOGUE

Taos, 1952

Summer was short in Taos and all the sweeter for its brevity. The sun unspooled its light, gilding the high peaks where snow still lay in hidden canyons, burnishing the rooftops of adobe buildings, and brushing the wedding party with shimmering gold.

Taos was, Glory thought as she gazed at her assembled friends and family, a place of magic – a perfect place to begin a marriage. That Ariadne and David Steiner would join their lives had been inevitable from the day they had met five years ago.

With a wisdom she hadn't known when she rushed off to Big Sur with Dimitri, Ariadne and David had schooled themselves to patience while David completed his medical degree and residency and Ariadne went to college to learn the writer's craft.

Although Ariadne was twenty and David twenty-eight, to Glory's brimming eyes they looked like children as they stood side by side under an arch of climbing roses to speak their vows.

When an equally youthful minister asked, 'Who gives this woman to this man?' it was Glory's cue to step forward with Dimitri on one side and Lawrence on the other.

'We do,' the three of them answered in perfect unison.

Then the minister asked, 'Who gives this man?' and the Steiners stepped forward, looking as happy and full of pride as she had ever seen them.

A gentle murmur of approval rose from the wedding guests. Although Glory couldn't see them behind her, she easily conjured up each well-loved face.

There was grandmother Miriam, still spry at eighty-four, and the ever romantic Tiny Czernik Broadhurst, a bride herself at seventy-

337

five, having met her husband in a retirement community in Arizona.

Dimitri's new wife, a history professor with a sharp wit, and the Monterey Konstantines had made the journey to Taos as well. Cal, so stylish and content, and Jeremy who wore his success so well, were probably holding hands. She suspected that Clarence and Ellen Ashton were too.

A frisson rippled down Glory's spine as she sensed the presence of ghosts amidst the living. Perhaps she was just a foolish middle-aged woman but somehow she knew that Sean and Rebecca were there too.

'Are you all right?' Lawrence whispered.

'I've never been better,' she whispered back.

Life hadn't turned out at all the way she had imagined when she left the Girard mansion all those years ago. She had lost everything that day but now she had it all.

Love had triumphed. Art would endure.

ALEXANDRA THORNE

THE ULTIMATE SIN

WILL THEY EVER BE FREE TO
LOVE EACH OTHER

Young, vulnerable and unaware of her beauty, Elke has given her hand to the elderly man who rescued her from poverty, and offered her his heart as well as his home. It's a vow that determined Elke has promised to keep.

But when she meets her husband's best friend, Patrick Pride, Elke is horrified to find him so attractive. With each visit comes the pain and pleasure of feelings to which neither dare admit, bound as they are in their respect for the same man.

Then Patrick announces his engagement to a social belle and it seems that neither will be ever free to love . . .

The *Ultimate Sin* is a heartmelting love story from the author of *Sophisticated Savages*, *Past Forgetting* and *Creative Urges*.

HODDER AND STOUGHTON PAPERBACKS

ALEXANDRA THORNE

SOPHISTICATED SAVAGES

'GOOD, RAUNCHY STUFF' – *Publishing News*

Texas was all in the past.

Caitlin Pride. Supermodel. Her face and her figure famous nationwide and beyond. A life of photocalls, catwalks and international assignments. Manhattan, Milan, Paris: only the best, the most expensive, the most glamorous.

But underneath the flawless complexion, the look that women worldwide sighed for, lay the long-buried painful memories.

And now Texas was luring her back. Daring her to face those memories of an unhappy childhood and a shattered romance.

Tempting her to love again . . .

HODDER AND STOUGHTON PAPERBACKS

ALEXANDRA THORNE

PAST FORGETTING

DARE SHE FORGET HER PAST AND PURSUE
HER PASSION?

Jade Howard's life has changed beyond her imaginings,
yet if her past were known . . .

Thrown together with the man of her wildest dreams and
desires, Jade must deny her true feelings, hide her
identity, even live a lie or risk losing everything. And
insatiable, jealous Hilary Delano is looking for clues.

Duncan Carlisle is a famous painter. Gentle, heroic,
passionate yet desperate not to fall for Jade's charm.

How can each resist the other's overwhelming
attraction? Yet how can their happiness be fulfilled
without Jade revealing her intimate secret?

HODDER AND STOUGHTON PAPERBACKS

ALEXANDRA THORNE

CREATIVE URGES

SHE WAS PASSIONATE, BEAUTIFUL, SUCCESSFUL –
AND SUDDENLY TERRIBLY VULNERABLE

Life is looking good for Liz Kant.

Passionately unashamed at her appetites for pleasure
and success, she is living life to the full. Her gallery in
Phoenix, Arizona and the artists she represents are now
attracting the attention of the New York dealers and art
experts.

The years of unremitting hard work, her eye for original
talent and her flair for presentation has brought the
rewards she knows she deserves. But suddenly everything is at risk: her career, her independence and her
heart.

As her longtime affair with Indian painter Alan
Longchase falls apart, her ruthlessly ambitious assistant
Rick senses his opportunity to insinuate himself into her
bed and her business. And the past she thought long
buried rises up to haunt her . . .

HODDER AND STOUGHTON PAPERBACKS